The Urbana Free Library

To renew materials call
217-367-4057

Apr 2013

	DATE DUE	
JUL 2 0 2004		
AUG 17 2004		
NOV 1 2 2004		

CALL ME THE BREEZE

Patrick McCabe

CALL ME THE BREEZE

HarperCollins*Publishers*

HarperCollins books may be purchased for educational, business, or sales promotional use. For information, please write: Special Markets Department, HarperCollins Publishers Inc., 10 East 53rd Street, New York, NY 10022.

First published in Great Britain in 2003 by Faber and Faber Limited.

FIRST EDITION

Printed on acid-free paper

Library of Congress Cataloging-in-Publication Data
    McCabe, Patrick.
        Call me the breeze : a novel / Patrick McCabe.—1st American ed.
            p.   cm.
        ISBN 0-06-052388-3
            1. Politicians—Fiction. 2. Ex-convicts—Fiction. 3. Northern Ireland—
    Fiction. I. Title.
    PR6063.C32C35   2003
    823'.914—dc20   2003056564

        03 04 05 06 07 ❖/RRD 10 9 8 7 6 5 4 3 2 1

What we call the beginning is often the end
And to make an end is to make a beginning.
The end is where we start from.

T. S. Eliot, 'Little Gidding'

CALL ME THE BREEZE

The End . . .

. . . is the beginning – that's what the ancients say. Well, we'll see. But first of all I want to get the rest of this stuff out of the way and leave it exactly as I found it for Bonehead.

'You can't be a famous writer and go throwing your papers around you like that,' he says.

And he's right, I guess. But he might as well be talking to the wall. I've always been that way. As soon as I was finished writing anything, I'd just shove it into a bag.

A Leatherette Holdall . . .

. . . to be precise. That's where he found nearly all of the material. 'Give me that!' he says. 'Till I put some order on it once and for all!'

So I did. 'There you are!' I says. 'It's all yours, Bone! You can do what you like with it, for all the difference it makes to me!'

He spent about a month on it, beavering away in his room. When he was finished, he presented it to me: 'The magnificent Joey Tallon Archibe!' he says.

But there could be no doubt about it – he really had done a terrific job. In place of the leatherette holdall, a neat little stack of marbled box files containing all my notebooks and ledgers.

I've had a really good time going through it. And if I was any kind of writer at all, I'd have made something worthwhile out of it, instead of just sitting here rambling half the night, filling up pages with discursive nonsense. I mean, it's not as if enough didn't happen!

Particularly during the seventies, when the old leatherette holdall found itself very much favoured – particularly by anonymous men who had a predilection for leaving it behind them in crowded public houses.

Campbell Morris

Although somehow you always felt that in a small border town like Scotsfield nothing serious would ever really happen. That most of what you heard was talk and would never amount to anything much.

But that was before the 'Campbell Morris Incident'. Campbell was a salesman who happened to drop by for the Lady of the Lake festival but ended up getting himself killed. It's impossible to say who started the rumours about him.

Either way it ended with him being pulled out of the reservoir and the cops going apeshit, raiding pubs.

It wasn't my business. I was too busy getting on with my life, pulling pints and thinking about Jacy. She was all I ever thought about in those days.

'He was a fucking spy! And that's it!' you'd hear them shouting late at night, full of guilt over what they had done. There had been six or seven of them involved, I think.

'How about we go out to The Ritzy?' they'd said, as the salesman drunkenly grinned. 'You'll see things out there that you'd never come across in Dublin or London.'

It was a ruse, to get him on his own. They used to show all these blue movies in a barn way out the country. They had dubbed it 'The Ritzy' and for a tenner you could watch the films and drink all you wanted. There was talk of Boyle Henry and the Provos being involved in its operation, but you'd never say that openly. 'I couldn't tell you anything about The Ritzy' was what you said if you were asked. 'I know nothing at all about any of that' – that's what you were expected to say.

And did, if you had any sense.

The 'blues', as they called them, were very popular. Bennett had always liked them. 'The best of crack,' he used to say. 'I always make sure to go out every Saturday.' But not any more.

After the salesman's funeral, Bennett had driven out to the reservoir and sat there for a couple of hours thinking about it all, and his part in it, I guess. He was discovered there a few hours later, slumped over the dash and poisoned with carbon monoxide.

Whenever I heard things like that back in those days, my reaction would always be the same: finish up my work, head straight home to fall into Mona's arms.

I used to tell her everything. The only other person I had ever talked to in that kind of way was Eamon Byrne, The Seeker. We had been at school together but he'd gone off to travel the world. I used to love seeing him coming into Austie's with the big long beard and the hair flying around his shoulders. Especially when you knew the reaction he was going to get. He always wore this hooded brown robe, the *djellaba*, and knew that it drove them crazy. He'd sit at the bar and roll himself a joint, without, it seemed, a care in the world. Then the two of us would just sit there, rapping for ages, about Dylan and Carlos Castaneda (*The Teachings of Don Juan*) and Santana, the band. He was a big fan of their album *Abraxas* and had brought me home a tape of it. I used to put on 'Oye Como Va' and 'Singing Winds/Crying Beasts' in the pub just to drive Austie wild. 'Fucking jungle music!' he called it, flicking his dishcloth and kicking crates.

The Seeker (he took his name from a song by The Who) was living in a squat in Peckham and working on an adventure playground. Just listening to him there, you'd be kind of hypnotized.

'Did you ever read T. S. Eliot?' he said to me one day, and I had to admit that I hadn't. To be perfectly honest, up to that point I hadn't read much of anything. I'd read sweet fuck all, to tell you the God's honest truth. Not since *Just William*, *Biggles* and shit.

I don't know why, for it certainly seems stupid now. A writer who doesn't read – sounds really impressive, all right. I think what had happened was I'd developed a kind of a block. 'I don't give a shit about that intellectual stuff!' I used to say, but, almost at once, would feel kind of ashamed.

That would be around the time that I got put out of the house for having the parties. The council had given me three chances, and this was the last one. There had been all sorts of complaints about black masses and shit, but that was just the old-timers freaking. We'd always have a great laugh, myself and The Seeker whenever we'd get round to rapping about those parties. It was all to do with me playing Black Sabbath albums, and The Seeker going around in his *djellaba* blessing people and making out he was Charlie Manson. One night he jumped out in front of this old lady and roars 'Yow!' right into her face – but with this luminous skeleton mask on. It scared the living shit out of her and got the pair of us done for disturbing the peace. To be fair to the council, though, they weren't that bad – after that they could easily have got away scot-free with giving me sweet fuck all. Which a few of them would have been damn glad to do. But the fact that my mother had had a hard life (she was in Cavan General Hospital for a while before being institutionalized totally – they wheeled her off gibbering about 'Chinamen') kind of helped my situation, and when she passed away they offered me this rundown mobile home on the edge of a tinker camp just a mile outside Scotsfield town.

I tried the factory for a while after flunking out of school – I drank a bottle of whiskey before Latin class and when the president asked me how ashamed I was (they found me asleep in a pool of vomit) I replied, 'No, baby, I ain't ashamed because when you ain't got nothin' you got nothin' to lose.'

Which of course is a characteristically acerbic quote from Mr Robert Zimmerman, the defiant Jewish minstrel – not something that the president of the college was aware of, as I was to find out very shortly.

So that was it then, down the road and don't come back, you and your Bobby Zimmerman, and then a spell in the foundry ladling layers of molten iron on top of limestone and silicone to make stupid sickles and scythes and then a month or two in that fucking meat factory boning hall before Austie the publican saved my life.

He'd heard that I'd been given my cards at the foundry – on account of me being 'a dreamer' – and that things weren't so good in the meat factory either, what with me drinking and missing all these days and shit.

One day I met him on the bridge and, after we got talking, he said: 'Out of respect for your mother, she was a lovely woman, I'll give you a try-out in the bar, Joe Boy. But you'd have to be on the ball. Not like I hear you were above in the foundry. Or the meat factory either, the way I've been told. You get what I'm saying here, Joey?'

'Yup!' I said, and I started on the Monday.

The Seeker would just puff on a joint and out of nowhere then say: 'Now Rabindranath Tagore. There's a man worth reading.'

I still have his books. There's one of them right here actually, well-thumbed and battered. *The Poems of St John of the Cross*. 'To Joey The Man,' it reads, '*from his old pal The Seeker – Eamon Byrne, Feb. '75.*'

4

That was inscribed just the week before he died – he OD'd in his flat in Clapham, South London. Another time, I remember, he had sent me over *The Wisdom of Hinduism*. And when I opened it what was there inside? Only this lovely faded primrose (he must have remembered I used to bring a little bunch to Mona), squashed flat but with every one of its petals still intact. And, inscribed beneath: '*We shall not cease from exploration, and the end of all our exploring will be to arrive where we started and know the place for the first time – T. S. Eliot,* Four Quartets, '75. *Keep believing, Joey! Your old pal – The Seeker!*'

Only for him, I might never have written anything. Whenever I'd get his letters, I'd want to read them again and again. He was always including little quotes like that. It made you want to try and express your own . . . feelings, thoughts, whatever –

They're all to be found here, in amongst these pages so diligently catalogued by Bonehead. Some of them are calm and, I suppose, somewhat measured, while others are more passionate and, at times, even frenzied.

Although none of them, it has to be said, are quite as legible as they ought to be . . .

19 June 1976, 1.05 a.m.

A bit wrecked. Just in from Austie's. Wild night. Fucking disco jammed to the doors. Was run off my feet. Feel like . . .

3.10 a.m.

Must have dozed off there. Feel like . . . I don't know. Life is funny. Sometimes I think I love Mona and other times I think it's because I'm afraid of her. I mean she's older – a lot older, man, you know? So strictly speaking it shouldn't . . . well, it shouldn't be, I guess.

There are times I weep when I get to thinking about Jacy. A catch comes in my throat and I can't stop thinking of that long blonde flowing hair. When I do, it's like a film with my face and her hair melting in and out of each other.

They found Bennett today. Someone was out walking his dog and he came upon the van. The cab was still full of smoke. Poor Bennett –

5

no more blue movies for him. I have a fair idea who the ringleaders were. Hoss might have been in on it – Sandy McGloin, for sure.

But that'll never come out. Everyone'd be far too scared to name names.

None of it's of interest to me. All that interests me now is love. Love, like The Seeker used to say, and truth and understanding. Poor Eamon, R.I.P.

I dreamed about him again last night. He's just sitting there, smoking his jay – then suddenly he starts to cry out: 'He's coming for me, Joey! The Big Fellow! He's going to . . . he's going . . .!'

But you never get to hear what it is the Big Fellow's going to do. All you can feel is his presence right there. As an icy wind blows by. And the next thing you know The Seeker is there – but with flattening beads of brackish blood pushing out of his mouth. I shudder when I think of it and I don't want to see it again. There was a needle too. A hypodermic syringe, just lying on the bare floorboards. I get headaches when I think of that and it makes me just want to stay in. Not to go out at all, or go back into work or –

But then I think of Jacy and it's like the sun is rising in your head. Just that way she smiles when she turns around, like she knows instinctively you're there. Blue eyes. Blue eyes and blonde hair. It's fantastic. I have taken up the guitar and am learning a couple of Joni Mitchell songs. I think she'll really like them. One is actually called 'California Sunshine' – isn't that amazing? The other is . . . I forget . . .

(Some of the scrappier bits of foolscap have no dates at all. This one I'm not sure of, but it looks like it comes from early June 1976.)

What Jacy Means . . .

The worst thing about Mona is her moods. One minute she'll be perfectly OK – smiling away there, grand and happy, with not a bother on her. Then the next thing you know she'll be glaring at you, making demands or cutting you dead. Looking at you like you're the worst piece of filth she's ever had the misfortune to lay her eyes upon.

Then other times she'll be taking you in her arms and covering you all over in kisses, saying: 'So, how are you today then? How is my best little boy? How is Joseph today?'

It's not a nice feeling, not knowing which it's going to be. It's the worst feeling in the world, to tell you the truth, and I've had it all my life – right from the earliest days when my father would come in, all smiles one night and full of simmering violence the next – and only for Jacy would probably have never known anything else. I often ask myself: 'Just what does Jacy mean?' She makes me feel secure and believe in love, that's what my Jacy means. She helps me and makes me want to – like The Seeker said – believe. Because that, more than anything, is so much of the essence, so important, more than all other things . . .

When she came to the town first, she was so beautiful that some of them couldn't wait to get started. Calling her this and calling her that. They called her a stuck-up bitch, but all I did was smile. And to tell you the truth, it wasn't so long after that that any time they spoke her name, a part of me would just shut down, and it was like they weren't in the bar at all.

All you'd see were these lips moving and over in the corner, the prettiest woman you'd ever laid eyes on, really. The kind of chick you never thought would stop for a second in your town. But she had, and they were so unprepared for it, it was all they could think of doing. Like the worst kind of backward hillbillies. Pathetic fucking bullshit, nothing more or less.

I knew what was going through their minds, of course, things such as: 'Why the fuck should we look at her? She wouldn't pass us the time of day!' and 'Flicking her hair like she's in the movies, fucking Californian whore!'

Maybe the reason I knew was that, before The Seeker, before I got reading, I might have thought along those lines myself. But not now.

Not now.

Not since that first time.

The First Time

I don't need any diaries to help me remember that. She was standing at the far end of the counter, and when she turned my heart skipped a beat. It was like a camera had caught the floating wisps of her hair in slo-mo. She was wearing a zippered blue denim jacket. There was a cluster of flowers on the scalloped collar. She was the spit of Joni.

Sinking her hands into the pocket of her Levis and fingering that lovely bead necklace, one exactly like you'd expect Joni to wear. You could tell straight away that she played the guitar. I could just imagine her, in a log cabin somewhere with the firelight flickering on her face as she looked into my eyes and strummed. I just stood there watching as she talked to her friend about Iowa, which is a state in America, of course, but apart from that I knew nothing about it. Maybe they were going on holiday there or something because you could see a travel guide with this coloured cover sticking out of her bag with a great big blue sky and waving golden corn and just that one word – *Iowa*. I even loved the way it formed on her lips. I would call her '*My Lady*'.

'A pint of Guinness,' she said, and it was like I was kind of swaying in space.

Afterwards, when I went home, I thought of her all night. *The One*, was all I could think, for that was how she seemed: *The One who is The Only One*.

30 June 1976

In Dublin today to score some acid but Boo Boo didn't have any. Said he'd be getting some at the weekend, that one of the guys he busks with is definitely scoring – windowpane, I think. So we just had a spliff and rapped about her and things in general. 'She sounds like a cool fucking chick,' he said and started what was probably the only argument I ever had with Boo.

'I don't like you saying "fucking", Boo Boo,' I said. 'Not when you're talking about her.'

There was a bomb scare in the Film Centre during Taxi Driver *but it turned out to be a hoax, not that it would have made any difference for we were too out of it to know what was going on. After that we went to Zhivago's to get more wine. Boo Boo met some doll he knew and she asked us back to her place for more booze and who knew what else. What else, as it turned out, being mostly Boo Boo blathering on about his band and what they were going to do, world domination starts fucking here. 'You've heard The Sonics,' he says.*

8

'You've heard The Voidoids, The Mojos.' He cupped his hands and blew the jay: 'But, baby, you've heard nothing.' The last thing I heard was him saying: 'And that man there – Big Joey – he's gonna be our roadie!'

Murder in Sandyford

I remember getting back early the next morning with a fucking ripper of a hangover. It was around eleven when I hopped off the bus and made straight for the pub. Austie gave me an unmerciful slap on the back as I sat at the bar digging into a steak and kidney pie – I always seemed to want to eat whenever I got nervous or excited. He said: 'Jasus but you're the happy-looking boy! Did you have a good time in Dublin?'

'Sure,' I said. All I kept thinking of while he was talking was the album – the one I got 'her'. Wondering would she like it. It was called *The Only One* by a band I'd never heard of – Spontaneous Apple Conclusion. I had come upon it completely by accident. *Which is a load of nonsense*, I thought, *for nothing ever happens entirely by accident.*

'Will you like it, Jacy?' I asked myself.

I didn't even even have to ask. I knew she would. Of course she would. The Only One. She who is . . .

> The Only One, she who is –
> the only one,
> driving beneath the Californian sun.

I wasn't listening very carefully to what Austie was saying now. But you could see that it was serious. He was telling me about the British Ambassador and his secretary. They had both been killed in Sandyford – blown up by a landmine.

'A crater twenty-feet wide,' he said. 'Now we'll be fucking for it. After the salesman, we'll be fucking tormented, we will. They're convinced they're all hiding out here! Fucking Provos – they're going to ruin my business! Why don't they all get around a table and settle it all, pack of fucking –!'

3 July 1976 (late a.m.)
Thoughts/Reflections to Self . . .

Some of the things I'm asked to do I don't like them any more, even though I used to look forward to them. I don't have a problem admitting that. But it's different now. Ever since Jacy all of that has changed. Now all I want to do is say: 'Go away, Mona, don't come near me tonight, don't ask me to –'

But she always gets around me, standing there with that crooked smile she has whenever she's been drinking. Running her fingers through my hair and –

She lifts her own skirt up. Ever so slowly, till it billows around your head like a parachute. And then it comes – that blissful feeling. When you put your thumb in your mouth and you see the glittering stretch of water with her just standing beside it, staring off out to the horizon. She doesn't speak but you know what she's thinking. 'Out there is the precious harbour. That wondrous place where we'll all feel safe. One day we'll get there, Joseph.' 'Yes, Mona. I know we will' you are about to say, but when you look again she's gone and all you can hear are groans.

(There is a little notebook here marked BAND NOTES. With some fantastic little doodles in it by Boo Boo. Kind of like Marvel comics, or Robert Crumb. I remember him laughing whenever he'd do them, to keep himself awake on the way home from gigs. Odd bits of lyrics, too, some of them really good. I don't think they were ever used, though.)

Psychobilly

Looking over the cuttings brings that time back, those first few weeks of the band getting together and Boo Boo setting his plans for world domination in motion. 'Make no mistake, this thing is going to happen. I know you don't believe it, Joey, but we're gonna prove you wrong. We're gonna take the place apart and you're in it, my friend, whether you like it or not.' He was right – I didn't believe him but he sure put the smirk on the other side of my face when I went down to hear them in Jackson's Garage. Some of the songs were fucking great, no doubt about it, especially 'My Daddy Was a Vampire'. The yowls out of Boo Boo during it were unbelievable, so much so that Jackson came round in his overalls with a face like thunder. 'What the fuck is going on here?' he said, but Boo Boo told him to lighten up. 'Easy, baby,' he said as he wound the microphone cable. Jackson knew his father, otherwise I think he'd have knocked the bollocks out of him right there on the spot. In the end, though, he just fucked off, wiping his hands with an oily rag and warning us all to '*Watch it!*'

I agreed to be the roadie all right – I didn't see why not if I could work it OK with my shifts in Austie's.

Keith Carradine

When there weren't many in, I'd maybe leaf through a novel or just stand there staring way out across the town. I could see it all plainly, me arriving in this deadbeat hole where she lived with her husband, some old motherfucker of a bank clerk who'd bored her half to death since the day they got married. I'd be standing at the edge of town in my long leather duster coat, the sun lancing off my eyes as I gazed first into the sky then up and down the drab, unpainted buildings that seemed to hold each other up all along the winding street. 'So!' I'd say. 'Old timer! 'Bout a room for the night, maybe, huh?' and he'd show me to the motel where I'd wait till dark, just oiling up my Winchester pump action. Then it'd be time to go. Soon as she saw me coming she wouldn't be able to speak. The pump I'd keep well hidden right in there beneath the duster, not thinking about producing it at all unless there was some kind of trouble. Which there wouldn't be for the jerk bankman or doctor or whoever she'd somehow managed to get holed up with wasn't going to be that foolish. For if he was –

'How you been then, Jacy?' I'd say, not taking her hand just yet.

'I . . . I . . .' was all she'd say. She wouldn't be able to speak.

It would be beautiful making love that night, running your fingers through her hair, her jeans cast away there on the floor beside the bed. 'I love you!' I'd say. 'I've waited all this time.'

'Joey,' she'd say. 'Joe Boy, my lovely darling,' just the simple sound of her voice making everything you'd lived till now nowhere close to living at all.

Nights I'd drift towards sleep with a single word on my lips. 'Iowa,' I'd hear myself whisper, and with its swell and ebb it would remind me of the sea, even though I knew there was no water there. I'd borrowed a book from the library, just an ordinary guide to the Midwest. Of course there was no sea there. There was in California, though, the Pacific Ocean crashing just beyond the Big Sur sands. I'd read about it in *The Family* by Ed Sanders, which Eamon had sent to me. 'Check this out,' he'd written. 'He used to play with The Fugs.' I thought he meant Charlie Manson but it was the author he was talking about.

The more I went through it the more sympathy I had for Manson. In the beginning his ideas were kind of OK. Called himself The Gardener and collected all the flower people. Maybe if the karma hadn't gone wrong, things might have worked out different. Who knows how it would have ended up? It was just that old karma going wrong, that's all. It was a pity but that's the way things are sometimes. They just go kind of astray. The karma gets . . . I don't know, turned inside out, I guess. According to Ed Sanders, he was a really good player. Guitarist, I mean. Maybe if the recording contract had come through, that might have turned things around. But it didn't. A shame. Yeah. 'I'm The Gardener. I collect flowers. I see they get light and then I watch them grow' he used to say to people as he drifted along the road. In the days when the karma was good. I wrote a short little lyric in the pub, just scribbled it there on a beer mat to pass the time when there was no one around. It's just called 'The Gardener' or 'Song for Charlie'.

> They call him The Gardener
> The flowers he collects are people
> They bloom in the Californian sun
> His name is Charlie, he lived out in the desert
> Charlie, Charlie, garden while you can.

Easing Up

When I told Boo Boo I'd been thinking of easing up on things he said that it was a good idea, especially the acid, he reckoned. Then he said he was going down to Glenamaddy at the weekend. 'I have to pick up an echo box,' he said, 'and I'm going to check out some support gigs with the showbands.'

'Good thinking, Boo!' I said, but I wasn't really thinking about that. In fact, all I could think about was how great it was that we were all getting ourselves together. Not that we'd been doing all that bad, but you don't want to spend the rest of your life in a bar sweeping floors and scouring glasses. I went down to another practice and the boys were coming on great. They'd managed to get an interview with Dave G on community radio. Also Boo Boo and Chico came back from Glenamaddy at the weekend and said they reckoned there'd be no problem – as regards the showband gigs, that is.

My heart was beating fast all evening in the bar just waiting for Jacy but in the end she never showed and later on that night I heard them saying she'd gone to Dublin. I know I shouldn't have dropped the acid tab but I was so disappointed that I –

But then the electric tingles started at the tips of my toes and before I knew it I was as happy as Larry.

Barbarella's

The pub was going great guns now, after the disco and the building and all was finished. The best of it all was the big paved enclosure in between the old bar and the new, the bit they called The Courtyard. They were going to have all sorts of functions in it, they said. The disco was stuffed nearly every weekend. I often went in for a few jars after work, admiring the decor and whatnot – neon strip lighting, a flashing multicoloured glass floor. About as up-to-the-minute as you could get. It sort of provided comfortable surroundings for the way you'd be thinking. About how you were going to break it to Mona, etc. The words you would use, what exactly it was you were going to say. It was like Austie's place and the way it had gone – an old-fashioned bar outliving its time and inevitably giving way to the new. 'Like I mean, Mona,' I said to myself, 'who would have ever believed there'd be a place like Barbarella's in Scotsfield? Things change. It's the way it is.' 'We can still be friends,' you could hear her saying, nervously adding: 'Can't we?'

'Of course we can,' I'd reply. 'That was never going to be an issue. It was never on the cards, baby. You know?'

It would be good saying that and I felt so good about having worked it out that I dropped another trip. And sitting there in my old caravan it was like looking out on a mystical country. 'It's just like Charlie's garden, Mona,' I'd say. 'A garden that could have been.'

Then I'd burst out laughing when I'd realize what I was actually looking at!

The Tinker Camp

For the so-called 'garden' was nothing more than a couple of old tents with the canvas rotted away and any amount of other old rubbish, including bicycle frames and bedsteads, a broken pram, a burst mattress and a dying-looking piebald pony standing tied to a tree. Not to mention God knows how many car wrecks. With anything that might have been of value on them long since stripped and sold. Travelling tinkers came and went but the only one there on a permanent basis was Mangan. In the nights when they came, you'd hear them all arguing, playing Johnny Cash and Elvis, getting violent then, and drunker, as the half-starved mongrels howled along with the galloping music. Sometimes you'd get edgy and you'd find yourself shouting: 'Can't you play something else for a change? Can't you play some other fucking song?' and standing there twitching, not realizing how edgy –

It was the acid, of course, mostly. Looking back that's plain to see, but in those days you mightn't attribute it to that. You'd think it was to do with Jacy and what kind of day you'd had in the pub. You'd be nearly in tears with frustration, trembling on the bed and repeating: *'Why won't they listen? Why?'*

As the dogs howled and the shrill, off-key rockabilly guitar scraped on through the night . . .

(You can tell by the shaky writing just how edgy those days could be.)

12 July 1976, 4.15 a.m.

The dogs the dogs the dogs! They never let them off the leash you see and that's why they howl like fucking dingoes. It really gets on my nerves. Why can't they let them off the chain for a while? Why don't they play something else? Why do they never play some other record for a change? I'm going to go out and tell them. Fuck them! Fuck them and their dogs! I don't have to put up with this! I don't! Oh, Jesus, I feel so cold.

Nervy

You could be particularly nervy, I remember, if a certain number of things were to happen. If Mona didn't come home, say . . .

That was what I was like the night they started up with this accordion, the dogs joining in, some fucker then screeching on a fiddle . . .

All you could think of was that, when she did come home, you'd say: 'I'll never say those things about Jacy again. Ever.'

'You'll never love anyone else,' she'd say. 'You hear me? You won't! I won't allow it, Joseph!' as she stroked your hair, and if you sobbed it would only be because she spoke the truth.

But then in the morning it would all be quiet again with the tinkers having departed and not a sound to be heard, from the woods, across the fields and right into the town. No Johnny Cash, no accordion, no dogs. Peace and silence would reign once more. And you'd take the record by Spontaneous Apple Conclusion out of the drawer and, without even thinking, you'd lift it to your lips. And kiss it. Kiss it as you spoke the single word: *'Iowa.'*

Ten Men Dead

I remember exactly when the argument started. We were all just sitting there, and the next thing you know they were at each other's throats. When he heard about it, Austie went fucking mad. 'Why didn't you throw them out?' he bawled at me. 'They have no business arguing about things like that in here! We have enough trouble with the cops as it is!'

It was to do with the Kingsmills massacre and the ten Protestant labourers who'd been assassinated on their way home from work.

'That's what we've descended to! A fucking sectarian murder gang! Well, if that's what it is, it's not my war and I want no fucking part of it!'

Carson was a well-known Provo. But not any more, by the sound of it.

'We need you so bad,' sneered Hoss, 'for all the good you've ever been.'

'Ten men dead in the snow, slaughtered for sweet fuck all!' he snarled, finishing up his drink.

'If you're not in it then stay well out of it!' snapped Hoss as Carson the former Provo banged the door behind him.

Big Sur

I wondered what The Jace – I felt I knew her so well now it was OK to call her that – made of all that stuff, the killing and bombing, I mean. It was a long way from California, that was for sure. I had a fair idea she didn't give a fuck. 'If that's how they want to live their lives, well, that's fine. All I can say is, include me out.' The unblemished sands of Big Sur stretching out for miles behind her and the Pacific surf crashing. I couldn't stop thinking about things turning out differently for Charlie if he'd gone down the road of Carlos Castaneda and stuff and not got stuck with violent revolution and shit – just how great it all could have been. I'd been reading in the Ed Sanders book about how they used to live in the desert and drive around in these dune buggies, and I'd see myself then just sitting on a rock, sharing a toke with Charlie. And him nodding as he said: 'You know what? You're right. You're right about love, you and Jacy.'

'Me and The Jace,' I'd say, 'I think we got it right. Two flowers in a beautiful garden.'

As, behind a monster spliff, Charlie 'The Gardener' twinkled!

Cops

Hoss got his name from one of the Cartwright brothers in the TV Western series *Bonanza* and was built like a brick shithouse. One man you didn't argue with was Hoss Watson for he'd take you apart without even blinking. Ever since the salesman's death the cops had been shadowing him because they were pretty sure he'd been in on it. And now that the British Ambassador had died they had got it into their heads he'd been involved in that operation too, because of a comment he'd made to the sergeant one night. 'Good enough for him,' he'd quipped, or something like that. But they had nothing on him they could make stick.

You couldn't move now without the cops watching you. One night I got talking to one at the corner, the radio on his hip spitting static. 'What do you think of this town?' I said, not really caring what he said, just to make conversation more than anything. He was a young fellow not much older than myself, looking at me with his face so pale. 'What do I think of this town?' he said. 'I think it's hell.'

I felt sorry for him that he had to think that. Thinking that about anywhere, in fact. Especially when things were going so well for me. Not knowing what to do when only minutes later I'd seen her and her pal coming out of the office where she worked. I ducked down into the entry and watched the two of them going up the street. The other chick I didn't know but she was completely different to Jacy. Definitely no Charlie Manson joints there, or trips in dune buggies, I kept thinking. She was just an ordinary country girl who, I figured, worked in the bank or some place, with this little skirt and jumper on her. But any friend of Jacy's was a friend of mine, I reckoned, and all I could think was that it was real good to see them together that way, just rapping away there the way chicks do.

In the nights now I couldn't sleep at all – just thinking of the flowers on her collar and the way she slung the bag across her shoulder. I wondered what was in it. A diary, some books, perhaps some dope. I wondered what she read. I had found myself being amazed by some of the writings Charlie'd been influenced by – it gave you a list at the back of Ed's book and I couldn't wait to get my hands on some of those. They sounded like fantastic reading material. Even better than the stuff The Seeker had given me. Lyric poetry. Philosophy. *'The printed word is the key to the truth. Knowledge is power,'* he used to say to The Family. There were quotes in there from *The I-Ching*. Robert Heinlein. Hermann Hesse's *Steppenwolf.*

I didn't know that one.

Library

Una Halpin the librarian got it for me. 'I didn't know you read so much,' she said. No, I said, I didn't – only lately. 'It's a fabulous read,' she told me then. 'I read it all the time.'

I couldn't believe my ears. *What next?* I thought. *Una Halpin starts the revolution with Charlie and Family? In that little crocheted dress she'd be a very likely candidate all right.*

But I thanked her anyway and went off to read my book. It was all about this guy, deep and complicated with so many layers to his personality that you got dizzy even reading about them. I'd sit up all night just reading it and smoking roll-ups, every so often lifting my head and turning to her to say: *'Your face in the light when it shines . . .'* and then smoothing back her hair, long and blonde and fine and just streaming out there to touch them stars.

I leaned forward to kiss her ear. And it was then I sang it softly: *'Oh but California/California I'm coming home'* – the Joni Mitchell song, of course. I could see her eyes shining and it did my heart good.

'Big Sur,' I murmured to myself as I closed old Hermann and fell on the bed. 'Big Sur, you're looking good.'

One night I heard her say: 'Let's just go, let's just take off and –'

'Where we gonna go?' I asked her and lit another smoke.

'Joey,' she said. 'Don't even ask such questions.'

We were rolling across the Midwest when I heard myself speaking the words.

'I feel I can tell you anything,' I said.

To which she replied: 'You can.'

'When we get there, what will it be like?' I asked her.

'It's like heaven, Iowa,' she said. 'I spent all my childhood summers there. And that's how I've always thought of it. With the golden corn swaying and the big blue sky seeming to stretch for ever – it's the way a child might imagine it to be. Paradise, you know?'

I could sense my eyes glittering. Glittering like that stretch of water I saw whenever I melted into Mona. Except that this was even more beautiful.

'How a child might imagine it,' I heard her saying again, as she slipped a cassette tape into the dash and the fluid country shuffle of J. J. Cale went sweeping out into the weighted air as we cruised on down the interstate.

'You like that one?' she asked me.

'"Call Me the Breeze",' I said, drumming my fingers in time on the hood.

'OK, I will, then! I'll call you that!' she replied, as J. J. Cale sang out and on we sped towards the heart of the sun.

Things were going from strength to strength for The Mohawks – the name they eventually settled on after hours of arguing. I had to work so I couldn't go to the studio but when I switched on the radio in Austie's there's Boo Boo going full throttle. 'Records?' he said. 'We don't make records, Dave. Psycho fucktunes is what we make. We piss on vinyl.'

'OK,' said Dave G., 'so what do you do apart from urinating on plastic? The music you make, could you describe it for us?'

'Sure I'll describe it for you suckers!' said Boo. 'The Mohawks from Scotsfield – you wanna know what music they make, what kinda sounds those mothers lay down? Well, I'll tell you what we are and what kinda sounds! We're the screaming psychobilly cowboys, a garage band with music to melt your brain!'

'And what might punters expect to hear if they go along to see you guys?'

'Expect the terror of low-flying Stukas! Hank Williams on amyl nitrate!'

'So there they are, folks! The Mohawks – a loud, dirty combo with lots of sheer, aggressive bad-ass attitude! And they definitely are not punk!'

'Punk's for queens!' sniffed Boo Boo as, with scabrous, paint-stripping guitars, the band launched into a driving, raw version of '76', one they'd written in the van in ten minutes flat.

> Thirty and thirty and ten and six
> How many's that? It's seventy-six!
> Seventy-six! Seventy-six!
>
> The British Ambassador's in the grave
> The British Ambassador's in the grave
> Number plate 6, 6 M-I-K!
> On this beautiful summer's day!
>
> Seventy-six! Seventy-six!
> What the fuck do you make of this?

The minute the show was over, the switchboard was jammed with calls of complaint, mostly from in or around the Scotsfield area. One woman said: 'Those foul-mouthed hooligans don't represent us!'

Dumb motherfuckers, I thought, as I lit up a spliff and had me a laugh. Then I opened up *The Family*.

And the more I read it, all I kept thinking of was that old good Charlie – the Charlie before things had to go and get themselves fucked up – hooking his thumbs into his belt and grinning: 'You're looking good, man!' not realizing for a minute or so just who it was he was talking to – me and 'My Lady'. Jacy strumming her guitar as she sat in the sun and Charlie slapping me on the back as he said: 'She's one good chick, man! One hell of a chick, believe me!' The two of us sitting there as he opened his tobacco pouch and thought for a long time before asking: 'You ever been to India?' I shook my head. 'I'm gonna go there one day,' he said. 'When the revolution's done. I'm gonna go up to the mountains and seek out the prophets.'

'A pity you didn't meet The Seeker,' I told him. 'He knew, man! He *knew* – you know what I'm saying?'

'Right,' said Charlie as he popped the rollie between his lips. 'Friend o' yours then, Joey?'

'Yeah,' I replied, 'he sure was, Charlie. He sure was. He's dead now. Overdosed in London.'

'That's where you're wrong,' he said as he exhaled a plume of smoke. 'He's not dead. He's sitting right there beside you.'

I was so stoned I could hardly think straight!

'There's always a frog beside the pond, Joey,' Charlie said then, and I thought about that for a good long time as the desert sun burnt on, trying to figure out what Charlie had meant, for you always knew he meant something.

Romantics

Sometimes after work I'd go into Barbarella's and have myself a few beers and, if she wasn't there, just sit there and think about stuff she might say – in a downtown club maybe, looking into my eyes with the smoke curling from the cigarette as one of our favourite songs was played. They were always playing our favourite numbers in Barbarella's. Sitting there with the table lamps glowing and a couple of dancers moving in the shadows we'd look at one another and smile, especially if the song – which a lot of the time it seemed to be – was 'I'm Not in Love' by 10cc. I liked that one and I knew so did she, the way it was about someone who was so deeply in love that not only could they not admit it but had to keep on denying it, it was so strong. Knowing that sooner or later they'd be forced to give in.

When I went home, I read some more of *Don Juan* and then opened up *Siddhartha*, the other Hermann Hesse book I'd just started reading. I sat up until dawn, really getting into it. I happened just by accident to notice in the paper that Martin Scorsese's film *Taxi Driver* was tipped for movie of the year.

Showbands

Any time you rang Boo now, or called to his house, he was below in the garage practising with the band. One night when I was working behind the bar he called by for a beer. 'Say, Joey, can you do Mount-mellick this Friday?' he says.

I nodded and slapped up the pint. 'Sure thing!' I says.

So that was my first gig with The Mohawks, lugging hired amplifiers from a weatherbeaten bandwagon into a draughty old country parish hall. The band that night was Magic and the Swallows, their lead singer a rotund headcase in a suit made of lightbulbs. 'Don't care for your kind of music much,' he said, 'but I'll say you've got some guts.'

We hung out for a while there after the gig, drank in the hall for a couple of hours, then headed home. 'Did you see the faces of the hoors when I was singing "Schizoid"?' Boo Boo said. Sure, we said, how could we not, it'd have been pretty fucking hard to miss them! But it was great gas and you could see Boo Boo was right pleased even if he didn't say it. As I drove, I kept myself amused with thoughts and dreams about me and The Jace (dune buggies scorch the roads of Ireland!), and when I came back to earth, we were coming into Navan. It was a fantastic fresh morning, the windscreen splattered with flies. All I can say is that it was just wonderful to be heading home, knowing she was there asleep, soon to rise and head for work in the shirt-factory office. I couldn't stop thinking of Magic and the Swallows playing 'It's Over' by Roy Orbison, and how if the words of that song were saying anything, they were telling me something about Mona and me. And how all things, no matter how special they might have been in the past, must eventually come to an end. The most important thing for me to remember, I reflected, swinging the wagon on to the main street (Boo Boo was always dropped off first) was that when feelings are that strong – as strong as mine were for Jacy – what you've got to do is face up to the fact. For if I didn't, I knew, all I was going to succeed in doing was prolonging the pain – for both of us.

Which was why – at home – I rehearsed in front of the mirror. So as to get it right.

I can see now that I was in denial about *Taxi Driver*. Even at that early stage, I had definitely been influenced by it to some extent. I suppose later on I just found it embarrassing to admit to, what with all the shit they wrote about me in the papers. But it doesn't matter now, does it?

Sure I was influenced. I was even standing like De Niro, for God's sake. With my legs apart and my two arms folded.

'Mona,' I said into the mirror, 'we've got to talk.'

Also: *'I've got something here for you. I think we ought to talk.'*

I held it out. Then coughed and said: *'It's a present, yeah?'*

It would make everything so much easier, I reckoned. I spun on my heel and grinned at my reflection.

'We'll always be friends, babe,' I told her. 'Now and for always.'

Then I blew my gunfinger and headed into town, unburdened and happy and walking as though on clouds.

The Now

One night, after a party in the bar, I put away so much drink that I thought: *This is it. This is the time. The Now. I'll go out to the caravan now and do it, without presents. Or flowers or anything else. Now.*

I had everything figured out, down to coming past the dogs, having my boot ready if any of them tried anything, and repeating to myself: 'This is it. This is the end of the line, Mona. I hope you'll understand. We've been special to each other for a long time now. Except now I've got to say . . . it's over.'

But I knew in my heart that it wasn't to be. I could see it plain as day the way things would really happen. As they did, in fact, Mona standing at the doorway of the caravan in an old coat, hissing: 'You're drunk. *Get in!*' As I fell inside, becoming so excited that I couldn't seem to hold on to anything. There was a steak and kidney pie that I took out of the fridge but I dropped that too and somehow – I think I must have stood on it – it all got mashed up on the floor.

Pies

Some of these pieces are so badly written it's a miracle I can read them at all. One minute scribbled in something close to Arabic and the next in these huge childish letters, ringed in red like this one – PIES!

Which I'd spent plenty of time thinking about because, although I knew they were turning me into a bullock, I still wasn't able to stop, all the time thinking: *I've got to build myself up, to keep my mind focused. Build up to that major decision! Keep your mind focused and eat eat eat!*

I don't think it really hit me, though, until one day Austie said: 'Jesus, Mary and Joseph, Tallon, you're gone into an animal. What are you trying to do to yourself at all? You keep on like this and you'll make Hoss Watson look like a clothes peg!'

We had a laugh about it but I can't say I was laughing very much when I weighed myself on the chemist's scales on the way home. I had gone up from twelve to sixteen and a half stone. I told myself I would have to work out a programme of fitness and discipline for I definitely was starting to look more like Hoss than Keith Carradine. It shows you how stupid I could be that there I was, working out my campaign of order and fitness right there in my mind – I had paid another visit to Dublin for the sole purpose of viewing *Taxi Driver* again; so much then for my subsequent denials! – and me halfway through another steak and kidney! Thinking about Jacy and thinking about Mona and how the 'programme' must be started once and for all. *From Monday on* – Total Organization! was all I could think. That was the way it had to be. 'There's no other way,' I repeated. 'Total Org. is the only option.'

(There is a torn piece of paper here marked 'T. B. is God's lonely man!' T. B. being Travis Bickle, of course, the character in the movie. And, underneath – can you believe it? – 'I must get in shape. Too much sitting has ruined my body. Twenty-five push-ups each morning, one hundred sit-ups, one hundred knee-bends.'

I must have copied it out in the cinema, if the crazily slanted writing is anything to go by. No, I remember doing it actually – scribbling it on my knee in the Adelphi on Dublin's Middle Abbey Street.)

Peace and Reconciliation Rally

'Are you at it again?' says Austie, pushing the pie aside as he hands me this leaflet about the peace and reconciliation rally they were planning for The Courtyard. It was Fr Connolly who had organized it, he told me.

'He knows the crowd above in Belfast who got the whole thing started.'

I had seen them on the telly, talking about setting up a movement for peace after three innocent children got run over. 'Maybe we could get Boo Boo and the boys to play at it,' I said.

'Like fuck we could,' said Austie, rolling a keg along the floor in front of him. 'Can't you read? The word is "peace", not fucking mayhem. Will you change that barrel there Joey and make yourself useful to fuck out of that!'

'*Peace*,' I said and smiled, giving him the 'V' sign just for a laugh. When I was changing the barrel, Hoss came in and I handed him the leaflet. He sneered, then rolled it up in a ball and tossed it on the floor. 'Doddering old bollocks of a padre,' he said. 'Nothing better to do with his time than talk to them mad bitches.'

'I think it's a good idea,' I said, although to tell the truth I didn't think any such thing. I wasn't thinking about it at all. I was thinking: *Soon it begins. T. O. Total Organization.*

'Peace with justice – that's all we've ever wanted,' Hoss said and flicked a flame from his lighter. 'And we won't have that until those cunts are gone.'

'What?' I said as he jerked his thumb at the telly where a British officer was addressing the camera, explaining some action or other in the South Armagh area.

They said it was going to be the hottest summer for fifty years. Eighty-three degrees Fahrenheit, according to the weatherman, average twenty degrees above normal. The fire brigade was up and down the street the whole day long, off out in the country fighting gorse fires and barn blazes. On top of that there was a water shortage. Then there was the bank strike, everyone cashing their cheques in Austie's. 'The country's going mad,' said Austie with a sigh as Paddy Cooney, the Minister for Justice, appeared on the screen and promised all-out war on the Provos. 'There is a huge round-up on the way,' he went on, 'and an awful lot of people will be getting an unexpected holiday.'

And Hoss Watson would be one of them, if the cops got their way. Sooner or later he knew they'd get him.

'A disaster,' he eventually admitted to me one night, drunk, mumbling incoherently about the salesman. 'A disaster, that's what it was, Joey. Things go wrong in a war, you know? The wrong ones get it. Campbell Morris was an innocent man. But the British Ambassador? He deserved it, for Christ's sake. He deserved everything he got. Because he was a spy all right, and make no mistake about it! I shed no tears for him, my friend! Even though I had nothing to do with it, I take off my hat to the volunteers who had!'

I managed to piece together a vague picture of what had happened that night with Campbell Morris. A few of them had decided they would act the big hard Provisional IRA men, drive him out to The Ritzy on the pretext of seeing some blues, then make a detour to the reservoir. Interrogating him all the way there in the car, accusing him of being an 'agent' and working for the British government. Snooping around border towns while pretending to flog pharmaceuticals. But then things had got out of hand: he'd started frothing at the mouth – Hoss reckoned he was epileptic – and they'd panicked. It all ending up with his body in the water.

'But they won't pin it all on me,' hissed Hoss. 'Those fucking cops, they picked on the wrong felon when they singled out the man from *Bonanza*!'

There was something about the way he looked at you . . .

You just knew he meant business. I didn't want to talk any more about it so I changed the subject. I started talking about football. But I knew Hoss wasn't listening to a word I said. He was miles away, breathing heavily and peering through the coils of smoke with narrowed, obsessive eyes.

21 July 1976, Late – Clock Broke

(in thick black pencil)

The Mysteries of Love!!!??

How is it someone can come, be just there, appear, and it's like you've known them all your life? Steppenwolf is about all those kinds of mysteries. Things I've always thought about but been afraid to say. I can just imagine Hoss if he heard me: 'Mysteries! Mysteries! I'll give you fucking mysteries! Reading too many effing –'

Except the truth is, whether he knows it or not, all of my life I've secretly liked books. Right from a very young age. Even if I don't know that much about them – yet. This being the first time since leaving school I've ever bothered with the library. And I know I have poor Una tortured. 'Are you here again?' she says every day, as off I go with a bundle. But I think she's getting used to me. And I know it's going to be worth it. Already I feel empowered. Like there's been a muscle left slack for too long. Next on the list is the rest of Hermann Hesse. For putting me on to him, gracias, Seeker. Thanks, Eamon.

I think of us sitting in the desert, just him and me and Hesse. Just talking away there about love. Where it comes from and what it means. I mean, you hear lots of things about it. You read about it all the time. But you never think you'll experience it. That's the thing you don't expect. The most wonderful thing about it is not just the ethereal other-worldly feeling, but that once it strikes, you know things will never again be the same. Even the simplest thing like walking past Jackson's Garage – whatever way the sunshine falls on it, the way it did today around two o'clock – you'll find yourself saying: 'Jackson's Garage – it's the same old garage and yet it's not. It's become something completely new. Somehow. I'm afraid I don't understand it. I genuinely do not.'

Which is perhaps the greatest thing of all about it – your not being able to understand. In the same way you can't comprehend why you are being so personable all of a sudden. And which, by the looks of things, hasn't gone unnoticed by a lot of other folks either! As Hoss said to me today: 'Well, fuck me pink, who's a happy camper? Monday morning and the shine off his eyes would blind you! I wouldn't mind some of what you're on, Tallon!'

Except that I wasn't on anything. Unless you meant an untroubled sea – the placidest ocean that's ever existed, to my knowledge. And which, if I'd been asked about it before, I'd have described as 'a load of bollocks', the way they all do in Austie's all the time.

But it isn't a load of bollocks. It is just about as far from being a load of bollocks as any human being can conceive, this fascinating mystery called love.

Boo Boo

I'd hardly finished writing that – it's like yesterday, that particular night – when the next thing you know there's this hammering at the door. Crazy. 'Who the fuck's that,' I says. Not Mangan again because if it fucking well is, looking for fucking sugar or toilet paper again, I'll –!

Then who does it turn out to be? Only Boo Boo with this chick from Newtown and a big pink cockatoo head on her. 'This is Anka,' he says. Turns out that she's German. Then what does he do? Announces that the boys have reached the final of the Battle of the Bands competition in Limerick. 'Every journo in the country'll be sniffing around. The word is they want punk. Every mag you pick up it's The Clash this, The Sex Pistols that! They want "white riots"? Then we'll fucking give it to them – street fucking guerrillas, Molotov cocktails! They don't know what they're talking about, fucking art school wankers – for that's all they are, no matter what they say!'

'You mind if I skin up?' says Anka, sticking her Doc Martens right in front of my face. 'Sure,' I said. 'Go right ahead.' I couldn't believe this fucking news!

'We're an unexploded bomb,' said Boo Boo as Anka slid her tongue along the gum line. 'Right, Joey?'

'An unexploded bomb,' I agreed. Then he opened his palm to reveal a sellotaped tab; good old lysergic acid like a little eye looking up at you. Saying: 'Well, hi there, Joey! *Eat me!*'

I didn't mind smoking draw. I had no problem with that at all. It was the acid I had begun to get worried about, and the effect it might be having on me. And I was feeling quite proud that I'd managed to cut it way down now that my life had begun to find direction. 'It's pyramid. The best you can get,' he said as he pressed it on to his thumb. 'Here, man. Take it!' I definitely wasn't going to do it. But when he popped one himself and she did as well, I just said: 'OK, one last time!' Then into the mouth and down she goes.

It was the mellowest feeling just sitting there listening to Boo Boo as he went on raving – this gig, that gig, all these fucking gigs – as Anka's dayglo head kept nodding: 'Mohawks – band vot iz seh best, ja?'

'You better believe it! Snarling genius from the bog's black heart!' says Boo, blasting a chord from an air guitar as the '*I Love The Sonics!*' tattoo rippled on his arm, living words of deep blue and red.

Outside, the moon looked in with these great big heavy-lidded eyes. I don't know what we started laughing about but we were still at it when morning broke. So we went into Austie's for a pint. There was talk of us going home around lunchtime but it was my day off so we stayed there drinking all day. 'Would you look at that!' says Boo Boo as Anka got sick out in the backyard. 'Jeez!' I said. This expanding yellowish pool full of all these amazing colours. We must have been standing staring at it for ages, a lake to us now studded with bright shining gems as poor Anka barfed up again. '*Bwoagh!*' she says and doubles over. 'I love her so much I'd eat it!' says Boo Boo as we staggered back inside, wrapped around one another like lovers.

A Sign

At times Austie's could have you in stitches. It could really be a fucking hilarious place with the boys all the business coming into the bar: 'Ah she's a great girl, my missus, I don't know what I'd do without her! Worth her weight in gold, she is!' Then, before you know it, rubbing hands and making plans after the disco to go out to the blues in The Ritzy.

I was rarely interested, in those faraway days being much too preoccupied with higher things. The only thing that bothered me then were the lies I'd think about them telling – not only to their wives but to themselves. Which, the more I thought about it, made me think something else about love that made it seem so really special. That if it was the real thing, it had the effect of making you feel like you were the only two people to whom it had ever happened. The only two in the world chosen to be so lucky. And almost feeling sorry for everyone else who hadn't been so fortunate. But who would think they had.

Then you'd find yourself saying: 'Ah yes! Those poor old fucks trotting out to dirty films! Who'll never know what the real thing is! Who'll never know love, I mean, not sex.' I'd sit there in the caravan for hours, really stoned, feeling sorry for them, strumming away at 'The Only One'. It went: *The Only One/When that day comes/In the burning sun/She'll surely be the one . . .'*

Or listening to them as they sat at the counter in the bar, muttering about women and going: 'I wouldn't mind shifting that, would you?' or 'Did you see the tits on yon?', and all of a sudden they'd seem like nothing so much as the saddest men in the world. Not being able to help the glow you'd feel growing all around you and seeing it, in a way, as a kind of sign that you'd been chosen. And why you'd find yourself writing in *Reflections* – just a children's copybook that I'd used as a diary –

25 July 1976

It's 3 a.m. or so and I just got home. Went to the disco after Austie's and waited but no show, at least not while I was there. I feel especially close to her tonight. They all went out to the blues but I had everything I wanted in Barbarella's – well, almost. They played you-know-what and I swear I was in dreamland. When that song is playing you just want to get the guy and say: 'You are in love, so stop denying it! Admit that you're in that place which is so pure and precious and wholesome . . .'

Just admit it for God's sake!

Am working 11–7 tomorrow so I better get some shut eye.

Love you.

Mona at Dawn

The cops pulled me in – by the looks of things everyone was a suspect now – and started asking me about Hoss, whether I thought he'd been involved in the Ambassador job or not and threatening to knock seven different kinds of shit out of me if I didn't co-operate. There was this guy Tuite from Dublin, the head of a special new outfit called The

Heavy Gang, who'd been sent down to shake the place up and come up with 'some fucking answers', as he put it himself. He had fists like fucking lump hammers and you knew he wouldn't be afraid to use them. 'You must hear plenty of Provo gossip in that place!' he said, meaning Austie's. I told him what I thought: that Hoss was innocent – of that job, anyway, I said. For I believed what he'd told me that night in the bar. When Tuite said: 'I'm not sure I believe you, Tallon,' I just shrugged and said: 'Believe what you like.'

That drove him mad – all you could hear before they threw me out on the street was: 'You're all in on it! You're all in it together! You all know something! I fucking well know – and I'll find out! You mark my words!

'You want to know what I think of this town?' he'd bawled at me then, clenching and unclenching his fists. 'I think it's full of felons, full of twisted fucking felons living treacherous felon lives! Provo filth – that's what it's full of!'

He went on and on like that, with spit on his lips. But I didn't care, because when you're in love that's the way it is. All you care about is a small soft hand and that windblown hair as she comes stepping right out of the ocean.

I had just nodded and said: 'That's fine.'

'Don't you worry!' he said. 'I'll nail that Watson cunt! And you'd better not be hiding anything, Tallon!'

The dawn was breaking when I got back to the camp. The dogs were at it again and I could see Mangan peeping through the curtain. The smack or two that Tuite had given me at the end had unnerved me slightly and now the dogs were starting to unsettle me too, so that's why I lost it a bit that night. *'Shut up!'* I shouted and swung the boot. Without even realizing I was doing it.

'You leave them alone!' I heard Mangan squealing from the caravan doorway in his nightshirt. 'You think I don't know what you be at? Who's that woman you have in there? Who do you be talking to at night? Eh? Who is she? I can hear you! You think that I can't hear you? Eh?'

'Leave it!' I growled. 'Do you hear me? *Leave* it!' and slammed the door behind me. As a result I needed Mona more than ever that night and it made me feel very confused.

'Joseph,' she said, 'you look pale . . .'

I couldn't think straight, mostly because deep inside I was trying hard to find a way – the best way of breaking the news. 'Mona, there's something I want to talk to you about,' I began to say. But when she looked at me and said: 'Come here,' all the words just withered on my lips.

When I awoke the sun was slanting through the window and she was sitting staring down at me, pushing my hair back from my –

'The place of peace,' she whispered in my ear. 'I'm the only one who knows where it is. And you know it. There's no one else who knows. Would you like me to tell you, Joseph? Would you like me to tell you where it is, that precious harbour? Would you? Tell me . . .'

I was groaning, thinking of an island out there across a stretch of cobalt blue water towards which the twinkling lights beckoned you, where you knew once you reached it you would always be safe. I groaned again.

'He used to sing it to me,' said Mona. 'His favourite song – "Harbour Lights".'

It was my father she was talking about. Sometimes she sang it too – ever so softly. I used to love listening to it, although you had to strain hard to hear her. I don't think she even knew she was singing it at all. It went:

> One evening long ago
> A big ship was leaving
> One evening long ago
> Two lovers they were grieving . . .

'But we never reached it, Joey. We never got to that harbour.'
Then she started crying. Stroking my face with her pale pink palm.
'But you will, Joseph. I'll help you.'

It was making everything harder now than ever. I heard someone moving about outside and then I saw a shadow moving past the window. 'Who's there?' I shouted and covered myself with a blanket. 'I said, who's there?'

There was no one there when I looked again but I was sure it must have been Mangan. I was sweating all over and although I didn't want a spliff I had one anyway, but it didn't do me much good. All I could think of was organization. T. O. – fixing on the words so much that it was making it harder for me even to put the two of them together. So I decided to gather my thoughts instead by writing them down on a loose piece of paper now yellowed with age and simply marked *Charlie – The Truth . . .*

Late – no date

Charlie the Gardener could have been good if things had worked out the karma if that had been meant to be we can all be good you know that Jacy if you follow the path of Siddhartha if you drink from the fountain of love for love is the drug love is all as she who is The Only One is I'm Not in Love but I am you see you see I am I – love love love love you Jacy The Jacy love is all is everything . . .

I must have fallen asleep.

Hoss

I felt sorry for Hoss after they took him in and gave him the hiding. The new law was that anyone caught singing a Republican song could be arrested and given a kicking. Not that they said that, but in practice that's more or less what happened. Hoss was in the middle of 'The Ballad of James Connolly' – '*God's curse on you, England, you cruel-hearted monster*' – when in comes Tuite and the Heavy Gang. Before you know what's happening they have him out the door and the next time you see him, well, all you can say is recognizing him – even up close – might have been a problem. He had three teeth missing and one of his eyes was the size of Detective Tuite's fist. They'd said they'd get him and so they had. It was clear now they had a licence to do whatever they wanted, the new emergency legislation taking care of all that. Which more or less meant if you had the temerity to open your mouth and say something they didn't like, you could well find yourself slung in jail, with fuck-all chance of appeal. Or pulled in so often it would make your life a misery.

It was around that time that Sandy McGloin reappeared. He had been away for a while. You didn't ask where. He was an old friend of Hoss's but just about as different from him as it was possible to imagine. Sandy was quiet and inoffensive, always neatly dressed in a grey or black suit and tie, standing at the end of the bar with not a pick on him, chain-smoking Major cigarettes and sipping Johnnie Walker whiskey, agreeing with everything you said. One night he even said to me: 'I wonder why they can't agree and put an end to it all, this business up in the north. What do you think, Joey – don't you think it's time it quit?'

I said I thought it was. 'Yes, it is, I think.' But to tell you the truth I was watching the door to see might she come in and didn't hear a word Sandy said.

When I looked around, the Minister for Justice was back on the telly. Now what had happened a young cop had been killed by a booby-trap bomb – in a town only twenty miles from Scotsfield. He said that this meant the gloves were off for sure and the crackdown was going to intensify. When the boys heard that, they all started laughing. 'That's what they think!' they snorted, and smirked over at Sandy. Knowingly. But Sandy said nothing. Just went on drinking and staring straight ahead, as if to say: 'I know nothing about any of that. All of that political stuff – it just goes over my head, I'm afraid.'

The only things he liked to talk about, really, were his wife and kids up in Belfast. He was always telling me that the day he was looking forward to most was when they could come to Scotsfield and join him.

'Thanks very much, Joey,' he said as I brought him his whiskey. 'Have a wee one yourself.'

But I didn't bother. Very soon my regime would be starting in earnest. For I had now finally reached my decision.

I don't think many of them went out to the blues that night. Sandy didn't anyway. He said he was going home. That was the impression he gave you – that he didn't mind other people indulging, but couldn't really be bothered himself. Once he showed me a picture of his wife. She was very beautiful indeed. 'She's a schoolteacher,' he told me. 'I don't know my luck.'

The Laughing Boy

I went out to The Ritzy myself for a laugh the next weekend. We all got a lift with Hoss and, despite what had happened with the cops, he seemed to be in great old form. There was nothing he loved more than telling yarns about Brendan Behan – the 'Laughing Boy' – writer and big-time IRA man of the fifties. A lot of the lads said it was because he looked the spit of him, with his wee short legs and greasy curls. 'So anyway,' he was saying, 'the Laughing Boy's in France without a tosser and he says, he says, how will I earn me a crust? So he goes over to Froggy: "C'mere, Henri," he says. "How about I paint a welcome sign over your bar to get the tourists in? Let me paint you a sign and your pub'll be fucking hopping!" "Right," says your man, "then away you go," and off goes Brendan, off he goes with his bucket and brush, and by Christ if next day the fucking bar's not stuffed – stuffed with English fucking tourists and Behan there half-twisted like the cat who got the cream. "By Jasus, how did he do it," says the owner. "How did he fucking do it?" Then he looks outside and what does he see in big bright painted letters – *en Anglaise*, as they say! – *"This Is The Best Fucking Bar In Paris!"*'

We were all in stitches after that, and then the blues came on. Mostly all you heard were grunts and groans. Some of the time it was OK but after a while you'd've had so much bad sound and out-of-focus scenes – as well as being tired from working hard all day – that you'd find yourself just drifting off to sleep. It was at times like that you'd see her, more clearly and far sharper than any dumb, stupid movie, blue or otherwise.

Waiting, maybe, in this little place in Mexico, with the dust all blowing around her and me just coming out of the haze to take her hand. 'I knew you'd come,' I could hear her saying. 'I knew if I waited long enough that sooner or later you'd appear.'

It was when I was emerging out of a half sleep just like that that I looked over and saw Boyle Henry sitting there, I suppose no more than ten feet away from me. I glanced a second time to make sure it was him for I was surprised, to say the least. For someone like him, the local bigwig councillor, was just about the last person you expected to see. No matter how much he might be involved. But there he was, his gaze fixed intensely on the screen as a masked woman, in close-up, parted her lips and mock-lisped: '*What is the secret of* The Blue Sextet?'

There was some kind of a party going on in a country house now and all you could hear was the vibrato organ music reaching a crescendo as the woman in the mask began to strip. During that scene – she was covering herself with a fan – I got to wondering had they ever gotten around to making a movie out of *Steppenwolf*.

When I looked again Boyle Henry was gone and there was a rolled-up tissue on the ground. I wondered what Mrs Henry – his wife in her younger days had been a local beauty – would say if you posted her that as a present. Not that anyone would be stupid enough to go and do the like of that. The way I was thinking, I found myself having a certain kind of pity for him. I could see myself saying: 'Boyle, can I tell

34

you something?' and explaining as best I could what it's like to be in love. To experience the mystery. How crystal clear it makes everything seem and how it can change your life. *Forbidden Photos of a Lady Above Suspicion* was coming on as I left, the Provo nodding as he opened the door.

Battle of the Bands

Well, were Boo Boo and the boys over the moon or what? I mean, invited to perform was one thing but to go and win it outright was far more than any of them had dared to dream, no matter what they might have said. And the standard was fucking high, there's no point in saying it wasn't, with a heavy metal band from Dublin looking like they were going to walk it and then this other crowd from Cork who did all their own amazing stuff. Turning in a scorching set and no fucking question about it. But when Boo Boo hit that stage like a man possessed you knew something really special had happened. The audience went apeshit and it really didn't surprise you. Scaling the amplifiers in his swallowtail coat and black pipestem trousers, he was like a miniature juju man, kung-fu chopping the air and sweeping his stovepipe hat, out of his mind on something. Except he was out of his mind on nothing, apart from the desire for fame, which he'd always been honest and upfront about. How many nights in the back of the van had I heard him at it: 'We're gonna do it, Joey, you wait and see! We're going right to the top, you mark my words! Right through the fucking stratosphere in our psycho mothership!'

The judge said he hadn't seen a band that could come close to them in years. 'Fucking right,' said Boo Boo, 'and we're going to see that's the way it stays!', as he hit me a karate chop right between the ribs. They won five hundred quid, a series of gigs in McGonagles, which was the 'in' place, and a bunch of hours studio time. All the way back you didn't hear a word. It was like they were all in shock. But you knew they were happy. It was all over the papers after that, '*Scotsfield's finest!*', like they were a fucking football team, when a few weeks before they'd have lynched the band. But no one was complaining, it was all part of the bigger game. There was even talk of a record deal now, at the very least a single. Around that time there was a call from *Scene*, a new music mag starting up in Dublin, requesting an

35

interview. 'I'll melt their fucking jackeen brains,' vowed Boo. 'I'll take their heads apart.'

The heading – on the very front page of *Scene* – was: *Scotsfield Psychopunk Speaks Out!*, with a photo of Boo sticking up his middle finger. It seemed there was nothing they couldn't do. Songs were literally pouring out of him. He even wrote one about The Ritzy – 'Hardcore'. He nearly wrecked the whole fucking place performing it for me in the caravan!

A Beacon on the Hill

Between the success of the band and the peace rally coming up, there was a great stir now in the town and everyone was glad of the opportunity to show the place in a better light. Especially Fr Connolly, droning on in the pulpit about Ireland having had enough of 'many young men of twenty' going out to die and why a decent, law-abiding town like Scotsfield would never collude with a minute crackpot element whose only achievement was to besmirch this country's name in the eyes of all good, right-thinking people. That was why he had invited the 'Peace People' from Belfast who, he said, had informed him that they would be more than delighted to come to Scotsfield. It was going to be the most wonderful night that the town had ever seen, he said, and that as a result of it we were destined to become a 'beacon on the hill'. But what was necessary was that everyone be seen to muck in and put their shoulder to the wheel for the press would be watching us like hawks. In the churchyard afterwards there was great excitement. It was like the sun had come out especially for Scotsfield.

Everyone went home in great humour that day.

Books Is Bollocks

I used always to leave my copy of *Steppenwolf* lying on the counter – you could tell now that it had been read a dozen times, if not more – in case she might come in and ask me about it, just catch a glimpse of it out of the corner of her eye. But it didn't happen. She always tended to concentrate on whatever it was she was doing at any one particular time. Whoever it was she might be meeting, or what she wanted to drink. But it didn't matter that much, not at all in fact, for it was just nice having the book there, thinking of how she'd read it too and how when the time was right we'd be discussing it together. Properly and intelligently. Taking our time. Not the way some of them would approach it, Hoss for example, or Austie himself, flicking through the pages growling: 'What the fuck is this? Me bollocks! Books is a load of bollocks, Tallon!'

I had known the band Steppenwolf, of course – lead singer John Kay – who'd done the music for *Easy Rider*. After work one day me and Boo Boo drove out to the reservoir and the two of us started singing it – 'Born to Be Wild', one of their greatest hits. 'Did you know they were named after the Hermann Hesse book?' I asked Boo. 'Fucking hippy cancer!' he snorted and flicked the jay out the window. Then, half stoned, he said: 'I've done a good song about Connolly, Joey.' 'What's that?' I said as I took a drag. '"Peacenik Fuckbrain Padre",' he says, and the two of us doubled up with the laughing. When the mirth had subsided, I got to wondering could Bennett hear us? We were parked in the exact spot where they'd found him. His voice coming drifting on the wind, stirring the leaves as though he'd never been gone at all.

Gig 2!

The night of the gig, McGonagles was heaving. I couldn't believe it myself, except that when we got talking to the punters it didn't take long to figure out that it was for the band from Manchester, Alberto y Los Trios Paranoias, not us. But they were damn good and no question about it. Which they had to be, I guess, for Boo Boo took the place asunder again. Doc Holliday on amphetamines, hurling himself across the stage rasping *'Psycho!'* and *'Hardcore!'* at the audience, who couldn't believe their ears. I'm not saying we blew Dublin's mind but we were asked back for three encores. We had a few jars with the Albertos in the dressing room after. I guess you could say they were a sort of satirical band, taking the piss out of everyone but most especially the punks. 'Fuck them middle-class weekend punks,' said Boo Boo, and they laughed. 'Scummy Dublin ponces living off Daddy's wallet!'

It was fucking great to be alive that night, that's all I know. 'Pity there aren't more places like McGonagles,' said Boo on the way home one night, 'Then we wouldn't have to do these country dumps, supporting every redneck prick from here to Ballyfuckways!'

Idea

The idea behind *Steppenwolf* was that you had so many different personalities inside the one person – any one person. It suggested that you or whoever you were, your soul – however you might like to describe it – was split into several selves and that you were like an onion, the more layers you shed the more emerged underneath. 'Fascinating' is not a word you would have heard me using much. Usually I'd have been embarrassed, to tell you the God's honest truth. I mean, you could imagine them if I had – you could hear them, couldn't you: 'Do you hear the fucker – "*fascinating*"!'

The truth, of course, is that I'd always wanted to write. I didn't know why. To discover things, or maybe to explain them. I thought it might help me find out who I was – and my father and mother. What all of it meant and who we *were*. It might, I reckoned, give me the answer to why I used to spend all day longing for Mona, staring out the window waiting for school to end so I could collect my primroses for her and then go around to her house for some bread and jam.

And sit there listening to her voice for hours.

It was in her kitchen that I first felt the urge. To write, I mean. To put it all down and examine it in some way.

Whether I'd have done any of it in the end – if indeed I'd be writing this – if a man called Johnston Farrell hadn't decided one day on coming to Scotsfield is literally impossible to say. All I know is – regardless of whatever difficulties we might have had later on – I definitely do owe him a major debt as far as kick-starting my 'creativity' goes. His writing classes opened up a whole new world. It's just unfortunate it worked out the way it did.

Of course, we couldn't have known that. Indeed, I think if you'd even suggested that we would one day become warring parties in a bitter feud, I think I'd probably have laughed in your face and I dare say so would he. But that's the way it ended up, I'm afraid.

Mass

It was hard to handle it when you saw her at Mass, kinda difficult at first to believe she'd be bothered. Going along to hear the likes of Connolly, I mean. He was hardly John Kay or Charlie the Gardener.

But when you thought about it, it was obvious she wasn't going to come to a little town in Ireland, then turn around and start making herself out to be something special. Going around thinking: *Why the fuck should I do the things you do? I'm from California!* Which only made her even more special, possessing that kind of insight. I did the best I could so she wouldn't see me looking, displaying what they called in the books 'an unmistakable yearning' (I think it was Hesse who said that – don't ask me where I saw it) so bad at times it was like it was physically trying to take shape so it could get out of me and touch her hair, lay its head upon her breast.

Connolly lowered his white head and asked the congregation *why*. Why was it we seemed to be turning our backs on the faith of our long dead fathers, to be selling our souls to television sets and paying nothing more than lip service to the laws of Christ. 'What would St Patrick think if he were alive today? He'd be horrified, that's what he'd be,' he continued. 'It seems to me we are producing the most unloved generation of children Ireland has ever seen. Oh, our children are well fed, well treated when they are ill. But they are growing up in a foreverness of infancy spiritually. Mothers are too busy and house-proud to talk or listen to the little confidences of small children. Pleasure-seeking and money-making are the top priorities. Easy to rush off to Mass and pile off out at the end as if there has been a bomb scare. "Pull a quick one" on a neighbour, cod the taxman, lie to teachers, read filth.'

He listed a whole load of other things that were wrong with the country, then sighed and placed his palms over his eyes and added: 'I could go on. But I won't. For what I want to concentrate on is the possibility of a new beginning for us in Scotsfield – no, not alone in Scotsfield but the entire island of Ireland.' His speech was so impressive that you could see some people were quite eager to clap. I was so dizzy from trying to get a look at her – there was a fat woman blocking my view – that all I could think of, daft as it seems, was Connolly on the stage in Monterey or somewhere, stripped to the waist going: *'This one's for all the people over there in Ireland! It's called "Peace Frog".'*

After Mass I waited in the grounds and tried to steady the trembling in my legs. Then – *suddenly!* – she appeared in the doorway. I especially liked the way she slid her hands in the pockets of her sky blue Levis. The way she nodded to her friends when she was listening to them, especially the bank girl. I was trying to think did I know any of the other chicks who were talking to her when I got this whiff of perfume and realized – how could I have missed it! – that that very second she had just gone walking past me!

But the more I thought about it the more I realized that perhaps it was just as well I had, for I don't think I'd have been able to speak, to be honest about it. The whole thing had happened so –

All of a sudden her voice boomed close by – *no, it was the bank chick's* – and then it was far away like the tiniest voice you've ever heard.

'Right! I'll see you out at the lake around three!'

Before I could say anything, this shadow fell and I looked up to see one of the boys from the pub standing in front of me, smoking a cigarette and asking me something. *'Shut the fuck up!'* I was on the verge of snapping. *'Can't you shut up for once when I'm thinking?'*

It turned out he was asking me whether there was an extension in the pub on Friday night. 'Yes! Yes!' I said. 'There is!'

'Austie's coining it down below, eh, Joey?' he said. 'Ever since starting the discos.'

I wished he'd stop tapping his foot. I wished he would piss off, whoever he was. I didn't even bother to look at him. I couldn't believe she was going out there. 'Ah ha, aye!' he kept saying, still jabbering away, his lips with a life of their own as his stupid head kept nodding away there behind the veil of smoke.

By the time I got home I was in a right state, I can tell you, but had never felt better or more . . . full of possibility, I guess, in my life. I stood in front of the mirror and jabbed the air with my 'gunfinger'.

'Yeah!' I said. For a laugh I sang 'Peace Frog', imagining that I was Boo Boo somehow mixed up with Jim Morrison and there were all these people in front of the stage. I looked at them in the mirror. 'You doin' good?' I said, and hooked my thumbs in my belt. 'I'm real pleased to hear that, people!' I said then. I attempted the Keith Carradine smile. There was a name for it. 'The enigmatic smirk' they called it. I tried it again. It didn't look bad. All told, I reckoned I could do it pretty good. 'Yip!' I said as I lit up a spliff. 'No acid tonight!' I added decisively – and had barely uttered the words when who raps on the door? That tempting little fucker Boo Boo! With two whats in his hand? California sunshines, surprise, surprise!

So you can imagine the state we were in after shoving down those!

At the Lake

Especially the next morning! I'd only managed to get in a little over two hours kip thanks to them skittish electrics going *swoosh* inside my bloodstream!

It must have been the hottest day of the year, and that was saying something considering what the summer had been like so far. When I got to the lake, who did I see lying out under the trees? Only Hoss and a gang of the lads from Austie's, drinking beer.

'Hey, Joey! Going in for a swim then, are you?' Hoss shouted.

'Aye! He's going in to get rid of some of that beef! Isn't that right, Barbapapa?' called someone else.

There were shadows playing around me – because of what remained of the acid, of course – sharp, angular ones that jutted out all of a sudden, and then of course, on top of that, the specks going *zit zat zit* so nimble and fast that one minute you were fired up with ecstasy then, the next thing you knew, enveloped by dread.

Barbapapa was a big kids' cartoon jelly man who was on the telly in the middle of the day – I'd seen him in the paper once described as a 'cuddly blob of pink ectoplasm' – and this was their private name for me. Any time they used it, they went into fits of hysterics. Hoss's pal was even hitting Hoss now as he repeated it, squealing: 'Did you hear what I fucking called him, Hoss? Did you hear me calling him Barbapapa?'

I think they must have been pretty far gone, regardless of what time it was, for Hoss tossed a can at me then but it missed by a mile. I wished you could make your heart go at the speed you wanted by just sitting down and concentrating. The opposite was the way it seemed to work, however. I could have sworn I heard them calling me again but I didn't turn because if the regime was to begin it would have to start with situations like this. 'Don't turn around,' I told myself. 'Keep looking straight ahead. This is the beginning. In this place it begins. Organization total. Total Organization. Just stare straight ahead.'

41

The squeals of the kids as they splashed in the water began to reduce in volume as I steadied myself and stiffened in order to focus completely and diminish the acid's power. I could feel it slowly beginning to wane.

Then, gradually, I experienced the most exquisite and gentle calm descending. Along with the tiniest reassuring hint of pride. Soon the time would come when we could talk about such emotions. But not without patience. Only through patience and discipline could that moment be delivered. I closed my eyes as I thought of her in slow motion, wading through the water. I could not – inappropriate as I felt it seemed to the moment – prevent myself from thinking what she might look like in a swimsuit. Before thinking: *Maybe she won't even wear one!*

Perhaps go streaking right along the shore right into the trees, the way she might in California.

Except she wouldn't, you see, for I knew she had too much class for that. I'd seen that side of her already, showing respect for the traditions of other people and cultures. I wondered whether she'd been to India, for example, the way that The Seeker had. Maybe that's where she learnt it, the idea that if you're in someone else's country you showed them some respect. Not turning around, going: 'My way – understand? *My* way's the way – there is no other!'

I was on the verge of saying: 'You know something, babe? You're absolutely right!'

But I was suddenly distracted by the sound of approaching voices and looked up to see the bank chick standing close by, my heart missing a beat. I was surprised by her patchouli perfume, which suddenly smelt sweet as it went floating by, and the cheesecloth Indian-style blouse she was wearing. I guess I hadn't expected her to be wearing that kind of gear. But then, that was what you did, I thought – pigeonholed people. Just because she worked in the bank didn't mean she had to be a straight. *No way!* I thought.

I didn't know what to say when I heard her saying: 'No, she *said* she was coming, but she had to go to Dublin!'

All that night I found it difficult to sleep. I could feel her presence hovering close by. I saw her standing on O'Connell Street, the thoroughfare on either side entirely deserted, as though there'd been a bomb scare. She was unwinding her hair and staring straight at me. 'Joey,' she was saying, 'how you been?'

The swirling colours of *Abraxas* – the Santana album – were fluid and fantastic in the sky behind her. She had just got back from her travels and was wearing a sort of padded oriental jacket with embroidered motifs of shimmering gold. It looked stunning. 'What?' I said. 'What, Jacy?' I sounded hoarse as I spoke her name.

'I've got something for you,' she said.

'Got something for me?'

'Yes,' she said. 'A special gift for you.'

She rummaged in her bag then and smiled as she handed it to me.

'It's hand-sewn, embossed in gold,' she told me. 'I found it in a little shop in Bombay. It was just sitting there, waiting for me. And I knew I had to buy it. As a special gift for you.'

'*Siddhartha*,' I whispered and ran my hand across its cover.

Then I kissed it again, that sweet and lovely book she'd given me, carried all the way from India to present to me in that empty street. I felt as if I was in a truly wondrous place.

As though I'd been reborn.

Rosa and Big Bertha

The day of Rosa and Big Bertha the place was packed. There had been talk of Fr Connolly arriving with a picket but he didn't show. I think he had enough on his plate with the Provos and their objections. Which, if you'd any sense at least, you tended to take very seriously indeed. They'd been going around drumming up dissent and tearing down his posters any chance they got, so I don't think the girls were too high on his list. The first thing was the football club mascot that they now called Horny Harry, having dressed him up in a sailor's uniform. The roars of them above the music! They perched him on the bar counter and every time his mickey went up – there was somebody in behind the counter squeezing a bulb or something – the place went half mad, egged on by the jukebox as it blasted out 'You Sexy Thing'.

'Horny fucking Harry!' howled a man at the front. 'If the wife got a look at that –!'

'Maybe it'd put a smile on her face!'

'And maybe hoors like you that can't shut up go flying out fucking windows!'

'Maybe they do!'

Then I heard someone calling: 'You're looking happy there, Joey! Old Harry must be doing the trick!'

'Something is but it ain't him!' I laughed, and Sandy McGloin said: 'You're a good one, Joey! No mistake! He's a good one, isn't he, Hoss?'

'Mr Barbapapa!' laughed Hoss, adding: 'I'm only kidding you, Joey! I'm just frigging around with him, and Big Joe knows it! Right, old sweat?'

'You got it!' I replied cheerily.

We were all in great form. During the interval, Big Bertha and Rosa sat drinking at the bar, enjoying all the attention that was coming their way, with enough drinks to quench the thirst of an army lined up in front of them. An old-timer had managed to squeeze in between them, beaming away like all his Christmases had come together. 'And what's your name, little fella?' asked Bertha as she vigorously rubbed his thigh. Boyle Henry was standing by the pool table in his yellow three-button polo shirt, stroking the cue suggestively as he winked over at the boys. 'No handling the merchandise!' was what his wink was saying. All of a sudden he delivered a mighty kick up the hole of the old-timer and said: 'You touchee, you fuckee – out on the streetee!'

There was a great laugh when he did that, and then it was time for the show proper to begin. They set up the ring in The Courtyard – a bit of a ramshackle affair, just tatty old canvas and breeze blocks. But it did the trick all right. They had decorated the place with pennants and flags – 'The games people play! At Barbarella's!'

The first thing Rosa and Bertha did was go down on their knees and get well stuck into Horny Harry. 'That's the stuff for the randy hoor!' shouted someone from the back as the disco beat thumped. When they'd given Harry as much as he could take, they pushed his cap down over his eyes and sent him flying out into the middle of the crowd. The old-timer caught him and pretended to copulate with him right there and then. 'Christ but he's the dirty bastard!' they guffawed. 'Get up on the crack of dawn, he would!'

Without warning, Rosa got a hold of Bertha and sent her stumbling backwards against the ropes. 'You made a big mistake there, lady!' says Bertha and comes charging at her like a bull and gives her the father and mother of a slap there and then right into the mush. 'Jesus!' gasped the audience in astonishment. Such a wallop! You could hear it all over the –

Then what does she do, when she has her on the floor? Starts bawling: 'You want it, huh? So that's how you wannit – you wannit, lady? Then that's what you fucking get!'

Where she produced it from, no one could say for sure. It must have been hidden underneath the canvas. I wouldn't say too many people in Scotsfield had ever seen a dildo before. At any rate, not one that size. Next thing you know she's pretending to give it to Rosa between the legs. Which did the trick more than anything they'd come up with yet, and all of a sudden there's not a sound to be heard in The Courtyard. Then the fighting proper started and, before you knew what was happening, the old-timer had got stuck in between them and was climbing on top of Bertha. 'That's it! Ride her, cowboy!' called Hoss as the old-timer turned to say something back but fell slap bang down on his face into the mud. Then Rosa came up behind him, hit him a smack and sent him flying back down again. This was the best yet. Some of the audience were weak from cheering. Rosa dragged Bertha past him by the hair, gave her a pretend punch in the stomach and said: 'Come on then, baby!'

The music was sweeping about the place like a big long twirling scarf, going: *'Una paloma blanca! I'm just a bird in the sky!'* when all of a sudden what happens? Bertha has turned the tables on her opponent and is slapping her hard, one, two, three, four, five times in the face. There were people turning their heads away.

'You think you can beat me, huh?', she snapped as she hit her, 'You think you can take on a champion like me? I'll show you what fighting means!'

Then she scissored Rosa around the neck and started bumping and grinding, with the sweat rolling off her. After that she banged her head a good few times against the floorboards until Rosa pretended to be passing out. But with one leap Rosa was back on her feet and Bertha was there beside her, taking a bow and blowing kisses right, left and centre. The old-timer was close to fainting at this point, covered in muck from head to toe, and I could hear him saying behind me: 'Do you think they'll be coming here regular? Do you think it was good? I think it was good! I hope they'll be coming here regular!'

Boyle Henry came climbing in through the ropes and, after holding up both women's arms and announcing: 'Ladies and gentlemen! The fabulous Rosa and Big Bertha!', went on to say that there would be two more shows before the wrestlers went back to England. Then he called for a big round of applause for the sexiest women in Ireland – all the way from England, of course! The roof was nearly blown off the place with yelps and piercing wolf whistles.

But once it was all over and the women had gone back to their hotel, the mood sort of changed and conversation all but died out in the bar. You could hear nothing apart from Austie saying: 'Well, so much for Connolly and his picket! All talk! That's all he is – just talk!'

Then, after a bit, one of the regulars stared broodily into his pint and said: 'Aye. Well, maybe – maybe, I was thinking, it wouldn't have been such a bad idea if he *had* come with his picket.'

'Ah now,' said Austie, and smiled. But not much – he was reading the situation from experience and could tell that they were all privately in agreement with the speaker. Like what they were secretly thinking was: *Those English prostitutes have made fools of us! Come over and make their money and then what do they do? Fuck off!*

For the next couple of hours, it was like you were afraid to say anything – no matter how innocuous – in case a fight might break out.

But I reckoned by now I'd learnt to deal with situations like this. Once upon a time I would have found myself picking up every detail, the sudden jerking of a head or the flick of a cigarette. Investing such gestures with a significance that was often misplaced. But not now. Now I was oblivious to such trivial ephemera. My reading – my acquisition, I guess you could say, of knowledge – seemed to be directing me towards a different, more important place. Along with the vibes I felt coming – *emanating* – from her. A calm was descending. A peace. I could see the glittering water, and there, just beyond, the twinkling, beckoning lights of a comforting, precious harbour.

Hoss said: 'Are you listening to me, Joey?' Some horseshit or other about a football match. I nodded and made eye contact with him, just to keep him happy. But I could just as easily have said: 'I'm not. No, I haven't been listening to a word you've been saying.' Because that was the truth – I hadn't. For the very simple reason that I was giving my attention to certain other words that he wasn't privy to and which I found a hell of a lot more interesting.

'It's up there, straight ahead!' I could hear Jacy saying. We were on a winding dirt road just off the interstate and heading for our new home in the mountains. I'd read all about it in a book on reincarnation I'd found quite by chance – if such a thing really, *truly* can be said to

exist – in the library. It was as though it had been hollowed out of the rock in expectation of our arrival, deep in the safety of its darkness, each tiny little detail meticulously and lovingly prepared.

Our special name for it was the Karma Cave, and the moment you laid eyes on it, you knew exactly what it was. Realized that you'd been there before, even if you couldn't say exactly when.

The first thing you heard as you approached it was the fragile tinkling of the wind chimes rotating slowly in the heavy afternoon air. There was a little silver tiger. And an elephant. I could hear those chimes so crystal clear.

'*Are you fucking listening to me?*' I heard Hoss saying. 'I said, Corrigan played a blinder! He won the match for them! He won the fucking match on his own!'

I cast him a blissful and unworldly smile.

The Councillor

I knew Boyle Henry had been in the back lounge that day, but hadn't realized who'd been in there with him until I came back in from the yard with the crate of Guinness and saw him running out after her. He was stubbing his Hamlet as he pursued her, the door swinging behind him as I heard him calling: '*Wait! Come back here, Jacy, for Christ's sake! I didn't mean that!*'

I could hear them arguing outside in the street. 'Of course I'll do it!' he growled. 'I'll do it now – tonight! If that's what you want me to do! Sure I'll fucking leave her! You think I wouldn't?'

I know it should have been the beginning, that I should have realized then. But if you had told me I don't think I'd have believed you – '*What? Jacy? With Boyle Henry?*' I'd have said, and laughed, dismissing it casually, before going in behind the counter once more to continue with my work as if it meant nothing to me in the world.

Except that it did, and when I looked again Boyle Henry had come back into the bar and was sitting over in the corner, colluding in whispers with the Provo who ran The Ritzy. Danny, I think, was his name. I saw him accepting money as it was passed to him under the table, a fat roll of notes bound with an elastic band. The blue-movie money, most likely. For Henry to launder through one of his many businesses.

The new hotel he was involved with, maybe, or the proposed shopping centre the council'd been talking about. I didn't know.

Or care. Right at that moment, there was only one thing I cared about, and that was the book I had open in front of me called *The Lyrics of Joni Mitchell*, running my eyes across the words of 'California' with only one thing on my mind: how we were going to reach it, the Karma Cave, despite this unexpected setback.

Arrive somehow at that precious harbour. The longed-for place you'd call . . . home.

Aviator Shades . . .

. . . cheap or not, can look real good. Especially when you're stoned out of your box. Boo Boo had given me some terrific 'Paki black' draw and I'd been blasting it all evening by myself. I was completely whacked as I ran though my routine in front of the mirror, folding my De Niro arms, grinning for a while just thinking about things. The black was so strong it could make you laugh at nothing. *'Phee-oo!'* I wheezed (there were tears in my eyes) and cocked my revolver. *Revolver!* Revolver my bollocks! There was no fucking revolver – the papers got that whole thing arseways. We didn't need no shit like that, me and Jacy, I grinned, and went *pow!* with my index finger.

Then I got down to the nitty-gritty. Pasting back my hair and going: 'So then, Jace!'

And: *'So, how you been?'* and *'I really like your hair, you know?'* Although I could never seem to manage the last part all that well. Eventually I decided to stick with the original: *'So how you been then, Jace? You doin' good?'*

I smiled and tugged down my jacket.

'You lookin' at me?' I said then, and continued: 'Yeah, Jacy, I'm lookin' at you. And you know what? I like what I see. No – *love* what I see. Because it's a mystery.'

I'd sit down then to contemplate. Before going through it all over again.

'I really like your hair,' I'd say. 'Your hair – I really like it,' as I blew a neat chain of smoke rings. Then I stubbed out the joint and said: 'That's the last one – this time for definite.'

I turned and pointed the gunfinger at my reflection.

'You got that?' I said. And then said it again. *'I said, you got that, Joey?'*

Laughing a little bit. But nervously. I mean, I knew what I was taking was a really big step. And that it wasn't going to be easy. But I knew in the end it would all be worth it. More than anyone could ever believe.

'Because then you'll be mine,' I announced impassively to my reflection. 'You got that, Jacy? Then you'll belong to Joey!' watching her face slowly melt into mine.

The Big Fellow in Banbridge

You'd hear the old-timers going on about it, looking around them with hunted eyes and muttering behind their hands. Like the day Willie Markham died when me and Bennett were kids. The neighbours had been coming in and out of the house all morning. 'It's not looking good,' I heard one of them saying, staring brokenly at the ground. Me and Bennett were sitting on the window sill, staring in. I had never heard anything like the sounds coming from inside that room. It was like someone was being burnt alive. You could see them all crying. It was then Bennett started on about the 'Big Fellow'. He could get very excitable, often coming out with things you didn't expect to hear. *'He's always there, Joey!'* he kept insisting, gripping my arm tightly and pleading with me, looking into my eyes as if to say: *'Somehow! Help me! Help me to stop him being there, Joseph!'*

Another day he told me he'd had a dream about him and that he'd been like one of the gangsters out of *The Untouchables*. Standing there smiling like your uncle, with a great big fedora and a brown suit covered in stripes. But when you looked again you could see he wasn't smiling at all. And that what he was holding in his fist was your still-beating heart with its blood seeping out through the cracks in his fingers. He was beside himself as he told me this. 'Why is he always there?' he kept repeating until in the end I had to beg him to stop.

'Don't talk about him any more!' I pleaded. 'Do you hear me? Do you want me to start seeing him too?'

Which I did. Years later, the night I first heard about The Seeker dying in Clapham. The Big Fellow was standing over him, examining the red tip of his cigar as though the decaying corpse meant nothing at all. Just another job of work. But then he looked towards me – and smiled. It was the most awful smile I had ever seen and even now it makes me shiver to recollect it.

I often wondered whether that was what Bennett had seen in those last few minutes in his smoke-filled cab. The Big Fellow standing out there on the grass by the edge of the water, examining his cigar. And then slowly turning to give him . . . that smile.

But Banbridge – I hadn't expected to encounter him there. We had been across the border numerous times by then and nothing untoward had ever happened. It wouldn't even cross your mind that something might, for the band had never been as busy; the stints we were doing with the showband Tweed were going down an absolute storm. They'd do Floyd's *Dark Side of the Moon* – their version of it was legendary – and we'd play 'Vampire', 'Hardcore' and 'Psycho' and, with the word getting out, the crowds turning up at the gigs starting to get larger and larger.

They really were good times.

Some nights the two bands even got onstage together, once – I think in Bundoran – doing a fifteen-minute rockabilly version of the national anthem that ended with the drum kit being kicked into the audience and Boo Boo roaring 'The Whores of Donegal' at this bunch of headbanging pink-haired punkettes.

But this time we were on our own, off up to the Harp Bar in Belfast. It turned out to be something else. Absolutely fucking mental it was. In the end they had to pull the plug for it looked like, if they didn't, the kids were going to tear the place down. *'Fuck you Belfast and your fucking pathetic bigotry!'* shouts Boo Boo from the top of the speaker stack, rotating his mace as he took the piss out of the Orangemen. I had an early start with Austie in the morning so we hit the road straight away once the gear'd been loaded.

I think it was about a mile outside Banbridge that we ran into the roadblock, but we never gave it so much as a second thought, for they were all over the place those days – just routine security precautions. There were three squaddies and the captain, and they seemed like the best of lads no matter what your politics were. They got a great laugh out of Boo Boo with his stovepipe hat. 'You're like one of these fellows you'd see in Belfast of a Saturday,' they said. 'What d'ye call them? Aye, those hot gospeller fellas! That's what you'd put me in mind of now!'

I was a bit stoned and, as I lay there against the side of the van, I had a great old rap with the captain, who told me his name was

Victor. 'I used to be mad about music myself,' he said, 'but it wouldn't be your kind of thing now.' Boo Boo laughed as he jabbed him playfully with the butt of the rifle then lit a fag and starts talking about something else. 'No,' he went on, 'I'd be more for the civilized music. Music, for example, that doesn't have any of them auld fiddles and banjos and – well, in general, that type of thing. Do you get my drift?'

I laughed at that. '*Sure do!*' I said.

Then he looked at me and said nothing. I flipped back through my mind to check if I'd said something wrong. The soldier to his left chuckled a bit, but he went silent when the captain threw him a frosty glare.

'*Sure do. Sure do*. I like the way you say that. I like the way you talk. Half American, like. Half Yankee. Hmm.'

He poked me in the stomach.

'You're putting on the beef, musician. I say, you're putting it on down here, all right! They must be feeding you well down south. I say, they must be feeding you well – are they?'

I laughed again.

'They are indeed, Captain,' I replied. 'They sure are doing that!'

Now he was laughing too and everything was fine. He shouldered his weapon and smiled as he said: 'But we weren't talking about that, were we? What's this we were talking about, Fat Boy?'

'Music,' I said. 'We were talking about music, Captain.'

'That's right!' he said. 'We were talking about music, Captain – real music, that is. Music, in other words, that isn't played by treacherous felons.'

'Oh now,' I replied, not thinking about what he'd said, being so out of it, I guess.

'No, the gig in Banbridge was really good,' I remember saying. Then I heard Boo Boo calling my name.

'Right then! I'll just take a look in the back,' the captain said.

I couldn't figure out what exactly was going on. Boo Boo was pointing towards the van where the other boys were now raising their voices. Were they arguing with the captain?

'I'm just taking a look,' the captain was saying. 'It's just routine procedure. There's no need to get upset now! I say, there's no need to go getting upset!'

I don't know who it was shouted '*It's a bomb!*' Then I heard Boo Boo crying '*Jesus!*' before stumbling back with his two arms out, the others running forward as if to catch him. Someone shouted: *'Get down for the love of fuck, Joey!'* Even now I don't know who. All I could see was this sheet of white light and the captain coming lunging towards me – suspended in the air, with this sideways grin on his face. I ducked to try and avoid him as his body, with a dull thud, hit a tree. The words were on the tip of my tongue – 'Now! Do you see what you get for trying out foolish antics like that!' – when I nearly passed out with the intensity of the heat and the sulphurous smoke that was filling up my lungs. The other soldier had taken off, running down the road with his jacket in flitters and the hair burnt off his head. A stupid thought came into my own head: 'I'll pick up that stick there and chase after him with it to teach him a lesson for this stupid fucking carry-on!'

Before coming around to realize just as I was about to do it that it wasn't a stick, for sticks don't have tattoos with *'I love The Sonics'* on them – or fingers, come to that. Then I heard this groaning, and what happens then? Out from underneath the wagon comes Boo Boo – covered in blood. I was just about to go over to him when – like rags being ripped – another fire started up inside in the cab and the windscreen blew out. 'Let's get the fuck out of here,' one of the boys was shouting, 'before the whole fucking thing goes!' Boo Boo was walking around in circles repeating: 'Where's my arm? It blew off my arm!'

One of the 'soldiers' came zig-zagging back down the road, his white face appearing out of the dark: 'What happened? Can you tell me exactly what happened?'

Before anyone could, the ambulance arrived, screaming. I froze when I saw him first – the Big Fellow. Just standing there smiling beneath a tree as the paramedics clambered from the vehicle. He waved genteelly and tipped back his fedora. It was at that point my whole body started to tremble as one of the medics took me by the hand, in a soothing voice reassuring: 'It's OK now. You're going to be OK now. Come on now. That's right. Take it easy.'

It transpired that there wasn't all that much wrong with me – outwardly, at any rate, I remember thinking, still afraid that my ever-so-slightly acid-tinged version of the Big Fellow might appear and cursing Bennett for ever having planted that seed – and they reckoned I'd be right as rain in a couple of days.

All I'd been able to think about as I lay there in the hospital bed – some nights I didn't sleep a wink at all – was Jacy and Boyle Henry.

And why I hadn't acted that day in the bar, whenever I had the chance, instead of getting myself into a state. But I hadn't been able to think straight, his voice – *'I'll leave her! If that's what you want, I'll leave her!'* – ebbing and swelling in my mind.

In the nights, I'd wake up and see her sitting with him, plucking motes off his jacket and laughing heartily at his jokes. Then I'd imagine her rummaging in her shoulder bag, taking out the hand-sewn *Siddhartha* and passing it over to him. I'd be on the verge of breaking down then. I knew in reality it wasn't likely to happen, but that didn't stop me thinking it. Or from hearing her say: *'You're The Only One, Boyle. You know that, don't you? Boyle Henry is The Only One.'*

Him and his stupid political bullshit. He didn't even know if he was a Provo or not. He was a member of Fianna Fáil, a consitutional nationalist party which at that time was fooling around, quite dangerously, with the Provisional IRA. There were even those who'd suggested that Fianna Fáil had set up the Provos using money that had been banked in Scotsfield, with a view to ultimately destabilizing the illegitimate northern state.

There were rumours too that Boyle Henry had been involved from the very start, his money-laundering activities being just the tip of the iceberg. Although you knew damn well that in his case that was all it would ever come down to – money, for the fucker would sell his own mother. He'd sell Jacy too. I knew that. Once he was finished with her, he'd pawn her off and not give it a second thought. And the more I thought about that, the worse things I'd find myself imagining.

Like the night I saw him in a dope-addled dream. I was supposed to have quit toking but I'd been allowing myself a spliff or two to help me get over the Banbridge affair. I found myself staring directly at him as he approached like an executioner across the stone floor of this darkened basement, the upper part of his body webbed with leather straps. He was wearing a hood, but you knew it was him all right. You could just tell. Jacy begged, but he wouldn't listen. She was strapped to the wall, naked.

When I awoke all the blankets were on the floor and the pillow was sodden. I went out to the toilet for a blast but it didn't help me. I was afraid to go back to bed and remained there for over an hour, bent double over the washbasin trying to make myself sick. When I eventually climbed back into bed, I was more or less certain it had passed. But as soon as I closed my eyes –

I pleaded with him: 'Don't hurt her, Boyle. That's all I ask.' He sucked his teeth and went '*Tsk! Tsk!*' just folding his arms and nodding, with a thin, patronizing smile.

I wouldn't have blamed him for despising me. I could see Jacy staring at me and I prayed I wouldn't catch her eye. For I knew what I'd find if I did. Something regretful, disappointed. That said: '*You let me down, Joey. Why?*' as the Karma Cave closed over. Her soft voice gradually fading: 'And now because of this, you'll be forced to wander for ever. You'll never find your way home.'

You'd see him at meetings, slicing the tape for some new supermarket in this great big fucking white suit of his, or in the *Scotsfield Standard*, making a speech, with his wife standing beside him. She was a doctor from a very wealthy local family (what they called 'old money') and was regarded by some as 'far too good for him', a comment he'd laughed at when he overheard it one night in the pub. 'Sure,' I remembered him saying. 'You might say that, lads. But at the end of the day whose cock is going inside her? It's not fucking yours, you can be sure of that! *Nada*, boys! The Lady Doc is mine, all mine, and that's the way it's going to stay!' In interviews, he always made sure to insist that it was her who had 'made him what he was'. 'The Queen' was a term he often used to describe her.

I started thinking about that so much and of the lies he had told to Jacy – I knew he'd never leave his wife – that I almost forgot about Banbridge. I visited Boo Boo in the hospital almost every day. But he wasn't showing much improvement. The nurse said to me: 'He had a terrible time all last night. He keeps on about his career being over.'

Which was correct, of course. There weren't going to be too many openings for one-armed guitarists. I tried my best to get through to him but it turned out to be no use. Half the time I don't think he knew who I was. Just turned over, gesturing half-heartedly with his good arm.

25 September 1976

Whatever happens I want you to know I love you. I cannot afford to take any more risks. I almost died without seeing you – loving you. Sometimes I fear he has a hold over you. I have hesitated and I know it's wrong.

Today I read: Do today what has to be done tomorrow; do this morning what has to be done this evening; death does not wait for you to complete your task.

I play 10cc all the time and it seems more beautiful than ever because I have accepted that I love you totally and denial even for the protection of oneself or whatever other unsatisfactory reason shall never be possible again. In the morning the sun opens out across the fields and I wake to see you, standing by the window. Tossing your hair and turning as the music softly plays, music that's full of – what's the word? – yes, yearning. 'Courage,' you say. 'Courage for what it is that's meant to be.'

There is only one way, I know that now. Total Organization. I have written a note to Una Halpin requesting the entire works of Rabindranath Tagore, who has written: 'The river and the waves are one surf: where is the difference between the river and the waves?'

These wonders of knowledge they empower me so. Exactly as Charles Manson said. There was a happy guy in the hospital who was into the Christian mystics. He says, What's all this shit about the Indians when the Christians have seers of their own? Good point. I told him all about The Seeker, how he liked St John of the Cross. He was impressed by that and he quoted him to me: 'See how the suffering of love is only cured when you – or when your face – is near.' He was talking about his chick but when he said it I couldn't stop thinking of how true it is – for us. I feel so fortunate having met these people. I have become as a magpie gathering jewels, acquiring random nuggets of wisdom. The Yogi dyes his garments, instead of dyeing his mind. You must always dye your mind. Dye it – how? In the colours of love.

I want us to be able to share everything together.

When I go to sleep she's there.

The Colouring Book

The cops had swooped on Hoss's farm and discovered explosives in an outhouse. So things were looking pretty bad for him. They reckoned at the very least he'd get ten years, which couldn't have come at a worse time after his mother had taken the stroke which everyone was sure would kill her. I never saw such gloom as enveloped the pub that night. Austie said: 'Do you mind the one he used to tell about the lighthouse? Behan was given a painting job above in the north, and the Orangeman says: "None of your slacking now – this is a hard-working wee country! So when I come back I want that lighthouse painted proper." And when he does, what does he find? The bold Brendan has painted *"This lighthouse is the property of Éamon de Valéra of the Irish Free State"* in big black letters all across the front! And the Orangeman goes fucking mad! Christ but he was a gas man!'

Out of nowhere, someone turned on him and spat: 'The man's not fucking dead! It's not like Hoss is fucking dead or something, you know! He hasn't even been convicted!'

But everyone knew it was a done deal no matter what was said, so they all went home early that night and there was only myself and an old friend of Bennett's sitting there in Barbarella's with a couple of half-pissed zombies dancing around their handbags.

'Where do you think he's gone,' he said, 'my old pal Bennett?'

You could see he was on the verge of tears and I didn't know quite what to say. I sat there for a minute as I sipped my drink, and then he said: 'All I can say is this, Joey. I don't know for sure but I know what I hope. That he's found his way inside that colouring book.'

I didn't know what he was talking about but he went on to explain.

'That's how he used to see it,' he said. 'Like this lovely picture that a kid might crayon, with a fabulous blue sky spreading over fields of swaying corn. That's how he always saw it, Joey. That was Bennett's vision of Paradise.'

Precious, I thought, and smiled as I saw him there, having reached home at last. 'If only it could be true.'

He looked into his drink, then turned to me and smiled as he laid a gentle hand on my shoulder.

'It is, Joey. It *is*. And I know he believed it. It's the end and the beginning, I used to hear him say. The end of sorrow and the beginning of happiness.'

'The end and the beginning,' I smiled. 'Just like the ancients say.'

'You got it,' he replied. 'The end of "The Now" and the beginning of . . . forever.'

No Date???

It's like there's this sense of . . . closing in, or something. Like you know the the summer will soon be over, the short evenings and the long dark nights of winter drawing in. It's almost like the gorse fires and those lazy days lying by the lake, like they happened somewhere else or something. In some distant, uncharted country. You go into the pub now and there's nothing, only these ghost-faces watching the telly, the pool balls clacking below in the back bar, and then the phone ringing in The Rockford Files *or something, making this vast and hollow sound. There's this enormous sense of . . . disconnection, that's the only way I can put it. And why I feel so . . . grateful for this . . . gift, for there's nothing else I can think of could name it. It's nearly pointless to even try.*

October 4
Thoughts/Reflections to Self

The things you dream, at times you feel them so deep it's like some-one is saying to you: 'Reality? There is no reality. This is the reality. The reality is you and you are the reality.' The pages you write becoming that reality.

'You know something, Joey?' I heard her say today. 'You want to know something about you? You really make me laugh. You make me crack up, man! You really do! That's what I love most of all about you. About my Joey. Joe. Joseph. Jacy. J–J. Love. Harmony. Forever.

The Layers of the Onion

> They call me the breeze,
> I keep blowing down the road . . .

She switched off J. J. Cale and climbed out of the pick-up, strolling across the sand to freshen up at a roadside pump. The water broke on her face like diamonds as she looked at me and said: 'You know what I think about you, Joey Tallon? You come on like you're this great big . . . like you don't give a shit, you know? Like you could travel the world from east to west and nothing would ever bother you, that you're just peeling off the layers we been talking about. You're just doing it to keep me cool, to show you know what's what. You're hip in other words.'

'Hip?' I said and tried to be it. I sucked my teeth and narrowed my eyes. Then I looked at her with the . . . *enigmatic smirk*. And I could tell she liked it.

She shaded her eyes and stared off for a bit. Then she said: 'You know, there are a thousand different Joey Tallons. A thousand different *yous*. That's what Harry Haller tells us. That's what we know from *Steppenwolf*. Ain't it? Like he says: "Man is a texture made up of many threads, an onion made up of a hundred integuments. The ancients knew this well enough, and in the Buddhist Yoga an exact technique was devised for unmasking the illusion of personality."'

She paused. Then she said: 'You are an onion, Joey. We are onions. But we got to get to that inner core. Shed those layers so we get to the onion's heart. Where inner light truly shines. Can you dig that, Joey?'

'I can dig it,' I said.

Then – I became alarmed – all of a sudden she turned away and stood with her back to me, her hands in her jeans' hip pockets. For no reason at all, I shouted: 'Come back, Jacy! I'll slim down! I'll get myself together! I won't eat any more pies!' And straight away felt so dumb, just about as dumb as you could possibly feel. 'Pies,' I felt like saying, 'fuck pies! And fuck Boyle Henry too!' Before realizing that I'd got it wrong. All she'd been doing was thinking again. She came walking towards me ever so slowly. Her gaze didn't flinch as her eyes probed deep.

'Two people love one another,' she began, 'there's nothing they should not share. The Hindus have a saying. "We must listen to the still small voice. The still small voice that's within us all. We must listen to it."'

She touched my hand. 'It's just that I don't think you're listening, Joey. I don't think you're listening to that small voice. And I don't think you're telling me everything. I want to know the you that we've been talking about. I want to know the real Joey Tallon. Tell me about him, Joey. That inner child. *The inner child, Joseph!*'

'The inner child?'

I swallowed as I said it. Then I looked away. There was no mistaking the tenderness in her eyes. It reassured me so much.

'Perhaps you're not ready for it yet. But I'll be patient. Then, when you're ready, I know you'll tell me. Slowly begin to shed those skins. You'll do that, Joey, when you're ready? Tell me then you'll give me your trust.'

'Yes,' I said. 'My trust.'

'That's all I want, baby,' she said. 'I want to know you and I want you to know me.'

She moved her hand to my shoulder and stroked the back of my neck.

'Then we can go to Iowa,' she said.

She paused for a moment.

'You hearing me, Joey?'

I could still feel her touch when I woke up I don't know how long after. I think I slept eighteen hours.

I spent the whole day reading, then drove up to Tynagh mountain to get the Karma Cave ready. Austie had lent me this beat-up old Bedford on account of what had happened to our wagon. The only thing I was afraid of was that I'd go and crash it on him, for I'd noticed since Banbridge I had become very nervous behind a wheel. But as soon as I entered our 'private world', particularly there in that little cabin stuck there on the side of the mountain which had once been a forest-worker's hut, any cares like that soon drifted away. It seemed so right just being there sweeping up the floor that I almost felt like falling to my knees. It was damp inside, having been deserted for years, but still was far from uninhabitable. The only other human being for miles was an old geezer called McQuaid, who I knew was spying on me from his own cottage across the valley. I'd see him at the window every time I drove up. But that didn't matter – he could do that if he wished. If that was his scene. Maybe one day he could even come and visit us, right there in that old Karma Cave. *That would be just fine by me, Mr McQuaid,* I thought. *You just keep on peering out that window, baby.*

As I strung up the wind chimes, I felt absolutely certain that my journey had been . . . I don't know – ordained, I guess. I closed my eyes and breathed in the incense. I could see the lights twinkling out across the bay. They said: *'You're here. It's been a long journey but at last now it's ended.'*

I spent the whole night in the cabin, fixing things up. For I wanted everything to be as right as could possibly be. All the surroundings to be as . . . *congenial* – is that the word? – as could humanly be made possible. I would see to it – I had to. It was my duty. It was part of the regime. Of the total reorganization that would set us on our path. That led to the core of the onion, with its primordial, lustrous light. It was essential that everything at the beginning be made as smooth as possible. Because the first layer, without a doubt, would have to be the most difficult. I knew that. Just as I knew that when that was done everything else would be easy. Once successfully dealt with, all the other layers would flake off like paper.

I stacked the paperbacks on the shelf and tacked up the wall hanging. Beside that, the Joni Mitchell songbook and guitar. I had finished a painting of Charlie Manson on a sheet of hardboard, which I nailed to the other wall. Underneath I printed: '*The Gardener*'.

I was a bit tired but I still had enough energy to draw a single eye – the eye that sees the truth – on the ceiling. The harder I worked, the more I thought of The Seeker as he sat at the bar flicking through Castaneda. '*The Toltecs say,*' I heard him musing, as he massaged his beard into a point, '*that if we save enough energy, a door will open to an unknown side of ourselves, the Nagaul, a side that it is not possible to think of or verbalize about.*' If you asked him how he saw himself – and people were always doing it – he'd think for a bit before saying: '*I'm a psy-warrior!*' Then he'd grin and look at you: '*An astronaut of inner space!*' he'd say.

You really had to admire him, Eamon. In his memory I painted a few logos right there on the wall: '*Stay high, love the Buddha!*' and '*You are the you of you!*'

Then, pretty exhausted but at the same time ecstatic, I tidied up the albums again – with Joni placed where she couldn't be missed – and headed back into town, thinking: *The shadows of evening fall thick and deep, and the darkness of love envelops the body and mind.* I was so engrossed in my thoughts that I almost drove into a sheep – I just saw it at the very last minute, stumbling wildly as it got caught in the headlights, terrified. I knew I would have to be that bit more careful from now on. There was no room even for the tiniest lapse in concentration.

The Dancehall

I was writing in my new diary – an accounts ledger (I had found a whole bunch of them, completely unused, dumped behind the bank) – when I heard this furious hammering. 'Will you give me a chance to get my fucking trousers on?' I says. 'Can you let a guy do that at least?' Turns out to be Chico, one of the boys in the band, all on for the dance. 'Let's rock,' he says. 'I'm fed up moping and brooding about Banbridge.'

So off we went to Oldcastle. We had a couple of spliffs in the car park and a few pints in a pub on the way, then fell into the dancehall, and who does Chico run into? Only this mad fan who never missed a Mohawk gig. Goes white she does. 'I can't believe it's you, the drummer out of my favourite band. I just cannot believe my eyes.'

'Well, believe them, baby,' says Chico, and gives me the wink and that was the last I saw of him. Off he sweeps into the crowd as I went backstage to have a word with the guitarist, asking him to play our song. 'No problem!' he says, so, man, was I happy camper then. All I had to do was sit there and wait for those first few opening bars: *I'm not in love, so don't forget it, it's just a silly phase I'm going through,* that floaty feeling coursing through you the very same as when you'd find yourself dreaming about being inside Mona's stomach all those years before, a tiny little baby sucking its thumb, in the original Karma Cave.

Against the odds, it had turned out to be a beautiful night, with all the windows thrown open and the warm air coming drifting right into the hall, the hippie chicks from Dublin hanging out in front of the stage, the Oldcastle headbangers pogoing up and down the maple floor. And as I waited for the song I don't suppose I was in that dancehall in Oldcastle, Co. Meath, or anywhere fucking near it, tell you the God's honest truth. For already I was halfway there, in the Karma Cave, where the only sound you can hear is the plinking of windchimes as cross-legged you sit, *Siddhartha*-style, three fingers touching your thumbs as you chant your mantra. The purple smoke of the incense writhing as yet another layer is dispensed with, bringing you ever closer towards that final goal, the unmasking of 'the illusion of personality', which, according to Hermann Hesse, had cost India thousands of years of effort . . .

I couldn't believe it when I looked up and saw Boyle Henry. He was standing right in front of me, grinning. There was a half-drunk woman hanging on his arm. I had never seen her before. Just then the first mellow chords of the song started up and my heart began to pound. Between that and him arriving – just out of nowhere – I became alarmed and wanted a spliff. *No! A pie!* I thought. And then: *No! No pies!*

'It's stupid,' I said to myself.

Fuck him! I thought. *Fuck him and her!*

'*Well, well, well!* Would you look who it is! How are they hanging, Joey?' he began as the guitarist adjusted the mike and announced: 'This one's specially for Joey from Scotsfield! Roadie with The Mohawks! Hope Boo Boo's making a full recovery! Don't let the bastards grind you down, lads, you hear?'

The woman's eyes kept swivelling in her head, looking up at him every so often as if about to say: 'I've managed to get off with Boyle Henry? It can't be, no, it couldn't be!'

He pulled a hip flask from his inside pocket and handed it to me.

'Always good to see a fellow Scotsfield man,' he said.

'What's that, Boyle?' I said, and put the flask to my lips. Then the word 'pies' came into my head again. That was always the way it worked. Just when it seemed OK I'd get afraid it would start up again, and sure enough it did. I spilt some of the whiskey and it went dribbling down my front.

'There's some gone down your jacket,' he pointed out, and laughed. I could see the guitarist trying to catch my eye.

'What?' I said. Boyle winked.

'I *said*, it's always good to see a fellow Scotsfield man!' he said again, and gave the woman's buttock a squeeze. I was bathed in sweat. You could fill a glass with it, I thought. Then, for no reason at all, I found myself thinking: *I would like to be somewhere else right now. In Austie's even. Washing glasses. Pulling pumps. You could fill a glass with my sweat. 'Two gins and a nip of sweat, sir. Yes, there you are!'*

'For God's sake, Joey, will you watch that whiskey!' said Boyle. 'You'll go and spill it again if you're not careful.'

'Ha ha,' I laughed.

He winked again and squeezed my elbow. 'Not a bad little piece, eh? Whaddya think?' he said.

I agreed – over-enthusiastically, I realized almost as soon as I'd opened my mouth.

'Yeah, sure! Fantastic!'

I handed his whiskey back.

'OK then, kid?' he said, reaching out to accept it.

'Sure thing, Boyle,' I said and gave him the thumbs up. My face was aflame.

'Well! Be seeing you then!'

He grinned from ear to ear as he sparked a Hamlet, looking dapper in the cream-white suit, as he said: 'Let's get dancing then, sweetheart!' Her eyeballs swam as she fell into his arms and he dragged her like a sack of potatoes across the floor.

The minute he'd gone I went back to where I'd been. *In the land before pies!* I thought. Then giggled a little . . . idiotically. I got to thinking of myself on Tynagh mountain. Sitting inside with both my legs crossed. In the lotus position. That was what you called it. I thought of the mountain and I thought of the sky. Then I closed my eyes. I must have looked pretty stupid sitting there in the dancehall with everyone sweeping past me on the floor. But I didn't care, because the calm was returning. You could feel it. *'Knowledge can be as a vast tree which yields more and more fruit,'* I repeated softly to myself. *'And, as to this knowledge, we must attend to that little voice. The one within which tells us: "You are on the right track, move neither to your left nor right, but keep to the straight and narrow way."'*

The band finished the song and announced the end of the set. 'Your next dance will be coming right up,' they said. Then, out of nowhere, I heard: 'Hey, Tallon! What the fuck are you at over there? Are you falling asleep or what?'

It was Chico, pulling on his coat, with the chick beside him. 'OK, man, I'm outa here!' he said. 'I can't stand this country-and-western bollocks any longer! We're going up to this baby's place! You staying or going?'

I said I'd hitch a lift. Which I did. I headed off shortly afterwards.

I must have been on the side of the road a good two hours before I looked up and saw the yellow Datsun approaching.

'Hello there,' said Boyle, pulling in as the door swung open. I climbed inside.

The woman was still all over him, her mascara streaking her cheeks. She slipped her hand inside his shirt and grinned blearily, stroking his chest. Boyle thought it was a great laugh. 'Sure as long as we're enjoying ourselves, that's the main thing! Would you say I'm right there?'

He grinned. 'Well, would you, Josie?' he asked me. They called me that too sometimes – Josie. I didn't mind it. The way I was feeling now they could call me whatever they wished. For the first time I felt that my little 'zen' session in the dancehall was really beginning to kick in and I was overjoyed. Now he had started telling me all about his plans. He was thinking of running for office, he said. 'Do you think someone like me might make a good representative, Joey boy? Boyle Henry as your local TD? Your man above in Dublin, whaddya say?'

If he didn't cut it as a Dáil Deputy, he might make the senate, he reckoned. 'I've a lot of good friends up there in the smoke, Joey. As well as around our own town. You think they like me, Joey? You figure they like Mr Henry in Scotsfield? I think they do! She does anyway, don't you, baby?'

He made a grab for her bare thigh and she dropped her cigarette in a shower of sparks.

'Baby! You'll burn us out!'

'Boyle!' she chuckled as she bent down to retrieve the cigarette.

He started going on about Fr Connolly then and his great schemes. 'He's a terrific idealist. You have to hand it to him. I admire a man like that!' he said, then adding: 'But this Peace Rally – now what do you think of that? Would you say now that's such a good idea?'

To which I replied that I didn't know and had no opinion on it at all. The only peace I cared about was to be found up on Tynagh mountain, although of course I didn't utter those words.

To my surprise, I started really enjoying his company then – and to feel bad about the way I'd been thinking. About him. And everybody else, in fact. I began to feel regretful about it all. But promised myself I'd make up for it. I smiled as Boyle pulled off the road and drove up to her house, promising me he wouldn't be long and giving me the wink as he assisted her out. She was completely incapable now.

He must have been about twenty minutes or so, and was still grinning as he climbed back into the car, shoving two fingers under my nose as he said: 'So smell that, Joey Tallon! Sweet as fucking roses, man!'

Chuckling to himself all the way along the Scotsfield Road. 'The yelps of her, Joe,' he says, practically jumping up and down in the seat. It was almost coming naturally to me now – and I can't tell you how good I was feeling about it – moving into that relaxing space. Where anyone could say absolutely anything and it wouldn't bother you at all. 'Sure,' I said, and 'That's right, Boyle.'

I must have dozed off for a bit, for the next thing I remember the car is turning off the road somewhere around Lackey Cross and Boyle is saying: 'Now listen, Josie, I might be another wee while up here, so the best thing you can do is stretch out here for a bit. Here, take another drop of Jemmy. But don't stir till I get back. And then we'll have you safe and sound at home in the campsite. You'll be OK then, Josie? Catch forty winks!'

I nodded and did just that as I watched him dodge the sudden shower as he made his way on up the lane, and it was like a warm and toasty hand had come to soothe my soul. I might as well have grown wings and been gliding over cool clear water, skimming it every so often just for the sheer fucking fun. Triumph was a word that came to mind just then – I had reached some special plain. And this was just the beginning. What would it be like in the Karma Cave? With *her* in the Karma Cave? I reckoned I was getting close to . . . I don't know. 'Delirious' was a word that I wouldn't have been afraid of using right then.

What time it was when the birds woke me up I couldn't say for definite. It was bright outside and it looked like it was going to be a really lovely day, but as yet I was too tired and hungover to appreciate it. I searched around for the flask. It was dry as a bone. All of a sudden – it was like the 'old me', I thought – I found myself becoming unnecessarily alarmed and thinking: *Oh no! He's gone and forgotten me altogether!* Which was stupid, of course, as I realized almost immediately – I mean, he was hardly going to leave the Datsun lying there at the side of the road.

So I just got out and went off up the lane towards the bungalow at the top of the hill, nearly breaking my neck over an old pushbike someone had left lying in the middle of the drive. 'Will you for fuck's sake wake up, Joey!' I said. 'Wake up here now, Joey Tallon! Just because things are getting a little easier now doesn't mean you can afford to start getting sloppy!' I grinned unconsciously, thrilled at the idea of this new confidence that appeared to be growing apace inside of me. The 'old Joey' might have been lying like a shed skin by the side of the road. 'Oh, Joey,' I heard her saying, 'I never dreamed it would be this good. You're so . . .'

She'd be lost for words. I'd toss her a smile.

There was nobody around when I got as far as the bungalow. Nobody I could see through the first window anyway. But when I looked through the second, who's in there? Boyle. As fresh as a daisy, it seemed, walking around chatting away to – guess who? – Detective

Tuite, with the pair of them getting on like a house on fire. All you could hear was Boyle saying: 'I'll make sure it's worth your while coming out here tonight, Mr Tuite. I know you're taking a big risk, but you know you can trust me. Which is more than can be said for a lot of the fuckers around Scotsfield. And believe me, I should know, for I've been doing business in it long enough. Fucking felons, wouldn't believe a word comes out of their mouths. But listen here. This information. We've got the lowdown on a couple of very important people. Who've made the big mistake of stepping out of line with some other very important people, if you get my drift. Not that it matters to me what they fucking do. Just don't ask us where we got it. All you need to know is that they shouldn't have crossed Sandy, know what I'm saying? And, if you play your cards right, Detective, what I have to tell you should see them put away for a very long time. But before we get to that –'

He clicked his fingers, then who comes in? Big Bertha, one of the wrestlers from the pub, and Boyle gets a hold of her. The pair of them having a great old time. The sort of time, though, best described as 'private'. And on top of which it might not be such a good idea to go barging in wearing your big Joey Tallon size twelves. Which didn't bother me in the slightest. Nope, not one bit.

So fine, I thought, *I'll just be on my way then*, and was about to do exactly that when the connecting door opens, and who's closing it behind him only Sandy McGloin, pale and lean in his grey silk suit and obsessively flicking his cigarette. He took a pull of the fag and winked over at Boyle. But Tuite didn't see him.

They started giving him the information then. I could hear them going on about explosives and weapons. I heard Boyle saying: 'Sandy knows where every one of these arms dumps is located. But he'd have to be paid. He'd be risking his life, as I'm sure you appreciate.'

Then he pulled a wad of money from his pocket and waved it. As if to indicate: 'This kind of money.'

It was obvious Tuite was surprised and confused by these sudden and unexpected demands but he clearly wanted the information so badly that he was definitely giving serious thought to the proposition. They continued debating and arguing for a long time. Then, with a flourish, Sandy produced a bottle of whiskey. They had obviously come to some kind of agreement. The detective shook hands with Sandy. Then turned to Boyle to do the same. I was on the verge of going back to the car when I heard a laugh, and when I look in what seems to have happened is that all of a sudden Sandy McGloin has turned into a comedian, which was certainly not what you expected from him, I can tell you. In all my time in the bar I don't think I ever heard him – a thin, cadaverous northerner, always on the alert, probably with good reason – crack a joke. But now there he was just chortling away, knocking back whiskey like it was going out of fashion and shaking his head, marvelling at how good this yarn of his was. A view shared by Tuite and Boyle, who kept passing the bottle back and forth. Then what happens? The connecting door opens again and in walks Rosa. Her and Big Bertha were a bit drunk you could tell, but not a bother on them, getting stuck right into their private show, with Tuite laughing a little bit shyly at first and raising his hands as if in protest. I could see him shaking his head and making as if to leave, with Sandy and Boyle dissuading him energetically. Then he was wavering as Boyle crooked his finger and Rosa came waddling over. Bertha's blouse was first to come off as she continued grinding for a while in front of Boyle Henry, before moving on to the still-protesting Tuite. He tried to push her away but she just threw her head back and laughed. So did Sandy. Rosa started work on Boyle, opening his fly as he showered her in notes. 'That kind of money,' I could hear him saying. 'That'd be what he'd require. Only the best for a first-class tout! Which is what you're going to be, isn't it, Sandy?'

'No,' replied Sandy, phlegmatically. 'I'm sorry, Mr Henry! I'm sorry to say I've changed my mind about that.'

Boyle, running his fingers through Rosa's hair, laughed when he heard him. 'Stop,' he said to Sandy. 'Be nice to the copper. He's a Heavy Gang man.'

'A Heavy Gang man, you tell me? Well, let's see just how heavy!'

Poor old Tuite was pale now, having realized too late exactly what was going on. Boyle Henry looked over at him and sighed. Then shook his head as if to say: 'So how does it feel? Tell us, detective. Go on now, there's a good boy. Tell the lads how it feels to be up the creek without a paddle!'

Of course, no detective would ever have given serious thought to meeting a Provo on his own, even one who had supposedly 'turned', which was obviously the story they'd spun him. But Boyle Henry was different. Nobody knew for sure how involved he was – and you could imagine him using all his respectable councillor wiles to convince Tuite that everything would be safe and above board.

I was so busy watching Boyle Henry – his body was rocking back and forth as he came in Rosa's mouth – that I didn't notice Sandy reaching into his jacket. The next thing I heard the gunshot and Tuite was buckling to his knees as Sandy looked pained, pulling the trigger again as he moaned: 'No, not that heavy at all, Mr Henry! Not so heavy at all!' A worm of black blood pushed its swollen head through the detective's lips. A spot of it got on to Bertha's white flesh. Just a paintbrush flick. She started crying but gave up, heaving on her knees as though realizing that any more sound was now completely beyond her. Unlike Rosa who started screeching and tearing at her hair. With the result that Sandy had to hit her with the revolver.

It got very bad after that, so bad I had to hide my eyes. I saw Boyle kicking her as she curled into a ball and covered her face with her hands. When they were finished, Sandy sat in a chair staring at the gun. Rosa stood there with her eyes pleading: *What do I do? Can you please tell me what I'm supposed to do now?*

Boyle, cool as ice, gave her his answer by smiling and gently placing a finger upon his lips. He blew some smoke rings as he whispered: 'Let's not think of doing anything silly now,' and I never felt such melancholy as I thought of the smoke shaping her name: 'Jacy.' Saw those smoke rings forming the words *'Jacy'* and *'No. You didn't get it wrong, Joey Tallon.'*

Because that's what I had been beginning to believe. That I had been deceiving myself through bitterness.

I hadn't, though.

For this was him all right. This was the man. The same one who'd been with her that day in the lounge and had followed her out to the car. Calling her name and making promises. A gloom descended on me then and, for some reason, I thought of the Garden of Gethsemane – I had always been fascinated by that story at school – when it's at last revealed what it is that Christ must do and yet how part of him wants it to pass.

'Let this cup pass from me' were the words I remembered from catechism lessons. That was how I felt now. With a heavy heart I found myself uttering the words: *The beginning.*

Then I looked inside again. For a few seconds or so, Tuite came to life briefly and tried dragging himself across the carpet before Boyle Henry accepted the pistol from Sandy and put a final bullet in the detective's head.

Instinctively, I found myself joining my hands and intoning her name. I kissed my fingertips and gave thanks without words for having been given this sign. Bertha stiffened her shoulders, about to cry out again, before Sandy spotted her. He waved his finger from side to side, frowning as he cautioned: '*Woo woo!*'

Then Boyle went over and lifted up the poker, before shoving it in the fire.

Jailbirds

I suppose, to be honest, when I embarked on these few ruminations last night, I was secretly hoping to stumble upon a novel. Hoping that by going through my papers I might somehow be inspired so that at least something like the beginnings of a new work might emerge. By accident, I mean, for it was definitely never going to be by design. I've tried that approach a thousand times, each time without success, and if it didn't work then it won't work now.

What I wanted, more than anything, was for the material to catch fire so it would go off and write itself, in the same way it happened that very first time, when I completed my book *Doughboy* in what can only be described as utterly adversarial circumstances. Miraculous being the only word to describe that experience.

Nonetheless, I still have to admit it's been quite enjoyable. Sifting through these piles of papers, eclectic meanderings, memos, correspondence and what have you. Bonehead has even pasted some newspaper articles dealing with my court case into a scrapbook. I don't bother much with them, though – it almost makes me sick just to look at them – and tend to concentrate on my own petty ramblings.

There is a mouse who inhabits this study (Bonehead has put his own name up on the door: *Seccratary* [sic!] *P. J. Stokes* – I mean, can you believe it?) and from time to time, you can see him poking his little rodent head out from behind the china cabinet, as though he's checking to see everything's all right. He's a dead ringer for the fellow who shared the cell with the pair of us back in Mountjoy. Or 'The Joy', as it's generally called.

The first day I arrived there Bonehead offered me a bit of friendly advice. Sitting on the bunk and swinging his legs, he pointed to the mouse, going: 'He's the only friend you'll ever have in here, Boss! That's the kind of kip it is, and don't go thinking different!'

He told me his surname was Stokes but that that didn't mean he was a traveller. He regarded that breed – tinkers and travellers and itinerant types generally – as being lower than 'that mouse there', well-deserving of their reputation as shysters and thieves and disreputable people to be dealing with generally. The only problem with that being that Stokes was a common tinker name. 'I'm no tinker! Do you hear me?' he roared out of nowhere, and hit the wall a thump. 'I'm not a tinker! Nor a traveller neither!'

I said that was OK and he calmed down then for a bit, puffing out smoke clouds from his rollie.

'I have me own house!' he barked again. 'And don't you mind what they tell you in here! There's plenty o' travellers in this dump, Joesup, but I'm not one of them! Pat Joe Stokes is a high-bred man!'

He was shaped like a barrel and as bald as a coot, wearing this stripey jumper that made him look like a bumblebee. On top of that he had a severe hare lip, which was why, of course, he referred to me as 'Joesup'. They'd put him in for – among other things (which, I later discovered, involved a fatal affray in which an itinerant had died) – stealing lead off a roof, which seemed a pretty traveller-ish thing to be doing to me (thieving scrap was their stock-in-trade), but you daren't say that or he'd go completely insane.

'You just remember, Joesup,' he said, 'I'm a businessman and not a tinker. Them fucking travellers – all they ever do is attack each other with rusty hooks. That's no way to be carrying on with your life. Have nothing to do with them when you're in here! They'll only rook you for every penny.'

One day a bona fide traveller shouted at him across the exercise yard: 'G'wan, Stokes! Lettin' on to be wan o' the buffers and you wan of ourselves the whole time! You have no house of your own! That house belongs to Mannie Maughan!'

Before the screws could do anything he had charged across the yard and had your man up against the wall battering the living shit out of him. 'Say I'm not a traveller!' he bawled. 'I have my own house! Say that!'

All you could hear before they managed to pull him off was: 'You have your own house!'

'And it's not Mannie Maughan's!'

'And it's not Mannie Maughan's!'

He dusted himself down as the screws pushed him past me. 'I'm sorry about that, Joesup,' he turned and said to me, 'but I like people with manners. Us Stokeses was always brought up to have manners. Not like those ill-bred fuckers, effing gangsters and robbers!'

I don't know how long I'd been in there before my speech began to come back. Where it had gone to I hadn't a clue – I guess I must have been in a state of shock. Which is not surprising considering the balls I'd made of the whole fucking thing. And all the shit the papers had written about it. The yellow press had completely gone to town. *'One-Man Army Runs Amok'* was one of the headlines from the *Irish Press*. The worst of all was the *Sunday World*. They had a photo of Robert De Niro – the famous one with him blasting away as he's coming up the stairs – and there right above it in bold black type: MANIAC!

In retrospect, it is a very debatable point as to whether the return of my speech was a good development or not, for once he realized what had happened Bonehead wouldn't leave me alone, making up for all those days and nights I sat staring back dumbly at him. He had gotten it into his head that every word the papers had written was true and started setting me up as some kind of hero. Shouting at the screws and everybody going past: 'Youse think youse are smart but youse are fucking well not! Joesup is the man – the man with the eyepatch will sort youse out! Look at him! Haw! He's like Moshe Dayan so he is! He's the boy all right! Took them on all on his own! Good man, Joesup! You showed them coppers! It was just like a film so it was – I seen it all on the telly!'

I used to go into a depression when he'd start all that even though I knew he didn't mean any harm.

One night I lost it and tore a newspaper into shreds. The article kept comparing me to Donald Neilson, the Black Panther who had kidnapped the heiress Lesley Whittle and kept her in a mineshaft, where she died. I just sat there on the edge of the bed, shuddering with grief as I thought of a motherfucker like that doing such a thing to a helpless young girl, and how they could compare me to him. For weeks I was so numb thinking about things like that that I thought the best thing to do would be to get a hacksaw, which I did. Using a trick I'd seen in the movies where you put one blade down your sock and slide another one up your sleeve. So that when they intercept the first one they're so delighted at having nailed you they don't bother their arses looking for the second.

I went to work on my wrists but didn't manage to execute that either. Getting nothing out of it except a couple of hours of blissful oblivion before waking in sick bay with Bonehead staring down at me. I think because we'd become such pals they'd started to think of us in there as queers, but we weren't – there was nothing more to it other than Bonehead getting it into his head that I was 'full of brains' and sort of like 'quality' or something, I guess you could say.

'Not like them fucking travellers!' he said to me one day. 'Hitler had the right idea, Joesup. People like that just have to be gassed-ed!'

Another time in the workshop he announced that people like me sort of had to be looked after. 'I read about youse boys, you know, in a book!' he said. 'Fellows like James Joyce and all! They're special kinds of bucks, aren't they, Joey? Brains and everything! I read books too, Joesup! Oh yes! My father was a great big book man! Tommy Stokes – could have gone to college if he'd wanted! What odds if he was an alcomaholic! But the drink did get him bad. He didn't mind himself, you see. And that's what you'll have to start doing. You can't just be carrying on like this. Look at the mess you've made of your arms! You can't be going on like that! You hear me, Joesup? You'll have to promise me now!'

After that fortnight in sick bay, we became pretty much inseparable. His actual name was Pat Joe Stokes, but they just stuck the two of them together so 'Pajo Stokes' he became. Except not even that so very much either, mostly Bonehead. The more I got to know him, the more I really started to think you could trust him, and, for me, the way I was feeling in those days, that was a really big development.

And, after all these years, it's great to be able to say that I was right. I don't know how many cups of tea he made me or how many cigarettes he rolled for me in those days when we'd tramp the exercise yard or lay about in that TV room, dreaming. Trying to forget. All I know is it made a hell of a lot of difference.

'We've all made mistakes, Joesup,' he'd say to me. 'And after I get out I'm finished with thieving. People only get the wrong idea about you. They think you're one of the Wards – or the Nevins. Or the "bad" Stokeses. And don't get me wrong, Joesup – there's plenty o' them! Do you know what I mean? They think you're lower class. So it's no more lifting lead for me. I'm thinking of going into cigarettes and whiskey.'

I told him all about Mangan, my tinker neighbour.

'Hitler,' he said as he flipped his rollie, 'Hitler had the right idea about what to do with them boys. Oh aye, don't talk to me about the Mangans.'

The mouse came out then and he fed him some more bread. Eddie Gallagher he called him, after the maverick Provo kidnapper. Some of the papers had said that was where I got the idea. 'Ah, good man, Eddie,' Bonehead would say, as the mouse tore into the bread. 'So what do you think of him, Joesup? Is Eddie looking good today?'

Then he'd look at him and say: 'You're a good one, Eddie Gallagher, but you're not as good as our Joesup. Joesup's the best kibbernapper of the lot!'

I used to hate him using that word but there was no point in me saying anything about it. Sometimes I'd just fall into a deep sleep and hope I'd never wake up. But even then you wouldn't be safe, for there'd be pictures in there that seemed to come drifting out of a fog. Almost as soon as your eyes began to close you'd feel them slowly gathering and there'd be a depth of unhappiness inside that dream that you almost could not describe. Which is hardly surprising when you consider some of the things you were remembering.

The Animal Pit

They dug Tuite up out of the animal pit near the tannery a week or so after the night at the bungalow, and it wasn't too long after that the rumours started. I think it was Austie got the one going about the detective's head having been practically hacked from his body. But whether it was Austie for definite or not didn't make an awful lot of difference, for pretty soon nearly everybody had patented their own private version, gravely setting down their drinks as they looked you right in the eye before declaring: 'It was the Red Hand Commandoes did this one.'

That was a made-up name employed by Protestant paramilitaries whenever they were involved in any casual killings. When settling old scores and things like that. Boyle and Sandy knew it would cover their asses no problem, people being only too ready to believe it.

'They branded him, you know. They burnt UVF into his back at least thirteen times.'

It was Austie who told me that the detective's penis had been severed

74

and stuffed into his mouth. 'That's the type of cunt you're dealing with when it comes to these Protestant bastards!' he said. 'It's not like the Provos, who'll hit a legitimate target, go in for the quick, clean kill. With the UVF, no job is done till the flesh is cut to ribbons. That keeps them happy.'

Everyone thought Fr Connolly was going to have a heart attack. 'Is this what we've sunk to?' he said. 'And our Rally of Peace and Reconciliation only weeks away? Do you hear me, people? An animal pit! An animal pit, I ask you!'

After Sunday Mass all anyone could think of was poor old Tuite lying there amongst the stinking, infested pelts. It was no wonder now that feelings were running high, especially with regard to the Peace Rally. 'You see?' snapped Oweny Casey, one of Austie's regulars in the bar later on: 'You see now the type of peace you can expect from the likes of those fucking animals?'

He slammed his pint down and spat the word 'peace' out of the side of his mouth. 'They'd know a lot about peace,' he sneered, and I was afraid the glass was going to shatter in his hand. This from a man who normally took no interest in politics.

'This time it's a fight to the death,' he said then. After that, someone happened to mention Campbell Morris and another argument flared. 'It's time we set aside our differences!' someone else pleaded. 'People can't be dying like this. He was an innocent man!'

'There's no such thing as innocent!' came the terse response. 'How do *we* know he was innocent?'

You could see there was going to be another bitter row, so Austie put everyone out. That night two public monuments were broken in the town and a barn set on fire out on the road. It might have been an accident. The trouble was nobody could say for sure and that had the effect of kind of making it worse. As well as that, of course, on account of Tuite being one of their own, the cops had gone crazy and given Hoss's younger brother a savage beating. Austie said if it kept on like this he'd shut the bar up altogether. He nearly had to do that when a couple of nights later they set upon this woman and started arguing with her about the peace rally. Even though she was trembling they didn't let up – it was like they didn't even notice. She was the secretary of the Peace Committee, whose job more or less was to oversee the entire rally. I froze when I saw Sandy McGloin going over to comfort her. He handed her a handkerchief and offered her a lift home.

'People's tempers are frayed,' he said. 'It's a hard time for the community, ma'am.'

Austie himself got drunk – a very rare occurrence – and kept falling about the place, asking would there ever be peace in the country.

I was handing Boyle Henry his whiskey – I know it seems strange and that people are bound to think: *But why didn't Joey Tallon inform the authorities? Why didn't he go straight down to the police station and say what he'd seen that night inside the bungalow?*

That it was my . . . duty! My *responsibility*!

But it's easy to say that. It's easy to look back now and say something like that. I knew Boyle Henry would have covered his tracks. That it would end up being my word against his. And who was going to believe me? Especially after my having been in trouble with the law, disturbing the peace that time with The Seeker.

But it wasn't just that. There was something awful about Boyle Henry. You could feel it. All you had to do was look in his eyes as he sat there at the bar. Remorseless is the word, I think. No it isn't.

There is no word.

'Thanks, Joey,' he said a week or so after the funeral, shifting on the barstool and wiping his mouth with a hankie. He folded it neatly and shoved it in his pocket. Then rubbed his thighs. 'Bad times,' he said.

'Yes, Boyle,' I said, my heart beating far faster than usual in case he'd fix me with those eyes and ask: 'Have a good time that night in Oldcastle, did you?'

As if he knew I knew something. Even though he couldn't have. How could he possibly have? There was no way. 'You were gone when I came back to the car, Joey,' he said then. 'I was worried about you.'

He smiled and raised his glass. Then he winked and took a sip before leaving it back down on the counter again. He reached in his top pocket and pulled out a Hamlet. I was working out what my response was going to be if he said anything more about it. But when I looked again he had turned his back and was staring at the boys playing snooker. At the other end of the bar someone was glowering into another man's face, the sinews in his forehead showing as he seethed under his breath: 'Tuite was no friend of mine either! But this is a bridge too far! Do you hear me? Those UVF fuckers have overdone it this time!'

I heard glass smashing outside in the street. Then I thought: *A glass of sweat, please*. I didn't want to think it but I did. I didn't want to think *Pie* either. I had to go down the back and rinse my face. When I came back Boyle Henry had set up a drink for me.

'I couldn't believe it when I came back to the car. There you were – *gone*!'

I didn't know what to say. He burst out laughing. I went for the drink and slugged some of it down. All I could hear was him laughing as he rocked back and forth on the barstool.

In the cool of evening, it was like the town was boiling.

The Karma Cave

I prayed that night and read some Hesse. I sat by the window and thought to myself that the last thing I wanted Jacy to feel was that I had anything against Boyle Henry. Any grudge or . . .

She might turn her thoughts towards jealousy then. And start thinking that I did it to . . .

That I wanted her all for myself. I *did*! But not like . . .

Not like that. And that was what she would think if I reported him to the police. No. No matter what he'd done, I couldn't allow that to happen. The truth about him would be revealed to her soon, but it would be nothing to do with anyone else. Just her and me. The Only Ones.

I carried *Steppenwolf* everywhere with me now and tried to memorize the Hesse passage I'd been studying. But I couldn't so I read it to myself while I was waiting across the road from her flat. It reads: '*He is resolved to forget that the desperate clinging to the self and the desperate clinging to life are the surest way to eternal death, while the power to die, to strip one's self naked, and the eternal surrender of the self bring immortality with them.*'

I had never thought of it like that – the eternal surrender of the self. I had always felt the opposite. That you never surrendered to anything and that, if you did, you were weak.

How wrong I'd been, I thought. I had put the book back in my jacket when I saw the bank chick coming out. I knew she had her lunch in the hotel across the road so once I saw her going in there I knew everything was OK. I wasn't going to need long anyway. It couldn't have been more perfect – the window at the back was open so in a matter of seconds I was inside. I just left the *Spontaneous Apple Conclusion* record – *The Only One* – where she could not miss it, directly inside the door. Like I'd just slipped it underneath.

I didn't want her getting to thinking that I'd been trespassing in her space. That would have been an impertinence. It wasn't time for that yet. I had dropped a little note inside the sleeve. It would have been beautiful just to remain there awhile. I experienced the most delicious out-of-body sensation when I saw – at first I couldn't believe it – *Steppenwolf* opened there on the bottom bookshelf. It was just lying with its pages open, as though she were saying: 'These are the pieces, Joseph, that I would like you very much to read.' I went over to it, and sure enough it was open at the passage dealing with surrender. If I had ever needed confirmation then this was it. It was like she was sending me a sign. A signal. Whatever. It was a blissful, revelatory moment and I would have loved just to stay running my hand across that para-graph, with the mote-dancing sun coming shining in through her bed-room window. But it was impossible. I sighed as I stared at her zippered denim jacket – the one with the cluster of flowers on the col-lar – neatly draped over the back of a chair. Even touching it made me feel . . . one with her.

And I found myself thinking: *Maybe I will stay. Just sit here and read!* But no. It really and truly was impossible for me to do that, I realized.

Not now that Total Organization had begun. This being the 'first test'. I reached in my pocket and produced my aviator shades. I put them on and gazed at myself in her mirror. I felt every muscle in my body stiffen. 'T. O.' – I mouthed the letters, trying to remember what I could from the movie: *Total Organization is necessary. I must get in shape. Too much sitting has ruined my body. Twenty-five push-ups each morning, one hundred sit-ups. I have quit smoking.*

I whirled, aiming the 'gun' in a lethal, two-handed grip. Then sat again and closed my eyes in meditation. Reflecting on Tagore. Think-ing of Hesse. But most of all, of her. And 'T. O.'.

There would be no more spliffs. No more pyramid or windowpane acid, no more anything. No more anything that got in the way of *us*, T. O. and '*The Plan*'.

*

I didn't want to walk away from what I'd felt in his car that night, before the slaying of Detective Tuite. Call it Nirvana. Call it whatever. I wanted it again, and I knew there was only one way to get it. By being close to her. To she. Who is the 'Only One'. Just before I left, I strummed it on the guitar. Ever so softly as the sun danced on.

> Driving together yeah we had such fun
> Me and her – who is the 'Only One'.
>
> Yeah she who is who am – The Only One
> Yeah yeah oh yeah she's – The Only One.

I spent the remainder of the afternoon – it was my day off – just squatting lotus in the caravan and reading. Then I drove off out to the Karma Cave and gave it another cleaning. It was really looking good now, with them wind chimes tinkling away and the scented candles burning in their little painted dishes. I opened out the *Abraxas* sleeve and tacked it to the wall. There was a quotation on it from Hesse's *Demian*. It read: '*We stood before it and began to freeze inside from the exertion. We questioned the painting, berated it, made love to it, prayed to it. We called it mother, called it whore and slut, called it our beloved, called it Abraxas . . .*'

I put on the record, the Afro-Cuban rhythms of 'Singing Winds/Crying Beasts' beginning to reverberate as I closed my eyes and opened them once more to drink in the painting's fiery purple-winged angel, its luscious mounds of citrus fruits, the stunning colours of its exotic flowers, the swirling sweep of the painted silk fabrics. The burnished amulet that gleamed, the ancient ruined temple, the lines of coloured candles. I sat on the camp bed and meditated. To others, once upon a time, it might have been nothing more than a dilapidated cabin long forgotten by everyone. An abandoned old shack way up there on Tynagh mountain. But to a man called Joey Tallon it was already beginning to look . . . beautiful's not the word – 'precious'. Precious is the word. To us it would be precious.

Just as I was saying that I flicked one of the little rotating mobiles and it struck the most magnificent note. It just seemed to hang there, perfect. I tossed my head back and drank in the air. Then I began my press-ups. The movie lines out of nowhere came drifting into my head: '*My whole life has pointed in one direction. I see that now.*'

Then I stripped to the waist. 'Vile!' I hissed through gritted teeth. I knew I looked disgusting and that it was going to take time. Remembering the words of the prophet to the effect that you must assist the self, I did twenty-five press-ups. Followed by another twenty-five. By now the sweat was literally pouring off me.

But I felt good.

Pies

I had the half day off and was down at the back of the bar playing pool with Chico when Boyle Henry walks in along with Fr Connolly. He comes over to me with his thumbs in his lapels and says: 'Man but you're some basket of fruit, Joey! Leaving your property lying about like that where anyone could come along and lift it! Father, do you know the things that go fecking on! The things that go on in this town!'

I don't think Connolly heard a word he said. He was much too pre-occupied with his own business. Then Boyle looks at me with this big grin and says: 'I didn't think you had it in you, Josie! As God is my judge, I didn't! But fair play to you for trying! *The Only One*! Ha! Well, boys, oh boys!'

I could feel the blood draining from my face, but before I got a chance to say anything he starts whistling and goes over to Connolly saying: 'I think the flag should go up there, Father!'

I wasn't feeling the best. You don't just give up draw like that, you don't just give up acid and all of a sudden – as if by some miracle – just come back to yourself. It takes time. And I could tell that Boyle Henry knew that – how fragile I was, I mean. But I closed my eyes for the tiniest of seconds and repeated to myself in silence 'It's OK, Joey!' and waited for the dread to pass. But then, unexpectedly, Chico startled me by saying: *'Are you listening to me, Joey? Then take the fucking cue, will you, for Christ's sake!'*

It took three attempts before eventually I managed to hit the ball, for all I could think of was, how does he know? Did he see me coming out of her flat?

What worried me most was that I was going to start thinking: *She told him. She must have!* which was the last thing I wanted to hear . . .

And was why I concentrated on *Steppenwolf* and her having placed the novel there. It couldn't possibly have been lying there by accident. *Could it?* I thought.

Of course it couldn't, I reassured myself. And smiled.

'Don't be dumb now, Joey!' I murmured, stretching right across the expanse of green baize. 'That would be impossible. Too much of a coincidence. It has to have been . . . a "signal", one she could give without too much risk.'

I looked over, expecting him to be staring back at me. Smiling, most likely, in that way of his that had the effect of almost sickening me, making my stomach turn over.

But he wasn't. He was standing on a stepladder arranging a string of small flags and pennants with the words 'peace', 'reconciliation' and 'rejoice' on them. The others were busying themselves with loud-speakers and cables. I missed the balls a few more times before Chico eventually lost his rag and said: 'Will you shit or get off the pot, Joey!'

I could hardly see the steak and kidney pie in front of me in its tin-foil tray as I sat up at the bar counter. The Olympics were on but seemed much louder than usual. 'You Sexy Thing' was playing on the jukebox. That seemed loud too, almost as loud as it had been the day of the wrestling. So did the fork, come to that, clanging against the plate. I tried not to drop it – but then I dropped it. When I made to get off the stool in order to lift it I looked over and Boyle Henry was standing right beside me, smiling.

'You're enjoying your pie there, Josie,' he said.

A glass of sweat, please, I thought. No, thank you. Knife. Fork. Pie. *No pie!* Sauce. Do you have any sauce? Salt? No! *Sauce!*

'Yes, I am, Mr Henry,' I replied as steadily as I could manage.

'I love pies,' he said. 'I love them with sauce. Smothered.'

He rubbed his paunch and laughed.

'Look,' he said, 'there's some on your chin. Hey, Austie! Get me a cloth!'

Austie arrived with a teacloth, and Boyle folded it into a triangle and dabbed at the sauce.

'That's better. You and your old beard. You can't go around the town like that.'

He leaned across and put his hand on my shoulder. Looking over to check if Connolly was there, he dropped his voice and said: 'You know what I'm going to tell you, you crafty old trespasser you!' he said. 'I wouldn't fucking blame you!'

'What?' I choked. He leaned in closer. His eyes were shifting back and forth – they were full of life now. Remorseless still, certainly, but leaping about with tremendous agility, like each one possessed a unique life of its own.

'Once – I swear to God it's no lie, Joey,' he whispered, 'once I was in a dive in New Orleans, me and a few of the boys – you can ask Austie if you don't believe me. We were in this dive down south like, with all the bucks we wanted to spend. Money no prob., do you get me, Joseph? Next thing your woman comes out. "Boys," she says to us, "we got 'em all –"'

His grin broadened and he rested his hand on my shoulder, squeezing it.

'"Boys," she says, "we got 'em all! Chinese, Japanese, Italian, Spanish, Jap or Jew! Right in behind those doors! You pays your money and you takes your choice! And that door of your choice – it opens up!"'

His mouth hung open for a minute, and then he said: 'What did she say, Joseph?'

I couldn't take my eyes off the spot of sauce that had got stuck on the tip of my nose. It seemed huge and brown, almost as big as the nose itself.

'What?' I said.

'Huh? How's that, Josie? Eh?' he said, and pinched me hard. I winced. He patted the spot, as a mother might to make a child's bruise 'better'.

'What did she –?' I began.

He drummed his fingers on his stomach. Beaming. He winked and said: 'Yes, Josie! That's the way she operates! You pays your money and you takes your choice! Then the door it opens up! *Austie! Austie!* Can I have a beer?'

After he got the beer he sat for an age with his two arms folded. Then he said: 'Joseph – may I call you that? After all, it's your real name, isn't it?'

'Yeah, they call it to me sometimes,' I said. 'Mona especially used to –'

Already it was too late. Her name had escaped my lips. He patiently rested his chin on his fist and gazed into my eyes when he heard me saying it. His eyes might have been saying: *Caught you!* It was as though they were saying: 'I knew if I waited long enough that sooner or later I'd catch you!'

'Mona,' he grinned. 'That'd be Mona Galligan, I dare say. She was friendly with your father, as I recall.'

'Yes,' I said and stared at the floor. The tiles were black and white and very grimy. I thought I had better clean them. *Ask Austie for the mop, ask Austie for it!* I found myself thinking with an alarming urgency: *Ask Aust–!*

His hand was squeezing my shoulder again, the other stroking his chin. He fixed me with a stare.

'Joseph!' he said. 'Look at me! Where did he ever go, that old father of yours? Where did he go, your old man Jamesy? Tell us, Joey, where did he go?'

I didn't reply. I tried my best to wrest my shoulder away, but without drawing attention to it.

'Did he have a wee girl maybe out foreign?'

'I don't know,' I said. 'I don't know where he went, Mr Henry.'

'What did he have to go and do that for? That was a bad thing to do. Poor old Mona, shovelling gin into herself then and going around quaking like a jelly. A Chivers jelly! Say that, Joey – a *Chivers jelly!*'

I looked away. He clapped me gently on the back.

'Ah well. Don't say it then,' he said. 'You don't have to say it if you don't want to.'

He sighed and sank his hands into his pockets. Then he continued: 'And your poor old mother, she didn't fare much better. That'd be the shame, I suppose. Shame is a bad boy, Joey. She mightn't give a fuck about him, and the way I heard it, she didn't. But the shame now, that would be different. That would be a different kettle of fish for a woman abandoned. Which is really what happened, Joey, no matter what way you might try to dress it up. Left on the dump so as he could ride all he wanted.'

He flexed his fingers and contemplated his nails. 'He was a good singer too, Joey. He used to sing at all the concerts. Do you know what he used to sing? "Harbour Lights", Joey. I wonder what harbour he sailed into? I know! The wee furry one, maybe!'

He clapped me sharply on the back and boomed: 'Aye! That'd be her! Eh, Joey? Eh, Joey?'

I swallowed. All of a sudden he erupted into song.

And then those harbour lights
They only told me we were parting!
The same old harbour lights
That once brought you to me.

He twinkled then and gave me a little shove. 'Wasn't he a desperate man now, doing the like of that?'

His eyes creased up and he laughed again. Then he said nothing for a while. He drank some more beer. The pool balls clacked. He licked his lips and gave his attention to the game for a while, commenting here and there. 'Nice shot!' he said, and: *'Lovely pocket, son!'*

Then, all of a sudden, he swung on his heel and blurted: 'Joseph?'

'Yes?' I replied.

He raised his left eyebrow. 'Do you think there'll ever be peace in this country?'

I said I didn't know. There were crumbs from the pastry on my lips. I tried my best to wipe them off. I didn't want him to see me doing it.

'Look at you, Joseph! You're all crumbs!' he teased.

I laughed a bit then stopped. Then I saw he was gazing at me and pointing at them – the crumbs. I half laughed again and tried to brush some of them off with my sleeve.

I was trying to think of what I was going to say next when he lifted up a piece of meat and held it between his fingers. Then he said: 'Joseph, will you open your mouth for me?'

Before I knew what I was doing I had complied with his request and he was pressing the cubed steak in between my lips. Without warning, he jabbed me with his fingers, real hard. I gagged.

'Oops!' he chuckled. 'Bit of an accident there! Sorry about that, Joseph!'

He grinned and was about to pick up another piece of meat when Connolly came over and announced: 'We'll have to be making tracks shortly, Boyle, there's someone looking for us up at the chapel.'

'Back at HQ!' the councillor laughed as the clergyman smiled and strode off again.

My stomach felt empty, like I'd eaten nothing at all. I was on the verge of calling out to Austie for another pie when Boyle came back and gripped my wrist: 'Like I say, Josie . . .' he continued.

Then, oddly, he dropped his voice until it became a mere whisper. The pool balls were seeming to take an age travelling the breadth of

84

the green cloth. It was as though he were in pain now as he spoke. As if tears were about to moisten his eyes.

'That night in New Orleans we could have had our pick, the choice of whatever it was we wanted, any sweet and juicy pussy going, Joseph my man, French, Jap, Chink or Jew, we could have had it. What do you think of that?'

He flicked his nail and sighed, still pained, even more so. 'Oh, Joseph!' he went on. 'If only you'd been there. If only you'd been there that night. Do you know where you'd have come with us?'

I flushed to the roots.

'No,' I said, 'I don't.'

'Joseph,' he continued, 'you'd have come with us. To the only place you could. And where's that? Joseph, *ask* me! Where's that?'

I wished he would stop it. Stop it now, *right now*!

I was on the verge of grabbing a handful of pie and saying to him: *'Shut up! Shut up now, do you hear me? Stop it and shut up or I'll mash this into your face! I'll mash this pie right into your face right here and now in this fucking bar! Do you hear me?'*

'Joseph,' he said, 'you're not answering me.'

'I didn't –'

'Ask me, I said. Say to me: "Tell me, Boyle, where's that?"'

'Where's that?'

'No: "*Tell* me, Boyle!" Mm?'

'Tell me, Boyle, where's that?'

He sculpted a female figure in the air, closing his eyes as he licked his lips, his body enjoying a sensuous quiver of delight. I thought he'd never get around to speaking. I wanted him to stop and yet I wanted him to speak. *Just say something!* I thought. *Say it, for fuck's sake say it!*

At last, his lips parted.

'That is,' he smiled, 'that is the American Door, behind which you'll find – behind which you'll find –'

'No!' I cried.

He shook his head and frowned sympathetically.

'I don't blame you for not believing me, Joseph, for it's not that often you'd see it round these parts but when you do, Joseph – Joseph, when you do . . .!'

'Austie!' I called, as I nearly choked on a meat cube. 'Can I have another steak and kidney pie, please?'

'That's right,' Boyle said, 'you do that. You have yourself another pie, Joey, but in the meantime listen. Listen to your old friend Boyle.'

I opened my eyes hoping he'd have gone away. But he hadn't. He split a match and started picking his teeth with it.

'But the best of all,' he went on, 'the best of all didn't come from New Orleans at all. Didn't come from Louisiana state at all. "Where did it come from, Boyle?" Ask your old pal that.'

He looked at the match, then tugged my sleeve.

'Go on then, Joseph,' he urged, 'ask me.'

I lunged towards the plate, forking a dollop of pie.

'That fork's dirty,' he said, before continuing: 'It doesn't matter now. It's gone. You've ate it. It's . . . *finito.*'

He sighed, flicking away the match. Then, rubbing his thighs, he went on: 'Anyway, where was I?'

His grin widened.

'Go on then, ask me.'

'Ask you?'

Top Cat exploded on to the television. He shot up out of a dustbin with a fish skeleton on his head. *'Hey T. C.!'* a mechanical voice squealed as the music speeded up and the characters tore off like things possessed.

'Yes. Ask me. *Ask me!* "Where did she come from, the sweetest juiciest pussy that a man did ever . . . if she didn't come from the state of Louisiana then where did she come from?"'

I wanted so much to do it – lift the plate right there and then, break it, and stuff the pie right down *his* throat.

'Ah, come on now, Joseph,' he said after a bit, 'I haven't got all –'

I couldn't help it. I know I ought to have kept my voice down. It wasn't a shout exactly, but it was an awful lot louder than it should have been. And I oughtn't to have cursed.

'Where did she come from then?' I snapped. *'Where the fuck did she come from then if she didn't come from Louisiana?'*

He looked at me as if to say *'Tut tut!'* and pressed his forefinger to his lips. 'Now, now,' he said.

He lapsed into silence then, remaining deep in contemplation. Then he looked right at me.

'California,' he whispered. 'California.'

He stood up straight away and brushed down his jacket. He gestured towards the empty tinfoil tray and said: 'I'm paying for that, Josie.'

'Where the hell have you been, Boyle?' called Connolly then, bustling in with an armful of his pamphlets. 'We've been looking everywhere for –'

'The Sunshine State,' grinned Boyle Henry, conspiratorially, 'the Sunshine State, Josie!'

'*State! State!*' fussed Connolly. 'We'll be in a right old state if we haven't got The Courtyard finished this evening!'

'Right so,' said Henry then, tugging down his sleeves.

'Austie!' I called. 'Would you have another pie there, please?'

'What?' said Austie, grunting. 'You haven't fucking finished this one, Tallon!'

'He's an awful man,' laughed Boyle, leaning on my shoulder. 'If he doesn't stop this he'll go up like a balloon! He'll be like your man on the telly – Demis Roussos! The girls won't fancy him at all!'

'*Go* up like a balloon?' snorted Austie. 'What do you mean, *go* up?'

'Ah yes!' laughed Boyle. 'You're an awful man. But there's just one thing. There's just one thing and you should know . . . you should really know it, Joseph.'

'What's that?' I said. I thought he was never going to speak.

'There aren't two "r"s in "darling".'

He gripped me by the shoulders and gazed right into my eyes. Then he moved in closer.

'There aren't two "r"s in "darling", are there?'

'No,' I stammered, 'there aren't, Mr Henry.'

He sighed exasperatedly.

'No,' he continued, 'there's only one "r". Only one "r" in "darling". And any man that thinks otherwise, any man that'd find himself thinking otherwise, well, he'd have to be a bollocks. But don't worry, your secret's safe with me. That's one thing you and me have in common – we can keep secrets. Right, Joey?'

He grinned and winked. Top Cat was running for dear life now as a black-masked burglar came chasing after him. The soundtrack raced hysterically along with them.

'*Hey, T. C.! Hey, T. C.!*' was all I could hear.

'Whaddya say, Joey boy? Huh? Well, Joey?'

I thought it was T. C. but it was Boyle Henry. He was hitting my shoulder short sharp jabs with his fist. Then he stopped and said: 'Right, Joey? Eh? Eh?'

'Will you come on out of that, Boyle, for the love and honour of God!' I heard Connolly calling.

'Right you be, Father,' replied Boyle Henry, all of a sudden relaxing and smiling as he said: 'Well, be seeing you then, Joey, old friend!' and walking towards the door before swinging on his heel to deliver one last cheery smile.

When I saw him doing that, not to mention his giving me the thumbs-up, it was all I could do not to grab what was left on the plate and shove the lot right down my throat. Then stand there shouting: *'Now do you see! Do you fucking well see now, Boyle Henry! I've eaten it! Are you happy now? Well, are you?'*

That night a familiar gloom took hold of me and no matter how I tried I couldn't manage to shake it off.

I'd indulged in two spliffs, you see, in an effort to banish the sound of his voice.

Betrayed my trust in myself, effectively.

Mangan

It must have been near midnight when I heard the knock on the door and opened it to find Mangan standing on the step. He had his dog with him. He was wearing an old Fair Isle jumper with tea stains all down its front. 'You'll be sorra,' was all he said. Sorra. The way he said it. *'Sorra'*, as a hesitant trembling took hold of his voice. 'If he hadna been chained up you'd never have hurted him!' he said and started stroking the dog.

'Why are they always barking?' I said. 'That's all they ever do. Why don't they shut up?'

I brought him in and, when the light hit him, I saw that he'd been crying. You could see that plainly. He kept stroking the animal's head and repeating, heart-rendingly: 'You'll pay for what you done, Joey Tallon! Now the whole town will know! For I'll tell them! I know what you be at in here! Don't think I don't see you! I seen you all right! I seen you – *with her*!'

He glared at me.

'Pulling at yourself and talking in women's voices! You think I don't know? I seen, you see! I seen! I seen you putting a wig on her! A long black wig – I seen it!'

'Shut up!' I said. 'You don't know anything, Mangan! You don't know what you're talking about!'

88

He squared up to me, quivering.

'I do!' he snapped. 'I know everything that goes on. You think I've been here in this camp for close on thirty year and not know what goes on? I know all right, and I know you hurt . . . you hurt my little –!'

'He's not fucking little!' I spat. 'He's not fucking little!'

Then I experienced a pang of remorse.

'He just wouldn't stop!' I tried my best to explain, but Mangan was already on his way out. He turned as he crossed the grass and raised his fist.

'I seen you and don't think I didn't!' he called. 'Through yon window. I seen what you be doing! Calling out her name! *Mona! Mona!* I know who you're talking about, sure enough! I seen her about the town, years ago, same black hair and all! Yes! That's what youse be at, you and her! You and your Mrs . . . *Mona!* Oh aye, Mona Galligan that fired herself into the reservoir! Aye! Riding the dead! Riding the dead – that's your game and don't tell me any different! For these eyes don't lie – dressing her up and talking to her! Lying there raving without a stitch on you, full to the gills with drink! Do you hear me, do you, rav–'

'Shut your mouth, Mangan! Get in there, I said! Get in there to fuck and shut your mouth! Who's going to believe the likes of you, a halfwit old tinker!'

He slammed the door and I could see him at the window, shaking behind the curtain. Afterwards, I couldn't manage to sleep a wink, worrying and wondering how he'd found out about me and Mona. But glad in a way that it had happened. Simply because the more I thought about it – and the Boyle Henry 'incident' – the more I realized that what all this meant was, *I was being challenged.* That this was my big test.

A sort of dry run, in a sense, before the *Big One*! Sure I had fallen, betrayed my trust, like I say. But it wasn't the end of the world. It wasn't *The End*. Far from it, in fact – it was a new *Beginning*!

I sat by the window. There was an old paper lying there, carrying reports of the Eddie Gallagher siege. It had been the talk of the country for weeks and I'd watched it every day in the pub. Day after day, with Austie giving me grief about being 'obsessed' by it.

Gallagher was a Provo working off his own bat with Marion Coyle to bargain his lover out of jail. They had kidnapped Tiede Herrema, the Dutch industrialist, keeping him hidden upstairs in a council house bedroom, besieged by police and army. I didn't like the way they'd gone about things. There was a lot of talk about the psychological torture and unnecessary pressure they'd put on the man. I didn't know whether it was true or not, but if it was, it was bullshit. That was what it was. That kind of thing didn't belong in me and Jacy's world. It wasn't going to be like that, no way. It was . . . *bad karma.*

But the newspaper reports gave me the idea for the bags of sand – my fallback if things went wrong. Joey Tallon, 'The Human Bomb'. (*'I'll take you all with me, you motherfuckers!'*)

A bluff, maybe, but I knew it could work.

Transfiguration

My eyes lit up as I solemnly repeated: '*You are on the right track, move neither to your left nor right, but keep to the straight and narrow way.*'

I threw out all my Rizla cigarette papers and a matchbox crammed with acid tabs. I will never be able to explain in words – even now, with all my experience – just exactly how I felt that night. I might have been Tarzan. A Tarzan of the mind, that is. I wanted to cheer: 'Fuck pies!' To stand there beating my chest. I wanted to run to the top of a mountain. I could have run up and down one for hours.

At the first sign of light I went into town, running. And got some food to make me strong. Even stronger! Some steak and kidney pies? No chance!

I had salad. Lettuce leaves and carrot. I bought them in the vegetable shop beside Austie's. Very tasty. And nutritious. That night I read some *St John of the Cross*: '*And then we'll climb high, high to peaks riddled with stony caves softly hidden away, and there we'll go inside and taste the pomegranate wine.*'

I felt . . . transfigured. That is the only way to describe it.

Mohawk

I headed down to the barber's. 'Just shave it all off,' I told him, 'but leave a bit running down the middle.'

'Is this for the band then, Joey? Is that why you want to be like a Mohawk?' he says as he plugs in the shaver.

'No,' I said, a trifle impatient, 'the band's broken up. Didn't you hear about Banbridge?'

'Jesus, Joey, I'm sorry,' he said.

'Just clip the hair, man,' I said. 'Just cut the fur, you dig?'

'Right you be then, Joey,' he said and got to work. 'I'll do you a Mohawk.'

I couldn't believe it when I looked in the shop window after leaving the barber's. At first I thought: *It's just a coincidence.* But then nothing ever happens that way – and I knew it. It was a signal, a sign, call it what you will. A fantastic bright orange palm-print shirt. Hawaiian.

I shoved it on and stood in front of the mirror. *'Are you looking at me?'* I said. *'Huh? Huh?'*

I slipped on the shades and the combat jacket.

'You lookin' at me, baby? You lookin' at me, Jacy hon? I sure hope you are because, you know something, babe? I love you!'

I'd fold my arms and vary the voice. Different emphases each time. Are you looking at *me*? You, are *you* looking at me?

'Hi, Jacy. Joey here. So how you been then? Doin' good?'

I was beginning to feel really comfortable now saying stuff like that.

I mean, the knowledge was something that had to grow privately within you. You couldn't go around spouting philosophy all the time. Like The Seeker used to say, *You are the you of you.* And this was the *me* of *me*, the Joey Tallon that belonged in the real world that you could see and touch. The Joey Tallon that had taken himself in hand and set off once and for all on his journey. I repeated the lines: *'My whole life pointed in one direction. I see that now. There has never been any choice for me.'*

Except that the difference between me and Travis Bickle was that he had always been lonely. He said: *'Loneliness has followed me all my life. The life of loneliness pursues me wherever I go; in bars, cars, coffee shops, theatres, stores, sidewalks. There is no escape. I am God's lonely man.'*

But that wasn't how Joey Tallon felt. Maybe once upon a time he had. But not now. No fucking way now, I repeated to myself. No way.

That night sleeping like the happiest bunch
of motherfucking lambs.

Primroses

It was Carmel Braiden from Old Cross Terrace who won the Poem for Peace competition. Boyle Henry presented her with the prize, and a lot of the Peace People from Belfast and Dublin had turned up for the ceremony. Carmel was very nervous reading it but she managed to get through it all right. All I can remember is: '*The world is a sad place/We see so much waste/Must we turn away, ignore/So that it happens for ever more?*'

That was strictly speaking the opening of the Peace Rally of Hope and Reconciliation. I was pleased to see it happening and hoped some good would come out of it, for everybody's sake.

Afterwards, I went out to the reservoir. It was a special place – always had been. It was where Bennett and the salesman and Mona had died. When you sat there listening, you could hear the rustling of the leaves, with the wind coming through them as though it were their voices trying to reach you in order to explain. What exactly it was that had happened and how they were feeling now. *Are you up there, Bennett?* I kept thinking, but not in a negative way. You could imagine other people there too. Other souls who had long since departed, who had once walked the streets of the town. Or stood there staring out across the water towards the thread of the distant horizon. 'He used to sing it here,' I heard Mona saying, 'and whenever he did, you'd imagine yourself way out there on the ocean's blue surface in this little boat, just lapping homeward. It always used to make me think of that whenever he'd sing "Harbour Lights".'

I didn't expect Mangan to understand the complexities of the relationship I had with Mona. Or to know what she meant by 'that precious harbour'. The place of dreams that her and my father never managed to reach. You'd hear mutterings in the town: 'He bucked her crooked then fucked off both on her and the wife, without even bothering to look back once.'

But that wasn't how Mona saw it, and I knew that. She had told me all about it when I'd visit her after school every day. I'd just sit listening for hours.

'I know he loved me, no matter what they say,' she'd say. 'And I'm sorry for the pain it caused your mother. But one day we'll reach that Place of Wonders, the wondrous place, and none of this will matter any more. And all the things that have ever gone wrong, they'll all have come right again. Because that's what it's like there, Joey. And he's waiting there, your father Jamesy, for my boat to arrive. At night, perhaps, when those lovely golden lights are twinkling. And when it does –'

She paused before turning to me and saying: '"Mona," he'll say. *"Mona!"*'

Sometimes she'd whimper when she said it, or fiddle about with tissues.

'Don't think bad of me, son,' she'd say. 'I know what the rest of them are saying. Because of what I done to my baby.'

'Don't worry, Mona,' I'd reply and want to climb inside her stomach so that *I* could become her baby.

'It could be you,' she said one day. 'You could be born again! To me! *Then* everything might come right!'

As I sat there I could have sworn I heard her. I listened again to the leaves softly stirring.

'*I'm hearing you, Mona,*' I said, then tossed some flowers into the air and smiled.

I used always to make sure to bring her primroses, which grew in abundance out at the reservoir.

Total Org.

As the 'plan proper' got into gear, in the days that followed I couldn't wait to get home, working harder than ever before – carting barrels, polishing mirrors, cleaning taps, all with the same purpose in my mind: *Total Org.* I had a little garden now beside the caravan and I tended it every day. There wasn't much in it, just a few cabbages, parsnips and carrots. And a row or two of peas. I thought of it as being a shrine of sorts, in honour of what Charles Manson might have been. The problem with Charlie was that he had made the wrong choices. He could have been Jesus but instead became the devil. He could have been the Buddha but chose to become Hitler. There were two gardens on earth, and I knew that now. In one there were flowers both tender and perfumed, and in the other there was nothing but evil. I stood up and stretched as I shook my trowel. Then I looked at the sky as wisps of cloud drifted across in the blue. The sun glinted off the trowel's polished metal. 'You made the wrong choice, Charlie,' I said.

Just then Mangan appeared in the doorway of his caravan.

'Who are you talking to, Tallon?' he growled suspiciously.

I shaded my eyes and smiled at him. Even things between the two of us had greatly improved of late. I'd started bringing him the odd cabbage or bowl of peas.

'*The Only One*,' I said. 'She alone has shown us this path. The others are but minions. Messengers. Signposts, really, on the road to love.'

'Who?' he asked. 'What others?'

I'd meant Tagore. St John of the Cross. Manson even.

'You cannot arrive until you surrender. And only with her can such a thing be possible,' I said.

He stood staring at me for a long time, then went back inside, muttering: 'Dead people don't fucking well talk! You're lucky they don't come and take you away!'

He slammed the door and I could see him peeping out through the curtain. But it didn't bother me now. I had never heard the birds sing so sweetly, knowing as I did that when the 'precious moment' came, we'd – all of us – be together.

'In the place where Love lies, Mangan!' I felt like calling out. 'In that resting place we like to call our home!'

But I didn't. I simply sat there in my garden, cross-legged, and shrugged. Just grateful that the knowledge I'd gathered had become like a kind of armour that protected me. 'Yeah!' I heard myself say. 'He loved Mona too, my father. He loved her and my mother both, if you wanna know the truth! You hearing me? Now they're all together, up there behind them clouds! Listen!' I said, and cupped my hand over my ear. It seemed so melodramatic that I almost burst out laughing. But I was glad I'd said it all the same. 'Naughty daddy!' I chuckled. 'Riding two girls at once!'

It was strange, uttering those words aloud like that, for I'd never have dared to before. It was like now that the 'moment' was close at hand – when we'd be together, Jacy and me – that I was practising 'surrender'. For there was nothing I wasn't going to tell her. Every skin and layer there was to be shed, I'd shed it. For that was what it was all about, Love. Mona knew that too. That was why I'd wanted to grow inside her. So that that second time I would know all about it, right from the very beginning. But, even better still, believe in it.

'He never meant to hurt your mother, you know,' she'd say to me. 'You'll really have to believe that, Joseph.'

That night in the caravan, lying with Mona, running my fingers through her long black hair, I whispered to her what my mother used to say whenever 'the nerves' came on. 'That fucking whore, that slattern bitch! That skivvy Galligan, the husband-stealer! But he left her too, didn't he? Where did he go? To the Far East? Did he go off on a slow boat to China? Is that where he went, Galligan? Miss him do you? Miss *my* husband?'

I didn't say anything for a while after that. Then I said: 'Other times she'd cry: *"Don't leave me, Jamesy!"'*

As the dawn came up I listened to some Joni, trying out some more chords. I pretty much had 'California' off by heart now. I sang some of it, although I have to admit it was a little off-key.

I could hear the surf crashing, rising up in slo-mo, washing on to the sand and retreating then without a sound. Sometimes it made you weep, the thought of the 'precious moment' being so close.

It seems extraordinary now, that depth of feeling, but it's evident here in every scrap of paper. No matter how illegible – and, believe you me, there are plenty of examples of that.

With quite a number of one's observations heavily underscored in pencil – a caution against wavering, sceptical tendencies, no doubt!

23 October 1976, 9-ish

Just back from the reservoir, sitting there thinking about us and the ordained life ahead. The open road and all its excitements – from Denver to Lincoln to Omaha and then across to you-know-where. Because that's the heart of her onion! It sounds funny when you put it like that!

Note to self: Is the world real? Is it an illusion? With form? Without form?

With The Jace, the answer is yes, it is real. Realer, in fact, than anything you could dream.

When I had finished writing, I closed my eyes and I could hear her saying she was glad that I prepared everything so carefully, gone out of my way to put so much effort into it.

I heard her saying: 'He's a very dangerous man. And that's why I appreciate you doing this, for that's what true courage is: knowing your fear and facing it.'

I thought: *Because it is true. Whenever I think of him, I shudder. Who wouldn't when you think of what he did that night?*

But love is stronger than any of that. Love and patience and discipline. Love and discipline will see us through. Upon discipline depends the heaven that men desire and upon it rests this world too.

1 November 1976

I got the plastic bags, and the sand I'll be getting tomorrow from a place not far from the camp where they're putting up a new estate. Went up the mountain and swept the place from top to bottom – again! If this keeps up it'll be the cleanest home in history! 'Home' – even saying the word makes me feel at rest. For that's now how it seems, anything it might have been before no longer having any meaning. Cave of Dreams most precious. Where you belong, where I belong. Where we belong. I know ... I am perfectly aware that the first two or three days will be hard. Until slowly the layers begin to strip and our two souls bond, entwine. The self, hidden in all things, does not reveal itself to everyone. It is seen by those of subtle and concentrated mind. What we must do is concentrate on the onion, take each layer one at a time. This is essential.

Remember: Time of its own power cooks all beings within itself. No one, however, knows that in which Time itself is being cooked.

A Good Laugh

On the way back from getting the sand I remember meeting a couple of the boys from Austie's. '*Hey! Travis Bickle? You lookin' at me?*' they shouted. '*Because if you're not lookin' at me, who are you lookin' at?*' Then they bawled: 'I just hope we don't get the weather you're expecting, Tallon!' laughing away at my US army jacket, which I'd buttoned all the way up to my neck to hide the sand. I did three or four runs so as not to look too conspicuous. Then I practised in front of the mirror with a couple of the bags strapped to my waist.

I drew with my gunfinger, then wheeled sharply. 'You doin' good then, Jace? You are? You feelin' OK? Your hair – it looks real good. Huh? Huh? Yeah!'

One thing I was afraid of was that they might slip, but they held pretty steady thanks to the duct tape I'd bought in Provider's. I did some exercises while still wearing them. They made it much more difficult, of course. But also much more beneficial. I did fifty press-ups. All the time it kept going through my head: *Thank God for this chance, this precious moment. I'm working long hours now some six days a week. It's a long hustle but it keeps me real busy.*

She is not like the others.

I sealed all the bags then tried to get to sleep as best I could. But it was hard. What I wanted more than anything was for it all to be over. That it all would end so it could begin once again – with each new day being born in the way it ought to have been the first time.

(All the stuff from Mountjoy Bonehead has pasted into a number of 'Jail Journals', essentially thick, bound notebooks with various items of correspondence clipped or stapled into them. The writings themselves are far from chronological – quite erratic, with some of them typed, others handwritten. Quite a few a mixture. There were long periods when I didn't write anything at all inside, being overcome by blackness, melancholy . . . I don't know – maybe just not seeing the point. Months could go by without me writing so much as a word. Even years.)

Jail Journal (subtitled: 'Diary of a Kip')

It has been hell in here for so long ever since I came through that fucking gate that I don't even like to talk about it, much less write down my feelings in a notebook like this or anywhere else. After the hacksaw business the screws never left me alone, in particular one of the kicking squad – kind of like Tuite's 'Heavy Gang' – who'd got it into his head that me and Bone were definitely queers. 'You needn't think you'll get out of it that handy!' he said to me one day when he came up behind me in the yard. 'Topping yourself with a hacksaw blade. It's not good enough for you terrorizing women but now you've turned queer-boy as well. Well, don't worry, my friend, I'll see you finish your term. You try that again and I'll bust your balls! I'll sort you out good and fucking proper, Mr Taxi Driver! You see if I don't!'

It came to a head and one day I lunged at him in the workshop. Which was a mistake for he had been waiting for it and I came off the worst. 'I'll put that other eye out for you, you half-blind fucker!' he said when he had me down on the ground. They didn't do that, but him and the rest of the kicking squad took me into the toilets and gave me a beating I will never forget. Bone said he'd get them but there was nothing we could do. I didn't talk much to anyone after that and to tell you the truth I don't think I ever would have if things hadn't changed in the fifth year when the new governor Mervin Recks was brought in to take charge. This would be around the time when the first junkies had started to appear, all these porridge-faced Dubliners with dark eyes sunk in their heads, traipsing around the place like *Dawn of the Dead*. Me and Bone were sitting in the TV room watching U2 one day (I couldn't take my eyes off Bono - he seemed so *sure* of what he was doing) when this fellow in a tracksuit sits down beside us and asks for a smoke. 'What are you in for?' says Bone, and when he says: 'I got caught with seventy grand's worth of gear!', asks him maybe could he get us a telly, or a couple of Walkmans at least. 'I'm bleedin' talkin' about *gear*!' says your man. 'Smack, you stupid bleeding tinker!'

Well, when he said that, you can imagine the reaction of Bonehead - it took three of us to pull him off him!

'How dare you say that to me!' he yells. 'I'm one of the Stokeses of Rathowen! I have me own house, you jackeen drug addict bastard!'

Much of the diary for those four years is quite banal and tedious, with one day the same as the next. There's this deadening rhythm going through it. And only for Mervin, to tell you the truth, I don't know . . .

Whether I'd have made it or not, I mean.

A lot of them said that he took a shine to me and Bone and that because of it we got far more than we were ever entitled to. I don't know about that but one thing I do know is that Mervin's arrival changed the fucking place for ever. I won't say the years after he was appointed were heaven but it sure did make it more bearable, the opportunities he offered you enabling you to forget the sickening smells that clung to the place, the stench of pisspots, fags and underwear changed once a week mixed up with that of overcooked food, disinfectant and detergent. It was as if the minute he came those smells kind of turned around and died. Which they couldn't have, of course, but you definitely didn't notice them. Not so much.

'I've seen you writing the odd time,' he said to me one day, and of course I denied it. Because at first I didn't trust him. As well as that, I was embarrassed. If I'd been full of shame about attempting such things before, well, as you can imagine – the kicking squad can work wonders for your confidence – I was twice as full of it now. 'No,' I said, 'as a matter of fact, Governor, I can barely write my name.'

If it had been anybody else, I suppose that would have been the end of it. But Mervin knew how to handle you and it sort of didn't seem like you . . . were being used, I guess.

So in the end, I confess, he got around me. We used to have these chats in his study and, during walkabout, he'd come into the cell and spend some time there. He couldn't get over Bonehead. 'Does he ever talk about anything else?' he asked me. Meaning travellers.

'Yes,' I said. 'He talks about football.'

He was football mad, in fact. Which really did my head in, for when he got started all you'd hear would be: 'Who scored the winning point in the All-Ireland Final in 1954? Go on then, Joey, who? Who?'

I never had the faintest clue. But Mervin did. He was nearly as bad as Bone. It was after one of those chats that the two of them cooked up the idea of the football tournament. The Mountjoy Gaels A wing we were called and what a collection of fuckers as ever was let near a football pitch! We had the little junkie guy, who turned out to be like a streak of fucking lightning, scoring a hat-trick on his first outing alone. Bone was in goal and didn't let one past. The only thing about it was he never shut up about it now. It was night, noon and morning football in the cell. 'We'll fucking take her, Joesup!' you'd hear him saying, pacing up and down the floor at all hours of the night. 'We'll burt the fuckers!'

Meaning 'burst', of course.

The tournament was, at first, exclusively kept inside the prison but, later on, other cons were allowed in for games. By the time the season was over, you could hardly see the rim of the wall there were so many footballs impaled on the razor wire. I'll never forget the day Boo Boo came in to visit and slipped me a tab of acid. Unfortunately it was the day of the final and all I can remember is the ball arriving at my feet and Bonehead going: *'Now, Joesup! Run!'* but being so out of it that all I could think of was: 'Look at those fabulous footballs! Those amazingly beautiful footballs! Man! Jeez!', with the nimble flicky flickies – your own private little solar system – going *phwoosh!* and all the lovely colours – mostly orange and white – bleeding into each other there on top of the wall. It was the most magnificent of visions. At least until I heard Bonehead shouting: 'You stupid bollocks, Joesup! You've gone and loosed-ed the game on us!'

Which I had. They won by three goals and a point to nil and the Bone didn't speak to me for a week. 'I'll never forgive you, Joesup!' he says. 'Why did you do it? You let me down!'

But then he went and forgot all about it, being much too busy tormenting a young fellow called Ward who'd just been put in for stealing lead. He couldn't go anywhere without getting a clip from Bonehead. 'Just because I lifted lead doesn't mean I'm like you!' you'd hear. 'Get away from about me, Ward – and all belonging to you! It's a wonder youse wouldn't go and do a day's work! Isn't that right, Joesup?'

Sometimes he'd just hit him a kick up the arse and run away. The poor young fellow didn't have the life of a dog. But fortunately he was in for just six months and, after he left, poor Bone was at a loss as to know what to do with himself. That's when he started reading. Westerns mostly, but generally anything he could get his hands on. 'Did you ever see a *traveller* reading?' he said to me one day, and before I could get a chance to answer, he'd said: 'No, you didn't, for they're too fuck-ing stupid, that's why!' going back to his volume like he's Head of Critical Studies, Mountjoy Jail.

(What I have to thank Mervin for, more than anything, is keeping at me until I admitted to him that, yes, I did scribble a bit, but not leav-ing it at that, insisting that I write down some of my experiences. He used to read my notes and stuff regularly, which gradually got me back into the swing of things.)

6 April 1984
The noise in the exercise yard you just would not
believe! This evening they were all talking about
the young fellow who hanged himself last night.
There isn't a blade of grass to be seen in the
fucking place. It's a long way from the reservoir
here and that's for fucking sure. But I don't mind.
I'm in no hurry out now. Sometimes I think: 'It's a
pity they didn't finish me off.' The kicking squad,
I mean. The minute just before I passed out beneath
this sea of scything boots, I could see all the
people lining up along the main street in Scotsfield. They were all there - Boyle Henry, Austie,
pretty much everyone I'd ever known in the town.
They were shaking their heads as they saw me coming. I was naked and covered in dried dirt.
Smelling of Mountjoy. 'That's him,' they said, 'and
it's good enough for him.' 'He reeks of cabbage and
dirty old drawers,' I heard someone say, as another
one mused: 'There's talk that he's gone into a
queer.' 'That's right,' came the reply, 'I heard
them saying that. With a bit of luck he'll get
AIDS, this new disease they're all talking about.
That will soon soften his cough for him. The way I
understand, the pain is like nothing on earth. Your
bowels collapse. Then your heart enlarges. And
bursts out through your -!'
    They were all laughing when I saw Jacy standing
in the doorway of Austie's. She looked like a

skeleton with hollow sunken eyes the very exact
same as a junkie's. She was shivering in a blanket
and pointing as she asked me in this cracked voice:
'Why, Joey? Why?'

The judge was standing in the doorway of
Austie's, writing in a ledger. Then he looked up
and said: 'Joseph Tallon, you have been found
guilty by a jury of your peers. My role in this
case is to protect the interests of the public
against the possibility of such heinous offences
being repeated. In view of your previous conviction
and the fact that you have put the victim through
the additional agony of having to give evidence in
this case, I direct that these three sentences –
comprising possession of drugs with intent to sup-
ply, false imprisonment and assault occasioning
bodily harm – are to run consecutively.'

When I looked again he had gone back inside with
the door marked 'Austie's' in gold leaf just swinging there behind him.

It was Austie himself who walked out of the crowd
and came over and knocked me to the ground with one
single well-aimed blow. Far away I heard my own
voice pleading: 'Harder there, please! Please, do
it again!'

But they were gone and all you could hear was,
why Joey why why oh why did you have to do it she
was really such a lovely girl and we know you liked
her why oh why did you do it Joey why?

There is a little booth which acts as a lost-and-
found point; in another part of the yard, prisoners
queue up to buy stuff at the shop. Others are waiting to go to the workshops. You can watch TV or
play pool in the recreation room. I managed to get
myself a Walkman – Boo Boo brought it in – but I
don't listen to the old music now. It's too hard
for me. *Abraxas* would only remind me of The Seeker
and Joni Mitchell. So I just listen to Bonehead's

country-and-western tapes ('Boys but I loves Daniel
O'Donnell!') and any other old rubbish I can find.
I don't care, so long as it takes me away from the
stink of boiled cabbage and the all-pervasive rank-
ness of other men's drawers.

(Even flipping through it is enough to make the gloominess start insin-
uating itself again. You almost go into a foetal crouch as you turn each
weighted and weary page, with talk of nothing – only strikes and abortion referenda, rain and misery in a country that seemed ruined.)

<u>2 May 1985</u>
Sleep broken all the way through the night. I woke
up and said: 'Don't let me think about her,' but
when my eyes closed again I saw them all coming up
the main street, sort of like in a movie but with
the sound turned way down. It was like a funeral
cortège, with Austie at the head of it dressed all
in black. But a funeral that was taking place
years ago with the hearse being pulled by two
plumed horses and the Big Fellow inside driving
it, wearing these breeches and buckled shoes. They
looked ridiculous along with his fedora, but he
didn't care. He just smiled at the mourners lined
along the streets as if to say: 'All in a day's
work!', and lashed the horses as they trotted
onwards. Now I could see that the mourners were
laughing too. When we got to the graveyard Jacy
was there, attired in this beautiful floaty print
dress – it alarmed me that it was a little bit
like Mona's – and a daffodil-yellow sunhat. When
she opened the coffin it was filled with light,
and when that had gone I saw quite clearly who was
in there beneath the lid. It was me – in a
starched white shirt and red tie, the one I used
to wear when I'd go to Mona's.
   'Hello, Joey,' she said and stroked my forehead
with her palm. 'How are you in there? Is it nice
being dead? Never mind, you're alive now!'

Hoss appeared then, directing the men who were carrying the cross. I can still feel the pain of the nails as they went in. But it was nothing compared to the shame when Jacy approached me on the cross and started tugging at the strip of cloth they'd tied around my groin. She chuckled into her hand and then turned to the mourners, going - not in a Californian accent now but in a really drab country Irish one, from around County Wicklow or thereabouts it sounded - 'Did you see the little yoke the fucker has in there? Tsk! Tsk!'

I died then and they all went back down to Austie's. I can still hear her saying that, and the more I try to block it out the louder it seems to get.

23 June 1985
There is talk of establishing a Prisoners' Revenge group to put a stop to the kicking squad and their intimidating bullshit. I don't know. Everywhere you go there seems to be violence. Times the bad feelings start coming again, then you get over them and think, no, it's not so bad in here. Maybe I'll survive.

(A lot of the later entries are undated — a sign of growing contentment, I think, and a preoccupation with Mervin's schemes. There is definitely a lighter touch to the prose, as in this little pen picture of our custodian.)

Mervin (and 'The Poetry Association')
Mervin, Mervin, Mr Governor Mervin, where the fuck did he come out of? Don't ask me - but what a guy! What a motherfucking cool fucking guy . . .!

What I mean by that is, he's so full of ideas and enthusiasm. And really good at imparting them. 'I think it would be a real good idea,' he says to me the other day in his study. 'Might get rid of the stink of piss!'

I couldn't believe it when I heard him swearing like that. But then, Mountjoy can get to him too, with its fucking grey walls and its fucking grey skies, with its endless fucking rules and interminable head-counts. At first I didn't believe his idea would work and nearly laughed straight out in his face. 'What would the dumb fuckers in here know about poetry?' I said. And was pretty damned cocky about it too, the way it came out. But not quite so much so after Mervin had done with me. 'What gives you the right to say that?' he asked me. 'Where's your evidence for such an assertion?' By the time he was finished with me I felt like I'd gone ten rounds with Rocky. I won't say that when I left the office I was a completely changed Joey Tallon, but one thing for sure – he had made me see how arrogant I could be.

'That's exactly the attitude that prevented you from writing!' he told me. 'That prevented you from bothering to articulate how you felt. Don't give me that shit, Joey! Get out there and form that Poetry Association!'

At first I thought I had fucked it in one! For the minute I mentioned it to Bonehead he started getting all fired up, suggesting all these ridiculous projects, such as inviting T. S. Eliot in to speak to the prisoners! (He saw I had been reading him and picked it up in the cell one night.)

'The fucker is dead!' I told him. 'Bonehead, T. S. Eliot is dead!', making no more impression on him than the man in the moon, before eventually having to grab him by the bollocks and rasp into his face: 'Will you fucking listen to me, will you? You can't invite in dead people!'

'Jasus, Joesup, will you take it aisy!' he says. 'Sure there's bound to be people that's alive can write pomes as good as him!'

I'm Reading!

In the end, anyway, we got it up and running, although it wasn't called the 'Poetry Association' and wasn't confined to verse. The name we decided on was the 'Mountjoy Literary Society', and after the first three or four meetings – which consisted just of me, Eddie 'Mouse' Gallagher, or perhaps what was a close relative of his who popped by the recreation room for a snoop – things began to pick up and, before you knew it, you were beating the fucking bastards off with a stick. Mervin managed to wangle us a grant and, after a while, we did start bringing in writers, although not well-known ones like T. S. and not because they weren't alive, either, but on account of our budget not stretching that far.

It was the making of Bonehead too, for that was where the 'secretarial' aspirations began, culminating in, of course, his compilation of the definitive 'Joey Tallon Archibe'.

He had even started to wear his glasses on a cord – or in his case, a shoelace – and I couldn't go anywhere now without him coming up to me with questions. I nearly pissed myself the day I came upon him in a corner of the exercise yard, leafing his way through Joseph Conrad. 'How are you getting on with that?' I asked him, and what does he do? Puts the hand up, as much as to say: 'Do you mind, Joesup? I'm reading!'

Literary Soirées

There were some fabulous nights you couldn't forget at our 'soirées', as I'd taken to calling them.

'*You fucking bastards you put me in the Joy/Me just a decent young boy! You put me in here where there is no joy!*' this fellow delivered one night – and that wasn't the worst of them either! Not by a long shot! Another time a junkie got up and started punching the air, all these rat-a-tat-tat smacks as he went blue in the face going on about '*smack!*' and how it '*fucks your bleedin' head!*' '*But they don't care!*' he says, '*'cos all they bleedin' care about is their share – of cash!*'

It was after that we got put in charge of the library, and I suppose it was there Bonehead learnt his other skills – became 'The Catalogue Meister', I suppose you could say – which has resulted, happily, as I say, in this quite extensive chronology.

He has even included on bits of wrapping paper little quotes – just random thoughts, I suppose you could call them – that he's found. One, believe it or not, in pencil on the back of a Rizla!

The worst thing about it was that it turned him into Hitler. 'What the fuck do you mean you don't know where you left it? That's library property! What are you, a traveller? You needn't think you'll lift all about here, you thieving cunt!' I heard him saying to this fellow one day. 'So you'd better go and find it! And if I catch you taking encyclomapaedias out of here again, it'll not be good for you! Them's reference books!'

Another great thing about it was I could get extra privileges for myself. Mervin saw that I had special entitlements, which he could justify to his board on account of membership of the library being up fivefold since me and the Bone took over. Although, to tell you the truth, I think it had more to do with Bone's eccentric style of management than any dramatic refinement of literary tastes. On the other hand, maybe that isn't quite fair, for the literary society was definitely turning a lot of people on. I used to love reading *The Poetry of T. S. Eliot* aloud, even though I have to admit there was a lot of it I still didn't understand, and *St John of the Cross*, which, despite the fact that it still reminded me of The Seeker and the old days, I was beginning to warm to again.

'I didn't know you were holy, Joesup,' said the Bone to me one night in the recreation room. 'You never said anything to me about being holy.'

Another time he caught a fellow by the shirt and fired him out the door. At that point I had to take action. 'You can't be at this, Bone!' I said to him, quite forcibly. 'You'll lose the pair of us our jobs!'

'I know,' he says and starts going all shaky, 'but he was cutting pictures out them special books to take back to the cell to wank with. It's not good enough, Joey!'

Then he shows me this book of Rembrandt plates and shakes his head, disgusted. 'Even an itinerant wouldn't do it,' he says, ruefully.

Diary of a Kip: 24 June 1985
We have had the best of crack all morning talking about these moving statues. This smack dealer called Crowe, who has just been locked up, was telling us about going down to Ballinspittle, where

the whole thing's been happening. 'You wouldn't believe it!' he says. 'Half the country is down there and swear they seen her talking. She came down off the plinth and walked over to a fellow. Apparently the auld bollocks couldn't walk and now he's kicking football!'

'Maybe we could get him on the team,' says Bonehead.

'They're coming from all over,' the dealer replies. 'Only the cops fucking caught me I could be down there making a fortune selling burgers.'

'Shut up, you fucker you! We don't want pushers in here!' snarls Bonehead the other day when an argument started. 'You're giving us a bad name!' Your man, of course, goes for him then! Bonehead never knows when to shut up.

There is great excitement too about the boxing. Barry McGuigan looks set to win the world title. He's from near Scotsfield, so I can imagine what the crack must be like in Austie's right now. I wish I was there. But I don't suppose they'll ever want to see me after what I went and done, stupid bollocks that I am. I have only myself to blame, no matter what the governor says. He's a great man to talk to is Mervin, he'll just sit there and yap for hours. 'What about your friend St John of the Cross – what has he to say about forgiveness?' he asked me. I could have given him a couple of quotes right there off the top of my head. But I knew there'd be no point. It isn't St John I want forgiveness from.

He says he's delighted with the way things have gone, both in the library and the literary society generally. 'Now,' he says, 'I have a proposition to put to you.'

Then he says – I nearly shit myself! – 'Did you ever think of putting on a play?'

Take Five!

That was the first time it had ever entered my head. At first I completely rejected the idea, but when Mervin said he would help – he had directed a lot of plays himself, he said, he was a member of an amateur company – I decided I would give it a go.

When Bonehead heard about it first, he said: 'What? You? Sure you couldn't do plays! We're in charge of libraries and pomes, Joesup, that's enough!'

But, of course, as soon as things got started, there was the fucker in the thick of it, running around with a clipboard, flapping his arms with the glasses swinging. It didn't take him long to learn the jargon. 'Take five!' he says to this crackhead who was playing the lead.

'Wha'?' says your man and looks at me with his mouth open, as Bonehead gives me this painful look as though saying: 'Do you see what I have to put up with?'

Diary of a Kip: 3 July 1985
Have been in the library all day, studying and getting ready to begin the play. Came across a great book called *The First-Time Director: A Guide* and it really is excellent. I can't wait to get started. It says in the book that it's like a general getting ready to go into battle, and that's exactly what it feels like now. You read and you read and you read and then you find yourself standing in front of the mirror going: 'This has to be a production that will set this prison alight! It has got to be something really special! Something that they'll be talking about for years. For years to come, you got that, Joey?' Then, adjusting this imaginary dicky bow as off you go, thinking to yourself: *This is gonna be a piece o' cake, pal! Dig?*

27 November 1985
All the way through Merv has been around, just in case anything might go wrong. He's like an anchor. A rock. He has made it all so very easy. It has

been plain sailing, a really terrific experience. Although of course I'm nervous, obviously.

<u>24 December 1985: A History of Mountjoy Prison!</u>
There was a huge crowd in tonight. The papers have picked up on the good work Merv's doing and they sent some reporters in. The crowd was mostly social workers, relatives and people from the department. But it was fantastic! I was shitting myself all the way through. Some junkie your man turned out to be! His performance as the narrator was terrific. He also played one or two other parts. There wasn't a sound as he delivered the speech: *'Your Petitioner thereby humbly prays Your Excellency will be graciously pleased to extend your clemency to Petitioner by remitting him to his family thereby enabling your Petitioner to spend his future life in loyalty to his queen.'*

It just shows you what can be done. It was basically the history of Mountjoy Prison from 1850 to the present day, with your man the junkie doing all the links. We took in the troubles of 1920 and the political stuff and then ended with the smackheads and all the rest of it. It was fantastic, even if I say so myself. *Mountjoy – A History* we've called it on the posters, all of which we printed ourselves in the workshop. There is even talk now of us starting a magazine. There is talk of all sorts of things.

Jealousy

I don't know where it came out of but when our 'Narrator', i.e. the junkie, came up to me one day out of the blue and told me that he'd had a poem accepted for publication in the *Irish Press* – they run a page that prints short stories and poems – I am ashamed to say that instead of being proud – I mean, we in the literary association had been the first to encourage him – what I experienced was an undeniable twinge of jealousy. I couldn't believe it as I felt it begin to assert itself and had to turn away from him, knowing I was on the verge of saying: 'So, what do you expect me to do about it?'

It was a dreadful thing to think for you could see he was over the moon.

That was the first night in ages that the depression came back. It enveloped me from head to toe, becoming so bad that at times I literally couldn't breathe. It was awful and I was mortified because I'd caused it myself with my attitude to the junkie earlier. I read his poem and it was really, really good.

But that only made me worse.

Diary of a Kip: 17 February 1986
The young junkie is really coming into his own
right now. He showed me some more stuff today and I
really have to admit that he's excellent. I have to
laugh at the way Bonehead keeps going on about him.
All you can hear now is: 'He's powerful, isn't he,
Joey? He can do some writin', oh yes!', which is
fine for a while but after a bit begins to fucking
wear, you know? In the end I had to tell him to
shut up. Just to give it a rest for the love of
fuck. Of course, he gives me his baleful look, but
I'm sick of that too.
Anyway, I have my own work to think of.

28 February 1986
I can't stand it in here sometimes, it's . . .
Barry McGuigan did the business the other night,
beating Cabrera really fucking well. And I bet
you'll never guess what? The junkie has another
poem written! Bonehead is going around quoting it!
'He'd bate T. S. Eliot any day, Joesup!' he says.
My, my, it's hard not to think what a literary
society we've created in here! One minute they
can't write their name and the next they're going
around quoting Four Quartets!
I can't get over the thought of Boyle Henry being

at the McGuigan fight. I saw it in the paper.
Beaming from ear to ear. Like he's his fucking
manager or something. He won in the election. He's
a senator now. My stomach turns –

11 March 1986
I can't stand this fucking place! And I wish Bonehead would fucking shut up! He wants to start a
film society now! 'What the fuck would you know
about films?' I said to him. 'There's more to the
cinema than fucking John Wayne!' Another fucker he
never shuts up about! 'Did you ever see it, Joesup,
did you? *True Grit*! Your man has the eyepatch the
very same as you! Man but that's some fillum!'

'Would you shut the fuck up about John fucking
Wayne!' I said. 'Give it a rest for the love and
honour of Christ!'

He went into a huff then and hasn't spoken since.
Good. For at times he drives me fuckingwell mad.
Film society! The whole thing's going to his fuck-
ing head!

Although, when you think of it, it mightn't be
such a bad idea. I've been reading a lot of the
reviews lately and there are quite a lot of good
ones coming out. There are some really good books
in the library too. I think I'll check them out.

Jesus, it can get you down in here. Rattling
handcuffs, walkie-talkies, whistles and headcounts
and then more whistles, and everything monitored by
wall-mounted video cameras. Maybe we should make a
movie with one of them. *A Day in the Life of Bonehead and Joey*, maybe!

They get up they walk around the exercise yard
they spend a while in the workshop then they go to
the recreation room and when that's over they go to
the dining hall and then go out for some exercise
then they get counted and wank in their bunks: THE
END.

Exciting, huh?

I was in the middle of trying to write something
again, just a couple of short lines about my feelings since the blues lifted – which you never
should say for then they're back in a flash – but
it's impossible. The problem is I just can't get
started. The whole cell's filled with balls of
screwed-up paper and even Bonehead started to com-
plain, regardless of any potential 'literary acu-
men' which his cellmate might be in possession of.

'Just write something and clane the place up
after you, can't you?' he says and sits down then,
grunting and reading. Reading, I might add, one of
the books I procured on cinema. He even managed to
find something about the Duke in that. 'Ha! Look!'
he says then, back to himself. 'There he is – the
pilgrim cowpoke with the one fucking eye! Ha ha!
Shoot the fuckers, Duke!'

I was in the middle of cursing – the young
junkie's face kept appearing and going: 'Well? And
the problem with your writing is what exactly, Joey?
You can't get started? Here! Let me help you!' –
when the cell door opened and in walks Mervin. I
rolled up the page and tossed it away in disgust.

'So! Gentlemen! And what are you reading, Pat
Joe?'

I threw back my head and scoffed: 'Why, he's
reading about the great directors, Governor. John
Cassavetes, no doubt, or perhaps Fassbinder, who
knows?'

Mervin threw me a look that should have shamed me
to the core. But I was feeling so bitter, it
didn't. Later, however, it did and I vowed to let
Mervin know. But that wasn't an awful lot of good,
was it? I could just hear him saying: 'Don't display the hauteur of the autodidact, Joseph. It
doesn't become you.' He'd said it to me on a few
occasions previously. He could read you like a
book, that Mervin.

There were times – when the downers returned –
that I wished that one day they'd just open the
door and say it was no use trying with me any more
– and fuck me into a hole – a proper one with a
bolted trapdoor. While far away I'd hear them saying: 'Well, that's the end of him! That's Mr fucking Writer gone! Mr Fat Fucker that thinks he can
write! We'll be having no more annoyance from him!'

'I have a proposal to put to you,' said Mervin,
sitting down and popping in a Tic Tac.

That was all he did, old Mervin. You sort of
expected him to smoke a pipe the way a decent governor often did. But maybe that was probably only in
the movies. As far as Merv was concerned it was Tic
Tacs all the way. *Pop!* And then these big ideas.

'I've been thinking about the Christmas concert!'
he said.

<u>22 November 1986</u>
This is the first time in ages that I have opened
this diary to put anything in it for, to tell you
the truth, I have been so busy and exhausted with
everything – getting ready for the concert – that I
just haven't had the time. Something which, to tell
you the truth, I am actually really fucking pleased
about for things have been going really, really
well. I had a letter from Dixie (the junkie poet)
and he says he's had a really lucky break and may
be having his first collection coming out next
year! Can you believe it? Well done him! Obviously
he has been a great loss to us with the concert
coming up for we have no actor that can come anywhere near, so after a while not knowing what to do
I decided to do it myself. It's just a little one-
act comedy so it's no big deal. Bonehead is as
nervous as a kitten and, to be honest about it, I
am beginning to feel sorry that I put him in it at
all. It was just an idea one of the prisoners came
up with, of a pretend interview with some of the

inmates, a sort of *This Is Your Life*-type thing.
Which eventually became *Oprah Winfrey Comes to
Mountjoy!* and resulted in Bonehead blacking himself
up and running around the place with his clipboard.
He brings the house down every time. 'So tell me,'
he says, 'did youse have an unhappy home life, did
youse?', getting them all to spill the beans and
really immersing himself in it, in exactly the same
way Oprah does, dropping her voice when she's about
to ask a grave, grave question. Except in a half-
tinker/traveller accent, of course. I think it's
going to be the highlight of the concert. Which is
going to be a variety show, really, with a couple of
good surprise items thrown in. One of which will be
Mervin reciting a couple of parodies by Service.
Robert W. Service, that is, who wrote all these
great poems about the American gold rush way back in
the nineteenth century. I had never heard of him but
loved his poems so much I headed off to the library
– the whole day had gone before I knew where I was.
You want to hear Mervin! He brings the house down
with that accent of his. 'Do you hear him, Joesup?'
said Bonehead. 'Dangerous Dan Mc-fucking-Grew! This
is going to be the best concert yet!'

I don't know about that. But I think that it's
going to be good all right. Mrs Recks is doing the
piano accompaniment for us. She is also helping out
with the directing. Her regular job entails music
teaching in a convent school so she really knows
her stuff. She's playing a few short selections
from an opera that I never heard of. It's called
The Mikado. Bonehead is in that one too – he's the
Lord High Executioner, going around with this axe
and a hood on his head. You want to hear him
singing – not bad at all. Before we got started
just the other day Mrs Recks was telling me all
about opera, in particular Gilbert and Sullivan.
They really sound like two fantastic guys! Very
witty! I must get all their records!

Merry Christmas, everybody!

For if this one isn't I don't know what one will
be. All I know is Mr Joseph Mary Tallon right here
in this cell with Bonehead 'Oprah Winfrey' snoring
like a trooper is one very happy camper indeed with
the concert having gone an absolute bomb! *The
Mikado* was a massive hit, and if that wasn't good
enough, Bonehead had them all in stitches with his
boot-blacked face and this great big rose on his
boobs! 'Did your father bate your mother black and
blue?' he says to one of the lads! Which just came
out, apparently, completely unscripted!

The governor looked great in his gold-rush gear,
and I have to say my own performance as 'Guard Mullanney' seems to have gone down a treat. The little
play was called *Occurrence at Tullanapheeb* and was
written by one of the writing-group members. It is
just a great bit of hokum about mixed-up identities
and odd situations in a tiny Irish village in the
fifties. I didn't have all that much to do except
every so often appear on the scene looking grave
and booming: *'What exactly is going on here then,
lads?'* But I really enjoyed it, and everybody said
they enjoyed the performance. Another highlight was
this old guy who had stabbed his wife thirty-seven
times over an affair she was having putting on a
short cabaret show based on Arthur Tracy, the
street singer. Actually, that's what he wanted to
call it, he said. *The Street Singer*. That would be
a good name for it. 'Good and simple,' he suggested. So I said fine. I can't tell you the effect
it had on me the first time he sang that fucking
song. And even on the night of the actual concert
it was hard for me not to start shaking. The
goosepimples were crawling all over me. For you
could see from the way he was delivering it just

what it meant to him too. He even wrung his hands
as if in pain as he sang: *'I saw those harbour
lights/they only told me we were parting . . .'*

I couldn't wait for 'Oprah' Bonehead to come on,
to tell you the truth, just to put it out of my
head. I found the whole thing so fucking moving. He
was close to tears himself when he came off.

Anything Is Possible

There were all sorts of things we got involved in after that, for I suppose you could say now that the handcuffs were off, if not in reality
then definitely in your imagination. It was like Mervin had pushed
open the doors of an old abandoned attic and thrown open all the windows. Had come stomping across those decrepit dusty floorboards
and inhaled for himself a deep draught of air. 'Smell that!' you could
hear him say. 'Drink a draught of that fresh clean air! For don't you
know it, my men – the possibilities are limitless now!'

And that was exactly how I felt. Which might seem strange to someone else with more education or experience, perhaps, but definitely
was the case with me and Bone. Sometimes I'd find myself waking up
and thinking: *What? I directed a play?* or *I acted as Guard Mullanney
in* Occurrence at Tullinapheeb? *Without making a complete prick of
myself? It cannot be!*

And for a brief few seconds or so I'd be lost in this kind of no-man's-
land before at last feeling the warmth creeping over me as I realized –
of course it was true! Yes, I had done all those things! With the help of
Mervin Recks, of course, but nevertheless I'd done them!

When I looked in the mirror now, all I did was smile!

'Anything can be done,' the governor said to us. 'There are more
strings to your bow than just artistic ones. You must always be prepared to extend your horizons.'

That was the day he put us in charge of the garden. And, before I
knew it, I was standing in the middle of rows and rows of peas and the
crunchiest-looking cabbages that ever you seen, all neatly laid out in
rows by the methodical Mr Bone. 'Charlie the Gardener' I called
myself, and laughed. 'I collect people, man, and I tend them like
they're flowers. I am the "People Gardener", man, you dig?!'

'No more of that chat of yours now, Joesup,' blustered Bone, 'we have these drillses to finish before the dinner!', as I bent down and set to work, with his great big corduroy arse parked right in front of my nose.

The Story of Me

It was around that time I got the idea of starting up the U2 fan club (with Bonehead, of course, once again appointed my fastidious assistant) because, along with Mervin, they were the people who had convinced me that anything was, as the governor had said, possible. For a start the depressions had lifted – hard to believe as it might seem – on a permanent basis. Which made me feel absolutely fantastic. I hadn't had to deal with one in almost two years now. And while Merv's advice was essentially the reason for this really encouraging development, it wasn't the only significant factor. I had been reading a lot of late about Bono and U2 and their attitude to things, and listening carefully to their amazing records and tapes. Their music just seemed to lift your heart and take you to places that before you didn't think you'd be ever be capable of going. Bono was so like Mervin in many respects. He handed you a guitar and said: *'Play it! Play that guitar!'*, and when you hung your head and said: *'No I can't!'*, he made you feel ridiculous for ever having said such a stupid thing. Then the next thing you knew you'd be out there in front of 80,000 people, pouring your heart out and sharing your thoughts with them. With The Edge, his guitar player, blasting a chord as you rolled around on the stage, going: *'Yeah! I'm Joey! And this is the story of – me!'*

Mervin was still on at me about my life story. 'You should tell it right from the beginning,' he'd say, 'and explain to people who mightn't otherwise know what it is that leads the likes of yourself to end up in here.' I have to admit that I gave it a lot of thought, starting any amount of would-be 'Jail Journals'. But it took me a long time to pick up the courage. I suppose I was afraid that everyone would say: 'I'm sorry, Joey, but this is a pile of horse's cocky! It's all spelt wrong for a start!'

I have to admit it. If Johnston Farrell did anything, he taught me this: don't worry about things like that. 'Shakespeare himself couldn't spell for nuts!' he used to say.

And it was later on in his writing classes that I really started putting pen to paper, with a view to writing something more substantial. So, whatever I've said about him, don't get me wrong – I definitely do owe Johnston Farrell a debt, regardless of what he's done. For, without his influence and guidance, no *Story of Me* would have ever got started. Never mind finished.

But the problem was that all along Johnston had had his own agenda. Mervin was a totally different animal. I remember him talking to Bone one day. Bone trusted him with his life and poured his heart out as he told him all about his father. 'He was just an old country fellow,' he said, 'with baling twine around his britches. But he wasn't a traveller, Governor! We had a caravan all right! But we had a house too – in Rathowen village! We only travelled *sometimes*! Boys but he loved them western books! He could read and everything, my father! Cowboys! Nobody could do the book-reading at that time, Governor! There was no pome societies then!'

Then he'd laugh, and so would Merv.

'It wasn't his fault he had to put us into the home!' he said then, as the governor put his hand on his shoulder. 'I hated those children's homes! All I wanted was to go back to our own house! To hear him read the books! He always read cowboys! John Wayne, Mr Recks!'

He'd get excited whenever he talked like that, trying to explain how he felt in this high-pitched voice. That was all he'd ever wanted, he used to tell me at night in the cell, and every time ending up saying the same: 'It wasn't me father's fault he put us intill the home. I hated them children's homes.'

His mother had died and his father had developed a drink problem – that was why he'd done it. It was great for Bonehead to get it all off his chest, for you could see he had never told anyone before. The day before he left the prison – three years to the day before me – he told me that he'd never thought it could happen that way, that in you come broken and out you go mended. 'I feel like I could burt the world with kicks!' he said. 'I've got all my plans worked-ed out! First I'm going to get a job and then I'm going to meet a nice woman and make her proud of me, Joesup! I'll see she never wants! And it's you I've to thank for it, you and Merv! So whenever I meet her you're to come around till see us! Promise me that, Joesup! Me old buddy – *De Man*! Promise me that you'll come around and meet this beautiful woman! The woman that won't care I was ever inside because – I don't have to tell you, Joesup, you *know*!'

'Because she loves you,' I said.

'Exactly,' he said, and shivered.

So you learnt a lot about people in the prison, once they felt they could trust you, anyway. I guess to tell the truth Mountjoy is where I learnt everything. And why, in a way, I was sorry to leave it. But I had the good sense not to dwell on that, for as the governor said as he was handing me his letter of reference, if I had learnt anything at all he hoped it was a sense of one's 'self-worth', as he called it, and how everything if you wanted it could now be considered attainable. 'It's not the end,' said Mervin as he shook my hand and said goodbye, 'but the beginning.'

I couldn't stop myself thinking about Bono as I stood there inside that office – of him clutching his mike as he tossed back his head and then, over the squealing feedback, his voice rolling out across the packed stadium as he pronounced that he *'agreed with the governor . . . that the governor knows . . . the deal!'*

And why, I suppose, in a moment of pure 'bonding' because I knew what he said was true and that the place he was coming from was genuine, I just went over and hugged Mervin and hugged him hard.

It was both the hardest thing and the easiest thing I have ever had to do, leaving Mountjoy on that summer's day, three years after Bone. Hard because I'd never again meet people like the governor, and easy because I knew that was nonsense, that was the old way of thinking. Because now, in the town of Scotsfield and everywhere else, absolutely anything was up for grabs. *Boomtown*, they were calling it in the papers now. I couldn't wait.

I had a tape of *The Joshua Tree* in my shoulder bag so I just slipped it into the Walkman as the bus took off down the main north road, and the twinkling sun that dappled the trees might have been the pure and uplifting crystal-clear harmonics of the guitar as played by The Edge.

Scotsfield Breakaway Bonanza

I was hardly back in Scotsfield a week, most of which had been taken up with me trying to get the mobile home habitable again – it was in an awful state – and was standing on the bank steps wondering what my next move might be when I looked up and who's coming barrelling down the street? Fr Connolly. He was all business, loaded down with forms – nothing to do with any peace rallies this time, but the 'Scotsfield Breakaway Bonanza', no less! He was full of it, rabbitting on nineteen to the dozen. 'A sort of variety festival,' he explained. 'A bit like the "Tops of the Town" jamboree we had years ago, Joseph – I don't know if you remember it – but a lot bigger and better, in keeping with the spirit of the times. For we've come a long way, Joseph, as I'm sure you can see! I'm afraid with your Sky TV and your multiplex picture houses you'll be a long time waiting for anyone to come out for your shows if you haven't made the effort! I think you have to work twice as hard these days, people are that spoiled! But still, it's good to see a few shillings going about for a change, isn't it? God knows, we were long enough without it.'

As if to emphasize his point, a stretch limo draped in streamers went honking through the town, followed by a long line of equally clamorous expensive-looking cars. 'They're all off to Dublin. Boyle Henry's young lassie's getting married.'

'Is that right?' I found myself saying, trying my best to camouflage my involuntary wincing.

'Aye. His wife wasn't well there, you know. They were afraid she mightn't make the wedding. But she's all right now, thank God.'

'That's good,' I said.

'Ah, she's a lovely woman, Mrs Henry. A real lady, and a terrific doctor! I can tell you that from experience, having attended her over the years. He thinks the world of her, you know. Adores the ground she walks upon, so he does.'

I said nothing.

'Sure he wouldn't be half the man he was only for her. "I'll see that husband of mine in the Dáil one day," I remember her saying to me, oh, way back, Joseph. Which she didn't, maybe, but as good as. And maybe he's better off being a senator.'

Senator Boyle Henry. I had to admit it sounded good.

'He's done Trojan work behind the scenes for a settlement in Northern Ireland, Joseph. Works night and day. Sometimes I'm going by late at night and I see him up there, going through his papers. Won't rest until every tiny detail is dealt with! That's the kind of him! I dare say only for him and hard-grafting men like him you wouldn't be seeing the changes that have come about in Scotsfield lately, eh, Joseph?'

I nodded and folded my arms, running my eyes across the roofs of the town. The shopping centre had finally been built – a brightly coloured American-style mall complete with all the high-street franchises – including the long-desired McDonald's hamburger restaurant. Austie's had been sold and was now a wine and cocktail bar – Doc Oc's – themed inside with a waterfall and exotic greenery and easy-listening music playing all day long. There were hanging flower baskets everywhere and a swanky Italian restaurant where the chip shop used to be. Stretched across the main street was a white banner with the name of his festival printed in red: 'Scotsfield Breakaway Bonanza – *cominatcha*!'

We got talking some more then, and when I began to elaborate on my experiences in the entertainment field in Mountjoy, he was all ears, he really was. For that was one great thing you were able to say about Connolly: he always saw the best in everyone. And if you had something to offer the parish, then he would be the man to spot it. 'So you produced a concert in there, did you, Joseph?' he says, and I nodded. 'Yes,' I replied, 'I was very involved in all that area.'

'It doesn't come as any surprise to me,' he said. 'I'll bet you didn't know that years ago – God bless us it must have been 1949 or '50 – we did a production of *The Desert Song* with both your father and mother in it. I'll bet you didn't know that, Joseph?'

I shook my head. 'No, I didn't,' I said. It took me completely by surprise.

'It was absolutely terrific. Of course, your father Jamesy was a marvellous singer. There was no one to touch him in those days, Joseph. Ah yes, they were great days. You couldn't move up the street the first night it opened, that show. Another great favourite of his was "Harbour Lights" by Jimmy Kennedy. But you'd hardly remember that. So you got on well above in Mountjoy then, did you, Joseph?'

'I was in charge of the prison garden too,' I told him.

'Well, that is just fantastic,' he said. 'I'm glad you were able to find something that you liked, for the time would hang heavy on you now, I'm sure, if you didn't. And what else did you do?'

I told him about the concerts and my acting stint as Guard Mullanney.

'Boys,' he said, 'but that must have been funny. You as a policeman – I just can't picture it, Joseph!'

'Anything is possible,' I found myself saying then, echoing the governor's words with a great big grin plastered across my face.

He shook his head and said: 'That's the attitude! If only we had more of that attitude in Scotsfield! But, you know something, Joseph? I think it's coming! I think the bad times will be soon behind us, what with this ceasefire and everything, people at last getting sense into their heads! The days of the killing and bombing and young men being sent out to die will soon be a thing of the past. Would you say so, Joseph?'

I said that I hoped so, because I genuinely did.

We got talking some more – I think we must have been standing on those steps for the guts of an hour and a half – and when he saw my letter of reference, I think that was what clinched it. Up until then he'd been a little bit hesitant – maybe he thought I'd come out of prison far worse than I'd been when I went in, having picked up bad habits from all sorts of rotten apples – but he saw clearly now that that wasn't the case. His eyes glittered as he stroked his chin and said: 'You know we'd be glad of any expertise you might be able to offer. It can be difficult at times to motivate people. You know yourself how things are in a little town like this.'

I thought for a minute before picking up the courage. Then I said it: 'But might it not be a problem, having me involved? After everything I've done, I mean?'

He contemplated his toes for a moment or two and then said: 'Yes, I admit that I can see there might be one or two on the committee who'd have reservations. But then isn't that what you hear on the radio these days every time you turn it on? That we must give priority to reintegrating offenders into our community now that all our political troubles seem to be coming to an end. I mean, if we can't extend the hand of friendship and reconciliation to one of our own, well, what is the whole thing then – only some sort of hypocritical farce? Anyway, Joseph, your father and me and your mother, God rest her, we go back a long, long way. I remember one morning coming out after Mass and there they were standing in the churchyard. We'll go for a drive, says I – I had the old Morris then – and that's exactly what we did. We went off and had ourselves a picnic. Do you know what your mother always called that day?' The day we had the "Picnic of Dreams", she used to say. And I hope it doesn't embarrass you, Joseph, but do you know what we used to call them in those days of *The*

Desert Song? The "lovebirds" – that's what we called them. For the pair of them, you couldn't separate them. The lovebirds, Joseph – that was their name. Out by the reservoir, walking in the spring rain, hand in hand. And two great people they were.'

He tapped his thumbs and then looked at his shoes one more time before saying: 'Well, I've dawdled about here long enough, I'm afraid, although it's been great chatting to you, Joseph. I'm delighted to see you again and to see you looking so well. Just remember that now you've paid your debt to society it's everything to play for in the little town of Scotsfield!'

'Exactly what Mervin said!' I beamed. 'The very words he used, Fr Connolly!'

'Everything to play for, Joseph! The field's wide open and you've got the ball, Joey Tallon!'

Then – surprisingly nimbly, for he was getting on in years now – he swivelled on his heel and was gone with a skip, off down the street with the black soutane flapping.

Well, after that I was as high as a kite, not being able to believe my good fortune. Hardly one day back and here I was, right back in the heart of the community like I'd never been away!

I went straight back out to the campsite then. Well, whatever about stretch limos, malls and flash eating houses, there was one constant in Scotsfield and that was it right there, in front of me, with no alterations whatso-fucking-ever, apart from a few new busted car wrecks and another mangy fucker of a dog. I knocked up old Mangan, who hadn't exactly metamorphosed dramatically either, squinting out the window behind the curtain and waving me away before I managed to get around him to let me in. As suspicious as bedamned, of course, not sure if I was playing games or not. But in the end I convinced him I wasn't – I had learnt a lot from Mervin there too: that if you're open and honest, people will generally respond. It might take a while but gradually they'll relax and you'll bring out the good in them also. I made clear to him that what was most important to me was that we put all our old differences behind us. The more I thought about it, the more I came to realize just how vast the treasure trove of skills that prison had bequeathed to me actually was. I seemed to be discovering new things all the time. It dawned on me now that I could communicate with people. Share their thoughts, anxieties. Tell them about my own. We could solve problems together now. By talking things through. It really was a terrific discovery. Of course, there could be no denying that it did help a little that your head wasn't full of cannabis smoke, not to mention lysergic acid diethylamide.

As soon as I'd finished talking to Mangan, I set about finishing my work. My caravan renovations, I mean. The guts of a week's hard labour on it and still it was looking a shambles. The young fuckers had been in, obviously using it for screwing. They had painted WEIRDO and DRUGGIE and KIDNAPPER on the walls and done an aerosol painting of me in the nip, with this great big giant eyepatch, of course. The eyepatch was bigger than the turnip-shaped man with this big long willie hanging down between his feet. But I didn't let it bother me and by midnight that night, the place, if not quite inhabitable, at least was a lot more bearable. I felt exhausted but proud and raring to go.

Breakaway Meeting

As we'd arranged, I called up to the presbytery the following afternoon for a preliminary meeting with Fr Connolly regarding the forthcoming festival. The more he told me about it, the easier it all appeared to be. For a start you had a lot more resources at your disposal than you ever would have had in prison and, of course, weren't being watched every minute of the day by a couple of disgruntled screws who didn't approve of you being allowed to do it at all. Which you had to deal with in The Joy all the time, for not everyone was as decent as Mervin Recks. 'No, it's a great idea,' I said to Fr Connolly as I gathered up my pamphlets and stuff. 'And it's great to be involved with it! Open up those windows, Father, and let that fresh air in!'

'It was great to see you again yesterday, Joseph,' he said as he opened the front door to let me out. 'And especially great to see you in such fine fettle! You look over those now and we'll talk again in a week or so!'

'Sure will, Father!' I replied as I gave him a big thumbs-up and almost went skipping off down the road I was in such a hurry to show off what I'd learnt in prison. Knowing full well in my heart that there would be a lot of people in the community who would be expecting me to come back with all sorts of hang-ups, complexes and chips or whatever. No chance was that ever going to happen now, not with people like Merv and Fr C. on your side!

'Tops Responsibility'

It was my job – or 'Tops Responsibility', if you like – to oversee the 'Tops of the Town' revue which Connolly had planned for a bit of a laugh and to go around the pubs to try and persuade people who might initially not be all that interested – and, as I soon began to realize, there were quite a few of those, let me tell you – to become involved. Yes, there was indeed a not insignificant number who hadn't, they made it clear, the slightest intention of co-operating with Connolly – particularly after the disaster of the original peace rally and, of course, everything that had emerged since about clerical child abuse and so on. I remember going into the pub one day and hearing Oweny Casey saying: 'There's only one thing now for them sky pilots after what's come out – castrate the whole lot of the fuckers!'

I have to admit I was embarrassed when I heard him saying that. Not on the priests' behalf but because of a troubled sleep I'd had the night before and a repeat of the Jacy 'funeral dream', which really did have the effect of upsetting me. Because when I awoke it was still there, lingering, ushering in a familiar gloom which hadn't visited me for a long time. I don't know how you'd describe it. It was sort of heartbreaking, really. Like being told for sure that you're free and then having thirty years added to your sentence.

All morning I hadn't been able to get it out of my head, their faces as they stood around chatting while I hung up there on the cross with my face the spit of Charles Manson's. So I suppose it came as no surprise that I was already pretty high when I got as far as Doc Oc's. To the extent of being so busy concentrating on wiping my brow that I misjudged the papers – I had put everything, in the style of the later Bonehead, into a folder marked 'Tops' – and let them all fall on the floor.

'Well, would you look who it is!' says Hoss. 'The Top Man! How are they hanging, Josie? Long time no see!'

'Hey! What you do?' laughed Sandy McGloin. 'You home, Joey, old pal? Well then, welcome home!'

Just then, Austie appeared behind the bar, grinning. I was taken aback, as for some reason I had expected him to be gone too. But no, there he was, large as life and serving away like old times. Except now decked out in a striped shirt and dicky bow with an embossed name badge on his waistcoat. 'Ah, would you look at him! Home is the hero!' he laughed and flicked his dishcloth, humming along with Andy

Williams. Hoss and Sandy were looking good too, both dressed in expensive suits and exuding the air of men who had things to do. Things that couldn't wait. Sandy owned the Texaco garage now, he told me, and Hoss had a few things going. 'This and that,' he laughed when I asked him. 'Bottled spring water, video shops! You know yourself!'

'Excellent,' I said. I was happy for him.

There was an old fellow at the bar and he shot me this filthy look. I heard him muttering under his breath as he turned his back on me. But I didn't mind – I had expected a little bit of that and, to be honest, there weren't all *that* many who'd been hassling me during my trips around the pubs.

Anyway, regardless of that, I got chatting some more to Hoss and let him know of everything we'd got planned. I told him that most of the ideas were mine and that Fr Connolly was more of an adviser. Which was effectively true, for that was what the priest had wanted – someone with fresh new ideas, which someone of his advanced years simply wouldn't have. 'The more help I can get, the better,' he'd said, 'for I don't have the energy any more!'

'I'll be pretty much in charge of drawing up the programme,' I said.

'You're drawing up the programme then, are you?' Hoss says. 'Then by Christ it should be good! It should be good then all right! Would you say so, Sandy?'

'Now you're talking, Hoss! Connolly knows what he's doing all right. He gets all the top men on his side.'

'The Top Men! Do you get it, Barba? The top men! Ha ha now, it's a good one!'

'The men on the inside track!' laughed Sandy, holding his pint aloft. He had softened a bit by now, clearly deciding to become more co-operative. 'Sit up there out of that and join us, Joey, and I'll get you a pint of porter,' he said and clicked his fingers to catch the barman's attention.

I did as he suggested and spread my papers, memos and what have you on the counter. As soon as I'd my first mouthful down, I began to feel considerably calmer and certain that, once I'd got their backing, a lot more support would be bound to follow. I rooted about in my briefcase and found it – the letter that the fan club had received from U2's manager. I had already written to them in prison telling them what their music had meant to me, how what they said had meaning far beyond their wildest assumptions, and how, in my experience, poetry, art, film and music had the power to heal men's souls.

And women's! (I had made sure to – what's the word? – *interpolate* that, having, on re-reading, realized that I'd foolishly gone and omitted it!)

As a letter, though, it was well put together and I was glad they were keeping it on file.

'So you think there's a possibility they might play here this summer?' said Sandy, and I could see by the way he was looking at me that he didn't believe it. Didn't believe there was a chance. I had to choose my words carefully in case he might start going around badmouthing the idea and making it seem like –

'No, Sandy, of course not! I'm not that stupid,' I explained. 'Obviously I am aware that they are a very busy group of people. A world supergroup, in fact. So, clearly, I'm taking a huge big risk. A gamble, certainly. But look, Sandy, anything is possible!'

'Now you're talkin'!' laughed Sandy. 'Anything is possible! Anything at all is possible!'

'I'll drink to that!' declared Hoss Watson gamely.

I was sorry the old fellow sitting with them had felt the need to be so hostile. But I shrugged. 'That's life, I guess,' I said to myself. Then I folded my arms and took a sip of my pint. I turned to Hoss and said: 'We're shooting for the moon here, Hoss!'

I remembered hearing Bono saying that one night in the recreation room when me and Bone were watching them playing Croke Park during the *Joshua Tree* tour. Shooting for the moon. Giving it everything, in other words.

'All or nothing. That's the Bono way,' I felt like saying. 'Sure, some of us might have done bad things in the past! But that can all be forgiven! If you go out and show what you're made of! What you're really all about – inside! Open your heart the way Bono does and sing out that truth the way that U2 do! And they know, more than most, just exactly what that truth is. Know, too, that if you want to find it – to go on that voyage of discovery, to travel to "the truth" itself – that you don't have to go to *India*. What I mean – and what *they* mean – is that you don't have to get behind the wheel of a beat-up van and tear off in a cloud of dust to some place you've never heard of.

'And why not? Because the truth is *here*, right here beside you – the frog beside the pond, like The Seeker used to say. It's in your local library, in the faces of your people. In *art*, in *film* and *music*. The truth is you – *you* are the truth. And you will find who you are by *doing*. Not by excessive *thinking*, which was the way I'd once understood things to be . . .'

And it's Fr Connolly I have to thank, I thought, *for enabling me through what is essentially pro-active engagement to grasp this single essential maxim. That we* are *because we* do, *in a sense.*

I was in the middle of thinking all that and wondering should I say anything about it to the lads when I realized that a gentle hand was resting on my shoulder. It belonged to Sandy McGloin.

'Well, if Hoss is getting involved in this Tops of the Town of yours, then that's an entirely different story! I think I'll change my mind and get stuck right in!'

'Fantastic, Sandy!' I said and gave him the soul-brother handclasp.

'It's great to have you home,' said Hoss. 'You must have great stories about your time in The Joy.'

I did, I told him, but they could wait. Right now the Tops must be given –

'Top priority,' laughed Hoss as a playful punch glanced off my shoulder. *'Boom boom!'*

I laughed and accepted the pint that had arrived. Then I lapsed once more into deep contemplation, making a private commitment to leaving once I'd finished that drink. I didn't want to start getting into sloppy old habits and let Fr Connolly down. The more I kept thinking of it, the bigger in my mind the festival seemed to grow.

In a way I suppose I was hoping that the Tops could lay to rest for ever the memory of the first peace festival and all the other things associated with it. That it could act as a sort of cleansing agent, become a kind of purifier, really, and that that was why it deserved to be a really big success.

A Disgrace

I couldn't believe my eyes when I got home one evening – about a month or so later, the festival preparations in full swing – and opened the door of the caravan. I had been out since early morning, distributing leaflets, and who did I see shadow-boxing inside? The bold Bonehead, large as life. Completely plastered however, as I was soon to discover, falling around the caravan with a huge sombrero on his head and in his hand a bottle of John Jameson whiskey. 'There you are! There you are, Joesup!' he says. 'You're the man! *You are de fucking man!*' and then starts into this story about the children's homes and how he can't sleep because of forgiveness. 'I can't forgive!' he kept repeating, with his fists up to his eyes. 'Some of the things they did to me in there, I haven't it in me to fucking forgive!'

The sombrero looked stupid and I told him to take it off. He got hostile then and said a friend had given it to him in a pub uptown. He'd met him by chance and they'd gone off together on a skite. 'And I thought that you were my friend, Joesup!' he said then and glowered. 'If you were you wouldn't say it was stupid. It isn't fucking stupid and I won't fucking take it off!'

He lowered another swig of the whiskey and shuddered as he sat in the chair. I had rarely heard him talk like that before – not as intense, at any rate – and I realized the more he went on how hard things were proving for him on the outside. He wasn't fitting in the way I was. Already I was feeling – because of Connolly and the Tops and the faith he was showing in me – as though I'd never been away at all. He wiped his mouth with his sleeve and glared at the streak of saliva.

'They interfere with you there till you don't know what's what!'

He kept threatening to cut himself with a glass. 'I'll do it, I'll fucking well do it, Joesup! Like I did to Ward that night we were robbing the lead! He asked for it! That's why they put me away, but I don't care! I'll do it again!' he says, and jumps up off the chair. I had no other option but to slap him across the face. Which wasn't a good idea, for then he starts to cling to me and whimpers: 'Every night she comes, Joesup, she comes to me. She's a beautiful woman – I told you I'd meet her! Every night she comes to me and says: "I love you!" We can work this out between us! Maybe you could go to . . . what do you call it, Joesup? Councillors! She wants us to go to councillors! They can fix it! They're brainy men!'

'She means counselling, Bone!' I said, and embraced him. I stroked his back to calm him down but he was still as stiff as a board.

Then he starts to mutter and mumble and make these leers into the glass. 'It's them that did it – came between her and me! I start seeing their faces the minute she touches me, every night! So I can't forgive them, Joesup! Priests, Joesup! Ruiners! That's what they are! Look at me, Joesup! I'm a disgrace to the Stokeses of Rathowen! Even my own father would turn in his grave if he could see me in the state I'm in now! After all my plans when I got out of The Joy! What I was going to do – she's going to leave me, Joey! For how can she stay? Fucking ruiners, destroyers! It's them! She says I'm well bred, Joesup! She said I haven't a drop of tinker blood in me! She says she could tell the first time she laid eyes on me!'

Then he starts weeping into his hands, and what I was worried most about was Connolly or someone appearing on the scene, for I could see how bad it would look and I didn't want that any more, not now, not ever, and that was why I shook him, shook him and shook him. 'No!' I said. 'No, Bonehead! Listen to me, please listen to me for Christ's sake, listen!' I told him I'd read about forgiveness. 'Forgiveness is –' I started to tell him. 'Forgiveness is –'

But it was no good. He wasn't listening. Then he got up and started walking around, like he didn't know where he was going, sniffling and staring disdainfully at my books. He looked at me with these wild eyes. 'It's no good, Joesup! We told ourselves lies! Them books does nothing for you! T. S. Eliot is better off where he is – down there. Below! He's better off there, I'm telling you, Joesup! For now he has no more worries!'

He spat.

'Books!' he hissed. 'Filling up our heads with shite! Shite, Joesup! To distract ourselves from –'

He touched his forehead with his fingers and didn't speak for a minute, then came over to me and held me firmly by the shoulders. I didn't like it. It wasn't what I wanted overheard.

'No, Joesup! We're just fooling ourselves, you and me! We try to forget but we'll never be able to – you'll never be able to, because you love her! Merv is a good man! He's good, Joesup! But it's lies, all of it! Not everything is possible! The past will always catch up with you! Just when you think you've left it behind you look up and it's right there ahead of you! It's the God's honest truth and you know it, Joesup! No matter wh–'

I didn't let him finish. Not that I was annoyed with him – why should I be? Because he didn't know what he was talking about. Maybe once upon a time I would have been. But not now. And not because of zen, either, or anything to do with it. But because I'd *found* myself – through *doing*, through serving and *giving*. Giving myself to others.

And I really didn't need –

'*No!*' I said. 'No! That's where you've got it wrong, Bonehead! You've got it wrong, you hear me? And now, if you don't mind, perhaps you might care to leave.'

He didn't say anything after that, just stumbled down the steps and shuffled off across the grass with Mangan's dog growling after him and Mangan himself at the window, drawing back the dirty curtain. I was on the verge of calling out: 'No, Bonehead! I didn't mean it! Please come back!'

I didn't sleep a wink that night, thinking over what he'd said, alarmed at finding myself wondering was he right. The next morning I couldn't stop looking at the books and thinking: *Is it shite? All of it?*

'But no!' I said. 'It *can't* be true!'

It couldn't be, it simply couldn't be! For if it was –

The next morning there was a note lying on the floor. It was from Fr Connolly saying the boy band from Dublin had confirmed. I felt a huge weight being lifted from my shoulders and at once gathered up my effects and papers and went into town with a renewed sense of purpose.

A Serious Disagreement (from '*Fr C. – asstd thoughts and observations*' – of which there are quite a number, meriting him, indeed, almost an entire notebook to himself!)

Whether or not Fr Connolly is aware of it or not, what he said to me the day I arrived up to his house with the present is the most hurtful thing addressed to me – ever.

I had been up since the crack of dawn, thinking . . . no, not thinking – *marvelling* over just how successful the festival had been, beyond the wildest dreams of me or Fr Connolly either. The Tops variety revue exceeded all expectations, The Two Lads, Nite-flite and the local stand-up comedian Jason X ('What do you call a Scotsfield man in a suit? The accused!') and all the others putting on terrific shows. There was a great little sketch from a few of the factory girls, written by themselves, called *A Day in the Life*, telling the story of a day on the machines. It was really great and just shows you how much talent is around. For the kids and the community in general, the karaoke in Doc Oc's proved a marvellous hit, having everybody in stitches. As I ate my breakfast, all I could think of was Hoss when he said: 'I'm afraid you're in dreamland, Joey, if you think you're going to get the lazy bastards of this town out of the pub for something the like of that!' Meaning the treasure hunt, which had turned out to be equally successful.

One thing was for sure: regardless of what events you had attended, the Scotsfield Breakaway Bonanza and especially my Tops of the Town – which won the *Scotsfield Standard* award for best overall contribution! – had certainly gone and put our town on the map!

I was over the moon about it all, but in particular the faith that Connolly had shown in me right from the start. And I'm sure there had been plenty who'd advised him against it – allowing me to have the first thing to do with it at all, never mind become the key organizer! I felt consumed, as they say, by gratitude. Which made it all the more difficult for me to understand – to even begin to understand, quite frankly – the attitude of the clergyman, which seemed to have undergone something of a transformation, and a dramatic one at that. Especially coming right out of nowhere the way it did. I had just been whistling away getting ready to take the present out of my briefcase – I had spent ages wondering what to get him – when the next thing you know his cheeks have become a bit flushed and he's walking around real fast and picking at his nail as he stammers a bit and goes: 'I asked you not to do it and you pretended you were going to listen! But since then you've done nothing but go your own merry way! Look, Joseph! Stop it! Can't you see you're being ridiculous?'

That whole morning I had nearly driven myself distracted trying to think of something to get him. I'd been thinking of all sorts of things – chocolates, cigs, a tie. And then it hit me! *A book!* A book, of course! For books are the expressions of –

We write our souls in them. And that was why in the end I decided on *The Poems of T. S. Eliot.* I got it neatly packaged up and all. It's not that I don't forgive Connolly for what he said that day. It's nothing to do with that, or because of all the work I'd –

But there was something two-faced about it. If the truth was that behind the scenes he hadn't wanted me involved, why had he bothered to employ me at all? I hadn't forced him. Why didn't he just get someone else instead of –

But then, I thought, maybe he was just under pressure and when things had got back on an even keel he'd return to himself again. I was in the middle of outlining my plans for the following year – I had already drafted a letter to Madonna's people and been on the phone to U2 again, this time, I reckoned, with a very strong chance indeed now that their tour was over – when, all of a sudden, he starts up again and snaps: *That's enough, Joseph! Do you hear me now? That's enough! Or why for heaven's sake can't you see what you're suggesting – it simply isn't appropriate! I've seen her on the TV, her obscene acts, I know all about them! But I'm not talking about that! Joseph, when I employed you to do this it was my intention to help you but that's not the way it's worked out. I won't let you make a cod of yourself! Do you think I don't hear what they're saying? Even in front of you they say it!'*

What I was most disappointed in that day was that up until then I'd felt so comfortable with Fr Connolly, just sitting there in his living room, sharing generally my take on things, maybe going on too long, which, I admit, perhaps I had. All the same, you still don't expect it thrown back in your face.

But somehow I don't think it was that, even if it did play a small part.

No, I think it was more what he'd been hearing in the pubs. What's most disappointing is that someone of his calibre would listen to those stupid stories, which are essentially parish-pump gossip – in effect, the antithesis of everything we'd been doing. Or trying to do.

Who cared what smart remarks a few malcontents such as Oweny Casey – who would never organize anything anyway! – had made, as regards calling me 'The Promoter', 'Billy Barnum' and so forth.

Or 'Paul McGuinness' – which I think was Hoss's contribution and which I actually thought quite witty – after U2's Dublin-born manager, of course!

'Very well then, Father,' I said and shook his hand, being as civil as I could about it.

Because there's no denying, disagreement or not, that I was still grateful. For his showing me 'the way'. The way of *doing*. Not just *thinking*.

I'd never have anything to do with him again, however. Or the Breakaway festival either. What's particularly saddening is that I'd discovered, quite by accident, The Seeker's quote in the T. S. Eliot book – '*We shall not cease from exploration, and the end of all our exploring will be to arrive where we started and know the place for the first time'* – and had been thinking just how 'salutary' – if that's the word – it was that me and Fr C. had gotten together like this and were discovering one another in such a good way. Almost like I was my own father whom he'd known around the time of *The Desert Song* and he was the age-old pal who understood everything you were thinking without ever having to ask. And then it turning out in the end that he understood nothing.

It was ridiculous but, against all the odds, I had one of the most beautiful walks of my life on that occasion, just taking off and rambling across the fields.

It was fantastic out by the reservoir, gathering your thoughts as the wind blew softly, as though it were ancient and had been doing it for ever. And which made me sad. Feeling sorry not just for Bonehead but for poor old Connolly too – who just didn't get the plot, really, when you thought about it – and writing in my diary when I woke up the next day: *'Knowledge is power and Connolly is powerless'*, which was sad, for who wanted to write those words? Not me, but they were what I believed, and if that was the choice I'd made, your roads diverge and there is nothing you can do.

The Arrival of Johnston Farrell!

(This appears on a page all by itself lovingly crafted in an absurdly baroque calligraphy totally at odds with the rest of the account, which is scattered over any number of loose-leaf pages.)

The Story of Johnston

When I saw the notice advertising the creative writing classes in the window of the Scotsfield Hotel, a couple of months after the row with Connolly, the last thing I thought was: 'This is something that is destined to change my life.' But that was exactly what happened, for in some ways Johnston was, when it came to creative things and attitude, not in his way all that different from Bono. For a start he *looked* cool, although he worked in the bank – he had just been posted from Dublin – with this fancy embroidered paisley-style waistcoat and his shoulder bag stuffed with books and papers. It was as though he wasn't just a writer, but, if he'd wanted, could have made a very good sort of 'up-to-the-minute' psychologist as well. Just considering things patiently as he listened to your story and said: 'No! No, please go on!' whenever you became self-conscious. But also being able to encourage you when you felt like giving the whole thing up. There were people there who, if it had been anyone else who was running the show – 'The Moderator', he called himself – would hardly have lasted a week. Somehow he got around them and coaxed them back in. 'You must remember to relax and let the creative juices flow,' was one of the things he liked to say. Another one was: 'Fuck syntax and spelling! It's what you've got to say that's important! That's all I want to hear!'

And, boy, did he want to do that! Sometimes we'd be there until midnight in the back room of the pub, just reading our poems and scratching out stories, then off to his house to drink vodka and beer! You want to see the amount of books he had there, and I'd thought *I* had books. It could be difficult at times, though, it's true. Because when you'd come back to the caravan, loaded up with booze, what you'd think was: 'No, Bonehead is right! I'm fooling myself reading all these old books! There's only one writer in Scotsfield and it fucking well's not Joey Tallon!'

Then, at the next session, Johnston would say: '*Everyone's* a writer, Joey! I'm telling you, you can do it!' and then what would happen? Off you'd go again, thinking you were Shakespeare and Milton all rolled up in one, with a dash of James Joyce thrown in for good measure. Speaking of which, sometimes Johnston wore a flower in his buttonhole, which didn't please some people at all. Coming out of the hotel after a class one night, I overheard Austie saying: 'Look at the cunt! I'll kick his "truth" down his throat! Him and his fucking flowers!'

But Johnston didn't care – just strolled off down the street, with his head in the air as if to say: 'Now don't disturb me! Can't you see I'm otherwise occupied with the creation of a masterpiece?'

Which was the great thing about the country generally now, and you only had to look at people to notice it. Gone were the days when everybody had their head down saying: 'Not only am I not engaged in the creation of a masterpiece but the likes of me – why, it is only with the greatest of difficulty I can tie my own shoelaces I'm such a near-simpleton!'

Even old Boo Boo had turned around and learnt some fabulous new tricks, having come through the wars and now well established as one of the most promising record producers in Dublin. I met him one day on a flying visit from the city and he told me he'd introduce me to Bono some time. 'I really liked his music in prison,' I told him. I hated that word 'prison'. Even with someone like Boo Boo it made me kind of sick to say it.

'It healed me, I think. It was a real big help.'

'Whenever you're up, give me a call and the three of us will go out for some beers.'

'Did you ever hear of Thomas Merton?' I asked him, but he shook his head.

'I read all about him in the library. I saw in the paper that Bono likes him. So does Merv, incidentally,' I added.

'Ciao,' said Boo Boo, 'I'll check him out,' and drove off in this big flash motor – an Alfa Romeo, I think it's called.

I couldn't believe it when Johnston Farrell told me that he'd gone to school with him – Bono, I mean. I nearly fainted when he said it so casually.

'I just can't believe what is happening,' I said.

'Tell me your plans for your story, Joey,' he'd say, '*The Story of Me*, as I've heard you calling it,' and we'd head off down to Austie's, as everybody still called it, swanky cocktail bar or not.

At first I was a little bit hesitant, but gradually I began to open up. He told me he thought it might make a great treatment for a film. I didn't know what he was talking about, but over the next few weeks he explained. He used to take notes himself, just jotting down bits as I was speaking. After a few jars, of course, it'd be hard to shut me up, especially when I'd start thinking about Jacy. I'd see all these things that I used to see when I thought about her – the interstate and Iowa and shit – and it would get me all choked up. But Johnston was canny – he'd just look away when he saw me get like that, and when it had passed he'd turn back. You would have trusted him with your life, that Johnston Farrell.

Only for him, I don't think I'd ever have found the courage to face the truth about Mona and admit that I'd lied about her. I thank him for that as well. And for explaining to me also that in a way what I'd said about her *wasn't* lying. Because, for me, in a special way she *lived* all right.

He said she was like someone from a favourite book you can almost feel walking beside you. What he called: '*An exceptionally well-drawn character, fleshed out with convincing detail.*'

He had just happened to say it one night in Austie's and I took it down. Another thing he said was that maybe I should consider calling it *Siege!*, but I didn't agree because I didn't think the story was really about that. It was more, I felt, about *feeling*, and what people are like deep down inside. What their dreams are. How they might journey towards peace. Find a peaceful place they could call their home. At first he didn't quite understand, he said, but when I gave him my diary from around that time (the 'Total Organization' ledger, in fact), he said things were becoming much clearer. He said that he found a lot of it funny – things like the idea of Fr Connolly singing 'Peace Frog', say, which had completely slipped my mind. It was that night, just as we were leaving, that he happened to mention that Bono and him had gone to the same school. Not making a big deal about it the way I might have done! Telling everybody you met, like an eejit!

No, just saying it matter-of-fact. Like it didn't cost him a thought. Which was the way things should be and the way Bono would have liked it himself. He had said it in the papers. *'I'm just a regular guy.'* The same as Johnston, the same as myself. Just regular guys in search of the truth. Fighting the good fight, as Johnston would say. His favourite writers were Gogol and Eliot. I couldn't believe it when he said that. 'Mine too, Johnston!' I said. 'Even though I don't understand it all!' Meaning Eliot. I knew about Gogol after reading him in the library. What a headcase! Noses in bread rolls!

'That doesn't matter,' he told me, 'as long as you hear the beat of its heart.'

He really could catch it in one, Johnston. I used to sit for hours by the window of the caravan wondering how he did that. Then I'd take down Gogol or Eliot and write like a maniac in the same way they did. I used to take *Dead Souls* out to the reservoir and read it there for hours listening to the wind bringing voices from the clouds. At the end of the book the character wanted to build a Temple of Colossal Dreams. I thought that was a fantastic phrase – and a fantastic thing to want to do. I couldn't stop thinking of it rising up there out of the trees, with these great big marble pillars with vines and greenery all around. I wasn't sure what the temple meant, to Gogol at least, but to me it meant *a new beginning*. A new *spring* was what it meant. That the past was over and all the old winters were dead, with the freshest of warm breezes blowing in a world no longer knowing deceit or duplicity or guile. *Now that anything is possible*, I'd think as I closed that book, *what you once dreamed, now you can do! Because you know it can happen!*

'It can!' I said to the utterly silent water. 'It *can!*'

Which was why when I got home I dashed off a few words to Bono, telling him about Johnston and how we'd happened to meet up and shit and how much his music had meant to me at a particular time in my life. I didn't want to use the word 'prison'. I couldn't believe it when I received a reply hardly three fucking days later! All I could think of was how the world had changed. It was almost like the temple had been built already and there was no need to go to the bother of doing it. On top of that, Johnston Farrell kept phoning – to invite me out to dinner, no less!

He was fascinated by my story, he told me, especially what with its being set in the early seventies. Which he'd read about but didn't *know*. Well, of course he didn't – I mean, back then Johnston Farrell would have been but a child!

This is fantastic! I thought as I rabbited on like a youngster myself. I couldn't believe that it sounded so interesting to him. But it did, you could tell just by his expression. Not to mention his notes! Jesus! He had even more than me! The big difference, of course, that his weren't written by a semi-literate gobshite! No, I don't mean that. That's just me being stupid. Once upon a time I would have meant it. But not now. Not since he'd educated me. And Mervin. And, through his music, the man who had written *The Joshua Tree*, along with his mates Larry, Adam and a fabulous virtuoso called 'The Edge'.

Letter

I really treasured the letter from Bono but I didn't want to show it to Johnston in case he thought it a bit kind of . . . I don't know – silly. 'You don't carry it *everywhere* with you, do you?' I could hear him saying. Which out of embarrassment – the new spring hadn't entirely arrived – I knew I would deny. But I did. I did carry it everywhere, all creased up in the back pocket of my jeans. It was covered in Guinness rings and cigarette burns and had lots of little notes in the margins. There were even a few little astrological doodles on it. I read it again:

Principle Management
c/o Windmill Lane Studios
Litton Lane
Dublin

Dear Mr Tallon

Thank you for your letter which we have noted and kept on file. Unfortunately Bono and the boys are in Miami recording at the moment and won't be back until late June. I will pass on your ideas to them and will be in touch.

Yours etc.
June Enright

The thing I was really looking forward to talking to Bono about was how you – anyone – can do anything if they truly believe in it. It is, in a way, the happy marriage of *considering* and *doing*. You *think* and you *act*. You *think* and you *do*. You . . . *go for it*! That was what the journey was. That was what it was all about. I believed that now. What I couldn't believe more than anything was that I was just going to stroll in and meet Bono, one of the most famous rock singers in the world, and it wasn't going to cost either of us a thought. Which was why I sat down with the guitar and strummed a few simple chords. Simple because that was how the new spring seemed. That it all had happened so effortlessly, and without any mystical old bullshit. As soon as I had the song finished I was on the verge of going up to the library and taking out *Siddhartha* with the sole intention of putting a match to it. Or tearing all the pages out of *Steppenwolf*. But then I thought, *No, that would be stupid. For the past is the past and the present is the present. The new spring is the old winter's son.* When I thought that, I reckoned it wasn't bad. Not as good as Johnston, maybe, but not exactly a pile of horse cack either.

Then I took the guitar and went out to the reservoir. It was particularly beautiful there in the dawn. After I'd played my song, I recited a few words from Gogol. The dew was on the grass and the leaves were beginning to whisper. I declaimed it the way Johnston did, like you weren't ashamed of what you were saying or, more accurately, afraid that someone was going to pop out from behind a rock, shouting: 'Shut up with all that shouting, Tallon! You and your fucking poetry, you great big one-eyed fuck!'

There were wisps of cloud floating out across the blue as I swept my hand and boomed: *'The spring, which had for a long time been held back by frosts, suddenly arrived in all its beauty and everything came to life everywhere. Patches of blue could already be seen in the forest glades, and on the fresh emerald of the young grass dandelions showed yellow and the lilac-pink anemones bowed their tender little heads. Swarms of midges and clouds of insects appeared over swamps; water spiders were already engaged in chasing them; and all kinds of birds were gathering in the dry bullrushes. And they were all assembling to have a closer look at each other. All of a sudden the earth was full of creatures, and the woods and meadows awakened. In the village the peasants had already started their round dances. There was plenty of room for festivities. What brilliance in the foliage! What freshness in the air! What excited twittering of birds in the orchards! Paradise, joy and exaltation in everything! The countryside resounding with song as though at a wedding feast!'*

I was exhausted, spent – but delirious when I'd finished.

'Precious Moment' Scene

We had been discussing Samuel Beckett at the writing group so I went off up to Dublin to get a few of his books – there were none in Scotsfield Library – and just by chance where did I pass? Only Windmill Lane Studios. At first I wasn't going to bother going in but then I thought of Johnston's confidence: 'Of course he'd have come out to say hello to you, Joey!'

So in I went, but as it happened he wasn't there. But June Enright, the girl who'd written to me, was sitting behind the desk and when I asked to see Bono she couldn't have been more helpful. Turned out they were still in Miami recording and that things were going real well. 'All things being equal, their new album should be out around this time next year,' June told me. Then we got chatting about this and that. Knew quite a lot about literature, did June. Wasn't that fond of Beckett, though. 'Doesn't quite do it for me, I'm afraid,' she said. 'I'd be more into the beats.' I wasn't all that well up on them, either, but they sure did sound interesting. '*On the Road* – now there's a book,' she said. 'By Jack Kerouac!' 'Sure!' I said. 'I've heard of that,' and told her about my own plans for going on the road 'when I get a few bucks together'. 'Whereabouts are you headed?' she asked me. It transpired she knew the States inside out and had been there with 'the boys', as she called them, over half a dozen times. 'Oh, here and there,' I told her. 'Midwest, the West Coast! All around!'

'Well, you get reading those beats now!' she said. 'Believe me, they'll blow your mind!'

And was she right! Straight away I went out and bought them. That Allen Ginsberg. 'Howl'! *'I saw the best minds of my generation destroyed by madness – starving, hysterical, naked!'* and all that shit. What good was Beckett after that? Three arseholes sitting in dustbins arguing about sweet fuck all and, just when you think it's all over – *thank fuck!* – they start it all over again? I had a good mind to do exactly the same with him – fire his books into a bin that I happened to be passing right there and then. But I had to study him for the group so I thought it'd be best to hold on to them. Instead I bought myself a baseball cap and sat there smoking. 'Dodgers' was written across the front and it felt real good just sitting there in the Clarence Hotel (which U2 own, of course), reading. I couldn't wait to get home to discuss all this new stuff with Johnston, who would know it inside out, of course.

It was hard not to think of yourself sitting there, maybe going through William Burroughs – another right fucking headcase, went and shot his wife with a crossbow, for Chrissakes! – when, whaddya know, next thing would walk in Bono. 'Hey, how you doin', Joey?' he'd say as I tugged the baseball bill down and answered: 'Hey, OK, Bono!' As I pulled some poems, or a film script, maybe, out of my inside pocket. Then after a rap – who knew, even discussing with him the possibility of him writing some songs for the movie, or the entire band doing the soundtrack – heading off to a drinking den, say Lillies Bordello.

If he felt like it, of course. Maybe meet up with The Edge and some of the other 'musos'.

Screenplay – A Real Possibility

The more I got talking to Johnston the more I started to feel, once and for all, the way you reckoned a real writer should. You nearly couldn't move in the caravan now I'd filled it with so many books. But not with mystics and 'the ancients' and all those fuckers – all they did was tie you in knots – but fiction from all over the world. 'That's it, Joey!' Johnston told me. 'Read voraciously! All the fiction that you can find! But I still think, deep down, that your story is a movie!'

Now that I knew how to do a treatment – up until now I'd only pretended, I hadn't a clue what he was on about, treatment this, treatment that, treatment the other – I'd just nodded and pretended I knew. I had a pretty good idea now, though, I reckoned, what with his advice and all the manuals I'd been reading. So a screenplay on the story was definitely beginning to look like it could happen. *The Life and Times of Joey Tallon* up there on the silver screen. With particular reference to a certain thing that had gone wrong once upon a time in his long-ago life.

I'd wake up in the night and see it all before me, the water lapping as we approached the shore where the lights of the harbour were twinkling. 'Soon we'll be there,' you could hear Jacy saying, 'over there in the land of Paradise. That is what your writing means, Joey. It can make it happen! Out of something bad something really beautiful can come.'

I'd wake and realize that I had never felt so empowered, not even since the very first reading years before of *Siddhartha* or the chats I used to have with The Seeker. It being so strong, in fact, that those memories seemed as nothing if not adolescent. *That's baby stuff!* I found myself thinking. *This is it, man, and you'd better believe it! This is home! This is the real deal. The real fucking deal and make no mistake!*

I let my beard grow good and long until it looked like Ginsberg's. Which meant, of course, you couldn't go up the town without someone shouting abuse. Such as 'Beardy' or 'Fucking ZZ Top!'

I'd go out to the reservoir to do some declaiming. 'You're like a prophet,' says this old fellow to me one day out there. 'Like John the Baptist or someone.'

I smiled when he said that and closed the book as we had a smoke together. 'We all are, my friend,' I remember saying, 'each one in his or her own way. In his or her own special way.'

Rejection

Unfortunately that would appear to be all that remains of a systematic chronicling of my earliest years of freedom. But even the most cursory sifting through the various papers makes it pretty much clear what transpired. If the 'Writing Class Notes' are anything to go by – and there are literally thousands of them – there couldn't have been a minute of the day or night during those creatively fecund times when the scribe was not busy blocking out some script scenes or just shoving down the barest bones of random ideas. There are even storyboards which I'd completely forgotten about, to be honest, and a weatherbeaten jotter called *The Movie Book*, containing the names of my favourite films – 1,357 to be precise. So I suppose it was no wonder that my skills began to be honed quite precisely and a new confidence was soon on display. Not that it was to make a whole lot of difference, for as this letter shows, the response from Dublin's Windmill Lane Studios to the first draft of my masterpiece – at that time entitled *Psychobilly* – was destined, sadly, to be somewhat less than ecstatic.

Principle Management
c/o Windmill Lane Studios
Litton Lane
Dublin

Dear Mr Tallon

Thank you for sending the first draft of your screenplay *Psychobilly* to us. Unfortunately Bono and the boys are out of the country at the moment as they are recording in Miami. I should point out that the studios are not actually engaged in film production at the moment and you might be better sending it to one of the other major studios who specialize in that kind of thing. However, we will keep your script on file and will be in touch when the band get back.

Yours etc.
June Enright

Which, however necessary, was a lie, of course. They didn't do any such thing, despite being bombarded with letters and phone calls. As far as I can make out, my efforts over the subsequent months produced only one response: effectively, a mimeographed copy of the letter above, which was not the response Messrs Burroughs or Ginsberg might have received. Something the author was more than aware of, as is plain to see from this frantically penned effort, composed in a frenzy one winter's evening after a plethora of vodkas . . .

Saturday Night (Late)
(No Date)

The reading tonight went really fucking well and I think my confidence is coming back. At first I was shaking but I could see Johnston smiling, giving me the moral support that I needed. So that when the time came to start, I just tore into it with everything I had. Wham! *You know what I'm saying? The way you go into something and hold absolutely nothing back?*

When I was finished I was exhausted, but the clapping went on for ages and Johnston made a bit of a speech. Actually saying, in fact, that I had performed it so well that at any minute he had half expected me to start taking off my clothes the way Ginsberg himself had done at the inaugural reading of 'Howl'. Afterwards the two of us went down to Austie's and had a really good rap – as usual. He is a fantastic guy, Johnston, with this amazing memory. He seems to remember things I told him months ago, and has a particular fascination, it seems to me, with the seventies. What's most surprising is – to me at any rate – given his extensive knowledge of English literature in general, how into *thrillers he seems to be. Especially when you know damn well he could write the most terrific poetry if he wanted to. Or plays. Or short stories. Anyway, literature one way or another, you can be sure of that. But any time you see him he's got a bunch of these daft thrillers under his arm –* The Devil's Conundrum, The Nairobi Connection, The Mexico Sanction, *you name it!*

I think he's trying to get me interested but all I can think of is Burroughs. And the gang. Ferlinghetti: 'Fuck you, man!'

I don't know what I'd do without him. For you need someone like him. When you're trying to find your feet – creatively, that is – you definitely do need a mentor. Which Johnston is happy to be. Unlike that other U2 bollocks!

Not that I've anything against Bono, not personally. But I mean, if he wasn't interested, why couldn't he just say so? And if he was too busy to do that, just get June or one of his other secretaries to write and say: 'Dear Mr Tallon, we don't want to be involved in this project but thank you for bringing it to us.'

That's all. That's not so fucking hard, is it?

I mean, you either want to do something or you don't. I have better things to do than hang around in offices twiddling my thumbs staring at rubber plants. Although no offence to June Enright, for you won't get a better person and I know that. She said she had been to Scotsfield once, actually. I can imagine it would be a long time before you'd get something like that out of Bono. 'Scotsfield? Oo! Where's that?'

But screw him, it's his loss. There are plenty of others who'll be interested in the project. Just as soon as I get my next draft finished. I've got some fantastic new ideas for it. I reckon I've identified all the problems – analyzing it at the class has been a really good help – and know pretty much what has to be done. Like Johnston says: 'You have to be brutal! Break it up! Deconstruct! Tear it apart! Explore it from the inside out!'

He was so enthusiastic that he got me excited too and I almost went and tore up my draft right there and then in front of everybody. I was on the verge of grabbing a few pages and going: 'Yeah! Right on! You got it, Johnston! Let's show those sum' bitches!' before I realized where I was. I calmed down then and listened to his advice, in a less 'Ginsbergian' manner!

But Johnston, as usual, saw the funny side. In the end we agreed that there was no doubt about it – this approach could only improve the piece.

The problem, essentially, I realized now, was that the screenplay was concentrating far too much on big-time Hollywood shit, writing it first and foremost with a star in mind – Nick Nolte, say, or Keith Carradine. When what it ought to have been doing was sticking far closer in texture and approach to the way things had actually happened.

'That fateful night!' or however you might like to describe it. (That's how Johnston refers to it!)

Softer, I guess, more tender. To hell with Hollywood and Keith Carradine and car chases. Fuck hand grenades and helicopter gunships. It isn't about that, for Christ's sake. Which deep inside I've felt all along but haven't had the guts to say. But now I have! For Cunthooks Bono (or should I say 'The Fly' – I mean, for fuck's sake – 'I am "The Fly", woo woo!'), without realizing it, has handed me 'The Answer' on a plate. Ironically, after all his bullshit encouragement in the magazines and newspapers – you can do it man, anyone can do it! – he has shown me how to find what I'm looking for. But he's never going to know it – indeed, why the fuck should he? So fuck him and his 'Joshua Tree'. Way I see it, Mr Bono my man, we're all on our own, so don't come around pretending that we're all in this *fucking thing together. Because we the people – the ones you think you're talking about – might believe Johnston Farrell. But not you. Not you, my man, Mr big-time rock star that's made fucking millions peddling packs of lies.*

The Author Is Published

Clearly, as I am sure you are already thinking, with this new-found confidence and professionalism that was on display, it could only be a matter of time before the eminent scribe hit his stride and made his mark at last on the literary world. Except that there you'd be wrong, I'm afraid, for it turned out to be a very long time indeed – and in circumstances that were very much not of his choosing, as shall be seen! (Writing *Doughboy*, in fact, in Boo Boo's flat, putting in ten hours a day!)

Even today I find it hard to believe that a major London publisher accepted it. For I hadn't edited a word – just wrote the whole fucking thing without thinking, hoping against hope it might make me feel better. When the letter of acceptance arrived, I couldn't believe my eyes. Boo Boo kept saying: 'You've made it, man! I always knew you would! Well, fuck you, Joey Tallon! You've gone and fucked them all, but good!'

What the letter contained was an offer to include my book in their spring lists. I just could not bring myself to believe the words as I read them, not to mention the money they were offering! But all of that was a long, long way off yet. A lot more water would flow under the bridge before Mr Joey Tallon's stellar literary career took off.

The Writing Classes – The Verdict

A career, however, which, all things considered, had got off to a pretty good start, I reckoned, with the second draft of *Psychobilly* literally writing itself. A very nice feeling indeed, let me tell you! I was over the moon when I'd finished it and couldn't wait to get it copied and pass it around the group for some constructive criticism. It wasn't to be, I'm afraid. I didn't have a row with Johnston or anything – I wasn't going to be that stupid, for I'd learnt enough now to know not to act unprofessionally and that, whatever comments people make, they are not meant to be taken personally. All the same I thought it mightn't be a bad idea to write him a note, get my thoughts down on paper, just to clear the air. Because I think he knew that I was a little downhearted when he and the others . . . what's the word . . . expressed 'reservations' about what I'd shown them. I think the problem was that I just wasn't ready, knowing in my heart that some of it wasn't all that good and didn't seem to know where it was going or what it was trying to say.

Which is probably why I cursed, although I didn't mean to. Any more than I meant to fling the manuscript to the floor and erupt: 'Who knows what fucking love is! How can you tell me that what I've written's not true! Come to that, who knows *what's* true? What's true, you sum' bitches, can you tell me that?', for that was just childish behaviour. Especially when everyone had been getting along so well. What bothered me most was their insistence on *story*. 'What does that matter?' I kept saying. 'It's the feel that's important! The *feel* is the motherfucker, yeah?'

It was at that point Johnston told me to calm down, and I did. I listened to him – of course I did. He was *Johnston*! I listened carefully to my friend and mentor and we gradually got back on an even keel. Or so I thought. Because then he started saying: 'What have the Romans got to do with it? Why did you include them and this piece about the Garden of Gethsemane? It doesn't seem to –'

It was at that point that I stood up and said: '*Right! That's it!*', taking my manuscript away with me. A lot of people said later on that that was the reason Johnston had left town, but that's not true, it really isn't. It's got absolutely nothing to do with it, in fact. It was nothing more than an unfortunate coincidence, the truth being that he had been transferred by the bank and had been thinking of giving the classes up anyway to devote more time to his thriller.

Which turned out to have a very familiar theme indeed, as I would later discover to my horror.

His big interested eyes in Austie's all now starting to make sense. Along with his curiosity regarding my battered old ledgers. Not that I minded. I had been glad to turn them over to him. After all, *he* had given *me* plenty. But he could have told me. He could have fucking *told* me! Then, when *The Cyclops Enigma* eventually appeared it mightn't have been such a shock.

Anyway, by the time I got home that night I was completely drunk and wanted to hear nothing more about literature. It was like I was back in the old days before The Seeker, before Ginsberg, before everything, when I didn't want to believe in anything at all.

I knocked up Mangan and brought in a bottle and stayed with him there till the dawn began to break. That was the first time we got *really* talking about things in a long time. It was the first time we'd mentioned Horny Harry and the excitement that day with the mud-wrestling girls. 'Imagine if you had a woman like that now, Joey,' he kept saying, 'that'd do whatever you wanted!'

I knew what he was intimating but I didn't want to address it directly. We both knew that he'd seen me with Mona – he'd fucking well made it his business to! So, to make it easier on us both, I said that I had seen inflatable girls for sale openly now in a shop in Dublin and if he wanted I could get him one, 'if that's what you want'. He flushed and looked away, drank a mouthful of whiskey and muttered: 'Aye! Aye! Maybe!'

We talked some more about this and that. When I was leaving he pressed some notes into my fist and I fell out the door of the caravan. As my head hit the pillow all these images came gliding down, then swooped away like ethereal birds, and once that happened I knew I wouldn't be able to sleep.

I sat down at the typewriter and it was as though my fingers had a life of their own.

Wonderful Pictures

By the time my new draft was finished – and this time I was a hundred per cent sure! – I knew I had something special in my possession and that this time there'd be no deconstructing and no giving opinions, no debates or discussions at all. Of course, there wasn't a *hope* of a studio ever touching it – I knew that the minute I'd finished it. It was much too individual for that – no helicopter gunships, blah, blah, blah. But who gave a fuck? It was pretty obvious to me now that if you wanted something made then you had to go and do it yourself. Otherwise you'd be humming and hawing like we seemed to be doing at the classes now most of the time anyway. Yes, Johnston Farrell's famous classes. Which had been useful for a while, no question. But now, I reckoned, if you wanted to progess, you had to move on to a whole new level. Fact was, I realized, if I wanted it made I had to do it myself.

And there was only one way of doing that: I would have to form a company of my own. Which wasn't as difficult as it sounded. I mean, I would have laughed at the idea too – initially, I mean. But after my theatre experience in Mountjoy and the information I'd picked up over the years in *Film Monthly*, *The Screenwriter's Guide* and various other trade publications, I figured I'd have a pretty good idea just how to go about it.

The first thing I needed was a name. '*Wonderful Pictures*. Wonderful Pictures, Scotsfield. How's that sound?' I asked myself, wondering what potential investors might make of it. *Pretty good*, I thought. I would definitely give it some consideration.

After reading my piece again, I definitely felt very proud. And confident, too. I clutched the typed sheets and gave them a kiss. I was exhilarated. If it had been back in the seventies and someone had asked me to explain why I felt that way, I would have said that I reckoned we'd peeled away every layer of the onion, now finally approaching its pure and untouched heart. 'And what is it like?' they might say.

'It's full of light,' I would have replied. I kissed the pages again and read:

The Seven Last Words of Jellyman: A Film Treatment by J. M. Tallon

The pick-up is parked in the shadows, some way down a dimly lit alley. Just up ahead there is a night-club with a neon-lit sign over the door. The sign is broken, and sputters and flickers intermittently. The guy at the wheel of the pick-up has his base-ball cap turned down, just so. Out of the shadows appear the hoods, waiting for the blonde-haired dancer, who's coming heel-clicking down the street. She joins them in the alley. At ten after twelve another figure emerges from the club. There are a few muffled exchanges as the doorman says good-night. You expect the sound of heels but it doesn't come. You can't quite see the figure clearly. Just as it reaches the alley the dancer walks out, fumbling in her handbag, eventually producing a cigarette. It is then the light hits the figure's face and you can see who it is – it's Joey Tallon.

'Got a light?' the dancer says again, this time with a smirk that is somewhat playful. 'So,' he replies, and you can see his grin, that familiar old grin from those bygone days, those Total Organization days. You can tell it by the clothes. US army jacket. Hawaiian shirt. Doc Marten boots. You can tell it by the Mohawk cut. He reaches in the pocket of his fatigues. This is the signal for the hoods to move in. They range around him in a circle, chewing matchsticks and wielding baseball bats. One of them swings, the implement crunching against his cheek. Then another lifts his way above him and – *pow!* – he brings him down. As his head hits the pavement for the first time he gets a look at her face, blurred as it might be. It is her. His beloved. 'So,' she says, 'how you feeling now?' Then she reaches in her handbag and he catches a glimpse of the flashing blade. 'This is how it should be,' she says. 'This is how it should always be. For those who destroy something beautiful. For those who poison the precious harbour.'

This should then dissolve to a vast whorled sky with a pale, anaemic moon hanging above a garden of the freshest green vegetation, so lush and full of . . . *newness*. He can recognize some of the people in it. They are from the town of Scotsfield, only dressed in ancient Christian robes. One of them, he should be seen to realize, is his mother. She is talking away to someone who also has her head bowed, but you can't see properly because it is crowded. All you can hear is: 'It's what he deserves.' Out of nowhere there is a terrific clamour and the next thing you know the Roman soldiers are climbing over the wall and coming in through the garden gate. The person you first thought was Christ is revealed not to be him at all. Not that it matters for they go right ahead and slice his ear. Then they hand it to her. 'Well, well, well,' she smiles, 'an ear made of

jelly. Because he wants to be a baby. He wants to be
born twice! He wants Mona to give birth to him!
Because his own mother doesn't want him. But, of
course, Mona is a Chivers jelly. So he must be a
jellybaby, mustn't you, Tallon?'

'No, he's not! He's a fully grown jellyman now!
Aren't you, Joey?' someone said.

She goes to him and makes him eat it. 'Here then,
Jellyman!' she insists. 'Eat your own ear.'

The Romans think this is great fun. They can
barely contain themselves as they observe him in
the throes of mastication. Then the centurion
sheathes his sword and says: 'Very well! That's
enough! This is serious business! Now we must proceed to finish it!'

The crucifixion is indeed a serious business.
There are grim expressions all around. All the town
is there. Quite a few reporters. 'Have you anything
to say?' they ask him, but he hasn't, for he still
cannot speak, his mouth being filled with blushing
plasma. 'Barbapapa,' remarks a bystander. 'You'll
remember him, of course. He was pink too.'

His mother arrives over then and folds her arms,
glaring at him for quite a while. After a bit she
spits at him and says: 'You're just like him, your
father that went off to China or wherever the fuck
he went! After he rode that bitch in heat Mona Galligan! Who, if you'll notice, is not here now. Why,
you fool, where is she? Where's that quivery whore?
How they used to laugh at her in Austie's when
she'd try to hold the gin in her shaking paw!
That's how she turned when she had her abortion!
When they ripped Jamesy Tallon's bastard out of her
above in Dublin!'

He shakes his head. The skies have begun to
darken. It breaks his heart that Mona isn't there.
The assembly falls to its knees as one.

It took Jelly a long time to die. Seventy-two
hours. And all the time his loved one was standing

there, she too with folded arms. As she said: 'These are precious moments to me now. His moans are music to my ears.'

Even as the tears of blood came rolling down his cheeks he couldn't avert his eyes – her fine high cheekbones, olive skin and the way she tossed her fine blonde hair. He knew she would wince when he spoke the words, turn away in utter disgust. But just to say them made his journey easy. Those seven last words that he would ever speak upon the earth:

'My one and only beautiful darling Jacy.'

The Acceptance of *Doughboy* a.k.a. *Blobby McStink*

Poring over these musings – or more accurately, perhaps, what are often nothing more than drug-fuelled discourses without any sense of form whatsoever, however sincerely expressed – what is hardest of all to accept – which blew my fucking head off, if you want to know the truth, and still does! – is the very idea of any of my memories *ever* having found a home. But they did, I assure you, the only sad thing being that the experience will never be repeated. Maybe what every ambitious author needs are situations *in extremis*, constant proximity to those knife-edge zones which seem guaranteed to keep the creative juices flowing. Maybe I should give Senator Henry a call. Tell him I've got writer's block. Announce: 'Your services are required once more, Mr Henry!'

Oh, and bring Sandy too! That's bound to improve my style! Do you know what I'm saying, Boyle? You made me an artist, you really did! After all, when you know you could have died at any moment, there's not much point in indulging in self-pity! No, it concentrates the mind just wonderfully and formerly procrastinating persons, although trembling like a leaf, find themselves saying: 'Now you either write your book or you don't, for it really is all you have left! Well, do you intend to write it, Joey?'

Which, to my amazement, I did. Where did it come from? Don't ask me! All I know is, there's no sign of a follow-up! No, sadly there won't be any more letters winging their way from literary London, to the effect that I'm the most amazing young writer that's ever arrived on their doorstep. What they said they liked about it most was the 'voice'. I was over the moon about that, for up until then I didn't think anyone would ever read books that were written in Scotsfield vernacular. And now, here they were saying this:

Kingfisher Publishers
27 Chatham Square
London EC1

Dear Mr Tallon

On behalf of our company I would like to thank you for submitting your manuscript to us. We found it very interesting indeed and would like to include it in our lists, with a view to publishing in the spring. Obviously there are some details which we would like to discuss with you, not least among them the proposed title – *The Amazing Adventures of Blobby McStink* – we are not quite sure whether this is intended to be ironic or tongue in cheek or what. Anyhow, that can be discussed at a later date. The advance we would be prepared to offer is one thousand pounds. In anticipation of your acceptance of this offer, may I take this opportunity to welcome you to our lists – and congratulations on a very fine novel.

Yours truly
Gail Marchant

Youth in Action Creative Arts Awareness Scheme

Such dramatic and unexpected notification of success was a very long way indeed from those barren old days after Johnston had taken his leave of the town, with the writing group more or less falling to pieces and a couple of attempts to ignite the old energies ending in dismal failure. I booked the hotel a couple of times myself but only a meagre scattering of people turned up, and when I tried to address them, starting off with a literary quotation the way Johnston used to, I found myself going red and my mouth becoming dry, with the result that everyone else got nervous too and in the end nobody wanted to read. I couldn't stop thinking that it had been, in fact – despite my repeated denials to myself – my own headstrong behaviour that had led to his sudden departure. The reassurances of the other members, insisting that he had – *yes, definitely!* – been transferred to a bank in Kildare, however, went some way towards dispelling my anxieties. It emerged then – I forget who it was he had told – that he had received an offer for his thriller, and this would also have been instrumental in his decision. I couldn't get this news out of my head when I heard it. Especially when, apparently, the book was set in Scotsfield! I felt quite proud, in fact, that someone would have bothered to set their story in our hometown, never suspecting for a moment that it might have been . . .

His near obsession with my ledgers just didn't register with me at all. Or all the probing questions he'd ask. I was just pleased for him, and all I wanted was a chance to see him. Relive once more those uniquely rewarding days. Days that had been so full of energy and creative ideas that you feared you'd never experience their like again and that what you were facing now was a virtual wipe-out of all the exuberant and confident things that had become so much a part of your life, a return to the bad old seventies with none of the good things ever having happened.

It became more and more like that, from morning to night just sitting there in the caravan drinking, going through notebooks and trying to make sense of what might be generously called 'handwriting'.

When all of a sudden, the door opens and who's there? Only – *guess who!* – yes, the one and only Fr Connolly, shifting from foot to foot and looking a little bit nervous, in one hand this basket of groceries and twenty cigarettes in the other. Nervous, perhaps, because I was tipsy, on the verge, in fact, of inquiring: 'So, who the fuck is this – Little Red Riding Hood?', but managing at the last minute to hold back so that good sense prevailed. He wanted to know if he could come in for a minute or two, that he had a 'little bit of a proposition' to put to me. I said of course he could, for to tell you the truth I was more than glad to have a visitor, the only other human being I'd set eyes on for months being Mangan, who was in a right-looking state since I'd got him the doll – I don't think he was ever off her – so even a priest near seventy was a major improvement on that.

After a few cups of tea we had forgotten our old differences and, in fact, he told me that he had read the present I gave him – the T. S. Eliot poems – from cover to cover and had found it very interesting indeed. 'I really appreciated your giving it to me, Joseph. I never meant to upset you. I was just trying to protect you. I know what they're like around this town. Particularly in some of the pubs. You have to be careful what you say for they'll . . . well, you know what they're like. They'd eat you alive!'

I nodded. I understood now. I appreciated him talking like that. He reminded me of my father. Or what Jamesy Tallon might have been, if he hadn't left us. In the same way, if things had been otherwise, Charlie Manson might have turned out fine. 'Life is funny, Joseph,' he went on, 'and complex. And maybe that's why we need the poets. To help us understand. Improve us.'

'Maybe it is,' I replied, catching a glimpse of myself in the mirror – not at all unlike Charlie now, with my whiskers and hair! – and reflecting that whoever they were, the versifiers I was reading, they didn't seem to be doing too much for me in that department. The understanding and improvement department, I mean. Fr Connolly was standing at the window now and talking about the town and its history. When he mentioned drugs, I thought at first he was trying to get at me, but it was just the regular raids that took place now in the new place – the 'Fuck Me!' hotel as they called the Lakeland Towers, a huge art-deco pile that rose up out of nowhere half a mile outside Scotsfield, everyone going *'Fuck me!'* as their cars came around the corner, with kids as young as fourteen scattering on to the street with their tablets of 'E'. Love stories weren't beginning at Barbarella's any more but there in Marco's, as they called their nightclub, with its non-stop dance music and Sensurround video walls. It had been built by Boyle Henry and a consortium of businessmen, one of whom I'd heard was Sandy.

'Practically every weekend now, Joseph, and say a word about it and they'll laugh in your face,' he informed me ruefully. 'I have seen so many changes,' he went on. 'I remember myself and your father, just walking out to the reservoir. He had all his life before him then. So had I, Joseph. There's things you dream will never happen. Father Gervais – I'm sure you read about him in the paper – that used to be chaplain in the children's homes. Myself and him were in college together. I'd never have believed it either. Your father was a good man, son, and maybe things were swept under the carpet. I don't know what happened to your mother, or Mona, God rest her, but life can be bitterly cruel, and nothing's worse than malignant shame. It may be true that the times now are better. That there's a clean wind abroad and the cobwebs are all blowing away. I hope so, anyway, Joseph. And that's what I've come here to talk to you about. Do you remember the Peace People? All those long years ago? Well, I'm sure you've been listening to the radio lately with all these political developments. Well, the idea is, the Peace People have come up with a suggestion: there is so much money available from the European Union now to fund all sorts of initiatives whereby a deserving local youth or adult might be given a chance – particularly those who have been involved politically in the conflict, as they call it now, although I realize you don't fall into this category –'

He broke off. Then resumed: 'To get to the point, Joseph. In keeping with the changing spirit of the times, they are setting up a trust . . . no, more a sort of award – this was decided only last night – called the Scholarship of Hope, which will be advertised both nationally and in the *Scotsfield Standard*. It would provide someone who has, for whatever reason, become somewhat disadvantaged with an opportunity to rebuild his life, the manner in which this might be approached to be agreed with a selected committee – it could be through work experience in the community, travel, whatever. It would also bring with it a small but reasonable salary which would take that person out of the welfare system and help to give them back their dignity and enable them to be self-sufficient.'

He looked out of the window. There was an old tom cat staring back at him through the rusted window of a wreck. 'Joseph,' he began again, 'I know we've had our differences and that both of us have said things that perhaps we shouldn't, but I really do feel you have abilities and talents . . . well, to come straight to the point, a number of us on the parish committee, not a majority by any means, let me be quite candid about that – we've had plenty of opposition, let me tell you – but we definitely feel that someone like you . . . well, that you deserve and might benefit from an enlightened approach such as this and that it definitely should be given a tryout, a sort of pilot scheme, if you will . . .'

He coughed and said nothing for some time. 'We are aware,' he continued, 'that for a man in your position securing employment – commensurate with your needs and talent, at any rate – might not be the easiest thing in the world. Consequently, myself and Mrs Carmody, the principal of the community college, were wondering if you might be interested in a little post we have been thinking of creating . . .'

He finished by saying: 'Obviously it would be for a trial period. What I mean by that is, Joseph, considering your past not everyone was in full agreement with our suggestion, and you would have to give me your word that . . .'

'Of course, Father,' I said. 'Anything you require in that department, absolutely anything at all! But, believe you me, you don't even have to ask, and Mervin Recks will tell you that! I haven't had much drink since I came home and, as for drugs, well, forget it! That was the seventies, man! It embarrasses me even to –'

He smiled then and that smile was so sunny it sent me right over the moon.

'There is never such a thing as not starting again, Joseph. Like I said, I know we've had our differences. But, like they keep saying on the radio, there is nothing that dialogue can't resolve as we've seen over the past year or so, with former enemies getting on, if not like a house on fire, well, at least not assassinating each other. Do you understand me, Joseph?'

I nodded.

'I understand you, Father. I'm hearing you loud and clear.'

I felt like I'd just been talking to Merv. *Look out for those midges, Mr Gogol!* I thought to myself as my grin spread ever wider. Already I could see myself striding up to that college, my head chock-full of ideas. I made a private decision to tie my hair back in a ponytail so I'd look like one of these trendy New York businessmen you'd see going to work in Wall Street, swinging that old briefcase, maybe dropping into the Fuck Me hotel to sip a latte and rap with a few of the trendy young yuppies you saw coming and going out of there, barking down mobile phones, closing deals and shit. *Yeah!*

'So I can take it that you're interested in the position and that I have permission to put your name forward for the Scholarship of Hope?'

I extended my hand and then gave him a hug.

'You absolutely have, Father,' I said. 'That you most certainly have.'

He was on his way out and about to close the door. I swung on my heel and, without thinking, shot him silently with my protruding gunfinger-

'Oh, and Father . . .' I said.

'Yes?' said Fr Connolly.

'*Thanks!*'

So, there you have it, and in all fairness now you really had to hand it to Connolly. For whatever way it might have eventually worked out – between the principal Mrs Carmody and me – at the end of the day it was Fr Connolly who'd pulled out the stops. Who'd gone out of his way to give a man a second chance and enable him to be reborn. Enabling me for the first time in my life to have a proper job, one you could be fucking proud of for a change. Not rotting in a factory or sweating in a fucking foundry ladling molten iron into a blast furnace and getting bugger-all money or respect for doing it. Not to mention hauling beer kegs and listening to the problems of every drunk in the town, whether in Doc Oc's or anywhere else. No, this was a post where you held your head up high because you knew what what you were doing was useful. But not only that – *important*, as influencing young minds is always important. Merv was an example of that. You get the guy that gives you a hard time – you want to take his fucking head off, blow away him and his family. Then the guy comes along that treats you decent. And what are you like? You're like a little lamb there, bleating. So I reckoned that experience would be pretty useful too. As well as the fact that I could relate to young teenagers in a way that came naturally, having been into draw and all that shit. All I kept thinking was, your life is following a crooked path and the roads seem covered in shards. Shards of the most lethal and jagged-edged glass. Then you look up one day and there's not a single one in sight. The way ahead is uncluttered and clear. For a long time you think that it's never going to happen. But you wake up one day and you know deep inside. You know you're gonna open that window and that road will lie straight ahead.

Shardless.

Incident in the Fuck Me Hotel

That was the day I went around to the Fuck Me, which, as I realized now, was how they referred to the hotel all the time. They *never* called it the 'Lakeland Towers' or even 'the hotel'. All you ever heard them saying was: 'I'm off around to the Fuck Me now,' or 'Do you fancy a drink in the Fuck Me?'

It was the first and last time I ever went into it, though. I didn't know Jacy was working there. In fact, when I saw her behind the bar, I really got quite a shock, and I found myself praying it wasn't because of me and what I'd done. Her face was pale and her eyes were tired, her once blonde hair lank on her shoulders. I was just coming across the floor, thinking how funny it was, all these smart suits with their laptop computers, demanding 'decaffeinated' in the Fuck Me hotel. Except that when she caught my eye, it very soon stopped being funny. I turned on my heel. I made it out into the street, but sweating, you know?

The next time I saw her was outside the same building, on the day that the Taoiseach visited with a bunch of politico dignitaries. I don't know what it was about – something to do with financial opportunities for local businesses within the European Community. There were shiny polished state cars parked all the way down the street, and Boyle Henry and his wife were in the back seat of one. Or, should I say, Senator Boyle Henry. I stood in the alleyway and watched the proceedings. He helped her out of the car and held the door open for her, then they all went inside. The Lady Doc was on crutches and had aged quite considerably too. But not so much as Jacy, who was there too, although you wouldn't have known it from Boyle's reaction. She might as well not have existed.

I saw them together another time. A couple of weeks after that, in fact, one wet night on my way home from the shopping centre, chomping on a cheeseburger and fries. It was late, and I was on the verge of running away as soon as I heard voices. They were coming from the entry at the back of Doc Oc's, and straight away when I heard them I knew who it was. I was on the verge of bursting into tears, to tell you the God's honest truth, and wanted to get out of there as fast as I could but wasn't able to help myself. I could hear him whispering: 'I love you, Jacy!', and it was then that I heard her crying. Every nerve end in my body was tingling as I edged further into the shadows then saw them there, standing underneath the porch light. Her skirt was bunched up around her waist and he was thrusting into her, in and out. Her head was thrown back and I could see her face – so pale. Her mouth was open and her eyes were empty.

'I love you!' I heard him say again, before he groaned and collapsed on top of her.

My heart was thumping as I heard her say – her head was lying on his shoulder now and her cheeks were streaked with tears – 'I always knew you'd never leave her. I always knew!'

'Ssh, baby!' I heard him say, and I could smell the smoke of the Hamlet as a wisp of it went drifting by.

'There were times I'd have done anything to be able to make myself leave you!' she said.

'Don't talk like that, Jacy!' he said.

'All the years I've been with you, you promised me that!'

'And I will, I promise you! I just can't do it right now! She's not been well!'

'Stop it, Boyle, don't lie any more. I know you're just using me. That any time you snap your fingers, you know that I'll –'

She got all choked up then and he comforted her.

'Please, treat me with some respect,' she said, and I heard him kissing her. I couldn't help myself. My head jutted out and I saw him pecking at her neck.

'I love you, Jacy,' he whispered, 'and there's nothing I'd love more than to spend more time with you! You know that! You know that, don't you?'

'I love you, Boyle!' I heard her reply. 'God forgive me, but I love you so much!'

It broke my heart. I couldn't bear to listen any more. I went stumbling home in the dark, and time and my name and my place in the world, they meant nothing to me at all. For all of that night and a long time afterwards.

The 'Can Do' Approach

There wasn't much cash, of course. In the Youth in Action Creative Arts Awareness Scheme, I mean. But, like I said to Fr Connolly, you don't get involved in the creative arts for money. Just seeing the excitement on the kids' faces when you were banging on about ideas – plus the actual projects you managed to see through to fruition – was more than enough reward. I went at it with an energy I didn't know I possessed. 'This is the harbour!' I'd say to myself as I barrelled down the corridor laden down with books and guides and arts brochures, whatever. '*This* is the harbour – it was here all along!'

The first thing I did was inspect the video studio which, I was informed by my supervisor, Eddie, I would have the use of. The equipment available to me, he told me, apart from the editing console, included three Panasonic AG456 SVHS camcorders, one DV Steadi-Cam, a Lowell and Strand Century light kit, four Olympus digital still cameras, a vast array of microphones, assorted video monitors and a Mackie eight-channel mixer. All I had to do was sign for it with my supervisor and book the studio whenever I needed it. 'Excellent,' I said, for I was absolutely delighted.

I also had at my disposal a small office, little more than a broom cupboard, really, but with laptop computer facilities and a telephone/

fax machine. So, I mean, what more could you ask for? I picked up the phone and went to work straight away. I shuffled my papers, scanning my movie treatment as I waited to get put through to Principle Management. Of course, at first I got the usual old spiel: 'Bono and the boys are in Miami . . .' I mean, they're *still* in Miami? Give me a break, you know?

But, I suppose, what with having a new kind of – what would you call it? – legitimacy, I suppose, it didn't bother me in the slightest. No, for this was it, the real thing, not like prison where you often felt that even with the best will in the world they were only allowing you to do certain things to take your mind off topping yourself. But here you could tell they trusted you. There was nothing like that on their minds at all. This was a normal, ordinary environment, with people coming and going about their workaday business, where you felt connected to the world as it lived and breathed! And, because of the confidence and trust invested in me – and just that little bit of power, I guess! – I had decided on a whole new way of dealing with things. A 'can do' approach as opposed to a 'Yes! I'll see that it's done before Christmas' type one.

Which entailed not wasting your time chewing the ass off someone who had no fucking influence, and biding your time – with immense patience and good manners – until you *did* get through to the head honcho.

'This is Wonderful Pictures here in Scotsfield,' I'd say. 'We have currently a number of projects in development and would like to offer a part in one of them to Bono. Also, we're interested in the use of "Where the Streets Have No Name" on the soundtrack of one of these, provisionally entitled *Jellyman!*, dealing partly with the political troubles in Ireland in the mid-seventies, and partly a love story. I was wondering –'

'*As I said, sir, Bono and the boys are currently . . .*'

That was the usual line. But I was ready for it. More than ready for it this time, señor . . .

'We may be approaching Joni Mitchell for the female lead,' I said without blinking.

'Joni Mitchell?' you'd hear then. That always got them going.

When I had all my phone calls made and any other little bits of business attended to, I'd sit down and type up some ideas (you want to see the little laptop! Talk about state of the art! I don't know how many times I nearly busted it, but I got the hang of it in the end!). All sorts of jazz, including some lightweight stuff too. Because one thing I was beginning to realize was that you couldn't be writing heavy shit all the time. You needed to give your brain time to 'chill out' from all the effort that went into making 'real art', or whatever you might like to call it. 'Scotsfield! An Investigation!', 'The Troubles!', 'Hell Is . . . 1976!', 'Love' – those were all very well. But they took a lot out of you. There was nothing more enjoyable than just to sit down and forget about all that stuff. Give it a rest for a while. Write about something else. Your favourite album or whatever. It could be anything. Anything you wanted in this wide world. Such as this little nugget. There is a whole fucking box of them sitting here. I practically wrote the whole college magazine myself, in between filming and other activities. 'Hot Platters' was a column I really enjoyed, and 'Celluloid Round-Up'. The kids enjoyed it too, they were always telling you that.

FAVOURITE MOVIE (FROM: *blag*, ISSUE 3)
A lot of the students on campus often come up to me and say: 'So hey! What's your favourite movie then, Joey?', and my reply always takes them by surprise. 'What's my favourite movie?' I say, looking like I'm gonna spend hours considering, you know, but then giving it to 'em right there and then. My favourite movie? There's no doubt about it at all. It's *A Walk in the Spring Rain* with Anthony Quinn and Ingrid Bergman, I guess because it's always reminded me of older folks around Scotsfield taking walks out by the reservoir. When they had all their lives ahead of them and shit. Not that it means anything much to you kids, for usually you just go away and start blabbing on about *Die Hard* this and Tom Cruise that. But I urge you, guys, get out there and rent it now! It's a really tender piece of work! You got it? Till next time – *gabba gabba hey!*

(There are all sorts of diary entries and notes from those first few weeks in the college. I had forgotten just how hectic it was, but when you read them all together they build up a fairly accurate picture, although there were a couple of little incidents I'd gone and completely forgotten about, such as the '*Ciao*' one with the principal – comprehensively detailed amongst the pages of the 'Community College Ledger'.)

Ciao!

On the way out this morning I met Mrs Carmody, the principal. She is running the place like clockwork. Driving her flash car and wearing a real smart suit – chic businesswoman-type. I had a bit of a chat with her, thanking her for her hospitality and everything, and found her great, I have to say. 'No, Joseph,' she said, 'I'm very much in favour of all the arts. I think that in the past we – actually, not just us, but the education system generally – have been remiss in our attention to them. As well as that, of course, there's the fact that they generate a substantial amount of revenue in Ireland. I mean, so keep up the good work!'

'Sure, Mrs C.!' I said, 'Ciao' – and she gives me this great big smile, beaming away!

Eureka!

I remember being in great humour when I got home that day and still in 'creative mode' after working on the mag. So straight away I got out the laptop and started hammering away on it like billy-o! Every so often I'd tilt the shaving mirror so I could get a good look at myself working there with the Hamlet cigar in my mouth – ha! Screw you, Boyle Henry! You're not the only one who enjoys a cigar! – and the caravan full of smoke like I'm one of those guys out of the movie *The Front Page*, maybe, or, better still, Ernest Hemingway! Although I wasn't sure if he had smoked Hamlets – or any cigars at all, in fact.

But who gave a shit? The thing was that work was being done and that one's 'creative muse' was coming along in leaps and bounds. I couldn't believe I'd been so fortunate in finding a place like the community college. It was like I'd been put on earth for the sole purpose of going about my business working in that place! I couldn't stop puffing on the cheroot as I thought that. Then I'd hit the keys! Did I mention that I didn't eat pies any more? Well, I didn't! Right now I wouldn't have been able to remember when I'd last had a pie on a plate. And never would again as long as I lived! For I'd discovered the solution: get that motherfucking head right down and focus on those stories. Which were now coming together great! I mean, there I was, sitting down at the table and writing about Mona, and the next thing you know – the story you want to tell, the story that gets to the heart – !

Eureka! I almost kicked over the table.

For it was like you could write anything now. It was like you could write a play. *A film script! A novel!* It was getting like you could write them all at the same time!

'Easy now!' I said, and puffed on the Hamlet. Then I calmed down. I read what I'd just written about Mona.

'Mona Galligan was in love with my father. She aborted her baby and became an alcoholic sometime in the 1950s. Then she drowned herself in the reservoir. I loved her very much and used to go to her house every day. When my mother would be cursing my father. It was with Mona Galligan that I first experienced the hunger for rebirth into a world transformed. They threw her baby – or what was left of it – into the sea off Howth Head in Dublin. She told me that one time when she was drunk. I don't think she knew she was telling me. They used to call her the Chivers jelly. Mona Chivers jelly was what they would call her because she shook so much with the gin.'

That's all I wrote. Which doesn't matter because I rolled it up and threw it away. And then got down to the real business. The real hard business of me and Jacy.

As I wrote, I felt like getting up and running away – many times. For I realized now, with each succeeding draft, that I was getting closer and closer to the truth. I remembered reading a piece by James Joyce where he said that, when you write, it's like what you're doing is drawing water. You lower the pail into the well of the subconscious and you wait and see what comes up. I was sweating like a pig now and the cigar had long since burnt itself out.

I could feel what was coming, feel it welling up.

No sumptuous widescreen Hollywood, no majestic sweeps, no stirring poignancy at all. Just the crisp black-and-white realism of truth. Like a TV documentary from the early seventies. I couldn't believe my eyes as I read it. I could see the movie in my mind already. This was how it looked:

The Plan: A Film Treatment by J. Tallon

We are in a small town in Ireland. It is near the border. There is a lot of excitement in the area today. There has been a constant stream of people arriving since early morning. They have come from all over Ireland and there is talk that some have even come from as far afield as Canada and the United States. Already an RTE camera crew has installed itself in Austie's Courtyard, in between the old bar and Barbarella's, where the Peace and Reconciliation Rally is scheduled to take place. Sightings of the major celebrities Mairead Corrigan and Betty Williams, the original founders of the movement, have been enthusiastically reported, but these have not been confirmed for sure. There has also been talk of a well-known BBC commentator arriving, but this also has not been verified as yet. The air of expectation about the place is palpable. Already the burgers and steaks are being ferried in in boxes and stacked up in The Courtyard in preparation for the festivities which will follow the solemn ceremonies. The 'Poem for Peace' winning entry has been enlarged and laminated and is on display in the hotel foyer for all to see. Many in the town are proud of what the young girl has written and without reservation share in the sentiments she has expressed, feeling good about it also because it sends out the correct message to the world at large, informing them of the degree of shame which exists in this community as a result of the violence being perpetrated in its name. There are also those who are not only ashamed but also very angry. Especially when news reaches them of another savage murder in Belfast, which has allegedly been committed by a member of the Provisional IRA. Quite a significant percentage of the townspeople harbour a deep animosity towards this organization and, sometimes, perhaps if alcohol has been consumed, they will give vent to these emotions. They will approach well-known people such as Hoss Watson or Sandy McGloin, stare at them for a minute while flicking a cigarette or something, then close one eye and say: 'So, what's your game?

What *is* your fucking game? Who do you think you
represent?' Then sometimes there's a fight, other
times there's not. Hoss might kick back his chair
and snap: 'No! Who do *you* represent? I've got my
war, you've got yours! So fuck you! You got yours
and I got mine – *capiche*?' But whether he does or
not there's a lot of bad blood, you can feel it in
the air. Fr Connolly is very proud. Now that the
time is drawing near, it makes all those long
nights burning the midnight oil seem sort of worthwhile. He has been up and down the town all day.
Everywhere he goes people stop to congratulate him.
'It's a credit to you, Father. A credit to you and
a credit to Scotsfield!' is what they generally
say.

On LLR (Lakeland Local Radio) the DJ is about to
interview the Peace People. While he is waiting for
them to arrive, he observes that the town could not
have hoped for a better day. The temperature right
now is close to eighty-three degrees Fahrenheit.
Which, he points out, is twenty degrees above normal. *'Phew!'* he says with a laugh. 'As I stand here
mopping my brow with my handkerchief, folks, I
might as well be in Florida it's so hot down here
in Scotsfield!'

The interview which follows proves to be very
moving, and the switchboard is jammed after it.
Mairead Corrigan tells him that when she drives
from her home outside Strangford to Belfast she
often stops to look at an amazing sight: *a field*!
However, it isn't an ordinary field, she explains,
but one covered in rows of a beautiful mixture of
blue cornflowers, white daisies and yellow wild
flowers. There was nothing she liked more than to
stand in the middle of this field and think about
the beauty of the flowers, she says, and how wonderful it would be if politicians could see it and
perhaps learn from it, thereby giving us something
more imaginative and creative to lift our spirits,

because the people of Northern Ireland are a beautiful mixture too.

There is an army helicopter overhead, but no one is expecting any trouble. It's just there for observation. As a kindly woman observes, coming out of the butcher's, 'It would be a heartless soul indeed who would try to disrupt or do anything to spoil such a devout and tranquil gathering as this!'

The Legion of Mary have all decided to dress in white today, and Austie's wife has been chosen to bear the 'Candle of Peace'. The band playing at the barbecue has been chosen by Fr Connolly himself, who heard them at a similar rally in Westport, County Mayo. They are called The Doves and they specialize in gospel and charismatic-style songs. Their lead singer is a big fan of the Peace People and has put in a special request with Fr Connolly for a private audience with Betty Williams and Mairead Corrigan afterwards. 'After the ceremonies and when the festivities are over,' he explains to Fr Connolly. 'I just want to tell them how good a job I think they are doing.'

Fr Connolly understands perfectly and assures him he will do his best. Then, standing in the middle of Scotsfield's main street, he joins his hands behind his back and emits a long, luxurious sigh of contentment, for never, after what must be nearly thirty years in this one place, has he ever, he reflects, seen as much activity 'up the town'.

Approximately two miles away, in a mobile home on the edge of a former itinerant settlement, there is a certain person who is not at this point exhibiting any sign of wishing to engage in these noble and uplifting community affairs. No, Joey 'Mohawk' Tallon is not at this point 'up the town' involving himself in any of the preparations nor offering his services in order that things might proceed like clockwork and present the town at large in a good and favourable light to the greater world outside. Act as an example to them in a certain sense. Not that he isn't pleased for them. He is. Absolutely delighted, in fact, that things are going according to plan. It suits his purpose perfectly. It's just that, for the life of him, he cannot sit still. Look at him pacing up and down! *A pie!* he thinks. Then: *No pies! A glass of sweat! No! No fucking sweat!*

Poor Joey is tired and can't think straight. Not surprising, really. For once more he has been awake since early dawn and his mind is a wall of death, with thousands of thoughts careering around it on high-speed racers. How many times does he have to drive to that mountain before he can say to himself: 'Look, the fucking place is ready! It's OK!' and just forget about it?

He sits down to relax. Opens a book. Closes it again. Presses his forefingers against his temples. In days, he thinks, it will all be over. He is happy about that. So happy, in fact, he would like to celebrate it with a spliff. But that, he is not going to do. He is not going to do that because it belongs to a time that was. A time before 'The Plan'. A time before 'Total Organization'.

A time before they set off for home, to that Karma Cave of dreams. Of course, he reflects, it will be like what he longed for all those years ago with Mona, a garden where you could surrender your all. Where dwelt all the ones you'd ever known – Bennett, The Seeker, the salesman. Your own father, Jamesy Tallon.

Except that, with Jacy, it would be even more special than that. The 'onions' of their personalities methodically stripped, layer by layer just peeling away to reveal within the shimmering, unblemished light of one another's souls. The very *essence* of each of those souls.

Before donning his aviator shades, he stared at his reflection in their tinted glass. He looked fine. It was all worked out. He had it all worked out. There was nothing to worry about now. He had been over it fifty times. He knew Jacy was working as a steward at the rally. That had been established. He had watched them practise again and again. He felt proud of her that she had agreed to give her services to the community in this way. When she could, just as easily, with all her knowledge and experience, have poured scorn upon it. But that wasn't Jacy's way, was it? That wasn't the way of The Jace. He knew that now, had seen it time and time again. Boyle Henry was working at it too. But he wasn't a steward. He was to be positioned miles away from Jacy, looking after the car park on the other side of town, encouraging drivers to park there in order to reduce the volume of traffic in the centre, which, if half the numbers they were expecting arrived, was going to be absolutely crazy. But which suited Joey perfectly. There was a simple genius attached to his plan. He would park the Bedford in the alleyway, then wait until she –

He pulled on his black balaclava – a simple woollen hat complete with two cut-out eyeholes – then leapt to his feet and stood in front of the mirror, barking: *'There's a van blocking the alley! That van has got to be shifted!'*

He practised it again.

'I said, there's a van over there and it's blocking the alley! That van has got to be shifted! It's got to be moved – right now!'

He pulled off the balaclava and sat down, drawing a deep breath. Then he smiled. A gratified, assured smile. Pies? No thanks. 'That van has got to be shifted!' he began again in a voice that was strong and firm, and was in the process of taping the bags of sand to his midriff – if anyone gave them trouble he would threaten to blow both himself and her up if they weren't guaranteed safe passage. A complete bluff, of course! He wouldn't harm a hair on her head! Who did they think he was? Eddie Gallagher? Marion Coyle?

Then the door started pounding.

'Who's that?' he demanded, his heart beginning to beat furiously. *This shouldn't be happening*, he thought. This was a time of Total Organization. He was on the verge of shouting: 'Go away!' when, almost in slow motion – he felt like exploding into laughter, for how could this possibly be happening when Total Organization was already well under way, when the regime at last was up and running, with every little detail worked out to the last – how could it possibly be –?

'Hey!' he heard Chico saying, as the door swung open. 'You going up to the peace gig, Joey? Hey, what the fuck are you doing with them bags of sand? Let's get going, Joey! Gonna be wild! The place is hopping! Let's go!'

He picked up one of the sandbags and chucked it against the wall. It burst.

'No!' cried out Joey. Anka stared at him and laughed. Then she picked up a bag and threw it at Chico. It hit him in the face. 'You little bitch!' cried Chico as he brushed the sand from his eyes. When their 'sandfight' was finished, the floor was covered in it. Sand, that is. There was only one sandbag remaining – the one that was duct-taped to Joey's waist.

'Look!' squealed Chico. 'Welcome to the beach!'

'Come on, children, you must get your buckets and spades!' yelped Anka as she went skidding across the floor.

Joey was white. Abstractedly he tore off the last remaining plastic bag. He tried to fight off the gathering bitterness. 'I've got to calm down,' he told himself.

He succeeded. He spoke to them with restrained and

measured breaths. He said he didn't want to go. 'I can't go,' he said. Anka thought this was great fun. She chuckled. Then fell over, crawling on to the bed, as Chico climbed on top of her and cried: 'Hey! Look at The Man!' It was Robert De Niro he was talking about. His picture was tacked to the wall. He was looking at them. That made Chico laugh. He grabbed Anka by the ass and growled: *You lookin' at me? 'Cos if you ain't lookin' at me, who are you lookin' at? I don't see anyone else around!'*

Chico sat on the bed and opened a box. It was a little silver box. It should have contained little buttons or pins. But it didn't. It didn't contain buttons or pins. It contained tabs. Little tabs of acid in sellotaped strips. 'Here, Joey, have a tab,' said Chico as he slipped one on to his own tongue. Then he gave one to Anka, who swallowed it promptly. 'I don't want any tabs,' said Joey. 'I've had it with all that. Those days are done. This is a time of Total Organization.'

Chico thought this hilarious. So did Anka. And do you know what she did then? Caught Joey unawares between the legs and pinned him to the bed. Then she stuck her finger in his mouth. And wiggled it around a little. Joey didn't mind it at first for it felt quite nice, to be honest. It was only when he realized what she'd done that he lost it. Chico was dancing around like an Indian on the warpath, talking in all these garbled voices.

'Those days are gone? *Oh no, they're not!* Those days are gone? *Oh no, they're not!*', every so often falling on his knee and training a pistol on the mirror's reflection, bawling: '*Thank God for the rain which has helped wash the garbage and trash off the sidewalks! Pow! Pow! She appeared like an angel out of this open sewer. Out of this filthy mass. She is alone; they cannot touch her! My whole life is pointed in one directon! I see that now! There has never been any choice for me!'*

It was only when he felt the microdot slipping down the base of his throat that Joey began to realize for absolute certain that he was right. What he had feared had indeed happened, i.e. that Anka had spiked him. Then he lost it completely, which, as he should have realized by then, was an absolute waste of time, for Anka and Chico were clearly tripping their skulls off. Chico's eyes in particular were like whirling frisbees.

It was hopeless.

The more Joey remonstrated, the less attention they paid him, before they eventually fell out the door and tore across the encampment, with the dogs howling after them and Mangan crouching fearfully by his caravan window. He was at a total loss now, Mohawk. He could feel the electric tingles starting already at the tips of his toes. *'You stupid -!'* he began, but never managed to finish the sentence. Some of the sand had gotten into his mouth. In the crevices between his fingers. What was he going to do? Perhaps he could put it all back into the bags! How could he? What an idiotic thing to think! All the plastic bags were torn! If he didn't think of something soon –

He could feel the edgy shadows beginning to congregate at the corners of his eyes. Everything becoming that bit too sharp. What to do? He'd read about orange juice and vitamin C. That might do it.

But it was too late! He realized that, yes, it already was much too late! He wanted, more than anything, for those tingles to stop. They had finished with his toes and were moving on through his feet and ankles and up then towards his shins and knees. Soon they would be marching on his stomach and giving him those cramps he hated. That was because of the strychnine which they sometimes used as a base, whoever made the fucking stuff. Presently, then, the tips of his fingers. *Before the tingling became total. Before the total became tingling.*

He experienced an irrational urge to laugh and ask himself a really daft question. 'What's your name, Joseph? Yes, what is your name? It's Joseph, is it? But what does that mean? What does having a name mean? Who are you? What is the *you of you*?'

He cried out, and thumped the wall forcefully. 'No!' he bellowed again. He wouldn't allow it. 'Don't start that!' he demanded. 'No questions! Or ideas swooshing around all over the place! Talking in different voices! Stay together, thoughts! Just stay in line!'

But they wouldn't. They went off again. *Tingle totalling. Total tingling. What is the we of we? The you of you. I am The Gardener. You are the garden*. He shook his head to try and dislodge them – these unbiddable, almost neon-lit philosophizings. He stuck his head into the sink and showered his face with water. The tap seemed like it was made out of rubber. Then a thought – 'Oh, this is ridiculous!' he cried – poked its head up out of the plughole. It looked like a worm with a swollen head, which it tilted just a little as it opened its mouth. Before closing it, then repeating once again: 'Iowa.' He slammed his hand down over that plughole. 'Ha!' he cried. 'That soon got rid of it!', but just as he was drying his face what did he hear? Only something moving over by the window, and when he looked over what was sitting on the sill? Only the same fucking worm like a happy children's doodle, some cartoon from early morning telly just tilting that head, lips opening and closing as it said: 'Joey, Iowa!' *Iowa Iowa Iowa.*

It was now or never. He ran off out the door. As soon as he was behind the wheel he felt himself once more. Everything – at last! – was on course again.

All Aboard for the Cave of Dreams

It's great, thinks Joey, *to be setting off now
once and for all on the journey to the place you'd
been longing for all your life*. 'What is this
place?' all of a sudden he heard someone say.
'Why, the Cave of Dreams!' he responded at once.
And, for no reason he could think of, he found
himself laughing. Which was bad enough in the
circumstances – after all, he was off to complete
'The Plan' and erupting into laughter for no
apparent purpose while you were doing it was
hardly going to –

Any more than allowing your eyes to well up with
tears, which, he had to admit, he was doing now.
Yes, permitting great gouts of tears – enormous,
transparent golf balls – to appear in the middle of
each eye before fragmenting right there and sprinkling all the way down his face. 'Oh dear!' he
sighed. 'I fear I am going to jeopardize "The
Plan"!'

But then, thank heavens, help was at hand in the
form of a quiet soothing voice that seemed to
emanate from somewhere beneath the leopardskin-cov-
ered seat. 'Leopardskin?'

'Hah!' laughed Joey, swiping his arm right
across his eyes to get rid of those fucking tears.
'Leopardskin!' he cried. 'I wonder who shot that
leopard!'

The brown and black markings spun athletically in
front of his eyes.

'Poor leopard!' he sighed then, trying not to
feel sad but not being able to manage it, that
silly old leopard rearing up at the glass – the
glass of the windscreen – and growling at him with
great big teeth. But then the voice told him to go
easy. 'Go easy there now, Joey Tallon! Slow down
and take your time. It's going to be fine. Things
will work out fine, you'll see!'

He really hoped they would. More than anything he

hoped that they would because after all you had to remember that he'd never longed for anything so much! 'Ah, the Cave of Dreams!' he murmured. 'The opposite of the Big Fellow – that warm soft place where you know you'll always be at peace!'

And with Jacy he knew he'd find that place. Together they'd create a whole new world. They'd turn to the Big Fellow and laugh in his face. Take his stupid fedora off him and tramp it into the dirt. 'How do you like that, buddy?' they'd say. 'You're all washed up!', before giving his cigar a wallop and knocking it out of his big fat mouth.

Then, without warning, it was as if the flick of a whip had caught Joey across the face. 'No!' he cried out and skidded off the road. 'Don't ever,' he heard the Big Fellow warn, 'don't ever dismiss me again like that!'

Joey was trembling and he wanted to apologize. He wanted to call back the Big Fellow. But he was gone. Perhaps he had never been there!

No, he had! He had definitely heard his –

Such beautiful singing. He had never heard singing like it. Where on earth was it coming from? Why, it was coming from the town, of course. He was aproaching it now, with its wavering amber orchestra of lit candles. The music brought him close to tears again, but this time ones so joyful –

He gave silent thanks that he was nearing the end of his quest. The end of his quest and the beginning of his –

Now that a calm was at last descending, Joey began to realize that he had never quite experienced a sensation such as this. It was as though it were a preview of the tranquillity he was destined later to attain with the beloved, whose name was Jacy, the one who'd been put on this earth, who'd chosen to come to this town –

When he had completed his prayer, he edged the Bedford slowly towards the alleyway and left the

engine running. 'It's going to be so easy!' the
soft voice reassured him. 'This is where your
preparation counts. This is the payoff, Joey. What
Total Organization actually means.'

He pulled the van in directly behind the alley.
Then he reached inside his jacket for the balaclava. It wasn't there! He'd gone and forgotten
that too!

'What was that?' he started suddenly –

'It's only a dog barking, asshole!' he told himself, gingerly opening the door of the cab. He
stood shivering by the van as the crowds swept in a
wave towards the main altar in the centre of the
square. The Legion of Mary were like ghosts dressed
in white. A wave of formless spirits, floating
half-people bathed in light. You had to hand it to
Fr Connolly, for he had certainly demanded 'Total
Organization' from his flock, with his bunting and
flags and powerful lamps. It might just as well
have been a scene, he thought, from some end-of-
the-world science-fiction movie.

Except that what it was, in fact, was a scene
from the *beginning* of the world. A movie calling
Jacy to the Cave of Dreams.

He smiled now. 'Talk about previews,' he mused to
himself. 'Those days after school when I'd dream it
all up with Mona, they might as well have been a
preview for this. For this "Cave of Dreams" can be
nothing but real. It's the way it's meant to be!'

He laughed when he thought of the 'leopard'.

Imagine that! he thought. *Getting it into your
head that a jungle animal was loose in the Scotsfield countryside! A jungle animal, I ask you!*

He could feel the presence of someone close by
and he froze. *Someone who knew*, he thought. *Who
knew all the details of 'The Plan'.* He could feel
his entire body going rigid and the gathering icy
presence that seemed to be all around him now.
'It's the Big Fellow!' he cried. 'The Big Fellow!',

starting as he burnt his fingers with the cigarette.

But it wasn't. 'No,' he stammered, 'it's just the
keys! That's all it is! I've forgotten the keys of
the cabin! How can I get into the Karma Cave? I've
forgotten the keys of the fucking cabin as well!'

But it turned out he hadn't, great big silly.
Went and found them in the pocket of his jeans,
where they'd been nesting all along. 'Dear, oh
dear!' he began to laugh as he reprimanded himself
inwardly. 'I really think I'd better get started
and stop all this old –'

It was only a matter of getting someone to draw
her attention . . . probably best be a kid.

*'There's a man over there and he told me to tell
you . . . he says a van is blocking the alley!'*

It would be dead simple after that. What Chico
would call 'a piece of piss'. 'Chico,' he hissed,
'don't talk to me about Chico! Or that bloody Anka
either! Giving me fucking acid –'

He didn't bother finishing the sentence, his
attention drawn to the elegant shapes that the purple candle smoke made in the air just in front of
Fr Connolly. Their 'purpleness' amazed him. *The
Smoke Ballerinas*, he thought you might call them.

*'Tonight, at the Peace Rally here in Scotsfield,
Fr Connolly Productions are proud to bring you –
The Smoke Ballerinas!'*

He had a great big smile on his face and was
about to watch them dancing when he realized the
enormity of what he was doing. Indulging in frivol-
ity at a time when –

'Shut it!' he cautioned himself and, ridicu-
lously, nearly burst out laughing anew.

It was time to begin in earnest, before he found
himself distracted again, for the tingles were more
or less consolidated now – from the top of his head
to the tips of his toes. They felt orange. That was
what you thought their colour was. In almost every

corner of your body tingles were arguing most vehemently. Constellations of tingles all living inside
each other. And engaging in strident disagreements.
Galaxies of interweaving planets, all –

'Shut up, Joey!' he barked before clicking his
heels militarily.

Then he almost swooned as he saw her emerging into
the light. She was dressed in white and wearing her
steward's armband, with her long blonde hair tied
back. Obviously she wouldn't be attired in denims at
a sombre function like this. But he hadn't expected
her to look quite so beautiful – and pure. It was
once again a testimony to her respect for other traditions that she had deferred to local practice and
worn just a white blouse and white skirt, which
swept dreamily about her knees. 'Oh, I'm so happy!'
he heard himself say as the kid walked over to Jacy,
clutching the money Joey'd given him. He felt really
proud he had managed to hold it together while giving the kid the instructions.

He watched her listen attentively, kind, then nod
as the kid strolled back to his friends.

He was on the verge of intoning another silent
prayer as his eyes drank in every moment of her
movements now she was walking towards the alley.
It was like a slow-motion flashback in a romantic
movie. *A Walk in the Spring Rain* perhaps.

'I love you, Joey,' he heard her say as they
stood by the reservoir water, the rain breaking
like small glistening diamonds on the porcelain
smoothness of her face. Which was all very well,
but why were people pushing each other out of the
way? Why was there one man cursing? A coldness took
hold of him when he saw Jacy rising up in the air,
falling, then, almost at once, clambering to her
feet and getting ready to run. What was she doing
that for?

He tried to focus his attention on her but,
effortlessly, the adroit acid tugged his mind away

as the constellations above him began to shift their shape dramatically. The Big Fellow, unmistakably defined, was looking down upon him then, his wry smile appearing suddenly but then gone. Nothing remained but the anonymous stars. They stayed just like that for what must have been over a minute before exploding into thousands of colours. Somewhere out beyond them a loudspeaker squealed and an announcement was made. But it wasn't the one that Joey had been expecting, announcing perhaps the beginning of the procession. Instead it said: *'Do not panic! Please do not panic! Please leave the square in an orderly fashion! Please do not panic! Leave the square in an orderly fashion!'*

'Jesus, Mary and Joseph!' someone cried as an orange flash lit up the sky.

'It's going to be all right! There may be no more bombs! Please do not panic!'

You could hear the anxiety in the loudspeaker voice. Fr Connolly had left the altar and was running in the direction of the hotel. There was another flash – this time on the other side of the square – and the telegraph wires came sweeping down. All you could hear was someone screaming: *'The child's been electrocuted!'*

There was another explosion then, this time inside the hotel, and every window in the place was blown out. The arc lights were swinging wildly, picking out random, terrified faces, as the tidal wave of bodies surged forward, almost craven, beseeching. An old woman stumbled past Joey and he could see the white of her torn brassiere. *'There's a second bomb behind the altar!'* someone cried. The loudspeaker clattered loudly to the ground and suddenly went dead.

He had lost Jacy again. Then she was back, running this time. He caught another fleeting glimpse and more than anything what he felt like doing was falling to his knees and weeping. For it had all come to nothing now, his weeks of organization! His nights of planning what he'd been going to say as he'd persuade her gently into the van, telling her the truth about Boyle Henry the murderer and the plans he had organized for the two of them together. Talking about California as they made their way to the cabin and of how it had been ordained that she belonged with him, not Henry, their twin destinies now inexorably entwined.

Now! He saw her again. Another split second, he knew, and she'd be gone. He could hear her calling Boyle Henry's name. The electrocuted child was surrounded by people. They didn't seem to know what to do. Its distraught mother was screeching, blaming everybody around her. The child was still lying there, open-mouthed and motionless. Some people were abstractedly vowing horrendous vengeance on the people responsible. There was a grown man crying in front of the bank, shaking, ashamed of himself, but not knowing what to do about it. Just as things were calming down and the first of the ambulances arrived in a swirl of blue light, a mains pipe burst asunder. Someone shouted: *'Fr Connolly is dead!'* but that was wrong because Joey had just seen him. Jacy kept calling out 'Boyle! Where are you, Boyle? Please help me!'

Joey wrung his hands. It could all have been so easy. Why did it have to happen like this? What if there was another explosion? She might be killed. He could hear her weeping now. He could allow no more time for thinking. Instinctively, he sprang forward and grabbed her with both arms. He clamped his hand over her mouth. A massive billowing wall of smoke enveloped the square as he hauled her towards the Bedford. She scratched his face as he tried to explain. Someone squealed *'There's going to be another explosion! Fr Connolly's dead! There's another bomb in the hotel!'*

He begged her to listen.

'Get in the van, Jacy!'

'Get your fucking hands off me! Help me! Boyle! Please! It's Tallon!'

She screamed again: 'It's Joey Tallon!'

There were pallid faces slowly turning towards them. The sirens wailed and the night sky flared. Ambulances were arriving from all directions. Crouching paramedics criss-crossed the square as the injured and maimed were ferried through the mayhem. 'Why did they have to do it?' Joey asked himself. 'Why did the Provos have to ruin my plan?'

'I'm asking you, Jacy – please, I'm begging you! Get in the van! I'll explain everything when we get to the mountain!'

'Let go of me, you! I've hurt my wrist! You've broken my fucking wrist!'

Just then, Joey saw his own veins splitting open. 'No!' he told himself, fishhooks trawling his gut. The blood spewed out of the fleshy aperture like the water-main plume in the square. *Oh God!* he thought. *Maybe I have broken her wrist!*

He would have to get himself together. Rivulets of water ran red across the square. Bricks and broken glass lay strewn everywhere. The mechanism of the town clock had been affected and was playing *'Holy God, We Praise Thy Name'* over and over again. A Volkswagen Beetle lay on its back.

'Get in the fucking van, Jacy! For fuck's sake, Jacy, get in the van! I'll explain, just give me a chance!'

'Boyle! Where are you?'

'Oh, Jacy! Jacy, don't!'

She called Boyle Henry's name again.

There was nothing else for it. 'Oh God!' he moaned as he swept her up and bundled her inside. Then the doors slammed shut.

'I'm so sorry!' he said as he clambered into the driver's seat and switched on the ignition. He thought of his veins again.

'No! They're *not* breaking open, Joey!' he
insisted. 'It's just the acid, don't you understand?'

But the drug had now taken hold and everything
from now on would be magnified a hundredfold. Especially his guilt over hurting her wrist. Because he
had. Broken it, that is. Must have, if her cries of
pain were any indication. He called her name, but
she made no response.

'Jacy!' he repeated, turning the Bedford on to
the Tynagh Road, trying his best not to repeat *My
veins are not splitting, my veins are not splitting*
and repeating instead: 'Jacy! Jacy! Are you OK?' as
the van gathered speed and he tore off into the
night.

But Jacy never answered that question. Or any
other that Joey Tallon addressed to her for the
duration of that journey. She had fainted. He had
hardly driven a mile out of town before he heard
the siren. 'Oh Jesus!' he cried. There was a cop
car in pursuit. He managed to lose it but he knew
now that he'd been spotted. 'Those fucking Provos!'
he spat bitterly. 'They've gone and ruined everything!'

The needle climbed as he sped on towards the
mountain, his teeth clenched, the dread within him
becoming close to unbearable. He reached in the
glove compartment to get his shades. His hand found
itself resting on something warm. Something moving.
On closer inspection he saw that it looked like
suet. Then he realized it wasn't suet. *Maggots!*

A solid body of them, pulsating. He sprang backwards in revulsion, asking himself what he'd wanted
his shades for. He couldn't remember. He searched
about once more in the recesses of his mind. No
use. 'Anyway, there were maggots,' he told himself
and then laughed like a simpleton.

Then a dart of fear and reality went shooting
through him. He knew he had better get himself

together. That much he definitely knew. Things had
gone very badly wrong now and if he didn't start
shaping up, he was gonna be in a lotta trouble. Oh
yes, that much was for sure. But he reckoned that,
given a little time, he might still be able to pull
it off. If he could just hold on until such time as
the acid began to wane. Things would be different
then. Of course they would. It was the only reason
he had lost it in the first place. It had made him
so fucking paranoid. He shouldn't have grabbed Jacy
by the wrist. He shouldn't have hauled her the way
he had, of course he shouldn't. How could you possibly begin to suggest otherwise? It was bitterly
unfortunate it had happened that way - that was all.

Obviously, now, every part of 'The Plan' would
have to be changed. Every single detail revised.
Things would have to proceed at a much slower pace
if he was to have any chance of bringing Jacy
around, any chance at all of making her understand.
First he would have to bandage that wrist. That
would be priority number one. 'Why did this have to
happen?' he asked himself again. But there were no
answers. It had happened and that was that. He
would have to deal with things as they *were* now,
and not the way he'd dreamed them.

Which was what he was trying to explain as they
drove, hoping that somehow she might take some of
it in. Although he knew it was unlikely, as she was
slipping in and out of consciousness. Suddenly she
cried out.

'*Boyle!*'

'Jacy! Jacy, please don't cry! Did you hurt yourself? I'm sorry about your wrist! Is it bad? I'll
fix it!'

He knew, of course, there was a strong possibility that the entire operation was now doomed. A
strong possibility that he might be fucked. For a
start, the roads would be closed. The place crawling with cops. But all of a sudden the sparkling

lava stream of the acid went surging through him
again and he found himself consumed by the most
absurd and brightly coloured optimism. 'But we
might be lucky!' he declared as he sped past some
trees. 'Hee hee!'

That, however, wasn't destined to be the case.
Joey Tallon had got it right. He *was* fucked. Had
been from the word go. The fact being that he had
hardly shut the door of the cabin behind them and
flicked on the radio before he realized that
already they were relaying non-stop news bul-
letins, heaping detail on declamatory detail
regarding the merciless devastation of a small
border-town peace rally by the Provisional IRA,
who had already vehemently denied responsibility,
insisting on joint UVF and British Intelligence
involvement. And the extraordinary circumstances
surrounding another incident (it was not clear if
they were connected): the apparent kidnap of a
girl by a local man claimed to be modelling himself on the Black Panther, Donald Neilson, and
also, perhaps, to some extent, on Eddie Gallagher,
the renegade IRA man, who, of course, was responsible late last year, along with Marion Coyle, for
the false imprisonment of the Limerick-based
industrialist Tiede Herrema.
    '*Bullshit*!' snapped Joey when he heard that, ran-
sacking a cupboard as he searched for some bandages. All he could find was some old torn cloth. He
laughed at the idea of expecting to find bandages.
'What? A first-aid cabinet? Oh yes! Very likely!'
he muttered, a trifle hysterically.
    He laid Jacy gently down on to the camp bed and
squatted lotus style for a while, considering his
options.
    Some time later, relieved, he drew back the cabin
curtain and saw – and a heaviness took hold of his
stomach, although the strychnine pains were easing

off a little – to his horror, gathering outside, what could only be described as a small army of policemen, with floodlights illuminating the entire surrounding area and a number of marksmen already positioned in the treetops and the roofs of out-houses and barns. He closed the curtains and paced up and down, edgily. The radio spurted out sud-denly: *'We're going back to Scotsfield now where our reporter has more news of the developing situa-tion there –'*

'Shut up!' he snapped and backhanded the transis-tor the moment he heard Travis Bickle's name, not to mention further nonsense about US army jackets, Indian haircuts and the 'eccentricities' some locals – in Austie's, apparently – had ascribed to him.

'This man', continued the cocky reporter, 'is said to be capable of anything. Tonight the town of Scotsfield holds its breath in fear for what might happen to Jacy Flevin, who at this moment is being held captive in a remote area of Tynagh Wood –'

He went to the window again. His heart sank when he saw Boyle Henry, casually leaning on the bonnet of his yellow Datsun. You could see him beneath the floodlights, chatting away to the cops. Smoking his Hamlet in his white suit, without a care in the world. The detective stepped forward, raising the loudhailer to his lips.

'There will be no deals,' he barked. *'Do you hear me, Tallon? What do you hope to achieve? It's only a coward who would kidnap a defenceless young woman! It takes courage to make the decision to give yourself up. So come out while you can, Joey, don't be a fool!'*

As time went on it gradually became impossible with the floodlights to tell whether it was day or night. They erected scaffolding outside, with a large blue nylon screen beside it. He racked his brains trying to figure out what that could possibly be for. Then it dawned on him. *They were going to storm the house!*

He found himself rocking in a foetal crouch and thinking of Travis Bickle laughing. 'God's lonely man, Joey? Well, you sure are now!' he said and walked away, before turning in slow motion to look back and laugh, blowing some smoke from his 'gun-finger'.

Jacy had been crying for most of the night, complaining about the wrist again. For the first time he began seriously to question if they'd ever make America . . .

It went against everything he'd believed as regards 'The Plan' to light up the spliff, after a long argument with himself eventually locating the pouch of Paki black which he had stashed in the drawer for the trip to California. There was some brandy there too but he wouldn't touch that. Not yet anyway. Unless Jacy wanted some. It might ease her pain. He thought about asking her. Then he blew a few puffs of the jay. It felt good. Yes, it did. It felt real good actually, he thought. It wasn't a bad thing to do, after all. It wasn't a bad thing to have done. How could it be when it calmed him down and helped him to cope with Jacy's accusing stare, which he could feel on his back, or enabled him to steel himself for the loudhailer's taunts? He stood at the window and pulled open his jacket. There was nothing for it but to try and bluff it all the way. To stick with the original plan. A couple of the buttons flew off as he tore at it. *'I'm a human bomb, man!'* he shouted. *'You don't know what you're dealing with! I'll take you all with me! The whole shit will come down, don't you fucking understand?'*

Then he winked at Jacy so that she wouldn't be frightened. After the third spliff, he felt much better and was half able now to meet her eye. His explanations slowly became more fluid, if not

articulate, as he gestured towards her wrist and
said: 'I'm sorry about that, you know? Jacy, I am.'

In a way, after the second night's tribulations and
anxieties had slowly begun to pass, he was not all
that surprised at the way things began to develop.
For all along he had felt that their connection and
destiny was such that it could survive almost anything. And that, if he could just manage to be
patient, she might slowly begin to listen. Give him
a chance to explain. *At last!* he found himself
thinking. *At last now she's doing that.*
  Which she was. You could feel it in the air – a
slight easing of the tension as he walked the
floor, flicking the spliff ash and trying to find
the . . . most appropriate words. Ones that
wouldn't alarm her. She had been through quite
enough already.
  'You see, I never expected this!' he went on,
trying not to pace about too much and also to control some of those sudden, jerky movements which
he'd very recently acquired and which, he could
tell, unnerved her. 'The IRA or the UVF or British
Intelligence, whoever the fuck it was picking it of
all nights!'
  Now that the central objective of 'Total Organization' had been achieved – his making contact with
Jacy – it did not seem such a serious transgression
to go back to the pouch now and then. In fact, he
persuaded himself, it could do nothing but help. By
loosening his tongue, further easing the appalling
tensions of those first few hours in the cabin.
  'Do you mind if I . . .?' he asked her. 'I just
got one or two more things to work out, you know?
It helps me to concentrate.'
  She shook her head and hugged her knees, in the
process forgetting about her damaged wrist. She
winced as the pain shot through her.
  'Did that hurt you, Jacy? I'm sorry,' he said as

he fired up the joint and drew its smoke down deep into his lungs. He looked at her and then looked away, his face flushing.

'No, Joey. I think the pain is easing now,' she replied – the first time she had spoken in ages, apart from her understandably bitter castigations. Then, to his surprise, she extended her hand. He was amazed to see her eyes twinkling.

'Can I have a puff, do you think? It might calm me down,' she said.

She smoothed back her hair and his relief was immense.

'Oh, Jacy,' he said. 'I'm sorry!' And he handed her the joint.

He couldn't afford, obviously, to succumb to sleep, but as he drifted off – *between the poles of the conscious and the unconscious, there has the mind made a swing*, he recalled from Rabindranath Tagore's *Songs of Kabir*, which The Seeker had given him many moons ago – he stiffened as he heard her say: 'I just want to understand, that's all. This "Total Organization" plan you mentioned . . .'

He relaxed a little more and skinned up another. He was stoned all right – that much he accepted – but still alert. He could hear the cops outside, still barking shit through that fucking loudhailer. He didn't care. All he wanted was to be there with her and forget the 'World of Outside', as he thought of it now. It was of no consequence. It was a stupid world, an empty one. A stupid fucking world of idiotic marksmen, tinkers' fucking dogs and bomb-happy warmongers. He sucked in the tangy smoke and exhaled as though in ecstasy. Then he bobbed his head a little while gathering his thoughts and explained: '"Total Organization" was about one thing, Jacy. It was about discipline!' he explained. 'Discipline, you know?'

She nodded understandingly. He handed her the long thin cigarette.

'Discipline,' she replied, and flicked the ash from the jay.

'If I didn't have that, if I didn't get that organized, I knew we'd never go on the journey.'

'We'd never go on what?'

'You and me, man. The journey. Yeah. Jacy and Joey. Joey Tallon and Jacy.'

'And which journey is that? What kind of a journey was it supposed to be?'

He drew long and hard on the joint.

'A journey to the West Coast. To California.'

She smiled and nodded, bobbing her head exactly as he'd done.

'California?' she said.

'Yes. But not just that. It's an inner journey too.'

'I know about things like that. My flatmate is really into that kind of stuff. She reads about it all the time. Hermann Hesse, the mystics. She's always going on about them. She wants to go to India. So tell me, Joey. Tell me about the inner journey.'

He was uplifted. She had called him 'Joey'. He knew he was fumbling a little for words because of the effects of the jay but he went on to explain as best he could about him and Mona, the longing for peace and a kind of rebirth –

'I want it to be . . . the way it should have been. For Mona, for my mother. For anyone who –'

He hesitated for a moment, then eventually found the courage.

'For anyone who's ever wondered what true love might bring . . .'

'What might it bring, Joey?' she asked him. Her arm was resting on his knee now. And all of a sudden it felt like the most natural thing in the world. Exactly as he'd expected. She tapped him gently on the thigh.

'Tell me what you think it might bring,' she said.

'It might bring you home,' he said.

He could see she understood.

'Do you know what my flatmate says? You've got to go there. That's what she says you've got to do. I want you to, Joey. I want you to come home,' she said.

That was the second beautiful thing she said. The third was: 'Don't mind them. Don't mind the world outside. There's only one thing that matters now and that's home. I want you to tell me everything, Joey. When it was you decided to embark on this journey and why you wanted to take me with you. Will you tell me that, Joey Tallon?'

He was on the verge of weeping. But he didn't. Just at the last minute he managed to pull back, a triumphant sense of achievement spreading right through him as she placed her small soft hand in his.

Well, after that, after those first few encouraging words and the gentle touch of her undamaged hand – assisted by quite a number of joints, it must be said – there was no holding Joey Tallon, who literally deluged his companion with information regarding his past and the reasons behind this 'journey' of his. Any time his explanations faltered, she encouraged him with whispers or just a look into his eyes and on he'd proceed – literally a damburst, it seemed, of sensation.

His eyes were red from the smoke of the spliff as he gingerly held her hand – he was still quite reticent but she understood that, like everything else.

'We used to talk like that for hours, me and Mona,' he told her.

She said she wanted to hear more. About Mona.

'Tell me about her,' she said, 'for I feel she's the key. She's the heart of the onion, Joey.'

They'd had a great rap earlier about Hermann Hesse in general, and *Steppenwolf* in particular.

Of course she had read it. He knew that from day one. That day in the flat.

'I adore that book, and Harry Haller,' she said. 'My flatmate is absolutely crazy about it. She's always telling me to read him. She talks for hours about *Steppenwolf*. I almost know it by heart from listening to her going on about it, for she never shuts up to tell you the truth –'

She broke off and tossed back her hair. Then she hugged her knees and said: 'No, I'm just kidding. It really *is* amazing. Harry Haller is amazing. And you know something, Joey? You remind me of him. You remind me of Harry.'

He was flattered by that and could not resist the temptation to impress her by quoting the novel.

'*Man is an onion,*' he said, '*made up of a hundred integuments. A texture made up of many threads. The ancient Asiatics knew this well enough and in the Buddhist Yoga an exact technique for understanding the illusion of the personality.*'

'I want to understand yours, Joey,' she said. 'Understand the illusion of *your* personality. Until what that means becomes clear to us, the journey cannot begin. And it's not just my flatmate talking. It's me, Joey.'

Well, if all Joey Tallon needed was the tiniest bit of encouragement to really get into his stride proper with the beautiful Jacy he certainly had got it now, and by the time the third night came around, there were very few corners of his personality that had not, at some juncture, been exposed. Very few layers of that onion which remained unpeeled. And boy did it make him, Joey Tallon, feel good! He couldn't recall ever having felt so terrific! And after having surrendered so much! Something he'd never have dared to do before – with anyone!

'It's fantastic, Jacy!' he told her. 'It's electric, feeling like this!'

'Let's dance!' she said, and he couldn't believe his ears. The song had just come on the radio. The one he had been telling her about. 10cc.

'That couldn't be just coincidence,' she said. 'Some things are meant to happen. You know that, Joey. So come on then, let's dance.'

He was so out of it now as he laid his head on her chest – she was a much better dancer than he was – that he was barely aware that either of them was singing until she placed her lips very close to his ear and he heard her crooning: *I'm not in love, so don't forget it. It's just a silly phase I'm going through . . .*

'Oh, Jacy,' he said, the words waltzing so luxuriously and effortlessly from his lips, 'it's so wonderful to be here with you.'

'Tell me about Mona again,' she said. 'Did you want to be her baby? Is that what you wanted, Joey? Or Joseph – wasn't that what she used to call you?'

As they lay there later, she told him to lay his head on her lap. 'No,' she had encouraged him, 'don't be shy now. Rest your head right here.'

The warm white cotton of her skirt touched his cheek and he thought he was in heaven. 'I know where I am now,' he said. 'I am staring out across the harbour. I am in the Land of Paradise. I have been here since The End. I will be here at The Beginning.'

He groaned quietly as she rhythmically stroked his crown and ran her index finger along the ridge of his hair. He was telling her about his father's singing now, barely aware that he was doing it at all.

'"Harbour Lights" was his song. Before he went, you see.'

'Where did he go?' she asked him. 'Can you tell me where he went? Take your time.'

Her fingers strolled languorously across his forehead. He never wanted them to stop. The rhythmic and hypnotic stroking of her nails.

'He went abroad and never returned. He set sail for some foreign harbour. As far away from this one as it is possible to get.'

'What do you mean?' she said as she laid her warm palm on his forehead.

'Where you and me are right now, Jacy. Here, in this harbour of peace.'

'That's nice, Joey. That's a nice thing to say.'

'It's true. It's home. It's the harbour with the twinkling lights that beckon. Do you know what I mean when I say that, Jacy?'

'Of course I do, Joey. And I think you know that I do.'

He nodded but didn't say anything. She began massaging his temples as she whispered: 'Sing it for me, Joey,' and he was about to demur before realizing that the soft words had assumed a life of their own:

> One evening long ago
> A ship was sailing
> One evening long ago
> Two lovers they were grieving
> A crimson sun went down
> The light began to glow –
> I saw those harbour lights
> They only told me we were parting . . .

'Far away and never to return,' sighed Jacy as he sang. 'Way across the sea. Where you and me are going, Joey!'

His heart sprang with hope as her hand softly stroked his cheek.

'To Iowa first,' he heard himself say, as his eyelids drooped. 'We'll drive across country till we reach those fields of corn. To –'

'Iowa,' she whispered, the three soothing sylla-

bles issuing from her lips like a ghostly wave
hushing in the cabin's stillness. Before:

'You haven't got long left, Tallon!'

The loudhailer's whistling feedback corkscrewed
into his consciousness and he leapt to his feet,
drawing back the curtain.

'Don't think you've got me, fuckers! This ain't
over yet! I want a car and a promise I'll be given
safe passage! Are you listening to me?'

He saw the detective raise the megaphone. Then
something silly happened. He started stuttering
and was afraid to say anything after that in case
he'd get the words all confused and end up saying:
'I want a safe car and a commitment to passage!'
or something like that. So in the end he just
snapped: 'Fuck you, pig! Pgghew! Pgghew! You got
that, huh?'

He was glad to hear Jacy's voice again, and to
see that smile as she drew him towards her.

He was so tired when he lay in her lap again that
he was glad when she said she'd do the skinning up
this time, because he knew that even if he tried he
probably wouldn't have been able to manage it. He
was just so fucking stoned and tired, that was all!
All he wanted to do now was get out on that road
and get the fuck out of Scotsfield once and for
all! His eyelids began to droop. Then, suddenly,
his whole body went rigid as he snapped: *No! I
won't let it happen! For that's exactly what they
want, those fuckers! They want me to crash out! But
no fucking way! No fucking way, right, Jacy?
They're just waiting for fatigue to set in!*

She nodded and dragged on the joint. 'Here,' she
said, 'just a little toke.'

He loved it when she ran those fingers through
his hair, what precious little he had of it. He
laughed when he thought of that. The blue fug of
the smoke was a turban unwinding magically in the

196

air in the eerie silence of the small hours. It was
so tensely quiet. Quiet, that is, apart from the
occasional bulletin on the radio regarding the
'ongoing' situation.

'You've got to get away from him, Jacy,' said
Joey. 'He's a dangerous man. There are some things
I could tell you. Things that would chill your
blood. One day maybe I will. You got to believe me,
Jacy. You got to come with me.'

'You know what's funny about you, Joey?' he heard
her say. 'It's that you're so gentle. You hear them
saying things about you around the town . . .'

'*Things?*' he smiled – Jeez, he was exhausted, but
he definitely wouldn't give in – 'Things like what
– Barbapapa, say? Or just big fat stupid Joey?'

'Maybe,' she went on as she exhaled the smoke.
'But whatever they say they're wrong. They've got
you all wrong, Joey. You are The Gardener. What he
could have been.'

They had spoken about Charlie for hours the night
before. How, for him, if things had turned out otherwise . . .

'You see flowers where others see only weeds. You
know what I'm saying, Joey?'

He smiled. Sure he did. A day from the past rose
up out of nowhere, shining.

'I used to bring Mona primroses,' he told her.

There was a pause and he luxuriated in the
rhythms of her breathing.

'What was it you liked about Mona? The more I
think about it the more she truly seems to be the
heart of the onion. The key to who you are, Joey
Tallon. There was something about her, wasn't
there?'

He thought of those first few days after Mona's
funeral when he'd go out to the reservoir to listen
to her soul.

'It would only last a moment, before it went back
far beyond the clouds, or wherever it is they go.'

197

'They go home, Joey. That's where they go.'

He nodded. 'Yes,' he agreed, 'they go home.'

She pecked the top of his head with kisses. Tiny little 'popping' pecks. They felt exquisite. She rubbed his chest with her palm and dangled her arm around his neck. She gave him another little peck. He was weak.

'And where do you think it is, that home? Where does Joey Tallon think that home is to be found?'

He swallowed and tried not to think again of his mother weeping by the sink in the shadows of the kitchen. Once she had screamed: 'So that's where he's gone – to ride prostitutes in China! That's what they're saying, isn't it? But it doesn't matter where he's gone! For he's left her with the bastard and me with the shame and to a living death in this fucking town! But I won't "living die"! I'll *die*!'

Her eyes had been the size of the plates she was supposed to be washing.

'I'll die! That's what I'll do!' she had insisted as she twisted the dishcloth tighter.

'But she didn't die, did she, Joey?' said Jacy. 'Your mother didn't die.'

'No. She got Alzheimer's and they put her away. She died then. That was when she died.'

'I'm sorry.'

'It doesn't matter,' said Joey as his fingers brushed her bound wrist, occasioning an agonizing wrench of guilt. He looked away and tried not to think of his father, out there beneath a foreign sky. Or of Mona, so pale and abstracted . . .

'Where did Joey really believe,' she began anew, 'that that kind of rest might be found?'

Her nails described little threads and patterns up and down his forehead. She placed another tender kiss on his shining pate.

'In the Karma Cave maybe? Is that what he thought? Is that where he thought he might find it?'

His saliva was thick as paste and his face was blotched as he tried to meet her eyes. But he hadn't the courage when it came to the crunch. However, he could feel his own eyes glittering with excitement as, at the very last moment, he avoided hers.

It was like all the skins were peeling away at once. If there is a millisecond in one's life when every ache is assuaged and every sharp-edged anxiety that is born of entombed, unspoken secrets in a single instant goes floating free, it occurred in that space just before the 'precious moment'. When Jacy had whispered in his ear: 'Tell me everything, Joey. I want you to surrender completely now. Let me take these glasses off.'

He could feel all his tensions ease as he gave himself to her totally. He could hear Mona's voice, he told her, calling to him from an island. Out of nowhere he heard, elegiac but vivid, the strains of 'Harbour Lights'. It was as though, he explained, he were on a tiny boat, alone in the vast silence of a cobalt ocean. Then there were strange lights winking on the horizon and bizarre sounds echoing in the darkness. They were calling to him, but Joey only heard Mona, her voice coming from a tranquil place that was rimmed by coral reefs and palm-fringed beaches. That was the only sound he could hear now. The others were far off and had nothing to say to him in any case. The bizarre sounds, they were the blades of helicopters. Mona's whisper gliding just above the lapping water: *'Come to the island of green-roofed temples* [was it perhaps where his father was? Was that where he had gone all those years ago?]*, towards this safe harbour sail. And sleep in the Cave of Dreams. For ever in the Cave of –'*

The twin prongs of the peninsula slowly opened in a 'Y' as onward he sailed and the first rumble issued from the mountain.

'Was it like this?' whispered Jacy. 'Move your head up further, my darling. Come on now, Joseph, don't be afraid. Move it right up – further.'

His head was positioned between Jacy's legs. He slowly closed his eyes and the feeling that enveloped him then was so tranquil and rare, such a calm as he had never experienced. But somewhere – close by – he was deeply embarrassed. Jacy understood, however. She massaged his temples again and scissored her legs. He was finding it difficult to breathe and trying, through gesture, to indicate that. But it was just to galvanize him, she said, to locate and identify that strength of purpose within him, and then to consolidate it. The *doing* rather than the *thinking*, she explained.

'I can feel the old tensions returning, Joey. And they're telling you to fight it. They're telling you not to surrender.'

He knew she was right. She was speaking the truth. He felt ashamed of his resistance, trifling as it was, compared to what it would, without a doubt, have been in the past. Before he'd *learnt* – from Jacy, and from *Steppenwolf*.

'You've got to show courage,' she insisted. 'It's essential for the journey. For the truth, the essence. Bring your head up further. Go on. Bring it up further, Joey. There's a good boy. Don't be shy.'

For a number of glorious seconds he vertiginously bobbed upon that lapping ocean. He swayed, light-headed, far out in the blue. Then felt her stiffening sharply as he choked: 'No, Jacy.' But she didn't hear him as all of a sudden the peninsula prongs closed. The winking of the lights seemed an anxious semaphore now. In her voice was the same rigidity that had invaded her body.

'Tell me what she called you, Joey,' she said.

Her rigid legs locked around his neck. He could feel the white cotton material bunching up in her lap. One of her shoes had fallen off.

'I said, tell me what she called you, Joey.'

'Jacy, you're hurting me! I can't breathe -!'

For a split second, he felt certain he'd blacked out completely. Once, as a child, he'd put a plastic bag -

'What did she call you, baby?'

A flaring meteor of hot ash coursed a perilous trajectory across the sky.

'Did she call you "baby"? Is that what she called you, Joey?'

A spume of lava like a deadly orchid mockingly, lyrically fanned its petals then, unexpectedly, swooped to devour an entire temple.

'That's it, darling,' said Jacy. 'Tell me! Tell Jacy how you like to put your head up between girls' legs! Tell us, Joey! Tell the world! Let's share your secret! What is it you want? What have you always wanted?'

The sky shone saffron. A giant wave reared silently, then fell, devastating everything in its path.

'I want to be reborn!'

'You want to live again!'

'I wanted to live life over!'

'You wanted to climb inside Mona!'

'I wanted to climb inside Mona!'

'You wanted to be her baby!'

'I wanted to be her -! *Tthht!*'

'That's it, Joey! That's it, Joey! Suck it! Suck that thumb!'

'*Tthht!*'

'You're safe in the Karma Cave now, Joey!'

'Safe and home with Jacy!'

'With her you'll be safe in this precious harbour!'

'Safe for ever in this precious harbour!'

She relaxed her grip, and he knew the 'precious moment' was at hand. He could feel it approaching with almost every fibre of his being. The precious moment he'd for so long craved.

'Safe for ever, *you twisted fucking bastard*!'

Huge blocks of steaming pumice bounced lethally down the volcano's side. The entire island shuddered in the wake of another explosion. The crimson lava streamed into his eye. A column of red ash swirled out of it as she raked her nails along his cheek. He heard her scream and, blurred, watched her falling towards the door. The door swung open before her and she tumbled out into the night. The mountain cracked and the zig-zag fissure that ran down its front almost discreetly parted to reveal a core of light, but not the one he'd been expecting. There were cries of panic coming from all over the island. The floodlights were beaming directly at him. *'Jacy!'* he called, and struggled to his feet. He shouted after her again as the cabin door slammed behind him.

There were one, two, three, four marksmen all in firing position with their rifles trained. But he couldn't see them properly because of the hot fire. *'Don't fucking move, you cunt!'* the detective barked as he placed his coat around her. Then turned on him: *'Don't even think about it, Tallon, you fucker!'* he hissed.

He tried to locate her to explain. But she was gone. Instead, Boyle Henry was there, close by the yellow Datsun, smiling. Smiling directly at him, as if to say: 'You see? You understand now, don't you, Joey? No matter what you do, *I'll win*!'

He brushed away the sparks – some of them had gotten into his mouth. He was still trying to poke the remainder of the joint out of the blinded hollow of his eye – there was ash all down his front – when he saw Boyle Henry giving him a cheeky little wave before climbing into the car, as a voice just beside him said: *'Can you look this way, Mr Tallon, I'm from RTE!'*

A Psychobilly Version?

Even though I knew that a lot of it was still too personal and would have to be fictionalized and modified at some point, there can be no doubt that I was absolutely over the moon next morning having finished the script. On my way to work I thought about Johnston and how he'd been telling us one night about this guy Balzac, who, at last having discovered how his novel was going to pan out, threw open the window of his bedroom and shouted: *'He's dead! He's dead! Listen, everyone – the old fucker is dead!'*

Although obviously he didn't say 'fucker'. It's just that I couldn't remember the character's name.

The great thing – not just having honed it down and getting to the essential truth, although that was exciting too – was the way the style was beginning to emerge – already I could see it all inside my head. What it needed, more than anything, was that *psychobilly* touch. Which would be in keeping with the milieu in which it was set, a trashy and sinister country-and-western Ireland of murder, paranoia and sentiment – a sort of rough and ready treatment of the original idea, not unlike The Mohawks' music. Unadorned, no bullshit. *Blam!* Just get in there and do it, no frills, no fucking around. A movie that could be put together not only pretty fast but relatively cheaply as well. By the time I reached the college, I had decided that was the way to go. I could see it all so clearly, frame by frame. And how it ought to be directed.

For a start, I was going to use amateur actors, there being no doubt in my mind after the workshops I'd been doing with the kids that almost anyone could hack it as an actor. Of course they could! If someone could pick up a guitar and start belting out psychobilly tunes, not to mention storm the arenas of the world shouting about Martin Luther King, the way that Bono and co. seemed to be able to do, then I didn't really see what the problem was with acting. It would be, in the words of Chico, a piece of piss.

'People have been acting since the day they were born,' I said to myself as I came striding in the college gates. Even guys like Mangan would be able to do it, I reckoned, regardless of what they thought themselves. And, having bought him a doll, I figured he owed me a favour or two. So I'd probably be calling on his services. For the part of one of the 'old boys'.

old boy 1 – Mangan, I thought, and laughed.

Unlocking my office, I thought, *Yes, guys like Mangan would be as good as anyone, educated or fucking well not! Once they were given the confidence they'd be more than able to cut the mustard.*

After my first two seminars – which went terrifically well, I have to say! – I made a start on the production script and blocked out the first six scenes during lunch that day.

The Set-up Scene

The very first scene I felt was pretty much well worked out. First of all we would see the tinker camp, with broken prams, car wrecks, dogs howling and the various beat-up old caravans, as the fire dies in the wee small hours, and then – *wham!* – one of Boo Boo's songs comes blasting right over the soundtrack as we zoom in straight away on her inflatable face.

What we would have to get – essential, I reckoned – was the sheer unfathomable depth of helplessness in the doll figure's eyes as he pushed himself deep inside her (the camera zooming in on the lettering *'Not a cardboard imitation! Not an undersized toy! Genuine life-size inflatable with three workable openings!'*). Then, perhaps, a bold black psychobilly logo:

Ireland, 1976! The Gypsy Camp!

On second thoughts, no, we wouldn't bother with that, I reflected, and scribbled it out. Instead we'd go straight away into the scene, with the camera holding on the eyes all the way through as he kisses her face and runs his hands through her hair saying, 'I love you, I love you, I love you.' There would be a torn old sofa. A tatty slipper. He is kissing her belly button and his trousers are around his knees. But we don't see his face – Mangan would never agree to it if that was the arrangement. Then all we hear is an almighty, unearthly squeal – I could do that voice-over myself – as he reaches his climax, and the coruscating guitars go squealing ahead, until they're spinning almost out of control . . .

Then we hear another scream and the camera, having remained static all the way through, out of nowhere goes *vroom!* and careers wildly across the screen. Straightaway back to the doll with her pink, plump cheeks and the oval red mouth that never makes any sound. I banged down my new scene title and, having considered it for a bit, was more or less happy with it. It read:

SCENE 1: 'The Lakelands' Saddest Fuck'

Swinging through the double doors on my way back to class after lunch, having got the rest of the scene finished to my satisfaction, I was positively exhilarated. I knew in my gut it was going to be a powerful opener: the camera ever so slowly pulling away, with the doll's button eyes just staring at the ceiling. It would be hard for Mangan to execute, of course, and I knew the old fucker would probably protest, even if we were just going to see his warty old back. But a crate of beer ought to sort out that, I thought – no, knew!

Plus the prospect of having other assorted items purchased for him in the backstreet sex shops of the capital.

Her Ladyship

Which was exactly what transpired, Mangan, already out of it after all the beer we'd drunk, practically tearing the camera out of my hands, in fact, as I outlined the project to him. Stumbling around the place pointing it like he's fucking Bergman or Bertolucci, framing me in the viewfinder with this great big leer on his face, going: *'Don't be thinking you'll blame it all on me! I seen you at it plenty of times! Talking away to her and everything, like she was your wife, haw haw!'*

He swung the camera towards her, as she lay there beside the bed with her head flopped on to her chest.

'I heard you! Mona this! Mona that! You were at it the whole time and don't deny it! Don't start saying different, Mr Film Man! Hee hee!'

Which I had to admit was true. I didn't see any point in denying it any longer, especially not to him, seeing as he was capable of far worse activities in that department himself. For I'd heard *him*! Anyway, I was completely shit-faced that night, not only because of the beer but also from the sheer excitement of his having agreed so readily to come on board with the project. I mean, he was the very first actor I'd asked!

Drunk as I was, just lying there on the floor of his caravan, I had this great feeling about the movie. That there was this kind of weird light around it, you know? That no matter what you did, somehow you just couldn't lose.

The only thing that went wrong that night was when I woke up back in my own bed, bathed in sweat and with Mona's pale face looking at me from behind the curtain of black hair as she trembled and said: '*He didn't really see us, did he? Tell me he didn't hear us, Joseph!*'

Meaning, of course, that Mangan hadn't been aware of our . . . relationship, if you could call it that.

'No,' I told her, 'he didn't!', instinctively turning from those penetrating dead doll eyes. I still lay with her sometimes, whenever the depressions would come on. They could be troubling, those eyes. They were eyes that said: '*I'm neutral. It's nothing to do with me. None of it. It's all the one to me, Joseph.*'

I didn't get to sleep for an hour or two after that. But the next morning I felt fine again, and why wouldn't I when I was about to embark on the project of a lifetime? The *real truth* about 1976 in an ordinary old backwoods country 'n' Irish town. A hillbilly, rockabilly backwater full of shady politicos, sex movies, female wrestlers and dead detectives.

Not to mention activists for peace getting blown to kingdom come!

I figured I had all bases pretty much covered, because if I was prepared to tell the truth about my own life – with the names subtly changed, of course – it wouldn't seem that I was being unfair to anyone else. No one would be able to say: 'You steal our story but you won't tell your own! That's not playing the game, Joey boy!'

No, that wouldn't come into it because it wasn't that kind of project. Truth and . . . *verisimilitude* – is that the word? – well, truth anyway would be of the essence.

I'd just sit there in my office, thinking, whenever the kids had gone for their lunch: *Yes! Here he is! Scotsfield's own Andy Warhol! The John Cassavetes of the lakelands!*, with everybody clapping as they presented me with some award, don't ask me what.

I had seen all of Cassavetes' work by now – they had a stack of his movies in the new information technology section of the library. I liked the way he shot his pictures and – I was quite prepared to admit it – would definitely be stealing some of his tricks. Lots of hand-held camera movements, in what they called on the back of the case '*cinema verité style*', as well as extreme close-ups and lots of rough-shod camerawork. I was still without a title, though. I had gone off *The Plan*, for it had begun to seem kind of . . . ordinary. As though it were just about me and Jacy and what had happened between us 'that fateful night', to employ a phrase of Johnston Farrell's, when, in fact, it had begun to open out now in all sorts of directions and encompass much more than that. I came up with about fifty possibilities, but none of them proved to be satisfactory.

However, it didn't worry me. I knew it would come in time.

(The proposed titles are extensively listed in the back of the 'Community College Ledger', along with all sorts of doodles and sketchy plot ideas. There is even a drawing of the principal with a shoal of arrows raining down on her and me storming off with my camera going: '*Fume!*' as this raincloud of rage gathers over my head!)

The Movie – Yeah!
(Early p. m. – we got the half day off)

The more I've been thinking about the movie, the more I keep thinking, The more fucking realistic the better. A real, in your face, yeah-this-is-the-way-it-was-my-friend-type approach. With lots of fuzz guitar and heavy reverb. (note: must talk to Boo Boo in detail about the soundtrack), *and actual newsreels of those turbulent times intercut with our improvised, videotaped footage. Some of it will be documentary-style, in other places hard-hitting drama. I can't wait to get started pitching it to some people, and if I wasn't having such trouble with Mrs Carmody – she called me into her office again today – I'd get on a bus and head straight on up to the smoke.*

Wait till I tell you! I couldn't believe it when I was rummaging through the paper this morning, waiting for the kids to arrive, and who did I come on? Only Johnston Farrell! 'Well, what do you know,' I said to myself, hardly able to believe what I was reading! Turns out his 'border-country thriller' (that's what they're calling it) has, apparently, had offers not from one but three *major publishers. And not just in Ireland either, where they're known for paying buttons, but across the water in London, where they say the money is big.*

I didn't know what to think when I saw his photo. Part of me felt kinda queasy and, I suppose, in another way – if I'm honest – kinda jealous. But then I thought: That's just fucking stupid, Joey! Small-town petty envy, that's all it is, and it's kind of beneath you, my friend, Joey Tallon! *So I knuckled myself on the forehead a bit and thought that the next time I happened to be up in Dublin I'd poke around a bit and search him out. I thought that was a pretty good idea, all right. Talk about old times and shit. I smiled and said to myself: 'Well, how about that! Good man, Johnston!'*

But even after thinking some more about how stupid it had been to be jealous, I couldn't put this other thought out of my head, and as the kids filed in couldn't stop myself from wondering. I'd keep seeing his face as we sat there in Austie's way back then during the long winter nights. 'Yes, Joey, tell me more!' I'd hear him saying – he was always writing things down – 'Was there a bed in the cabin? At what point did she cry?' He even asked me where she had gone to the toilet, for fuck's sake! Mad! And I began to feel a twinge of resentment. I did, and I won't deny it!

But after a while I decided I was just being paranoid, and the session with the kids that day turned out to be so good that all I could think as I handed around the sheets – 'The Films of Cassavetes', which I'd photocopied from a film book entitled: Movies of the Great Directors *– was when would I get a chance to jump on a bus and hit the city. To rap with Johnston, my good old buddy, whatever disagreements we might once have had now consigned at last to the dustbin of history.*

The Community College Ledger
(*Film Production Notes* – dateless)

Withdrawn from the Scholarship of Hope!

All I can say is if not being able to figure out scenes in your script or having difficulty with what they call in the actors' manuals the 'motivation' of a character is like walking around with a stone in your shoe, well, let me tell you there are plenty of other kinds of problem too. Chief among them being people who one minute are clambering all over you telling you how great you are, and the next are clicking their heels and going past as they give you this look . . . all I can say is it would freeze the fucking desert! Not only that, but now they've informed me they've withdrawn me from the Scholarship of Hope competition . . .

The worst part of it is not knowing what you've done wrong. For at least if you knew that . . .

I don't know, it's fucking bothering me, that's all I know!

26th . . . Late evening, here in the caravan

Well, in the end I decided I could take it no more and demanded a private meeting with Fr Connolly, who's really getting on now and I know would rather not be bothered with things like this, but I just had to speak to someone.

'What's the use of saying one thing and then going back on it, Father?' I asked him. 'Then how is anybody to know where they stand?'

We had a good long chat in his office and he asked me what exactly I had been doing. I gave him the whole lowdown. About being in the process of making a feature we could maybe sell to the studios with a view towards clinching a three-picture deal. Obviously I kept the detail to a minimum. I mean, I might be stupid, but at the end of the day the man is a padre so I wasn't going to start on about life-size synthetic dolls or any of that business. 'It's essentially about rebirth,' I told him, and he looked kind of sad when I said it. Like it was something he wouldn't mind experiencing himself. Anyway, I said goodbye to him and he said he'd do what he could, fair play to him.

Which wasn't very much, apparently, for two hours later who comes bursting into my office (well, it's not actually mine as such – I share it with Eddie the supervisor)? Only Mrs Carmody, with this fucking face on her like she's about to have a stroke. Then she starts going on about money again. At first I was afraid I was going to blow my top, but fortunately not – good sense prevailed – and I permitted her to rabbit away. Then I said: 'But at the beginning of the year I was informed that I was entitled to spend what I liked. That there was loads of money in the kitty for equipment. All of it coming from Europe. That's what they told me, Mrs Carmody! They really did now, and you can confirm it with your colleagues if you wish!'

That, she said, was the last straw, then glares at Eddie as she throws this bill on to the desk with the various bits and pieces that I'd ordered since I came meticulously compiled into a neat little list, with each place and date of purchase marked, as well as the model and brand name. I stared at it for a minute, then coughed politely. I suppose I was hoping to spot some small error on their part, the better to enable me to argue my case. But there was none that I could see. Whoever had written the list had done their job and done it well. I coughed again and scanned it carefully one last time. I could feel her scowling at me. I read:

Item
Pelco VS5104 4 by 1 sequential switcher – £50
Magna Tech MD636-C mag film dubber w/long life, 1, 3, 4 track heads – £6,000
Canon DV camcorders (3) – £4,290
Olympus Digital still cameras (2) – £1,280
Nikon ED 50–3,000 mm zoom lens – £1,000
Asstd equipment (inc. Lowell and Century Strand kit) – £2,300

'Are you aware that the total cost of these items is over fifteen thousand pounds?' she said.

'Is that how much they are?' I replied. It was a stupid answer, I realize that.

'Yes, it is, as you very well *know*, Mr Tallon!' were her final words as she spun and stood in the doorway.

I didn't quite know what to say. I stared at her for a minute then looked away, regretfully. I was sorry that it had come to this. All I had wanted was to get along with everybody. With Carmody. The staff. Everyone. It was just a pity it hadn't worked out that way. Eddie attacked me too, once she had left. He told me he was sending the great bulk of the equipment back. And that he had '*no fucking intention*' of covering for me any more. 'You fucking got that, Joey?' he snapped. 'Always too far! You always push it too far! But not with me! Never fucking again! Got that? You got that, Tallon, you fucking –?'

'Charming.' That was all I could think as he slammed the door. I lifted the list to look at it one last time before putting it away and starting work on my script, which, unlike certain relationships in Scotsfield Community College, was forging ahead with a life of its own.

It was something that really did lift my heart! I just couldn't wait to direct it, make it come alive! Take it to that final stage! See those characters live and breathe in whatever way the kids might choose to interpret them!

And what fucking good kids they were! Already you could tell there were some fabulous actors amongst them. *And actresses too, don't forget now, Joey!* If not world class, then definitely fucking close.

It was all I could do while sitting in that office, tweaking this scene and that, not to fling down my pen and go running off to the video suite to grab the nearest camcorder and – fuck the begrudgers! – shout *'Action!'* as loud as I could.

The Return of Bonehead

That afternoon, when I was coming in after lunch and talking to one of the kids who was asking me about Cassavetes, I let this great big yelp out of me when I saw a vision, a wee fat man so nimble on his feet but with not a screed of hair on his head, being led along the corridor by one of my students.

'*Bonehead!*' I called and pressed the shutter-release button on the Canon camera I happened to be carrying. Well, you want to see the face of him, putting the hand up to cover his face – '*No, please! No, please!*', like he's this big fucking celebrity! – as I framed him in the viewfinder, calling out: '*Over here, Mr Stokes, if you please!*' and '*Ladies and gentlemen! We present: "The Return of Bonehead"!*' Us all having the best of a laugh then until, predictably enough, one of the students goes: 'Sssk! Sssk! Here she comes!', and who's there at the end of the corridor? Yes, Mrs Carmody, principal, immobile there with her hands on her hips as if to say: 'So is this what you call *creative arts* as well? Is this what he calls *creative arts*?'

Which made me decide it would be best to call a halt to that little episode and take Bonehead off down to the staffroom for tea. He was in his element being introduced to all the teachers, putting on this accent so they would think he was educated too.

I never fail, even now, to laugh when he puts on that voice. 'Yes indeed, I've studied quite a bit myself, *akshilly*!' he says. It can be hard to hold it together once you hear him saying stuff like that, especially when the half-tinker inflections come peeping out, although you wouldn't want to let him hear you saying that! He'd go fucking loopers!

So then after school we went out for a drink and I've never heard him sound so good.

'Well, fuck me pink!' he says. 'Boys but you're the man, Joesup, so you are. I always knew you'd do it. You've landed on your feet now, all right! The head buck cat in a swanky college! You're in charge of the whole shebang?'

'I wouldn't say I'm in charge of it, Bone,' I said. 'I'm more of a facilitator, yeah?'

'Do you hear him! A – *what*? You're a long way from Mountjoy now, Tallon, you boy, you! You effing facilitator, you! How the hell are you doing, Joesup?'

All I could say to him was that as far as I could see it wasn't me but him who had come this long way he was talking about. 'No sign of the sombrero this time anyway, Bone, eh?' I said, as he laughed and said: 'Aye! Do you remember that! Me and me frigging sombrero! Sure I only wore that for a laugh now, Joey, as you well fucking know!'

After that we got well stuck in and he told me all the news. Turned out that he'd met someone else and got on with her like a house on fire. 'She's the making of me, man,' he told me. 'I adore the ground she walks on. The last woman, she was good but . . . well, we had trouble like . . .'

He turned away and I noticed it again – that flinching from your gaze I'd seen in Mountjoy – as he mumbled something indistinct. I hadn't a clue what it was. It only dawned on me later that he'd been on about the children's homes again. I went to the toilet then and when I came back he was fine. It was like nothing at all had happened.

'But here, that's enough about me! How the fuck are they hanging, me old friend Joesup?'

He gets a grip of me then and stands a couple of feet away, appraising me sunnily. 'Let me look at you!' he says. 'Well, whoever would have thought it? The Tallon boy! The fucking one-man army, becripes!'

'Hey! Hey! Come on!' I said, and hit him a punch. I didn't want to hear that stuff, not even in jest. All I wanted to know now was the truth and for everybody else to know about it too. And very soon they would.

'Sure,' he said, 'sure thing, old friend. Have another whiskey! Man but it's great to see you! You and Pajo Stokes was always the best of mates! Right through the bad times, right, Joesup, old pal? And always will be!'

He told me he was living in London now, working at the fly-tipping, the only problem being that there were a lot of 'tinkers' in that line of work. But it paid good money so what did he care, he said. 'They live their life and I live mine, Joesup,' he told me. It really was terrific to see him sounding and looking so good. And the way he spoke of his new woman – well, it was shit you don't hear often. 'Love' (or, more accurately, 'lub'), he reflected, drifting away as he said it, 'you hear them going on about it in the songs – Daniel O'Donnell and that – but you never really think it'll happen to you. Did you ever think that way, Joesup?'

'Love is like armour, Bone,' I told him. 'Once you've got it wrapped around you, you're damned well indestructible!'

'Now you're talking, Joesup!' he said. 'That's exactly the way I feel since meeting herself!'

I gave him the soul-brother handclasp then left him at the bus, for he had to get back to Dublin to catch the plane for London in the morning. We stood in the square for a bit while the engine was still running. 'One way or another you'll keep in touch, OK? Sorry I mentioned that stuff before. That auld one-man army stuff! Sure it's all auld shite! What do you and me care, Joesup? All we care about is that we're mates! That's all in the past now, Joey! All in the past, just like Mountjoy! The only good thing about that place was Recks! Am I right, eh, Joey?'

'Right!' I said and gripped his hand again.

'You know what's the best part?' he said. 'The nicest part of all? Getting to where we are now, Joey. The place that you never think you'll get to at all. It's like the end of the journey. And it makes it all worthwhile.'

He paused and then said: 'Congratulations, Joesup. You've done powerful for yourself. Mr Recks would be proud of you, so he would.'

Tttht!

Spontaneously, I embraced him. And remained there till the bus was gone. Then I went back up the town and dropped into Doc Oc's to make a few notes (the time was drawing near – first day of principal photography, that is!) and have a nice glass of wine to end the day.

It hadn't been my intention to remain there very long but when I became aware of Austie staring across at me with this tense expression on his face, I began to get the distinct impression that it might not be a bad idea for me to consider perusing my notes elsewhere. He kept wiping the counter with the dishcloth in slow, methodical arcs, smiling in the direction of Hoss Watson – now, as I'd learnt, the proud director of Lake County Spring Water ('the freshness of the nineties!') and looking every inch of it in his tailored Armani suit, but still very much 'one of the lads' – who was standing over by the pool table, cleaning his nails with the point of a dart and craning his neck towards the back of the bar. It was then I saw Boyle Henry slowly turning to look at me with a smirk on his face – not so much 'enigmatic', it has to be said, very much more 'contemptuous'.

Which made me do what can only be considered a very stupid thing. I started gathering up my books and getting ready to leave, but at the same time trying to make it look casual. As though it were a spontaneous act and nothing at all to do with them. But on the way out I dropped some of the books, then carried on across the street as though

I hadn't even noticed. I could hear Sandy McGloin shouting: *'Hey! Barbapapa! You forgot your books!'*

I was so dehydrated when I got back to the camp that I had to drink five glasses of water. 'I'm fine now,' I said to myself. But then I began to sweat. However, not to worry, I reassured myself as I lay down on the bed. It was a new doll but the same Mona. She was wearing her black wig with the centre parting and her long floaty dress. The wig looked a little lopsided, so I did my best to fix it, trying to steady my hands as I did so. I didn't put any lipstick on her. On Mona. Except that it wasn't Mona. It wasn't Mona Galligan, was it? Never had been and never would be. But I laid my head on her breast anyway. I lay on her breast. No, I didn't. It was between her legs I lay. Between her legs, way in under that skirt. And do you know what else I did? I sucked my thumb. I sucked my thumb and lisped: *'Tttht!'*

And then it was like I'd never been in the pub or seen Boyle Henry at all, safe for ever with her in the cave of wishful dreams.

Sandy Serious?

I was still feeling a little bit off colour the next morning so I took the day off and went off out to the reservoir to do some work on my script. I had made myself a lovely little hideout there – a sort of quiet little cove all covered over with briars where you could work away to your heart's content. So as soon as I arrived, I got stuck in and, after an hour or so of intensive labour, *bingo!*

Which if you find yourself believing, then sorry to say you are a very credulous person, for actually bingo nothing, and even after another two hours all I had managed to write were endless pages of disorientated rubbish. Even the handwriting itself was hard to read – might as well have been Swahili or Arabic for all the sense it made.

But when I reflected – I was on the verge of tears a couple of times and I know that must really sound stupid – I began to realize that it was only because I was still tense after the incident in the pub. Particularly because of the look Boyle Henry had given me. I tried not to think about it and after a while I gradually began to settle down and relax. I crossed my legs and performed some exercises, the way the author advises you to do in *Becoming a Writer* by Dorothea Brande, another of my favourite books. It emphasizes that you should let whatever is bothering you come out and never ever try to impose your will, for it will inevitably affect the material. Now, as I felt them fading away – cares or anxieties or whatever you might want to call them – I had no intention of doing any such thing. All I was concerned about was sitting there and writing away to my heart's content.

With Gogol's water flowing ever so gently and the birds chirping merrily beside me.

After the success of that session – triumphant banishment of cares! – I tried my level best to make sure that every day, come rain, come shine, I always managed to get an hour or two out there after school. Preferably in the evening or what you often hear called the 'gloaming'. I loved that word and sort of employed it as a mantra whenever I'd be doing the exercises. Which I happened to be in the middle of one day –

'*In the gloaming as the silver water –*' I was murmuring softly to myself, slowly closing my eyes as I did so.

'*Boo!*'

It was Sandy McGloin. '*Boo!*' he cried again, lunging at me, 'Boyle Henry's looking for you!'

I didn't mean to cry out '*Jesus!*' but it had slipped from my lips before I was able to do anything about it. That amused him.

'I'm only joking you, Joey!' he laughed then. 'Sure he's not looking for you at all!'

He flipped open a packet of cigarettes and asked me did I want one. I said, no, I'd given up.

'Tell me,' he said as he dragged on a Major, 'When I said just now that Boyle Henry was after you, did you believe me, Joey?'

I said no. Actually what I said was: '*No!*' and '*I'm not sure!*'

Words you don't want can sometimes leap out.

'No,' he went on, 'he isn't after you. What would he be after you for? Sure all that business with you and his woman Jacy, that's all in the past now, Joey. Isn't it?'

I nodded. Vehemently. 'That's right. It's all water under the bridge, Sandy. At least I hope so.'

He cupped the cigarette in his hand and stared at it as he said: 'If anyone ever brings it up, I'd hurt them.'

Then he looked at me with a sad, appealing smile on his face.

'I'm serious, Joey,' he went on, as he pulled on the cigarette, 'because we have a duty to forget all these bad things that happened. It does no one any good to dwell on their past. You kidnap someone, terrify them, whatever. You do your time, and that's it. You've paid your debt. End of story.'

He smiled and went off about his business. As he was going past the sycamore, he turned on his heel and called back: 'Be seeing you then, Joey. Like the waistcoat, by the way!'

Unconsciously, then, after he'd said that, I found myself tugging at it with a kind of uncertain defiance. It was a paisley-patterned waistcoat, kind of similar to the one that Johnston used to wear but without the tortoiseshell buttons. All of a sudden I laughed when I became aware of the umbrage I'd taken. Realizing he had probably meant nothing at all. Just his peculiar idea of a joke – making oblique comments about people's dress. But of course, when you thought about it, that wasn't so unusual. People of Sandy's generation, they passed remarks on everything. The kids now, they were much different. A lot of them had actually admired the waistcoat, in fact. As far as they were concerned, you could wear whatever the fuck you liked. You'd see them coming and going in their black polo necks with their zippered brief cases all set to get started on their scripts for the day and they really just did not give a toss. The likes of Sandy and his generation, given half a chance they'd spend the next twenty years talking about a pair of trousers if they thought they'd get away with it, never mind a paisley-patterned vest, as the Americans call it.

I decided to forget all about it and, chewing on my pencil, began to work anew. I laid my hand on my brow. The sweat had almost completely gone. I felt triumphant. I looked at the tops of the trees and it was as though in one bound I could have cleared them!

'Life is beautiful!' I exclaimed, and set to like a demon. And in less than fifteen minutes I had written over ten whole pages, the world for as far back as I could remember never having seemed so good. All I could think of as I made my way home was how I could ever have been so stupid as to worry my head about Boyle. And whether Sandy McGloin had been serious or not! Which made it all the more ridiculous when I broke into a sweat passing by Boyle Henry's house and caught a glimpse of his wife moving about inside. But I did. The perspiration was rolling off me, in fact.

And as I sat there naked to the waist – I'd taken off my shirt and hung it over the sink to dry – I tried to see reason and convince myself of how stupid such a reaction had been, which is a much harder thing to do than you'd think.

Those Ten Pages . . .

. . . have survived all right in a box file in the archive. But they make absolutely no sense and are mostly concerned with the songs of the birds and the noise the water was making. Another piece from the same file written around the same time on, for a change, beautiful vellum, wherever that came out of – a certain principal's office, most likely – is, in the main, much more comprehensible.

Some Notes by Joseph Mary Tallon . . .
The Reservoir, Towards Dusk . . .

Working on the script and reading Dorothea Brande every day has consolidated the sense of inner peace and I can feel it getting stronger. It's a really wonderful feeling and, I think, all the better for having been earned. It is obviously also bound to pay marvellous dividends in terms of the script's actual quality. I feel emboldened – is that the word? – even my using it being testimony to the veracity of what I'm saying. Meaning the manner in which everything seems to be conspiring to assist me in my quest as a – inverted commas here, I guess – creative person! What I find particularly helpful, it must be said, is the feedback I receive from the students regarding the nature and quality of my work. That has become increasingly beneficial.

There was a visiting group here from Sandymount in Dublin, and they told us they found a lot of the psychotherapy work we've been doing very interesting and original. It isn't, of course, directly connected to the creative studies course as such, but the possibilities of it seemed so powerful that when I came across the text by Dorothy Heathcote completely by accident during the course of my researches I felt it was much too valuable an opportunity to pass up. I thought it absolutely incomparable, in fact, dealing as it does with the nature of personality – our fears and anxieties and so forth. There was no doubt in my mind that it was related, however indirectly, to the work we were doing on the Youth and Creative Arts Awareness Programme.

At first, I have to confess, I was just the tiniest bit sceptical about some of Heathcote's assertions and suggestions. But not now. And not just because it has worked for me either, but because I've witnessed its effects on others. Some of the students, for example, have really come out of themselves. And it doesn't have to be anything complicated, with lines to learn and blah blah blah. You don't need that. So much of it lends itself to improvisation. Take for example our script of The Big Fellow, *the bones of which I put together in a few minutes lying here on the grass by the reservoir. When I embarked on that project, I had nothing, only a sheet of paper containing the merest skeleton of the idea. I was out there on a wing and a prayer, to be honest with you, and did not have the faintest clue whether it was going to work or not.*

All I had said to the students beforehand was that I was going to work from this 'blueprint of words' to try and devise a piece that would enable one to confront one's fears. So I filled them in on the entire story concerning the Big Fellow and how me and Bennett had heard our neighbour Willie Markham dying in his house long ago on an otherwise beautiful summer's day. His voice rattling like chains in a bucket as we gazed through his window and saw them all crying. With the Big Fellow standing in there, staring at them and smiling his wry but arctic smile.

Once I'd told the story – I went into great detail, describing the bubbling tar and the kids playing ball – I recruited one of them to play the Big Fellow character.

Myself, I donned my aviator shades, the US army jacket (yes, I still had it), the orange palm-print Hawaiian shirt and my Doc Martens. Became, effectively, for the purposes of the session, the old me.

The student in question, I have to say, was excellent. He did exactly as I requested, stood there immobile, casting a long shadow of . . . foreboding, I guess. Then I set about him, jabbing what was supposed to be a pistol – in reality, however, a walking stick – at his throat as I shouted: 'Fuck you! The Big Fellow! What a bollocks! You think I'm afraid of you? Well, phoo-ee! But somehow I don't think so!'

When he didn't respond – it really was a wonderful performance – I demonstrated to the students how the sole effect of it was to enrage me further, shouting as loud as I could until I became so hoarse and exhausted that I began to sink to my knees. 'The Big Fellow! Him and his big fucking hat! And his great big fucking cigar!' *I cried.* 'You're a miserable fucking lousy fucking cunt! A big lousy, fat-headed bastard! You wanna know something, you fuck fuck fuck?'

There were some of them a little concerned, you could see that. And a number of them did ask whether it was necessary for it to be quite so realistic. But that's when I got up and took my clipboard from my assistant. I flicked my tongue against the back of my teeth and then tapped two fingers on the clipboard.

'No,' I explained as I paced the grass the better to order my thoughts, 'You see, that's the way not to do it! That's the way to the anger that rebounds on you! And who does it tear apart? The Big Fellow? Do you see him looking scared? Do you? Ask yourself!'

I looked at them over the top of the clipboard. My eyes widened as I inspected them all individually. The air seemed to literally vibrate with anticipation. 'Well?' I asked. They shuffled about a bit but didn't respond. Why would they when they knew the answer? I nodded a number of times in an attitude of deep but authoritative contemplation and said: 'No! There's only one person that that course of action will tear apart. Only one person, friends. And that person is –'

There was no need to state the obvious. There was a general air of recognition and assent.

'Now,' I continued, 'now we'll see what happens when you re-route that anger.'

So we went through the whole thing again, the big difference being that just when I was supposed to begin my outburst as I had in the first dramatization, this time I cast the walking stick as far as I possibly could from me and embraced the student as warmly as I could. There was a bit of a laugh when I did it too hard and my actor went: 'Ow!'

But they got the point as, in an inspired move, he sank to his knees, supplicant. I clapped heartily.

'You see!' I cried. 'The aggressor has sheathed his sword, knowing it to have become redundant!'

We had a great discussion afterwards about violence and its corrosive nature. One of the Sandymount visitors actually said that it was one of the most illuminating sessions she had ever experienced, and that was something coming from someone who'd been giving lectures herself for years. On our way home I invited some of the students out to the caravan for a drink and ensured they were aware of the depth of my appreciation. I have a feeling in the years ahead we're going to hear more from some of those guys. And gals – excuse me! Oops! There you go again, Joey!

I opened a letter I'd received from the Ulster Bank regarding the whereabouts of Johnston Farrell. I felt myself consumed by admiration when I read about his having left the financial game now once and for all in order to become a full-time writer. 'Hey, Johnston, my man!' I said as I thumped my palm with my fist. 'You're showing us all how to do it! You're setting the standard here!'

But accepting that placed a lot of responsibility on my shoulders too. So, straight away, I got out some paper, writing away throughout the night.

When the morning light at last crept in, I have to say I was feeling triumphant. Except that when I read what I'd written, it didn't seem to make any sense. It was like something a druggie might come up with, in fact. Except I wasn't on drugs any more, was I? I was so taken aback, I thought: I'll send it off to Allen Ginsberg! There's a chance that he might like it!

I still remained somewhat perplexed, however. So I had a cup of tea and, when I'd drunk it, went back to my masterpiece to read it again. I was full sure that this time it would yield up its meaning.

But it didn't.

(The following piece I found stapled to the back of an 'Asstd Jottings and Observations' notebook and covered in heavy ink and pencil markings, not to mention various circles and exclamation marks!)

Thinking Back on Dr Carmody – Here in the Caravan Late – No Date

You know something? When you look back on anything you do, there are always going to be things you regret, and that is as true of me as anybody else and what I would have to say when I consider my position right here and now, having had a chance to weigh up the pros and cons and to try and be fair to everyone, if I had a chance to do it all again, one thing I would do, I have to say, is make a much greater effort to understand Dr Carmody's position. To realize that when someone comes barging into your office in a highly emotional state, nine times out of ten you'll find there's a good reason.

For the truth is – and I can see that clearly now – that she wasn't exceeding her authority, which I, at that time, considered her to be. Perhaps what I had difficulty understanding was that although I was in charge of the Youth Community Arts and Drama Lab. (inc. Cinematic Arts) – a completely separate endeavour but still under the umbrella of the Creative Arts Awareness Scheme – my overall responsibilities were, in fact, very limited. She, on the other hand, was directly answerable to the management committee of the college and the various cross-border committees without whom the project wouldn't have existed in the first place. She also, remember, had, on top of this, to run her own day-to-day affairs. So I think I may have jumped the gun there.

No, I would acknowledge that I definitely did.

It's just that I was so taken up with everything I was doing – my head was scrambled with all the suggestions the kids were giving me and which I had requested from them, of course, as part of the 'brain-storming laboratory' experiment (there were students running in and out every five minutes with notes and cassettes and CDs) – that I think I was beginning to think the place couldn't properly function without the activity of my little 'Andy Warhol-style factory', as one of the kids had called it despite the fact that he was way before their time. Some of those kids were really hip to the beat. I feel so embarrassed looking back on it now, though, I really do, especially when I think of the speech that I made, turning the pen around in my hand and staring at her like she *was* somehow answerable to me!

Some of the things you say . . . I can remember little enough of it, to tell you the truth. All I know is there was a lot of stuff about 'privilege' and 'duty' and being 'imbued with a sense of responsibility'. Towards seeing the job through, I think I meant. 'I've put a lot of work into this, Dr Carmody,' I remember saying to her, 'and it means a lot to me. I have a lot of responsibility to these students. I'm not going to start something and then abandon ship halfway through – and if you think I am, then, Doctor, you've another think coming. That's not what we're about here.'

It was at that point she lost her temper, directly after which everything went completely askew. And not a little unpleasant, which is regrettable, for she is not entirely blameless either, a lot of the things she said being not only without foundation but quite unnecessarily vindictive. 'Do you think I'm the only one who's noticed this, what's been going on in here of late? You running around the place giving orders and winding the kids up to high . . . doh – it's a school we're running here, Mr Tallon, not a –'

'Not a! Not a! What are you talking about Carmody! Say what you fucking mean, madam!' I was on the verge of demanding, the fact that she was on edge having a similar effect on me. But fortunately I didn't. Not that there'd have been an opportunity now she'd really gotten into her stride, pacing up and down, taking her glasses off and putting them on again as she continued: 'Can you please explain to me all this technical jargon you use? Do the students know what you're on about half the time, do you think, Mr Tallon? I was going by the hall, why, only last Monday morning, and I stopped for a moment or two to listen to what you were saying – quite frankly, I didn't understand one word of the language you used! Post-modern this, exegesis that! Where are you getting all this? Honestly!'

I think it was her saying that more than anything that stopped me in my tracks. It flagrantly trivialized all the studying I'd been doing, and was so much at odds with the enthusiasm I'd been getting from the kids. She asked me something then, but I didn't respond. I suppose the dominant emotion I felt was hurt. I know it might sound childish, because at the end of the day you're supposed to be a professional, but slighted – yes, definitely – was the emotion I felt. As well as that, I knew in my heart and soul she'd been building up to this. Someone doesn't call into your office on all sorts of unconvincing pretexts without having something they want to get off their chest. It's just that they're finding it difficult to do it. That is what decided me once and for all on abandoning my strategy of seeming 'compliant'.

'Look!' I said. 'Look, Doctor! I've had enough of this!', slamming both palms down on the desk and eyeballing her. Catching my breath as I demanded – almost plaintively, as I guess I can acknowledge now – 'Why, Dr Carmody?'

I could see she was taken aback, but I had had enough experience of her and what she was capable of than to go and start underestimating her now. But even then I wasn't quite prepared.

What I had to endure after that can only be described as 'deeply upsetting'. She proved to be what can only be described as unrelenting – insatiable, perhaps, might be a more apposite word – in her desire for . . .

I have never seen anything quite like it, to be honest with you.

'Don't you realize,' she hectored, 'don't you realize you are on pro-bation here – which has already, in case you hadn't noticed, been con-siderably extended – and that your special circumstances – in the light of the peace process and the changing atmosphere in the coun-try – were not without significance in your appointment? Not to mention the persistence of Fr Connolly! Whose philanthropy in your case is beginning to seem quite misplaced, regardless of his friendship with your mother after your father . . . abandoned you! Look, I know your family circumstances were difficult, that your father's absence and your mother's . . . emotional difficulties have adversely affected you and that Fr Connolly wants to do all he can to help, particularly after your time in prison, which I know must have been difficult. And don't get me wrong, for despite your atrocious actions in whatever year it was – 1976 – I'm all for rehabilitation because I think the community as a whole will benefit if we address these problems in a humanitarian manner. It enriches us too, Joseph, I know that! But where is the evidence that this sense of duty and responsibility is reciprocated? If we want to find out just how much you care, Joseph, where would we look? Or are you treating all of this as some great big joke? Do you think the community is a cow to be milked? Is that what all this means to you? Some great big silly old joke to you? Because that's how it appears to me, if you don't mind me saying so!'

I responded glumly as she stood there staring with her hands on her hips. 'No,' I said, 'I don't think it's a great big silly old joke. I'm sorry, Dr Carmody, if that happens to disappoint you. But the fact is, I don't.'

I lowered my head, but without losing dignity. When I raised it again, she was standing over by the window with both her arms folded. A few of the teachers were making their way across the quadrangle towards their cars, laughing about something. She turned and continued: 'Why then do you continue to flaunt the most basic of requirements to behave in this flagrantly irresponsible manner? Have you any idea just how parlous your position is and that only for the aforementioned well-meaning clergyman your position within these walls, which you may or may not have noticed is a second-level educational institution attended by very impres-sionable young people, would most certainly have been reconsidered long ago?'

So that, then, was what she thought of my scripts and workshops and the little experimental films which we were doing as a run-up to my forthcoming 'main feature'.

Very well, Doctor, thank you for that, *I remember thinking to myself.* At least that much is clear.

But I needn't have thought she was finished yet. She was drawing her breath again and plucking at her bowstring in preparation for the discharge of one final arrow, both lethal and perfectly aimed.

'Which I could understand,' she continued, 'as I say, if you were capable of communicating your ideas and intentions to your students, instead of going off on tangents and saying, which you do, as far as I can see, literally the first thing that comes into your head. I've listened to you, Mr Tallon, I've heard you, and if it doesn't make sense to me, heaven knows what the students must think of it!'

It was only through drawing on reserves of self-control which I wouldn't have dreamed were at my disposal that I succeeded in holding my tongue. I felt like coughing politely and responding: 'The students, in my estimation, Dr Carmody, appear to have no difficulty with it whatsoever.'

But there would have been no point. She was still rabbiting on, sighing, folding her arms, unfolding them. Then turning to glare and go 'Hmm hmm hmmph?'

I remember being so seriously aggrieved by her outburst that after she was gone I was numbed *and literally incapable of moving for at least five minutes.*

It's only now that I can understand her position and see that what I had been attempting in those days – although it must still be considered a worthwhile experiment! – might have been asking too much of the students. Even so, there can be no doubt that many of them did, in fact, benefit from it, and in so many different ways. And maybe will one day succeed, having pursued a career in film or the related arts.

Further Reflections on Dr C. and 'The Confrontation!' (from the actual 'Community College Ledger' itself, some weeks later) (After lunch – free class until 2.15 p.m.)

You know something? There can be be no doubt about it. People are the strangest bunch of fucks. I mean, there's you-know-who, the most fantastic woman who just couldn't do enough for you in the beginning have you this Joseph have you that Joseph remember there's lots of money available oh yes the arts it's wonderful absolutely wonderful to have someone with your ideas on the staff I'm sure you'll waken us old fogies up ha ha oh yes and then next thing you know she's looking at you like you're fucking Saddam Hussein. Oh fuck her, man! I got work to do!

Later – 4.25 p.m.

The class this afternoon went really well. Some fantastic kids in there, make no mistake! All I can say is, if Carmody has got one thing wrong, it's to start thinking that she's gone and put the brakes under me. 'Once and for all sorted him out, the famous Mr Joey Tallon! We won't be hearing from his like again! Oh no!'

Well, what a mistake to go and make, you silly girl, Mrs C.! One big motherfucking whopper there, I'm afraid! Yep, one great big giant boo-boo, I'm sorry to have to say! But for which there is one happy dude who will remain forever grateful! And do you happen to know who that might be, Mrs Drive-the-Big Motor-I-Own-the-School?

It's fucking me, lady! Mr Joey fucking Tallon, that's sitting right here!

Eureka! Reprised

I began to realize that all she'd done – far from dissuading me from making my movie or ever writing again – was to, in fact, provoke quite the opposite, i.e. a galvanization of resolve. Which – *eureka reprised!* – was the very moment that I'd been waiting for. Once and for all to put an end to my dithering!

And the instant that I'd made that decision – to make myself a movie, in other words, not *some time* but *right now, this very second, any movie!* – I took myself off down the corridor, filling my arms with equipment from the technology room. As much as I could carry – Canon camcorders, eyepieces, Minolta Maxxum 28mm zooms, long-lens cameras, tripods. Then I went and got some of the students and instructed them that it was time to get our ass in gear. They responded immediately like a well-oiled military machine. I was amazed. But isn't that what they say? That creativity can employ adversity and use it to its own advantage?

Well, that's what happened with us that day, let me tell you! That was our experience. Like it was something that had been waiting to happen.

'Action!' I kept calling as we shuffled off down the corridor. 'Action on a rainy day!' for it was pouring out of the heavens! But that wouldn't stop me now, that was one thing I knew for sure! Nothing could stymie this project, a little short called *Joey's Movie!*, shot on video and only three minutes long, in preparation for the 'main feature'.

(The 'movie diary' turns out to be more readable than the others. All of it written in fountain pen and black ink – 'very intellectual'!)

The 'Movie Diary': *A New Beginning!*
(p. 25 onwards . . .)

There is no doubt about it – once you take a decision and resolve that you're going to stick to it, you are a new man. So hey, Mrs Carmody, thank you for that! Maybe I'll credit you on the movie! But now I gotta go – you wouldn't believe the work there is to do, even on a project like this, which is nothing compared to the big Hollywood stuff. But it's not that kind of movie, is it? And often independent low-budget pictures can do the most amazing things, come along to these festivals and knock the socks off everybody. So here's hoping we get the picture I've been dreaming of! Between you and me, I'm harbouring high hopes . . .

Pre-Production Notes . . .

What I find quite difficult to express is the sense of achievement I'm getting from simply having decided once and for all. From just going out and making the decision to get things up and running and stop this . . . procrastination. For I have been faffing around — I realize that now — thinking up all sorts of excuses so I wouldn't have to bite the bullet. The script isn't ready, we haven't the money . . .! All the usual shit that you read. But when is a script ever ready, and what production company ever has enough money?

Anyway, I was on to the caretaker in the community hall (they've built a new extension with all the European money! It looks fantastic!) and he reckons there should be no problem once we get the paperwork and the deposit sorted out. Which surprised me, I have to say! What a change from the old days! Deposits! Paperwork! I told him we were rehearsing a very important play so there shouldn't be much interference on set. We want as little intrusion as possible, I said. 'No problem,' he said. 'We're expecting delivery of a new set of lights which I'm sure you'll find useful. Thanks to the European money combined with the Access funding which has just been approved, they ought to be state of the art! The new stage too is absolutely second to none. A long way away from the community hall of old, Joey! Yes indeed!'

Which is a pretty good sign, isn't it? I have a terrific feeling about this movie. Well, gotta go. Am auditioning some kids in the office at twelve.

Technology Suggestions . . .

I think I'll shoot it on 8mm. The camera I bought — it just arrived today and looks absolutely fucking stupendous! No doubt Carmody'll be down complaining. 'What's this I hear about a brand new camera?' It doesn't matter now. The way things are beginning to look, it's like this project is literally unstoppable. We are going to rehearse in the hall today, run through the first scene just a couple of times and establish the feel of the movie. There is great interest building. All the kids are talking about it.

Notes from 'The Shoot'

(There is no shortage of these, mostly concerning camera directions and ideas for 'plot development', which are interesting considering the completed film was a little less than three minutes long. Most of them, however, appear more concerned with actors and the problems the director encountered . . .)

The Shoot: Day Two (Afternoon)

That fucker Mangan! Jesus, Mary and Joseph. I don't know how many times I've told him! How many times do I have to explain it?'Look,' I said, 'it's just the story of Mona. After my father left she went off to Dublin. Do you understand that? She goes off and has an abortion! Which breaks her heart, right? Which leads us then to her relationship with me! And I'm thinking, "OK then, Mona, I'll be your child! And together we'll transform the world!"'

It seemed pretty simple to me. Except that he looked at me as if I had just asked him to recite the entire works of Shakespeare. 'I can't do it,' he says, and starts hiding behind his hands. 'I nivver acted in fillums before!'

'Right then,' I said, making sure the kids didn't hear me — I didn't want to embarrass him — 'if that's the case I'll get someone else to do it. But that's the last errand I'll ever run for you in Dublin!' (I got him a stack of blues last week.)

And I meant it when I said it. Does he think I have nothing better to do than go running up and down to the city doing messages for him? Ever since acquiring Luscious Linda ('Not a cardboard imitation! Not an undersized toy! But a genuine, inflatable, life-size simulated sex object with two working love openings!'), he's become obsessed with the subject of sex. At night you can hear the fucker groaning now. He's far worse than I ever was! At least I had a name for my Mona, and one that I never changed and never had any desire to change. He has a different one every fucking night!

Anyway, in the end he relented and said: 'All right, I'll do it, Joey!' as I led him back to the set.

And, boy, what a performance he turned in. 'Mangan,' I said, 'you're as good as Burgess Meredith! No, better! You'd top Jason Robards any time! Fantastic! The best old-time actor I've ever laid eyes on! The camera loves you, Mangan!'

He was chuffed, and when we all sat down to watch the rushes you could see him starting to swagger a bit. It was like he was on the verge of clicking his fingers and demanding this, that and the other. 'You there!' I could hear him saying. 'Go and get me fags! Get me coke! Get me beer! And fast!' It was hilarious to watch!

I can't be enthusiastic enough, though, about the performances we've so far seen. What's the word? Cathartic, I think. It's been fantastic so far. Here's hoping for tomorrow.

(There is a drunkenly scrawled note stuck in here with the rest of the papers which is . . . well, let's say it doesn't readily yield up its meaning. That's because I never wanted anyone to know about what I'd seen that day, coming home happy as Larry after the day's shooting. There are only a couple of words on it, actually. 'The Only One' and 'Heartbroken'.

. . . It happened. I had just come out of the newsagents, collecting my magazines, Film Monthly, Empire, Hot Press, et al., *and was crossing the street when I saw Jacy. I went white and my first impulse was to run.*

I know since the first night I seen her that she's been working as a receptionist in the Fuck Me hotel ever since the shirt factory closed. Boyle Henry probably got her in there seeing as he's one of the owners. I blanched as I saw her swaying in the doorway of Doc Oc's, trying to light a cigarette. Her hair was hanging down in front of her eyes and her handbag was lying on the ground. She dropped the cigarette and bent down to pick it up. I ducked into the phone box in case she might look over and see me. She started laughing half hysterically to herself and then went stumbling on up the street. I touched my temples as I closed my eyes and spoke her name: 'Jacy!'

I went into a tiny, anonymous bar and spent the rest of the night there, shivering. The old owner stood by the window, bemoaning the changes in the town and how nobody any more cared about anything. 'Fucking like dogs from morning till night, falling about the streets, tearing around in their foreign fucking cars. The fucking dollar is all they want, everything else can go fuck itself. Including Jesus Christ! Not that I care – soon I'll be gone and they can do what they like. But in the past in this country I believed in the future.'

'So did I, my friend,' I said, as he poured me another drink and I heard the mighty surf crashing, 'so did I.'

Day Three (Post-Wrap)

Having finished the film, the way I feel is that I could do absolutely anything. Just get my hands on a camera and start shooting my major feature right here and now! It has been a wonderful experience and I see so much more clearly now the pitfalls and problems, etc. Obviously the visual quality of I Want to Be Born 2 (the title we've agreed on – a cast decision, picked from a number of my own suggestions) leaves a lot to be desired (it can be quite foggy at times, the titles rolling from side to side at the beginning, some unsteady camerawork – not all of it deliberate in the Cassavetes style – and a few little problems with the dialogue – due to wind noise you can't hear some of it). But it is a first effort after all. Problems such as these will be ironed out with Psychobilly (not the final title), which we should be getting up and running very shortly. And, in any case, the piece itself is so original (forgive my immodesty but I really do think it is!) that I don't think an audience will be all that bothered.

It opens with the camera tracking along the rubber doll's legs – we've bought a new one specially (hope Carmody doesn't find out, for we borrowed the money from the kitty!) – and then taking in the pubic hair – for which we had to use horse hair, for they don't come supplied with that. Before coming to rest on Mangan as he disappears – pretend! – inside her, all of him seeming to vanish.

That's it, more or less. It's a very short film, remember. With one of the students, v/o, going: 'I want to go back! Please let me go back! To live in the cave of our dreams and there at last to be once again born!'

You just know when something is good, don't you? And there can be no denying the response Mangan's performance received – astonished, rapturous, I don't know what word you'd use or what one might be most appropriate. None at all, maybe, or none that exists. Especially when I played them the music — Handel's 'Hallelujah Chorus', which is really going to be stupendous, especially when experienced in tandem with Dead Souls — the lovely passage about the coming 'new spring', what else?

The music and the prose rise together — fusing — as we see Mangan slowly disappearing under the skirt — 'No! We don't need to see your face! It's gonna be OK!' I kept telling him! — and the screen is consumed by a sheet of blinding light as — boomph! — he's gone, at last one with the world.

The only hard job I've had today, the thing went so fucking well, was persuading the students to stop clapping for a while so I could tell them to stop praising me and convince them that, if anything, film is a collaborative art and that no one person's contribution is more important than the next man's. 'Or woman's!' I corrected myself, to the good-natured amusement of a lot of the chicks.

The more I think of it, the more I want to dedicate it to Mona. To label that cassette with these typed words: 'In Memory of Mona Galligan — A Film by Joseph Mary Tallon: I Want to Be Born 2.'

(There is just this one single page of foolscap – with a drawing at the top of me posting the package! – headed, in what is clearly triumphant lettering:

Off She Goes, Me Boys!)

. . . Was up at the post office this morning and have sent the video cassette off at last! It was like everyone knew I was doing it. They were all chat!

'You look in good humour!' says your man behind the counter as I handed him the jiffy bag. 'Pay day, I suppose?'

'I guess in a way you could say that, all right!' I said, but didn't elaborate.

Which, of course, in a sense, it genuinely is. Pay day in so far as all our hard work now looks like it is going to be worth it.

The more I stood there, staring at the pasted label – Attn. The Commissioning Editor, Debut Series, New TV Drama, BBC Broadcasting House, Portland Place, London WC1 – the more insignificant it all began to seem, this occluded little world of Scotsfield. Worrying *about Carmody, Boyle Henry, et al., who probably isn't even aware of the way he'd looked at me in the pub that day. This town is so small and you see people so often that after a while you start to imagine things. I feel stupid for ever having allowed myself to think along those lines, not to mention investing a throwaway comment regarding a waistcoat with all sorts of pointless significance. Sandy probably just meant it as a joke. Yeah. Course he did. Yeah. I'm sure of it.*

The Big Issues

Which was why, all the way down the street, having cleared my mind of all that nonsense, I went back to what, I suppose, you might call the 'big issues' – like the magazine says! Ha ha! – life and death and why we're here.

And the more I did so, the more I couldn't stop thinking about myself up there on the director's chair, considering the best possible composition of an upcoming shot, now possessed of a belief no mystic had ever inculcated, my books and notes tucked beneath my arm as I swung into Austie's a completely changed man, from that day on only thinking one thing: 'So hey! How you doin' there, y'all? It's Wonderful Pictures from the town of Scotsfield! And we're here to shake your tree!'

The End of Misunderstanding

Which I suppose you could think of as *another* new beginning, the beginning of the end of misunderstanding and all that other stupid imaginary stuff that seems to go along with it – eyebrows that had never been raised and smirks which didn't exist but which resulted in you vacating pubs almost the minute you went in. Getting it into your head that it was you, specifically, they were all looking at. Not to mention thinking: *There he is! There's the kidnapping fucker! The same treatment as Detective Tuite, that's what he deserves!* When clearly now that wasn't the truth or anything remotely approaching it. The more I thought about it, the dafter it seemed that I'd even considered it for a second.

Extract

(from *J. T.'s Nineties Diary*, a separate book with asstd random entries – not in chronological order – often scribbled in when the 'ledger' was not immediately to hand)

Turns out I was right. About the misunderstandings and so forth – if today is anything to go by, at any rate. I was just sitting in Austie's going through my notes, trying to look as if I wasn't paying much attention to what was going on around me but actually, in fact, trying to determine once and for all if I had imagined it all or not. Without a doubt, I'm absolutely delighted to be able to report! For Boyle Henry was there, sitting with some fellow down the back, in the exact same place as before. But this time not even bothering to look in my direction. Far too busy talking business with your man and working his way through a great big feed – you want to see the grub in Doc Oc's! They do the most amazing lunches now. As a sort of celebration – from now on, no more of this 'paranoia' nonsense, for there's no other name for it, really – I decided to treat myself to the fillet of lamb with spiced pumpkin purée and green beans. 'There you are, maestro!' says Austie, and slaps it down in front of me. As I worked my way through it, I reflected on just how good an idea it had been to conduct that 'little experiment', which, really, in a way is what it had been, the road ahead being totally unimpeded now because of it. If I fucked up this time it would be nobody's fault but my own. Except that that wasn't going to happen.

Then all you can think is: It's all systems go! *It's only a matter of days now before the movie starts shooting! It's the most wonderful feeling and the only thing I regret is that Mona or my mother – Jamesy, even, the abandoning old fucker! – won't be there to see it, talk about it, enjoy – whatever.*

From the 'Community College Ledger':

'Complaints, complaints, fucking complaints!'

(This is scored at least seven times across the middle of the page in bright red felt-tip marker and underlined quite heavily.

Then it reads:)

I had a really good time reading over the entry from a couple of weeks back about the pub and the misunderstandings and how the movie would be so good if everyone could be there Mona and the old man and everyone . . .

But there's always something, isn't there? There's always fucking something!

(The remainder, however, as if written in a frenzy, is quite impossible to decipher. There are, though, some other pieces dealing with the subject, the most illuminating, perhaps, being this one from later on in the ledger.)

The Nature of 'The Complaints'

I have never quite been able to manage to establish the source of the recent complaints for certain but I have my suspicions regarding the cleaning ladies, for there were no other people around the set that I could see. Anyway, whoever it was, it has got back to me that someone had observed one of the students 'having sex' while attired in an Apache headdress. Which shows you the level of absurdity that rumours can attain, with all kinds of half-truth stitched in along with what can only be described as utter fantasy. Sure there was someone wearing an Indian headdress – what do you expect when you're making a pastiche Western? (The idea for which the students had come up with themselves, incidentally!)

It was short – a little sideline project, which was very good, actually – written by one of the fourth years. But having sex? Nonsense. Not that I'd have had anything against it, in principle; it's just that it didn't happen, that's all.

There was also talk of spliffs being smoked. I don't know for sure if there was – maybe one or two of them went out during break for a blast. I couldn't say one way or another. It's just that I had more to do with my time than breathe down their necks every second of the day God sends.

'For Christ's sake!' I said. 'I've a film to shoot here!'

Which I had. And the script was giving me trouble, real trouble! So I would have been able to do without the aggravation. 'This shit I can do without!' I said one day, really losing my temper. 'So come on, let's try that again! Hit it one more time!'

The kids, somewhat cowed now, set the scene up again. But we had
a great laugh afterwards when we had a drink in Doc Oc's, which
was getting as bad as the Fuck Me with the amount of palmtops and
organizers and fucking cellphone ringtones prr prr prr. 'You really
had us frightened,' they said. 'We never seen you like that before!'

'Well, that's the way it can be sometimes! It's not gonna always run
smoothly!'

'Especially when people keep interfering! Sticking their stupid
noses in!'

'Exactly!' I said. 'You got it now, my man!' and we all had ourselves a really good chortle.

I don't know what time it was when at last I rolled home, with so
many images just flying through my head like black-and-white playing cards going flip flip flip, as all these titles for the 'psychobilly'
movie came swooping in my sleep: Death of a Salesman, Reservoir
Death, Murder on the Irish Border. *And the one which seemed most
insistent –* Stories from the Animal Pit, *the animal pit meaning Scots-*
field or Ireland – being decided upon – eureka three! – *the following*
morning as I sprang up in the bed.

(Piece ends here with, once again, heavily scored in bold black type:)

THE ANIMAL PIT
A film by Joey Tallon

Which, of course, never did see the light of day!

Error of Judgement

Even now, Bonehead maintains it was all my own fault and that if I
hadn't gone blabbing about it to Austie things might have turned out
differently.

Which he'd be better off not saying, to tell you the truth, for it gets
on my fucking nerves when he does it. And we only end up squabbling
again.

'Oh, what the fuck do you know, Bonehead!' I said to him. 'You
know sweet fuck all about it! Anyway, it might just as well have happened that way as any other fucking way! It's all the fucking same in
the end!'

Whenever you talk like that, of late, it drives poor Bonehead crazy. Crazy! Especially when you remind him that he once thought along those lines himself. 'But that was different! We had nathin' then!' he says. 'Sweet eff-all is what we had! Things are so much better now! Look, Joesup, you've got a lot more going for you than most people! Once upon a time you had an excuse! But not now! Don't be an eejit, Joesup! Don't throw it all away! It's here, Joesup! Ripe for the taking!'

No point in telling him it's not. Or elucidating any details I might consider relevant regarding my little 'error of judgement' that particular day in Austie's.

I'd had a dream the night before in which I'd seen every detail of the 'forthcoming' movie so crystal clear it had gotten me all fired up, all . . . consumed by a desire just to share the experience . . .

'Do you understand what I'm saying, Austie?' I kept repeating. 'What it is that I'm trying to do? Yeah? What I'm about here is *sharing the idea*! No more misunderstandings! Let's lay it on the line! Are you hearing me here, Austie?'

'I'm hearing you,' he said. 'It's not as if you're not shouting loud enough!'

I remember laughing at that. I shouldn't have, maybe, but I did.

I tapped the bar counter with my pencil and tried to articulate further, inwardly, it seems to me now, being just that tiny bit amused as I caught a glimpse of Austie's 'intelligent' look, with his chin on resting on his hand and his brow so tightly knitted, as though he were thinking: *Ladies and gentlemen: Tonight on the* South Bank Show – 'Cinema!', *with Austie Hogan!*

At any rate, I proceeded. 'The idea originally was for a hard-hitting, extremely realistic film set in the Ireland of the 1970s, a dirty, uncompromising, high-octane narrative called 'Psychobilly' about the life that was lived here at that time. Using our own very town here as a sort of . . . example. A microcosm, I think, is the word.'

'Yes, it is!' agreed Austie as if he knew, sagaciously adding: 'That's what it would be now, Joey!'

'But now I think I'll go less for realism than a wild experimental approach. Just turn the camera loose and see what it comes up with! When you've a good tight script you can afford to operate like that. You getting my drift here, Austie?'

'Uh-huh,' he replied.

'A sort of Cronenberg/Cassavetes style, with some Andy Warhol influence. Maybe with a dash of Buñuel.'

'Bunwell,' nodded Austie.

'With original music by Boo Boo, I hope.'

'The fellow whose arm went west!'

'Exactly!' I continued. 'And which is one of the central events which we will be dealing with in the movie. There will be others, of course, which I've decided to approach maybe more in the Cassavetes mould. Yes! For those sections I'm more inclined to retain the idea of black and white. Sharp, crisp realism. Hard-edged monochrome. Documentary style. Like it happened *then* but it's also happening *now* – you still following me? You see, Austie, there's something really immediate about monochrome even though it's not used much, not now, obviously. The effect I hope to achieve is that, while we'll know it's the past, it will still hit us hard. We'll allude to each and every single tragedy. Within reason, of course! The band being blown up, the Peace Rally atrocity and, of course, the senseless slaying of Detective Tuite by Sandy and Boyle Henry. Subject matter which is obviously sensitive but will be treated in an appropriate manner.'

It was at this point that Austie stood back from the counter and gasped: '*What?*'

This, of course, was the moment of the *error of judgement*, for up until that moment he'd already lost interest. He wiped the counter, then looked quite stunned as he stared at me again and said: '*What did you just say, Tallon?*'

To relieve him a bit, I laughed just a little and tossed my head back: 'Oh, no real names of course! I mean, I'm not that stupid! No, we'll fictionalize all the names and ensure there's no problem like that. I mean, it's not about compromising people in that way. What it's about is the truth. Isn't that what they mean when they use the term "*cinema verité*"?'

Austie frowned just a little then sucked his teeth as he flicked the dishcloth across his shoulder and spread both palms on the counter. Then he fixed me with his gaze as he frowned and said: 'I couldn't tell you what they mean, Joey.'

'Well,' I sighed and stretched my limbs, 'I think I'd best be going!' Then I thought for a minute as I waited for that final crystallization. I moulded some shapes in the air with my hands and said: 'I'm thinking *Faces*, Austie, and I'm thinking *Hands*! I'm thinking *Killing of a*

Chinese Bookie! But most of all, I'm thinking truth! *The Peace Rally! Tuite! The Animal Pit!* The very heart of the seventies at last laid bare so we can know the truth about ourselves! Am I making sense? Why, I might even call it *The Animal Pit*! What do you think?'

'*The Animal Pit*,' repeated Austie in a monotone.

It was only when I got out on to the street that I realized what it was I'd forgotten to say. When I went back in, Austie was talking on the phone. I heard him using the words 'Animal Pit' and 'Tuite'.

'Austie!' I said as he slammed the receiver down abruptly and swung on his heel, grey-faced.

'What do you want?' he snapped as he turned sharply like he was trying to hide the telephone. I was a bit wrong-footed by this abrupt and unexpected change of mood. I had intended to tell him about the Big Fellow but now there didn't seem any point.

'If you've got something to say, just say it!' he said, then realized what he'd said. And the way it must have sounded.

'Do you hear me, Joey?' he laughed then, wiping his hands. 'I think I must be working too hard!'

It was only just then that I thought of the pies and felt the blood coursing up towards my face, in that way that always happens when you know you've been talking too much.

'*Well? Well?*' I kept hearing him say, like he was standing at the far end of the bar. Except that he was standing right in front of me.

'*Well? Well?*' was all I could hear.

Someone came in then, and he turned and walked away. I stood there looking as he chatted to them behind his hand. Then the two of them turned and looked in my direction. They gave me the very same look Boyle Henry had done. That first time. I didn't know what to think then. I was almost on the verge of calling for a pie, managing to pull back just at the very last second.

My head was buzzing as I fell out into the street. To make matters worse, I caught a glimpse of Jacy coming out of the Fuck Me and had to duck into the bookies in order to avoid her. My heart was pounding as I heard her going past. She was dressed in a cheap imitation leather raincoat, carrying a bag that was swinging all right, but it wasn't the patchwork shoulder one you saw her with in the seventies. It was the type you might see your mother with.

Or anyone. Just then I saw Boyle Henry pull up and the door of his car swing open. It was a new one, with smoked-glass windows. When I looked again she had already climbed in and, indistinctly, through the smoked glass I could see him leaning forward to give her a kiss. I winced.

'Do you want to place a bet or not?' the bookie kept saying to me. I didn't know how long he'd been saying it. I couldn't stop thinking: *Where did she go, that Californian girl who surfed in the sun? Where could she possibly have –?*

'Do you hear me, Tallon?' he said again, and just to keep him quiet I put a bet on some fucking horse.

'There you are!' he said as he handed me the slip, then smiled as if all was well.

If only he knew, I thought to myself as I opened the door on to the blinding street.

I didn't sleep very much that night, tossing and turning and thinking of the bar, with Austie standing wiping a glass before looking up and saying: *'That's him!'* as he pointed at me sitting there, reading Hermann Hesse. Except it was a Hermann Hesse novel without any words. The pages were completely empty. When I heard Austie saying that, I started flicking frantically through it in the hope that some print might magically appear. But it didn't. The pages remained obstinately blank. Then Austie wiped the glass again and looked up. Now *his* face was blank. With just a slit for a mouth, which piercingly but insouciantly remarked: 'Oh, it's him all right. It's Joey Tallon. He used to work here, a long time ago. Ah yes. But that's what it was – a long, long time ago.' He left down the glass and looked up again. But this time he was different. He looked like Charles Manson. But not the good one, the gentle gardener. The other one. There was only one thing for it, I realized, as I shifted about in the sodden, tossed bed.

And that was to do some writing. *That will keep me busy*, I thought. But I couldn't manage to get the pen to stay steady on the page, so I put on my clothes and went off out to the reservoir. I was on the verge of tears when I heard Charles Manson's voice – the sinister one – ever so gently stirring among the leaves. It said: 'I'm way up here, Joey! How are you doing? Are you OK? You don't look too good! You don't look so fucking good, man! You look like shit! You look like hell!'

That was as much as I could take. 'You may think so,' I said as I tried to locate where I thought he might be, far beyond the massive bank of cloud, 'but that is where you'd be wrong, my friend! You see, I'm feeling just fine! Because today's the day!'

And it was. It was the day of days and nothing would stop me making it special. So I fought with myself far down deep inside and said: 'Now don't be dumb! Don't go screwing it up!'

Except that I wouldn't be because, after an invigorating draught of the fresh clean air, I was already starting to feel OK. I listened acutely to the leaves as they rustled, and who did I hear coming through on the breeze? Was it Manson, he of the wild hairy mane and the crazed, glass eyes? No. It wasn't. It wasn't Charlie Manson the ruthless psychotic hippy killer. It was The Seeker. My old pal Eamon Byrne. And he sounded so peaceful. More content than ever I'd remembered him. *Up there in the precious harbour*, I thought as I found myself smiling.

Then I went off to get me some breakfast. All the better to fortify myself for the long day's shooting ahead. It was going to be great. I could feel it now in my bones. What sleep did I need, I asked myself. Being up all night imbued you with a kind of alertness, the kind of nervous energy that could only improve one's work, ensuring that you missed not a single detail.

It was a tremendous feeling when you realized that. Aware now as you pulled on your 'shooting gear' – the waistcoat and black polo neck, plus the eyepiece strung around your neck, of course! – that everything in the end had come good, regardless of whatever sweats or revisitings of old anxieties there might have been. Not to mention ridiculous dreams about Austie No-Face.

'I must tell him about it sometime,' I laughed as I strode towards the college, thinking of him laughing whenever he heard about it, tossing back his head as he wiped another glass, going: 'Oh now! Me flogging whiskey without a fucking face! Can you imagine it, Joey? Can you just imagine it now?'

Which indeed I could, no problem at all. For right at that moment I could imagine almost anything. But not in a bad way. Absolutely not. In a really terrific way, in fact, that made everything once again seem possible. Yes, we were back on track, I thought to myself, and as I strolled through the gates I just could not stop myself indulging, for that minute or so before it was time to start working, in the idea of a certain Joseph, now a celebrated film-maker, fêted internationally, with his name in lights over the cinema facades of the world. His movies written up in all the trade papers, waving to fans from some balcony or other.

'I'm going to put Scotsfield on the map!' I told the kids in my pre-shoot pep talk. 'You wait and see if I don't! Yes, kids, this is gonna be the one! And every one of us is part of it! *The Animal Pit*! A major motion picture, produced and directed by Joseph Tallon, and distributed by Wonderful Pictures!'

The Big Fellow scenes, once we'd begun in earnest – there'd been a few technical hitches – started rolling like clockwork. The student who played him – a different one this time, a stouter chap – looked really good. I got him to dress up in his grandfather's hat and suit – a fabulous, wide-lapelled brown chalkstripe. *'Give me a smile!'* I barked through the loudhailer, and started the camera rolling. He looked absolutely great in the viewfinder, tipping back his fedora and waving, with this fiercely hideous grin on his face.

'Look out, you fuckers!' he shouts out suddenly. *'He's the buddy you don't wanna see!'* then he goes and strangles one of his classmates, shaking him like a puppet.

'Louder! Louder! Gurgle louder!' I cried at the top of my voice until I was practically blue in the face, at one point jumping up and down. The student he 'killed' was kind of blue as well, but what a performance!

'Jesus Christ!' he says as he tumbled away. 'I thought for a minute you were really going to do it.'

'Excellent,' I said, 'really excellent,' nodding to myself as I swung the loudhailer.

The scene after that also went very well. It was the part of the movie where the Peace Rally's just started and the Big Fellow is making his way through the crowd, in those final few seconds before the bomb goes off.

(The situation here – now! With erstwhile archivist and general Man Friday Bonehead, right here in Dunroamin', this fabulous, rambling country retreat of ours!)

The Oprah Winfrey Show

What I have to admit is that – regardless of whatever emotional crises or problems I might have had – and I do not intend to condone them or attempt to justify myself in any way – of late the outbursts have been particularly horrendous, with 'you fucking ignoramus' being the least of the abuse Bonehead's had to endure. Which is dreadful when you think of the way things were at the beginning when the two of us first moved in.

When I'd begun to believe that what I'd been longing for might now actually be possible. Even the nameplate on the gate – 'Dunroamin'' – making me chuckle when I saw it. *Can you believe it?* I thought as I shook my head – Bone was paying the taxi – *Joey Tallon's found his fucking home at last!*

Of course, the trouble usually starts when there's alcohol on the job, or, in Bonehead's case, whiskey, which drives him absolutely crazy. Once he starts he's impossible to shut up.

The Oprah Winfrey Show was the best of the lot – a reprise of his turn all those years ago in Mountjoy, of course. When I looked up from my drink that night – I was absolutely plastered by now – what the fuck did I see there in all its glory? Only this headcase with a 'pencil mike', i.e. a biro into which you talk, with his face blacked up as he bawls: *'Ladies and gentlemen! Youse is all very welcome to the* Oprah Show! *Today we are very privilegeded* [that was exactly how he

243

said it!] *to have as our guest one of Scotsfield's finest writers and fil-lum-makers! Well, excuse me, what am I talking about? Why, one of Ireland's finest writers and film-makers! Yes, one of its best artists who only last year saw his first novel published and now is working on number two!'*

Which he shouldn't have bothered saying for it only got me riled up again and I feared I was going to get bitter as my fingers tightened around the glass and I heard myself saying: *'Don't start that shit now, Bone!'*

But, thank God, it passed.

For I know how hard it was for him to understand my having been offered a shitload of money to write another book and not being able to come up with it. The truth being that I don't know how I managed to write the first one. I'd been more than prepared for the world to wipe its arse with my efforts!

And, after all the negative convictions, to end up lionized by London publishers, asked for my opinion on this, that and the other. Hailed as 'fresh and original', not to mention as 'Mr Triumph of the fucking vernacular'!

Although the *London Review of Books*, obviously, didn't bother to include the word 'fucking'.

As if that weren't surprise enough, to arrive then at a literary dinner and be seated beside my old mentor, Johnston Farrell, now a celebrity beyond his wildest dreams on account of the runaway success of his 'gripping, suspenseful thriller, *The Cyclops Enigma*, set in a dark and troubled landscape in the Ireland of the nineteen seventies'.

A subject, as I am sure you have guessed, I happened to take more than a passing interest in.

Although I didn't mean for the whole thing to become so heavy, with me needling him constantly throughout the meal and glowering till long after it was over like the worst kind of soak imaginable. But it had been building in me all evening and what made it worse was that you could see that Johnston had started believing all their guff, every-thing they'd been saying about him and the book. Which was really embarrassing considering, if you're honest, that *The Cyclops Enigma*, while OK as a thriller, was a crock of cack-handed old bollocks – if you're talking about telling 'the story', that is. The proper fucking story, I mean. The only one *worth* telling.

'You'll never know because you don't fucking *feel*! If you *felt* you'd have fucking told me!' I slobbered sourly. 'You'd at least have bothered to *discuss* the fucking thing! Let me know what you intended to use!'

There was plenty from my diary that he'd gone and rewritten, but in the stupidest of hammiest prose, more than adequately complemented by the lurid 'Gothic shocker' jacket, complete with Kalashnikov-wielding hooded psychopath crouching against a backdrop of mountains.

'You know what you're like, Farrell?' I remember snarling. 'You're a soap-powder salesman, that's all you are! And you'll never be anything else! But don't worry, Johnston, they'll love you for it! Already you can see how much!'

They were lining up to talk to him as I turned on my heel. He didn't bother replying, for you could see he was much too hurt. Or – who knows? – maybe just the tiniest bit guilty. If not, indeed, a mixture of both.

But, bullshit and all as his book might be – and, believe you me, *The Cyclops Enigma* fucks up on so many levels – it can never be taken away from him that he was one motherfucking good teacher and those first few months after he arrived in Scotsfield will always remain close to my heart. With him strolling in there to the Scotsfield Hotel, with all his books and papers underneath his arm and that good old waistcoat looking splendid!

'How are you then, Joey, my man?' I can hear him say. 'We've got lots of work ahead of us tonight!', and it does me good just to think it!

I suppose, in a way, when I took out this stuff and started going through it, I was secretly half hoping that something might come leaping out at me, the way it seemed to do that very first time when I found myself writing as if by some weird unnamable magic. Scorching along like the hammers of hell and ending up with the guts of a finished book, all of it scribbled in a matter of days in Boo Boo's Dublin flat.

But that's not the way it happens, I'm afraid, and you can search all you like from the year 1976 to the year ten fucking million, but if it isn't there and isn't meant to be there . . .

. . . well, then you're fucked, aren't you? You're the one-off man, the one-hit wonder, the naive fluke artist who just happened to get lucky that one special time. Which is the way, if I'm honest, I perceive the situation to be. Irrespective of Bonehead's heart-warming and extremely flattering aspirations on my behalf. I'm sorry for saying that, Bone, but I can't render it otherwise. I would if I could but I can't, that's the truth. Because that's the way it is with art – it always suits its fucking self!

If you don't believe me, then take one fucking look around this poxy room. Christ! It's like a rubbish tip now with all this paper! And not so much as a whisper of a novel in sight. Nothing, only a stack of notebooks and diaries, not to mention box files and ex-Bank of Ireland ledgers. Into one of which – there are a few blank pages at the back of this one – I shall now proceed to enter my pen picture of a boot-blacked Oprah!

What a scream Bonehead is as he climbs over chairs and shoves his mike into the faces of the audience. *'So! Whatcha tink, young fella?'* he says. *'You're a Scotsfield man! Whaddya tink of the achievements of Joseph Tallon?'*

'The achievements of Joey Tallon?' he replies in answer to his own question, with exaggerated biliousness. *'Why I always taught he was a bollocks dat couldn't write his own fuckin' name, to tell you da troot!'*

Then asking me to come up and show the audience how much weight I'd lost – almost four fucking stone, actually, ever since accepting the Kingfisher commission! *'Yes! Look at him, folks! Where are the old pie days gone now, Joesup? Eh? Maybe you'd tell us dat!'*

I hadn't a clue how to answer that, because these depressions are different from the old ones. Once upon a time you could handle them a little by keeping yourself busy, walking, eating pies or whatever.

Now, all you want to do is stare out the window, drinking vodka or whiskey – anything you can get your hands on – as the little oblong cursor keeps pulsing away on the computer screen as if to shriek: *'Hey, Joey, can't you do it? Hey, Joey, can't you do it?'*

Before answering: *'Joey can't do it! Hey, Joey can't do it!'*

Whenever he had finished his speech about me there would be a few more 'interviews' along the same lines. And then, when he'd gotten a bit drunker, that dark look would come over his face and you'd hear the venom in his voice as he slowly turned to address 'Mr Boyle Henry', delivering his *tour de force.*

'You bollocks you, Henry!' he'd snort. 'It's you's to blame for everything! Why couldn't you just let Joesup make whatever pictures he wanted? But no! Because you were afraid he was going to steal all the limelight from you, weren't you? You and the blondie bird! Like a fucking auld twig she is!'

Funny as it might have been at times – and there's no denying it was, the wicked way he twisted up his face like the most spiteful and hateful old crone – I didn't want him saying that about Jacy. And whenever he did, a row inevitably developed.

'I asked you not to say it! The last time I told you I didn't want you saying it. And now you've gone and done it again!' I'd find myself snarling – the words would be out before I had the faintest inkling – and there we'd be again, in the middle of another outrageous scene.

'Don't fucking say it, I said!' I'd growl, as uncompromising and black as ever I've been. 'Don't *ever* say that about Jacy!'

As he stood there, half helpless, always utterly bewildered.

'But look what she did on you, Joesup! Can't you see it? She was as bad as him!'

Once it was said, when the words had been uttered, I cannot tell you the effect they had, the sheer depth of loathing they elicited within me. With it always ending up the same way – me losing it and flinging myself at him. Grabbing him in a headlock and bawling: 'Take it back! Take back what you said about Jacy!'

And ending up by just releasing him as I lay there in a heap, no strength in my limbs to sustain what I'd started, just enough to manage to croak: 'She called me The Breeze, you see. That's what you'll never understand, Bone. That's what you – or anyone else, by the looks of things – will never be able to understand!'

Which is a lie, of course. She didn't. At least, not in the way I wanted. But it had still been good to see her, simply to be in her presence. And to be privileged to observe that, despite all that had happened, she was still as beautiful as ever.

I suppose you could argue that, in a way, all along my film was an attempt to deal with my relationship with Jacy. Of laying those old ghosts to rest. A way of saying to her: 'I know I done bad, baby. Do you think you could ever find it in your heart to forgive me?'

For, since those days, what I'd longed for more than anything was absolution, then, ultimately, I guess, deliverance. Which was why in the script I'd rewritten that scene so often – the one I liked to think of as the 'precious moment', that 'nanosecond' when forgiveness happens against all the odds. When she stands with her hands in the back pockets of her sky blue Levis, just staring out through the French windows across the expanse of the Big Sur sands – you can hear the crash of the surf – before turning with a smile to answer that question. *'Forgive you? Is that what you're asking me to do? Of course I forgive you – ain't that what lovin's all about?'*

How many times I've rewritten that scene I can't even begin to remember. All I know is that I just loved sitting down and starting on it all over again, seeing it each time in a totally different light, the kind of picture you want to go on for ever, although knowing in your heart that it can't, for there is only one kind of movie in store for the likes of Joey Tallon when it comes to 'Forever' or 'Eternity'. A low-rent, straight-to-video 'disaster flick' in which the author goes out in a blaze of glory, still dreaming, incongruously, in flames!

Which is certainly a long way from where I'd expected to end up – no, not what I'd anticipated at all – back in those early days of 'Joey Cinema', as off I shot once more through the streets with my eyepiece swinging, explaining my incipient 'project' to everyone – I was as high as a kite on the energy of doing that alone!

'What it's about, if it's about anything,' I would expound, 'is not just me and my demons. And it definitely *is* about that! For I'm not alone in this! No, if *The Animal Pit* is about anything, it's about a community that at long last faces its fears! With me as the central character, obviously! Or someone who is to some extent based on me! You see, what we've got to do is face down the beast! To look in his eye! To effectively exhume . . . *the animal pit*, if you know what I'm saying!'

Most of the time they didn't, of course. They didn't have a fucking clue, to tell you the truth, although you couldn't have persuaded me to believe that then!

'Sure!' I remember them saying. 'That's what we've got to do! Face down the beast, Joey! Right you be then! I have to go on now and get my tea! See you then, Joey, ha ha!'

It doesn't take too much to read between the lines there now, does it? But no, off I would go, absolutely delighted with the account I had given both of myself and my masterpiece. I must have been the fastest director who ever stood behind a camera – the fastest walking, that is, not the fastest 'working'. Tearing about the place with my pockets full of memos. All these ideas on a wall of death going scrambling around in my head like crazy, arguing with each other from morning until night.

One minute it would be Cassavetes, the next Martin Scorsese. I was even reading about the Indians (Satyajit Ray) and the Japs (Kurosawa) in the hope that I might pick up something from them.

Sleep, once and for all, became a thing of the past, the only respite I could manage being a stolen minute or two out by the reservoir. Or maybe a nod at the counter in Doc Oc's, which had sort of become my unofficial office, so delighted was I that I had dispensed with my idiotically paranoid 'imaginings' re. Boyle Henry et al.

There were a lot of people turning up uninivited to the shoot in the new Theatre and Artbase (the community hall extension), yet another massive whitewashed structure in the centre of town entirely funded by European money, which discomfited me not a little – as had all the paperwork and deposit business – but was a difficult problem to solve. For it wasn't as though we had the resources to employ security. Which in any case wouldn't have been appropriate, because one of Artbase's principal tenets – one of the reasons it was established indeed, and why it adjoined the Scotsfield Sports Complex, which was thronged with people coming and going throughout the day – was that its facilities should be available to all. And in any case, I was only too aware that in a small town like Scotsfield you could very easily ruffle feathers by acting the big shot and refusing people entry. So I just used to say: 'OK. Let them in. Just so long as they don't interfere.'

Quite a lot of the time I didn't take any notice, for I really had enough to be thinking of than be bothered with who was there and who wasn't. But I have to say I did get a jolt when I looked up one day and saw Fr Connolly, pale with anxiety and wearing that same old expression I had come to know so well. The one that seemed a mixture of concern and bitter anger and which fixed on you and said: 'You promised you wouldn't do it!' And, as if that wasn't bad enough, I started to get all flustered when I saw him, dropping the eyepiece and forgetting my directions. The kids asking then: 'What do we do, Mr Tallon? What do we do now, Joey?' and frustrating me further, making me shout: 'I'll tell you, OK? I'll tell you! Just wait, can't you? Can't you just wait for a fucking second? Huh? Huh?'

It wasn't until the next day that, during a break in filming, I began to work out my strategy to deal with all this. I mean, I knew I had to be tactful with these 'casual observers' who, with the passing of time, seemed to be becoming increasingly more casual. I knew I couldn't turn around and throw the whole lot of them out. Perhaps I could have done it on the very first day, but I had permitted it to go beyond that now. I don't know exactly at what point in my thinking it was – close, I seem to remember to that stage where I was on the verge of deciding to get a circular printed, a sort of a flier, really, just to explain my position. I looked up and saw Boyle Henry and Sandy McGloin. Standing in the wings, both wearing tracksuits and carrying squash racquets.

I hadn't been expecting them, and the moment I laid eyes on them I launched straight back into my work, barking orders and waving my arms. A lot of it didn't make sense. Half the time the cast would look at me, then bump into each other as they did what I'd just requested of them. One of them somehow went falling over a sofa, which made the rest of them corpse and crack up laughing.

I lost it then, which was really stupid of me. But I couldn't help it because the pies had come back. *Why don't you make a movie called* Pies, *Joey? I found myself thinking. That would be a good idea! Make a movie called* Pies *and, who knows, perhaps Boyle could star. Mr Boyle Henry, that is. Mr Henry. Mr Boyle. And Sandy. The famous Sandy McGloin. Sandy 'Waistcoat' McGloin, that is. Oh yes!*

They stood there, smiling. When Boyle Henry caught my eye he raised his racquet and gave me a great big broad appreciative grin, nodding as if to say: *'I approve of what you are doing here, folks!'*

Before I knew it I was shouting at the kids: 'Just what the hell do you think you're doing? I told you to stand over there! Do you hear me? Are you stupid? Listen to me, you!'

It was ridiculous, I know. But I couldn't help it. The more I said to myself: 'I made a mistake there for sure, but this time I won't repeat it! I'll rectify matters, this time!' the more I'd go and do the same thing over again, spitting out sentences and waving my arms. When we had finished, Boyle and Sandy came over. Boyle asked me a question. I can't remember what it was. It was something to do with the content of the script. I knew I hadn't answered it to his satisfaction, for the only thing he said in response was: 'I see,' stroking his chin, as though vaguely dissatisfied, and turning over the substance of my reply in his mind.

He waited for a while as if expecting a better attempt, but I couldn't think of anything. *'Put that down, Jason!'* I shouted at one of the kids who was fooling around with the props. *'Put it down, I said!'*

Now I was explaining the plot in detail. In retrospect, it was not what you'd call in the trade 'a very successful pitch', considering, as one must, the manner in which it was delivered. For, by this stage, my face had become incandescent and the sweat on my brow was like a broad strip of cellophane that had been thumbed on there.

'I see,' Boyle Henry repeated patiently, nodding.

He was running his tongue along his upper lip and frowning. Because they were both wearing tracksuits, the smell of perspiration was very strong. Sandy didn't frown. He was still smiling, but not for a second averting his eyes. I had to look away from him because I couldn't make out what he was thinking. Then I started walking up and down. Stroking my *own* chin to try and marshal *my* thoughts. 'Get back here!' you'd cry in your mind, as they skittered away off again – your thoughts, I mean!

'Go on,' said Boyle Henry.

'I don't know what you've heard, Mr Henry. I mean, I don't know what they've been saying about us in the pubs or, you know, wherever. I mean, you know this town! It's impossible once the rumours start to know what to believe! So let me fill you in, yeah? Boy, it's warm! Isn't it warm, Mr Henry? Do you think it's warm? Are you sweating? *I* am! But then, of course, you've been playing squash! Where was I? Yes, of course! This film-making is a tiring business! Do you know what I think? I think a pie is what I need! Do you hear me? Pies! *No!* We must get this scene right! As you can see, it's the scene with the salesman! Or is it? Is that the scene we've been shooting? It must be! It's the one I've blocked out for today! Yes, it's the scene dealing with the murder of Campbell Morris the salesman all those years ago. Which has absolutely nothing to do with you at all, Mr Henry! Nothing at all in the wide world! No, solely Bennett and the others! Not that it would matter if it had! Do you think I'd mind? Of course I wouldn't! And I know you wouldn't either! Because you're an intelligent man and you know what's necessary in this day and age. You know, yes, you read all the papers. You know that we've *all* been involved in things. You, me! We've all done things we're not proud of! Gosh, Mr Henry, it's warm! So many bombs in one little town on the night of Fr Connolly's rally. *Boom!* How many people dead? How many maimed for ever? *Ouch!* Mr Henry, what kind of a carry-on is that? Then turning out it wasn't the Provos at all. British Intelligence, in fact! To discredit the IRA! Yes, strange things happened back in those days! And we've all done our share, let's not pretend we haven't! Yes, we're culpable too, Mr Henry!

You know that word? Of course you do! It means we're to blame, *yes, yes, yes* and a thousand times *yes*. Me for Jacy, yourself and Sandy for what happened to Detective Tuite – yes, a particularly brutal murder indeed, even by the standards of the time. Red Hand Commandos, my eye!'

Of course, it's pretty obvious now that it was a dumb thing to mention their names, just about as dumb as you could get, I reckon, and which I realized the very second I'd done it, no matter how high I was or confused or whatever, was pretty fucking foolish, and that's all you can say about it. As was what followed.

'No, Mr Henry, but of course I'm going to change your name. What would I go and use your real name for? You ask anyone here who's involved in the salesman scene, the simple fact is there is not a name, not one single name that hasn't been changed and it will be exactly the same for the scene with the detective. Should be really good fun, actually, coming up with all these new identities. In a movie that I hope will put Scotsfield on the map! I mean, you know the international arena, Mr Henry, from your politics and travels, yeah? They won't be expecting a film like this to come out of little old Scotsfield! A movie concerned with forgiveness and deliverance shot in an Irish town. It will be fantastic! A first, Mr Henry! Yep! You bet!'

A brief gust of dread went blowing by as I caught a glimpse of his penetrating expression. But almost as quickly it was gone when I saw him smile. And, once again, I was beaming, immersing myself in my subject matter, working myself up to a dramatic closing sentence as I opened my eyes and, drawing my breath to explain a little further, began to speak.

But they were gone.

The Night Visitor

With every sound that night I kept thinking: *Ah, Boyle! Come in!*, fast-forwarding the videotape, as it were, to the point where Boyle and Sandy would appear, reassuring me they understood. *'Ah! So that's what it was all about, Joey!'* they'd say, magnanimously grateful, as Boyle put his arm around me. *'Let's have a drink then!'*

A few times I thought I heard them and got up to open the door.

There was nothing, though, only the church bell sounding as it came on the wind.

On the Street

A couple of days after, I met Boyle on his own just happening to come out of the shop with his paper, and told him I would be more than willing to continue our chat. But he said he hadn't time. 'I have to see a man about a dog,' he said, shadow-boxing a little bit as he gave me a twinkly smile.

For Sure

I had a pretty good idea he'd come the next day, though. He didn't, however. I reckoned he'd been detained due to pressure of work. Things came up unexpectedly and shit.

Taking Its Toll

I was becoming a little bit concerned, though, for the incident had begun to affect the shoot. Given even the slightest provocation, I would now find myself, quite irrationally taking the face off the actors. At one point one of the students – my very best pupil, in fact – became so frustrated he actually turned around to me and said: 'Maybe we should forget all about doing this fucking film!'

'No! No!' I said, and calmed myself down. But I heard later that it had really been touch and go. The cast *had* been thinking of walking. I don't know what I'd have done then.

Never did a more relieved director pick up a megaphone to shout *'Turnover!'* and *'Action!'* than me that very afternoon, I can tell you!

The Roman Senator

I kept thinking: *If only Boyle would come out and have a talk with me, because I really don't think he understood what I meant about Tuite.*

One day I lost it in the pub. Austie stared at me, wiping the counter slowly and steadily in that almost zombie-like way.

'You see, Austie,' I explained, 'I know there's been some confusion. But it really is very simple. How can I put it? You ask yourself: What is the theme of Joey Tallon's movie? What, in a nutshell, is *The Animal Pit* dealing with? Well, I'll tell you, Austie. The very same as I'll tell Boyle when he has a chance to come out and visit. *The Animal Pit* essentially tells the story of a small border community and the series of events that affects it over a twenty-five- or thirty-year period. But, far more than that, much more important – are you with me, Austie? – it's fundamentally a *personal* journey. A personal journey for you and me, and for all of us who have been in some way involved. And we've *all* been, in some small way! Take the scene with the salesman, say. The "salesman scene", yeah? Do you think Bennett when he came in for a drink that night expected to leave a miserable few hours later complicit in another human being's murder? Another human being with a wife and child? A man called – *Campbell Morris!'*

I lifted my drink and looked around me. Then I said: '*I think not, gentlemen!*'

It's hard to believe that I used those words. In fact, to be honest, it's difficult to keep from laughing when you think back on it now. Not to mention what followed – becoming completely carried away when someone shouted a few words of encouragement, something like: '*Good man, Joey!'* and '*Tell it like it is!*' That more or less did it – I was away again!

So you can imagine my reaction when I looked up, in full swing, and saw Hoss Watson, snapping his cellphone closed as he came swinging in the door. He stood there staring at me. And gave me this look. I can't describe it. It was . . . it had the effect of . . .

I nearly went through the roof, to tell you the truth.

No! I kept thinking. *No! Don't say anything else. Steady yourself and say nothing more. For a little while at least, Joey. It would be better.*

But it didn't happen.

'Yes,' I continued, obsessively playing with the eyepiece, 'that's what the salesman scene is about! If it's about anything, it's about gazing into the darkness, into the very depths of that steaming pit. Let's look at what there is to see in there! And instead of bodies, pelts and innards, instead of steaming offal, innards, turn around and film – *what?*'

I paced up and down like some swaggering Roman senator, thinking *Hoss* and *Pies* as my heart kept thumping. Then I stopped in my tracks and found myself thinking: *He'll probably come out tonight.*

Meaning Boyle, of course.

'Here's a pie for you,' I thought of him saying, as I saw him standing on the step with a tinfoil tray.

'Good man, Joey!' someone shouted.

Instinctively, I whirled, frightening the life out of some old geezer who'd drifted off into a trance, and asked, rapid-fire, clicking my fingers with a quite pronounced hoarseness now on display: 'Instead of darkness, then filming – what?'

I paused.

'A *new beginning, ladies and gentlemen!'* I declared. 'A pit, in a sense, that's swamped in light! Where we'll find deliverance – through *purgation*! In there, in that horrible pit of guts, locating the source of our triumph! That will become our rebirth! The *old*, essentially, giving way to the *new*! Out of that rancid hole, the scent of newness rising, bringing with it the essence of a new spring. And what is the essence of that new spring?'

I lowered my head, then raised it.

'Ladies and gentlemen of Scotsfield,' I continued, 'today when we film the salesman scene at a location not far from this bar, I hope that what it will constitute, effectively, is the opening of that first bud, the very first "popping" of this "new spring"! The spring of which Gogol has written [I can't believe I remembered it! But I did! Perfectly!]: *"Suddenly, having been held back a long time by frosts, it had arrived in all its beauty, and everything came to life everywhere! Patches of blue could already be seen in the forest glades and on the fresh emerald of the young grass dandelions showed yellow and the lilac-pink anemones bowed their tender little heads. What brilliance in the foliage! What freshness in the air! What excited twitterings of birds in the orchards! Paradise, joy and exaltation in everything!"'*

I paused then coughed. Hoss considered me impassively. I noticed, perhaps for the first time, how much weight he had lost since the old days, and how well he fitted into his tailored Armani suit. Further indication of a redundant skin shed, I estimated. Before proceeding: 'And which belongs to us here in this little town! This town of ours that we call Scotsfield! It belongs to us here just as much as it does to any of the great nations of the earth, whether America or China or Japan or . . .'

I couldn't think for a minute and had to ask someone for a hankie. It seems so stupid now but it was Hoss I went over to.

'Hello there, Hoss,' I said. 'I was wondering, would you have a hankie?'

A web of sweat-streams masked my face. He stood there with his arms folded. I wasn't one hundred per cent sure whether he'd answered me or not.

'A hankie, Hoss. I was wondering, would you have one?'

'Are you fucking deaf? I told you I didn't!'

It was all I could do not to run off out the door. But instead I threw myself back into my speech, as if hoping I'd exhaust them and that maybe *they'd* do that – get up off their stools and exit. I was praying I wouldn't run out of things to say.

'The new spring,' I continued, 'this new spring which has been held back a long time by frosts. The frosts of deceit! The frosts of denial! The frosts of self-deception, people!'

That led into another big quote from Gogol, the bit in *Dead Souls* where he's describing the green thickets 'lighted up by the sun'.

'The green thickets,' I concluded, *'falling apart and revealing an unlit chasm between them, yawning like the open mouth of some huge wild animal.'*

And I have to say, in retrospect, that, in theatrical terms, it really was a pretty good performance – the Gogol parts, at any rate. But afterwards I was completely floored. I could just about find my way out when I'd finished. As I was going through the door, I heard Hoss calling my name. But when I turned to answer there was no sign of him. Everyone had gone back to either playing pool or watching *Big Brother*. With the door just swinging there, I might have been watching it all from the top of a church steeple.

I was going past the Video Emporium when I looked up to see Jacy in the doorway talking to the doorman, the Provo from The Ritzy days. She seemed nervous and pale, obsessively flicking her cigarette. I heard him say: 'Boyle says he'll meet you there at half eight, Jacy. He got delayed last night. Problem at home, you know yourself.'

'Sure I know,' she stammered, fumbling in her handbag for a lighter. She was wearing the red imitation-leather coat.

Then she turned to him and, drawn, snapped: 'You think I'm a fool? You take me for a fool, do you, Danny?'

Danny – that was his name, I remembered, bowing my head and keeping on walking.

'Hey, Joey! Joey!' I heard him calling. 'You not talking to the people?'

I couldn't bear to turn and face her.

'Ah, come on now, Barbapapa, don't be like that! Come over here and talk to your old pals, why don't you?'

I quickened my step and hoped I wouldn't trip.

I didn't sleep that night either, being completely convinced of Boyle's imminent arrival. So I was a bit tired the next day but I couldn't afford to cancel any more scenes.

'No, sir!' I said as I strode along the road. 'Today all our pages will be shot in their entirety!'

I was going through them individually, working out all the important details when . . .

. . . the car with the smoked-glass windows pulled up noiselessly behind me. Boyle was wearing his panama hat. He leaned out the window and said: 'Well, Joey! Off to work then, are we?'

All of a sudden I found myself stupidly tongue-tied and completely at a loss. But, as I'd been secretly hoping – actually, been pretty much convinced – it transpired that there had been no need – yet again – for any of my misplaced concern.

'You're worrying your head about nothing, for Christ's sake!' he assured me. 'I'm fully behind you and your efforts! That's what this town needs – more men with vision! It was the lack of them that kept us behind for so long. You and me, sure we're old pals! Do you remember the night we were together in Oldcastle? Oh now! Keep her going, Joey, yeah? Any help I can give you!'

I couldn't believe it as I watched him drive away. The new spring had definitely arrived when you were hearing things like that. There was only one thing you could say about it: it was wonderful.

When I got to the hall the cast were waiting. As I swung my loud-hailer I felt like shouting into it: *I love you all! Because you've made this possible! Every single one of you – I love you! I just want you all to know that!*

I couldn't stop thinking about the 'Temple of Colossal Dimensions', which Gogol had described so magnificently in *Dead Souls*. And of how similar to that my film was, being a kind of theatre . . . of true forgiveness, I suppose you might say. Whenever I thought of Jacy and all the things I'd done – not to demean all those other poor people who'd suffered, for beside them my story was of little consequence – I wanted to fall to my knees and weep.

All I kept thinking of was how good it had been of Boyle to level with me like that. And clear the air in that life-affirming way.

And why, when he put a call through to my assistant (a really good kid called Morgan) and asked whether it would be OK for him to drop by the reservoir later on that day as he'd heard we were shooting some scenes out there, I hadn't the slightest hesitation in saying: 'For sure! Tell the man – absolutely! Absolutely! Of course!'

He arrived straight after lunch, and I pleaded with the cast to give it their best shot. 'We've a really important visitor here today,' I said. And, happily, from the very first second I shouted *'Action!'*, I could tell they were going to give it everything. Absolutely everything those fucking kids possessed!

(These pages – fax sheets actually, which still survive in pristine condition – contain the germ of story I had given them to work from. The dialogue and action they made up themselves.)

Story Treatment: *The Animal Pit* – Salesman Scenes

It was a fine summer's day in the small border town of Scotsfield. The Lady of the Lake festival was just over and everyone was in good spirits and trying their best to keep it that way, still laughing, joking and lingering about the streets.

So it was not all that surprising that Campbell Morris, an English travelling salesman who happened to be in town on business, should decide to treat himself to a drink or two before continuing his journey to Dublin. The first bar he sampled was the Step Down Inn but it proved to be just that little bit too quiet for his tastes, so he finished up his beer (*'No! We don't sell pale ale in here!'* the barman bluntly informed him) and proceeded further down the street to what was an impressive-looking building indeed (*'Barbarella's - where love stories begin!'*), which looked like just the place for him!

'If there's action to be had in the town of Scotsfield then I've a feeling it's to be found in here,' mused the Englishman to himself as he pushed open the door and went inside. That was the great thing about Ireland, he thought, as he sipped his beer and accepted his change from the barman, who introduced himself as 'Austie' - you were hardly in a town five minutes before you were made to feel like you belonged in the place. Already he was beginning to give serious consideration to not returning to Dublin at all - but actually booking into a hotel and -

'Hello! My name's Hoss!' declared the bullish, red-faced man who'd just finished playing pool. 'You're on holidays then I take it?'

'No,' he replied, 'just passing through. I'm a salesman, actually. Just over from London.'

'Oh, London,' said Hoss. 'Many's the time I was in it. Do you mind if I join you? A Smithwick's and a Guinness there, Austie, if you please!'

Well, what a time he had with Hoss. Or Hoss Watson, which he informed the salesman was his full name. The man was a scream with these stories of his, an absolute fucking scream! 'But wait till I tell you!' he'd say, as he grabbed your elbow. 'Then the Borstal Boy says . . .' He was full of these stories about Brendan Behan, about whom all the salesman could genuinely say he knew was that he was an Irish author of some sort. But apart from that, knew nothing.

'Oh, by cripes, he was a good one!' went on Hoss. '"What sight do you most want to see in Spain while you're here?" says the customs officer. "What sight do you most want to see while you're here?" And what does the Laughing Boy say? "Franco's fucking funeral!"' The whole bar exploded when he said that. As it did when he told the one about this

Behan fellow painting a pub in Paris. '"This is the best fucking pub in Paris!" He painted that above the door! Can you fucking believe it, can you, Campbell?'

Campbell Morris had to admit that he couldn't. As he had to admit that for as far back as he could remember he hadn't enjoyed a night like this . . .

'And the night's young yet, eh, boys?' laughed Hoss as yet another tray arrived laden down with drinks all purchased for the visitor. They wouldn't let him put his hand in his pocket. The only thing was, Campbell had to keep reminding himself, he'd have to, at some point, book into a hotel. And he was on the verge of doing that when out of nowhere the singing started. Someone produced a guitar – he said his name was Bennett – and launched into a country-and-western tune. Well, this was music to Campbell Morris's ears all right, for there was no one he liked more than Hank Williams. So, without being asked, he stumbled up to the podium and started into 'Jambalaya', and within seconds the whole place had erupted.

'Good man, Campbell!' bawled Hoss as Bennett, the spit of Willie Nelson with his beard and collarless shirt, winked over and gave him the thumbs up.

Whenever the bellicose Republican songs started up after that, Hoss squeezed his arm and told him not to worry, it was only the boys letting off steam. Which Hoss needn't have worried about, for Campbell was oblivious to any intended slight. Even when the singer – a different chap now – punched the air with a vengeance, nearly strangling the microphone as he snarled: *God's curse on you, England, you cruel-hearted monster!* The ironic thing is that if Campbell had responded to it, for clearly the sentiments were being addressed towards him, the singer would, conceivably, have been satisfactorily mollified if a craven acknowledgement of his country's grave misdeeds had been forthcoming from

Campbell in the form of crushed and compliant body language. The positions reversed, as it were, with Campbell playing the part of the browbeaten, craven subject. But such a response never materialised. Indeed, if anything, the opposite was in evidence, with Campbell, completely inebriated, following one Hank Williams song with another, slapping the counter and calling for drinks, now clearly having the time of his life.

It was at this juncture, or close to it, that the murmurings began.

What exactly it was that Campbell had been asked, he wasn't even sure himself. He was far too busy singing Hank Williams. Then someone asked him what he thought of the Queen, and he responded by saying she was a great old girl. Strictly speaking, at the back of their minds, everyone present knew that the whispered allegation of 'spy' was not just a little absurd. But then, as someone else said: 'What about the Littlejohn brothers that were convicted a couple of years back of working for MI5? No one at the start would have believed it of them. And look what they got up to.'

Then someone mentioned the case of the soldier in Cavan who had been working in the meat factory for over a year before his links with British intelligence were discovered.

'Remember,' someone said, 'it's easy to operate around the border and there's plenty of information to be got. And what better cover than a salesman?' If Campbell had been a trifle more conciliatory and perhaps demonstrated a little more comprehension of the situation in Northern Ireland, especially when asked about Frank Stagg the hunger striker ('*Oh, for heaven's sake, why didn't he just take his food!*' he replied), things might have panned out differently. No one could say for certain who came up with the idea of the reservoir. 'That way we'll know for certain,' they said.

'We'll ask him a couple of questions. A few fucking questions won't do any harm! That way we'll know for sure!' You could tell, the drunker they became, that some people had started to think of themselves as desperados now, although in the normal run of things they'd have been terrified to think they'd be associated with subversives and were seeing themselves now as some kind of defenders of a dead striker's honour.

Initially, Hoss was against the idea. But then, he thought, it couldn't do any harm. Bennett, also, thought the whole thing 'fucking crazy'.

'No fucking way!' he snapped. 'The man's just drunk!'

But they kept on at him – 'We're all in this together' – so in the end he relented. It was him drove the van, in fact. 'Just do the driving,' Hoss had said, 'and make sure nobody does anything stupid. Just throw a scare into the English fucker. Do that much at least, so he'll keep his lippy mouth shut in future. I'm not going. It's too risky. The cops are watching me day and night. I'm relying on you now, Bennett. To keep an eye on things in case they get out of hand.'

Which, as we know, they did.

(*The Animal Pit* – End of Salesman Scene)

I stood by the water with my megaphone, stroking my chin as the kids took their positions directly under the sycamore. Then: *Action!*

'*That's it!*' I bawled through the megaphone. '*Now get stuck in – and give it everything, guys!*'

'You fucking cunt!' they kept shouting at the salesman. 'You needn't think you'll fool us, you fucking spy!'

You could tell just by looking at it right there and then that it was going to be the key scene. There were some really great lines, particularly when they all began to get hysterical – 'We'll have to puncture the body! It won't sink unless we do! We'll have to puncture the body! Oh, Jesus Christ, what have we done? What have we done to this innocent man!'

'He wasn't innocent! You can't afford to start thinking he was innocent!'

We got a good shot of them dumping him in the water.

'Print that!' I called and gathered the cast about me. 'Tonight when you go home, I want you to think about this! Tomorrow we'll be filming the pub scenes, the planning of the "interrogation", etc. So I want you to think about an innocent man. I want you to think of a world coming asunder. Of Bennett pleading: *"Don't do it!"* and the Englishman just lying here, convulsing. I want you to think of their hysterical utterances the very minute they realized what it was they'd gone and done: *"Big shot! Coming into town and acting the big shot! What did he have to come here for? Why couldn't he have gone somewhere else? Why? Why couldn't he?"'*

I looked over just for a second and was delighted to see Boyle absolutely riveted to the action! You could tell that – without being too big-headed about it, I thought – the smoothness and professionalism of it had taken him somewhat by surprise.

For I didn't think he *really* believed I had it in me. An instinctive ability to organize people. To bring out the best performance, which is the first real skill of any director.

'I want you to think of all those things,' I continued, very assured and in control now, 'and I want you to ask: What made it all happen? I want you to ask this question: Can we ever be absolved?'

Then I said I wanted to read them something. It was a poem I'd come across in the paper. That very morning.

'Cast,' I said, 'I want to read you this!'

They irritated me a little by taking a long time to settle down and I was on the verge of saying: 'Oh, very well then! I *won't* fucking read it!'

But in the end they dutifully complied and there wasn't a single sound to be heard. Apart from the leaves.

I cleared my throat and flattened out the paper. Then, with my eyes, for all the world like little cameras, panning across them, each and every one, I declaimed the poem to the best of my ability. *Now there's a poem about peace!* I kept thinking. *Not like Carmel Braiden's pile of rubbish that won Fr Connolly's prize!*

There wasn't a whisper. Rapt is a word I might employ to describe the waterside atmosphere. As I reached the climax, I declaimed:

I get down on my hands and knees and do what must be done
And kiss Achilles' hand, the killer of my son.

They applauded as I finished. Then they began to drift off home-
wards, with the usual valedictions of 'See you tomorrow', 'Ciao', and
so on and so forth.

I strolled over then to have a chat with Boyle. He was ecstatic, he
told me. He said that he just couldn't believe the performances I'd
managed to 'elicit' from the cast. That was the word he actually used!
And it made me think that even Boyle must want to get in on the 'creative' act if he's starting to use words like that – 'elicit'!

I couldn't believe it as I stood there rapping. That I'd ever been
afraid of him calling. Late at night or any other time. It embarrassed
me, in fact, when I thought about the imaginary conversations I'd had
with him so many times in the caravan. In which I'd hear him giving
vent to certain 'reservations', if not outright disapproval!

The truth was that he couldn't have been more complimentary. I
even began to wonder was he overdoing it a bit – in front of the actors,
you know? But all the same it was great to hear.

Then he said: 'Do you mind if I smoke?'

'Not at all,' I replied as he lit up his Hamlet. The twists of blue
smoke went waltzing past his nose, smelling sweet in the summer air.
Then Hoss arrived up in a Land Rover and said he was sorry he was
late, that he had been looking forward all morning to the filming.

'Ah, you missed it, Hoss!' said Boyle. 'You were great in it. You
should have seen the young fellow doing your part! He was terrific, so
he was!'

Hoss wanted to know all about this, so I explained as best I could.

'The most important thing for us to realize,' I said, 'all of us who
were involved – in whatever way – in this, is that the film isn't in the
business of blame.'

I collected my thoughts and continued: 'That's not what it's all
about, Hoss,' I said, reassuring him, for this was one of the queries
which kept coming up: would real names appear in the final cut?
Appear at all, in fact? In *any* cut . . .?

I shook my head, vehemently.

'*Of course not!*' I explained. 'It's just to help the actors achieve . . .
that feel of gritty realism, yeah? For ultimately what the movie's about
is not what happened out at the reservoir that night in Scotsfield or

anywhere else for that matter. It's about what has happened in our *hearts*, and how it really is possible for art, when it acts as a mirror to the soul, to become a powerful agent for transformation and rebirth! If not outright absolution!'

'Sounds good,' said Hoss. 'What do you think, Boyle?'

'I wish I had his brains,' said Boyle. 'It's been humbling, Hoss. That's as much as I can say.'

I just heard Boyle say that and no more, I was so busy trying to articulate my own feelings. To frame them in language that would do them justice.

'I suppose in a sense I want it to act as a symbol for Ireland and for what has been going on here this past thirty years. Do you know what I'm saying, Mr Henry?'

Boyle nodded eagerly.

'Of course I do,' he said. 'And let me tell you this: I'm impressed. Are you impressed, Hoss?'

Hoss said that he was.

'I'm extremely impressed,' he said. 'Very, very. Right, Boyle?'

'Very, very,' agreed Boyle Henry.

'Extremely, extremely impressed,' affirmed Hoss.

Then Boyle tapped his cigar and winked at me: 'Do you hear Hoss, Josie?' he said. 'Using all the big words!'

I smiled. Then I continued: 'So, in effect, what I'm saying, Hoss, is that your character – the character Hoss as he appears in the film – could effectively be almost anyone! Anyone who happens to get caught up in a conflict! It's got nothing to do with you *per se*!'

You could tell he was immensely relieved by that, with whatever anxieties he might have had now more or less dismissed for good, it having become perfectly clear that what I was engaged in was not some kind of hastily cobbled together biopic along the lines of *Scotsfield! That's the Way It Is!* Some miserable little 'cheap shot', a tedious, whistle-blowing exercise that would end up achieving nothing but leave a bad taste in everybody's mouth.

'No, Hoss!' I continued as I folded up some chairs. 'What we're after here is just one thing, and that thing, my friend, is the *truth*.'

I was delighted to see him loosening up so dramatically after that – that was clear from his broadening smile. Because, I mean, if I was in the business, I thought, of *blaming* people, whether it be Hoss Watson or anyone, regardless of what they had done, and I knew Hoss'd done

265

plenty of things . . . Of saying: 'You, Hoss, did this!' Or, 'You, Hoss, did that! It was *you* killed such and such in the year 1973! It was *you* possessed explosives in the year 1976!' – if that was all I was doing, then my picture was redundant right from the very start.

What about all the others who had perpetrated deeds of an equally heinous nature? Were a selected band of unfortunates to facilitate their convenient exculpation by shouldering all the blame?

No, I wanted to show things as objectively as possible and open up the audience's hearts, so that the like of what we'd witnessed in our times would never occur again.

'So do you get my drift then, Hoss? Mr Henry? It's not a biography, really, as such.'

Boyle nodded. So did Hoss. Then he said, as he folded his arms: 'I'm getting it, Joey. I get your drift. It is, in a way, kind of like, how would you say it? Kind of a version of *The Three Stooges*.'

'*What?*' I said, quite taken aback to hear him saying something like that. But when he explained what he meant I began to understand – kind of.

'Using real people and actors, I mean,' said Hoss. 'Like Curly Larry and Moe. Because they were real people, weren't they, Boyle? I say, weren't they, Mr Henry?'

'*They sure was, Hoss!*' laughed Boyle. '*They sure was!*' Then he ratcheted Hoss's nose, and Hoss went: '*Ow!*'

'*Take that, ya mallethead!*' laughed Boyle, then said they'd have to be going.

'Well, Joey, my friend,' he continued then, 'I don't know how to thank you for allowing us to see this picture! Do you know something? Keep this up and Joey Tallon won't be going to Hollywood! For *Hollywood* will be coming to *him*!'

'Thanks a lot then, guys! Really glad you enjoyed it!'

'We did, Joey!' said Hoss as he unlocked his Land Rover. 'Keep up the good work!'

'Good luck then, Joey! We'll be seeing you soon!' called Boyle as he flicked away his cheroot, climbing into the smoked-glass motor. 'And remember this: we'll be seeing you!'

'For we're your biggest fans! *Oh yes!*' called Hoss as he tore off across the grass, churning up the mud while his fingers wiggled out of the window. Before, I could have sworn, forming themselves into the shape of a 'V'.

Dandelion Clocks

As I sat there long after they'd gone, listening, with my eyes closed, to the stirring in the leaves, I couldn't stop thinking of the way that he'd said that *'Oh yes!'* and kept analyzing it over and over. But in the end I took myself in hand: 'Stop this now, Joey!' I said. 'We don't want you starting that old bullshit! That doesn't belong here now. Those are feelings from a faraway world that no longer has any relevance! You were wrong about Boyle and you're wrong about Hoss! You *didn't* hear a chuckle as he drove off through the field! There was nothing noteworthy about his fingers! That was your imagination, that stupid overworked imagination of yours, so stop it now and forget it! Start living right here in the *here and now*, and bear witness to your own philosophies! For what sense will it make if you don't? You, the one who's been crying out for a new way of seeing things. A new vision and order that will enable us to jettison the ghosts of the past. Then what do you do? You go and fall at the very first hurdle, the very minute that you've been tested! Reacting in that same old tired and predictable manner.'

'That way has failed us, Joseph Tallon!' I cried aloud. 'And failed us a thousand times! How many false prophets has this country had? How many times have the people been uplifted only to have their hopes, as so many times in the past, literally dashed to pieces before their very eyes? Is that what you're going to be party to? Is that your intention, Mr Joseph Mary Tallon? Are those your intentions as you're sitting here today?'

I rarely addressed myself by my full name. But I was pleased now that I had. It made me feel kind of . . . *whole.*

Which was a feeling that kept gathering inside of me as I lay there beneath the tree gazing across the still water where the midges were whirling and rapiers of light fenced with each other without making a solitary sound. It was mesmerizing; that was all you could say about it.

'Yes,' I continued, 'this is what it means to be whole! To utter your own name and listen to the wind bearing redemptive messages from that place of peace and rest, then blowing across the water bringing them to all who desire to hear them.'

You just knew as you lay there you were in the presence of the others. Where were they exactly? You couldn't tell for sure, but you knew they were very close by. I rooted about in my shoulder bag and located my *Dead Souls*. I opened it up and rested it right there on my lap. I closed my eyes and listened again. To the soft wind blowing. 'Ssh!' I said as I raised my hand. 'Was that Bennett I heard just now?'

I listened again, thinking of him there in his van by the water, unable to bear the guilt of his involvement in the Campbell Morris 'incident'. Trying to steel himself to follow through with the decision he'd made some days before, the silver water's sheer still surface now seeming anything but peaceful.

'How you doin', old friend?' I asked him. I could feel him all around me. 'What's it like? Is Mona there?' I asked, and the sun's sudden wink as a cloud passed it by might have been his smile.

'You'd better believe it,' he said. 'I remember when we were kids we used to say how it might be like the colouring book of a kid. The big blue sky and the golden swaying corn. And sure enough it is. That's what it's like up here now, Joey. You approach it from afar, the harbour drawing your boat safely home. At night you can see them twinkling, the lights that give signals to those hard-pressed, lonesome souls.'

Well, I can't tell you how contented . . . no, *not* contented – that's a lacklustre and anodyne old word for the emotion I'm trying to express – more like close to *incoherent* I became after hearing Bennett speaking those words. Now, after everything good that had happened, with the kids being so terrific in performance and Boyle Henry being so receptive and encouraging and everything, whatever unease I'd been experiencing was clearly nothing more now than old-fashioned paranoia. A tangle of infuriating brambles that served no other purpose than to impede the clear path of truth.

There were also, of course, the immense possibilities which my plans for Wonderful Pictures were suggesting inside my head. Not to mention another little project I had started on, a piece of prose fiction which I thought might end up being a novel, although I'd never written one in my life!

Ideas just seemed to keep popping up out of nowhere. I just could not believe my good fortune on this earth, I really and genuinely could not! With the result that it was all I could do not to run over to the nearest Friesian cow and give it a great big kiss on the forehead! Which I didn't, on reflection thinking the better of it, for you never knew who might be watching, and that just might be a little bit too much for them. 'Fukken kissin' fukken cows!' you could almost hear them saying. 'What next – riding sheep?'

I did, however, open up my *Dead Souls* and begin sonorously reciting my favourite passage, my voice gliding right across the still stretch of water as I gestured expansively. I was so full of belief because of the way things had gone that I think I must have thought that I was Charles Laughton! *'The spring,'* I began, *'which had been held back for a long time by frosts . . .'*

Then, soliloquy completed, I lay down once more. It was so comforting beneath that sycamore, with all of them around you (Bennett jerking his thumb: *'Would you look at the lazy big bollocks!'* and Mona going: *'Always mad for the books!'*) making you feel you were *already* at home, in that place where nothing would prove unacceptable. Where you could say: 'I'm the Prophet of Spring,' or, 'I'm Cassavetes the Second!' and no one would ever bother saying: 'Oh, would you shut up, Joey Tallon, you and your nonsense and your fanciful ideas, when everyone knows you're a great big stinky blob, that's all you are and everyone knows it – and all you'll ever be!'

(It's hard to believe – and to this day I still can't get my head around it – that you could submit a typescript with a title such as that – *The Amazing Adventures Of Blobby McStink* – and on the strength of it be told you're a fucking genius! But I'm afraid that's what happened – 'Joey McDoughey the Stinky old Blob' and his smelly old stupid old life story turning out to rock the meek-mannered world of letters! Look out, James Joyce, there's a new kid in town!)

I kissed the grass and bade her – and them – *adieu*, their voices all beginning to fade as I made my way once more back to town.

Until they'd vanished altogether, retreating back behind the clouds until the time would come for us to talk again, for all the world like little dandelion clocks just floating away on the breeze.

The Temple of Colossal Dimensions

The only thing was that once the film was finished – or 'in the can' as they say in the trade – I found myself at a bit of a loose end, kind of in-between projects, I guess you could say. But in a totally different way than before, because what had happened now was that at last I'd grown up. My experience in the college and in shooting the picture –

at least that's how it seemed to me – had shown me how, if you can manage to believe – really and truly, I mean – then things will somehow just fall into place. The days of standing around moping, waiting for Johnston Farrell-type figures to appear like a troop of 'soul cavalry' to offer you some form of example or guidance, or of twiddling your thumbs every day down in Austie's, half-cocked from drinking beer – not to mention screwing up your head with fucking lysergic acid – were a thing of the dim, distant past.

As I strode about the town, I felt now like I owned it. Or that at least there was a tiny little part of it that would now forever be all mine, which was a hell of a lot more than I'd ever had ownership of before!

I couldn't stop thinking that if someone had come up to me, just right there and then as I walked around, and said: 'I say there, Joseph! I know you're probably busy with your film-making but we've just got this slight problem! You see, we've to come up with a poem for a special occasion because our usual fellow's gone and let us down. Well, actually he hasn't, he's been taken sick, in fact, and we were wondering – we know it's short notice – do you think you could help us out?'

'In a jiffy!' I'd say, without even having to think. It was as though I'd been fitted out with the most fabulous suit of burnished armour. 'Look! There he goes!' I could hear them say as I came across the square, clutching my Gogol and swinging my shoulder bag. 'There he goes! Joey Tallon! Scotsfield's only true living genius! Do you know what I'm going to tell you? There's nothing that fellow can't do!'

However, somewhere deep within me, there was the tiniest twinge of concern regarding Hoss's fingers sticking out the window of his Land Rover.

Then I'd meet Boyle Henry in the newsagent's buying his paper or just passing by on the street, and the very minute I did, would feel so foolish!

'Oh for heaven's sake, Joey!' I'd say to myself and wipe away the perspiration, most of which, really, was caused by the heat. It was turning out to be a very hot summer, just like old times. There was talk of water shortages again and the fire engines were at it the very same as before, charging out the country to douse the numerous gorse fires and barn blazes. What with my thinking so much about forgiveness and having so much time on my hands, it was on an otherwise ordinary day in the middle of July when I was coming past the Fuck Me that I experienced a kind of revelation. Another 'eureka' moment, I guess you could call it, when I found myself thinking: *What about a manifesto, Joseph? A film manifesto, perhaps!*

Which I reckoned would be a way of getting it all down on paper so that people would know what your actual philosophy regarding your chosen discipline was. And you wouldn't have to be going: 'My film's about this,' or 'My film's about that.'

It would all be there for everyone to see, like your ordinary political philosophy, essentially, except in a more creative and artistic vein. I was sitting in the café sipping a latte and scribbling when I thought of a title that came to me so suddenly that I swear to God I nearly had a seizure!

'*The New Spring Manifesto!*' I heard myself saying, the words arranging themselves as if in Day-Glo right there before my eyes.

I think everything I have ever believed or considered believing was included there in that very first draft. I didn't stop writing until I looked up and saw the waitress standing staring at me with this lazy expression, announcing: 'We're closing!'

I rolled up my document and, shoving it into my shoulder bag, headed off down to Doc Oc's to see who might be around – maybe some of the students, who would definitely be interested in this startling new development!

'You're beginning to frighten me, Joe Tallon!' I said as I bounded towards the pub. 'What I'd like to know is just where they're all coming from, these cracking new ideas of yours?'

It seemed to me incontestable now that the reason all this was happening was to make up for all the bad old times, those fucked-up days of the 1970s and the dreary grey days in prison. The 'Day of the Second Chance' had arrived with a bang, opening up door after door. I didn't deserve it, maybe, but boy, now that it was here, was I going to take advantage of it!

To celebrate 'eureka' – and I know it must sound silly – I decided in Doc Oc's that I wouldn't have a drink or any of their fancy gastronomic dishes but instead a great big pie! Yes! A great big steak and kidney! As a way of saying cheerio to the past! To those anxious days of no opportunity when, frightened, you stuck your face in one of these and didn't dare lift your head!

Not now, I'm afraid! There was a different approach to the old pies now! Why, they even had them specially made! None of your microwave slop in a jacket of tatty old cellophane! The very best of home cooking, the most 'nutritious' pies in Ireland, I was told! And low calorie too!

'Good!' I thought as, with my knife and fork almost defiantly clutched, I launched with a vengeance into a sample and it was all I could do not to let out a cheer. I could see Austie staring down at me, but I really didn't care in the slightest. All I kept thinking of was my 'Spring Manifesto'.

There was a politician on the television talking about the changes that had come over the country lately and the clean wind that seemed to be blowing throughout almost every corner of the land. I chuckled and walloped another forkful of steak good and hard down into my gullet.

'*You ain't seen nothing yet!*' I exclaimed as I imagined myself on that TV screen, talking away there in place of the newsreader. Clearing my throat as I opened the document and sombrely intoned: 'And now – the "Spring Manifesto"!'

All that night I couldn't get to sleep. I could have sworn I heard a knock, but it was just someone rattling a bucket. 'Oh, for heaven's sake! Not Mangan again!' I mumbled irritably and went to the window. And sure enough there he was, filling his pail at the pump.

I smiled as I heaved a sigh of relief and climbed back into bed, proceeding to consider, in some depth, the predominant strands of my philosophy. But most of all allowing myself to dwell for some considerable length of time on the magnificent idea that was the Theatre of Forgiveness, my fabulous 'Temple of Colossal Dimensions'!

It was the cornerstone, essentially, of the manifesto, a jewel-encrusted edifice so bright your eyes could barely gaze upon it, incredulous at the sight it presented, having risen so dramatically from the interior of the dankest swamp – that of the soul of Joey Tallon and of everyone in Scotsfield town.

The Prophet of Spring

Reflecting on all these developments from what, at this stage, might be considered – I don't think I've the will or imagination left for anything else, to be honest! – a reasonably objective viewpoint, I suppose I'd have to say that what surprises me most is . . . well, how I got away with it, basically.

I mean, to succeed, in the first place, in getting the things printed. My 'manifestos', I mean! Did the printer or his assistant never examine the content, for God's sake? At least take a *look* at the sort of thing they were running through their machines?

It certainly doesn't look like either of them had ever bothered, for I don't remember experiencing even the slightest bit of hassle, with them just accepting the copy without a murmur and going off then about their business like I'd dropped them in the local *Greyhound News*. In another way too, of course, in the beginning at least – before it began to seem like the whole town had been papered over with 'Prophets of Spring' manifestos – it would all have seemed as little more than a laugh. In the way that I heard an old fellow say, when I was giving a speech in the square (it seemed like a natural progression from directing, and any politician that was worth their salt would surely sooner or later have to develop their public speaking – at least that's the way I'd been rationalizing it): 'He's at it again, that Joey Tallon! Since he started above in that community college, they can't keep him quiet! The only way of doing it might be to tie the fucker down!'

Which I have to say amused me no end. Except that that wouldn't even do it. For now that I'd glimpsed *possibility* – of a specific, particular kind – I really did see how practical, useful change – as well as the spiritual kind – might be effected and nothing now would stop me till I'd finished. Not even Carmody, who did her damnedest to ruin it, demanding to know why I was pasting up posters.

'You have no business putting those up in this school!' I found myself told after she walked in on one of the impromptu lectures that I had started giving to a number of the particularly zealous students in a rarely used seminar room. Which happened to be, unfortunately, on 'transgressive' or 'unusual' cinema, which we had been discussing of late, having just viewed David Cronenberg's *Shivers*, rented for that purpose.

The 'Cut Short' Lecture

I simply coughed and proceeded. The students were extremely attentive. It was, in essence, an unofficial *ad hoc* film studies group. I had no difficulty in departing from my script as I had been up until very late the night before memorizing the essential content. I stood at the window organizing my thoughts before turning to say: 'The movie you have just been watching seems, on the surface, to be a very simple story. But is it? A lot of the critics have suggested that it operates on a much deeper level than we think.'

I had read that in one of the film magazines and was only throwing it out as a suggestion. The plot of the film was, indeed, on the face of it quite uncomplicated. In it a number of women shared an apartment in a building in Montreal. I knew it was Montreal because it said so in the article. Otherwise I wouldn't have had a clue. Nothing remarkable happened for a bit, with one day being pretty much as the next until, then, one of the tenants kicks off her shoes and climbs into the bath to have herself a good long soak and wipe away all the cares of the day, the hassles of working in the office and shit. Then the plug goes *plup!* and the next thing you know there's this flotilla of foot-long parasites poking their heads through the plughole like pink mini-submarines, for that's the only way you could describe them, the camera homing in as they make their way towards the woman's private parts as though they've been programmed to do it or something. It doesn't just happen to her, though. Very soon it's taking place all over the city – the very same thing and in exactly the same way. Hundreds of flesh-bombs on the loose. It transpires that what they are, then, is parasites who infect the victim with venereal disease and make them go rabid for sex.

That led to a discussion on the topic of alternative cinema generally. I was in the middle of talking about that when I saw her. She had her arms folded and was livid. I was on the verge of saying: 'Hello, Mrs Carmody'.

But I never got the chance. I couldn't believe it. She actually came over and grabbed the book out of my hand.

'Who gave you the authority to set up this impromptu lecture?' she spat with venom.

The Good of the Community

What she didn't say to me in her office that day simply wasn't worth saying. Then she sent Fr Connolly out to the caravan in an effort to make me 'come to my senses'. He said I was on the verge of being dismissed. But I talked it through with him and – ha! Tough shit there, Dr Carmody! – he left having to admit that I had been making sense.

I was a bit cute there, though, to tell the honest truth, ensuring I had plenty of quotes from the Bible and *St John of the Cross* to accompany my arguments so that they would make the padre feel good. And, boy, did he feel good! No doubt thinking: *Yes, Joey's done his homework! And it can't be denied that he has the good of the community at heart!*

The good of the community? Why that decent old fuckbrain padre doesn't know how much! I remember thinking.

Like I explained to the kids, by the time we were finished and our film had acquired distribution, etc., etc., and been seen by thousands of people, the town of Scotsfield would be like the star in some magical widescreen extravaganza, one you'd be literally incapable of turning away from, complete with soaring, heart-lifting soundtrack.

'And how has this come about?' I asked the next day as I tapped my pencil. 'Because it had the courage to look into the animal pit! To hold its gaze as it stared in there to behold the . . . *writhing maggots!* But also [I paused] to discover . . . *the chickens!*'

'Also to discover the chickens!' I boomed as I engaged my rapt class without flinching.

The Chickens of Forgiveness

What I meant by that, of course, was 'The Chickens of Forgiveness', a little story which I'd related to them and some weeks before reprinted in my pamphlet – I used to get the kids themselves to distribute them, which wasn't strictly kosher. I mean, it wasn't their job. But they were fantastic about it, they really were, making no complaint at all.

'Sure thing!' they'd say. 'We'll see you right! We'll see these chickens hatch!'

And did those birds lay eggs or what? I don't know how many people – just ordinary folks you'd meet on the street – came up to me after reading it: 'You know something, Joey?' Or, 'You know something, Mr Tallon' depending on who they were. 'That chicken story is one of the most meaningful and moving parables I've ever heard in my life!'

Which indeed it was. I had come across it completely and utterly by accident, and it really did exert a powerful influence over me. Although, admittedly, at the time it didn't take all that much to get me going, discerning import as I now was in the simplest and most mundane of things, quoting *St John of the Cross* every chance I got. I had really come to like his verse, especially after his help in winning Fr Connolly around.

One day I ran into Austie, finding myself declaring: '*My soul – no longer bound – is free from the creations of the world.*'

'Sure,' he said, 'sure it is, maestro.'

I knew by the way he said it that it didn't mean very much to him. It didn't matter. I knew I was never going to bring everyone with me. 'Nobody ever does,' I said to the kids. 'A small band of devoted followers would be infinitely preferable to a horde of uncertains!'

It was Mangan who heard it first, the 'Parable of the Birds', I mean, or whatever you might like to call it. I couldn't sit still as soon as I'd read it and ran straight over to tell him. '"Chickens of Forgiveness"?' he kept saying, all the time trying to kick the used condom back in under the bed where I wouldn't see it – he'd just been at his doll, whose head was still sticking out from under the bed. 'What kind of chickens would they be, Joey?' he croaked.

I made sure to take my time and explain. He kept nodding as I spoke, but I knew he wasn't listening as he tried to nudge the wigged head back underneath with his boot.

'Will you leave it alone, Mangan!' I said. 'She's of no consequence now!'

He spluttered into a fit of coughing, turning puce again before nodding compliantly as I paced about the caravan and continued: 'You see, Mangan, there was this Christian woman, although strictly speaking I'm not a Christian – a *Springian*, perhaps, but not a Christian specifically – who owned two prize-winning chickens. One afternoon, the birds worked their way out of her yard and into her neighbour's garden. The neighbour, known for his hot temper, captured both birds, wrung their necks viciously and threw their lifeless carcasses across the fence into the woman's yard. The woman was undoubtedly hurt and considered giving the neighbour a piece of her mind. Instead she took the poultry home and prepared two pies, whereupon she took one to her neighbour and then apologized for not being more watchful of her chickens.'

I paused. 'Mangan?' I said, suddenly stabbing the air with my finger. He started, taken aback a little – I suppose I was used to being direct with the kids. 'What do you think the man's reaction was?'

I could see his Adam's apple squirming as he swallowed. He was plucking at his pocket with the crook of his thumb as I heard him reply: 'Jeekers, Joey, I don't know!'

I didn't mean to shout as loud as I did.

'He was speechless, Mangan! Speechless!'

And I left his caravan straight away. I had a few other ideas I wanted to jot down.

A Letter to the Council

There was talk of us improvising another short film based on the story – I had prepared a basic storyboard and the barest bones of a script – but we never actually got around to doing it. Which is a pity because the kids were a hundred per cent behind it.

'Let me be the chicken!' says one of them. 'Yeah, Joey! I could do it!'

They could be little fuckers at times! You know, taking the piss!

But what an image, if we'd ever managed to get around to shooting it! A close-up of the shocked man's face and the two crusted pies just sitting there steaming . . .

And then – *blam!* – in great big block letters, in emerald neon, say:

THE CHICKENS OF FORGIVENESS!!

It would have been absolutely fantastic, but I was so busy with my posters, it was pretty much impossible to get around to it. I simply hadn't time for everything. Then there were other ideas, one of the most exciting ones being getting a campaign started and actually going out and building the thing – the Temple of Colossal Dimensions, I mean. I could not stop thinking of the reaction of tourists when they'd come into this little village, expecting the usual old rural stuff, nothing much to write home about. A couple of tractors parked on the road, say, or an old stray dog just scratching its ass when all of a sudden they turn a corner and – Jesus! – the 'Fuck Me!' hotel paling into insignificance as they gasped: *'Can you believe it? Can you fucking believe your eyes, Mabel?'*, this magnificent polished white marble structure then rising up before them out of nowhere, with Doric columns, majestic colonnade, the *works*!

The great thing about that being that it would no longer just be a spiritual thing at all but our own private colosseum in memory of the dead built by our very own selves.

And the more I thought of it the more plausible it began to seem, because when you're dealing with something practical like that, something that people can actually see and feel and touch, it can excite people's imaginations. It's very hard to drum up support for an idea or philosophy. But with an actual *building* . . . I reckoned they'd be queuing up to give us grants – cross-border bodies, European Regional Funds, you name it!

Not to mention the enthusiasm that the locals would demonstrate. I reckoned they'd soon be throwing money at it, not to mention volunteering their labour. I dreamed up a slogan: *'The dead! We work to make them live!'* and of getting Fr Connolly to announce the scheme at Mass whereby every Saturday each man woman and child in the Scotsfield area would give of their time, free, gratis and for nothing, to construct this edifice with their own bare hands so that it would belong to the community in a way that had never before been thought possible.

It never happened, though, even though I wrote to the council. Spent hours composing the letter, in fact, in between trying to contact people with regard to what was happening to the movie scripts and video cassettes I'd sent them, something which was really beginning to irritate me. I mean, it was months now and – apart from the usual letter of acknowledgement – I hadn't heard back from any of the distribution companies. Which, as I had learnt from my experience long before with Mr Bono, meant sweet and effing fuck all! After polishing the first few paragraphs of the letter I put through another few calls and managed to track down a certain Simon Elliott.

'Just *what* the hell is going *on?*' I asked him. 'You could at least give me your opinion of the picture! A lot of those kids have worked damned hard on it, Mr Elliott!'

He was very polite, of course – as usual – and then says: 'I'll put you on hold,' and before you know it you're into 'Pop Goes the Weasel' or, even worse, Latin American pan pipes, as you stand there waiting for the fucker to come back. Which, eventually, he did, and what's the verdict then? 'We'll be in touch as regards your film, which the board have pencilled in for viewing tomorrow. Thank you!'

'Yes! And thank *you*, Mr Elliott!' I snapped and slammed down the fucking receiver. *Jesus!* I thought. *You think the hard bit is going to be coming up with the* ideas! *Coming up with the ideas and then getting them on to the screen! But no! It's not true! That's not the hard bit at all! The hard bit is getting the fuckers to watch it! Fuckers like Elliott with his half-English accent!*

I don't know how long I was working on the letter altogether. The guts of one whole night, all told, I reckoned, with my *Roget's Thesaurus* and dictionary beside me. That might sound over the top but I didn't want them – the council – treating this as some Mickey Mouse scheme, along the lines of new traffic lights or the widening of a road. No, sir, this was a whole different deal, a new departure, the beginning of a massive, big-thinking adventure. I scanned it one more time, then popped it in the post before heading up to the library to see if Una Halpin had got me my book.

Since finishing the movie, I had started reading up on historical figures, basically trawling around for ideas, with a view perhaps to preparing a major biopic of a significant historical figure – perhaps a spiritual leader. Such as Gandhi, perhaps, but he'd already been done. Maybe even Éamon de Valéra, the President of the Irish Republic who had fought the fight against the British.

But that was all over, I thought then; it was the opposite of that we wanted. I was after someone who had nothing to do with so-called 'freedom fighters'. The opposite, in fact. 'Peace' men. The 'good' Charlie Mansons, in other words.

Perhaps even Jesus Christ himself, I thought, wondering could I play him myself now that my hair had grown long – not unlike The Seeker's, actually – but thought that might be too ambitious and cost the kind of money we just didn't have. Unless, I grinned as I came in through the library doors, we actually 'shot for the moon' and went further than ever before. I asked Una whether she had a *Who's Who*, and sure enough she did.

'There you are, Joseph!' she said, and put it into my hand. I was so taken with this new idea that I went and forgot my biography of Martin Luther King. All the way out to the caravan, I couldn't stop thinking about Harvey Weinstein. I'd been reading about him in *Variety*. One of the most influential movie producers in the world, they reckoned. *'You wanna do what?'* I could hear him saying.

And all that kinda shit, before he'd have to admit that it was one hell of a good idea! 'Jesus Christ reborn in this tiny little Irish village? I gotta say it has a ring to it!'

I would call him first thing in the morning, I decided.

What the fuck! I thought as I slid into bed. *What's the harm in ringing up one of the most important movie producers in the world? I mean, all he can say is no, like Elliott, and I might as well get a refusal from someone who's important as some skinny little jumped-up cunt with a name like that!*

I couldn't believe it the very next day when, after only half a minute (I timed it!) – *So much for you, Elliott!* I thought, as I gave the air a chop – I got straight through to his secretary, an absolutely fantastic chick who told me that Harvey was 'power breakfasting' but would be back around eleven or twelve – could I possibly call back then? 'Could you possibly call back then, Mr Tallon?'

'Could I possibly call back then? *I sure could!*' I chirped. 'Absolutely no problem at all!'

The fact that when I called an hour later I was told he'd been delayed – it was a different secretary this time – but would take my call on Wednesday didn't faze me, not in the slightest. At least I knew I was dealing with someone who had genuine demands on his time, what with doing deals and signing contracts and what have you, not like cunthooks Elliott and his ilk who had nothing to do except file their nails and switch on weasel machines.

I was over the moon at these new developments and had gone into town to work out my pitch – '*Hi! Mr Weinstein! Joey Tallon here, I called you a couple of days ago, yeah? It's about my movie on the life of Jesus Christ*' – then the basic points of the story. I was thinking of him being born maybe in a room over Austie's pub then crucified on the Gaelic football field. It was while I was turning all that around in my mind that I looked up and who was there? Boyle!

'Joey!' he said, and I replied: 'Mr Henry!'

I hadn't been expecting to see him and it wouldn't have been so bad if I had – I wouldn't have started my usual 'rabbiting on'.

'Ah, Joey! Joey! Hush with that now!' he said. 'We have things to talk about!'

He told me then that he had an important message for me from the council. That he'd been looking for me for the past few days, in fact. He went on to say that they had received my letter – under the dual mandate system he could be both senator and a serving member of that body – and that all of them were 'very, very excited indeed' by its contents.

'It's only a matter of them doing the figures,' he said. 'I mean, it's a wonderful idea, this temple!'

It's hard to believe it now, but I heard him uttering those words. Boyle Henry! Boyle!

It almost brought tears to my eyes when I heard him speaking in that encouraging manner, tolerant and patient and genuinely magnanimous. It was all I could do not to grab his hand and kiss the back of it, I was so genuinely relieved and grateful!

And I think he knew that's what I was thinking, for just then he pulled back a little and said: 'Ah now, Joey!' as his eyes twinkled a little and he said: 'Sure there's no need to be getting too excited! Wait till we have something concrete! Such as a temple, for example!'

Then he burst out laughing. Before saying: 'Well, goodbye then, Joey! OK?'

'Sure thing, Mr Henry!' I shouted after him.

I understood. He was right.

'See you then!' he called back and strode across the road to the Fuck Me, on the roof of which the beautiful flags of Europe were all fluttering away in the warm Scotsfield wind.

When I got home, straight off I wrote in my diary:

The Caravan
Thursday p.m., 12 October 2001

Met Boyle Henry completely by chance and he's given me some wonderful news! It seems it's only a matter now of them totting up the figures and deciding on the plan's feasibility. Obviously this does not mean it's going to be built for absolute certain, *but it's a very good sign that they're taking it very seriously indeed. Boyle says that if the cost isn't prohibitive they definitely will draw up a plan and submit it both to the Pax Cross-Border Fund for Reconciliation and Peace and to the various European Regional Fund Schemes that cover this type of thing. 'There's loads of money available,' Boyle said. 'It's just a matter of us getting our hands on it!'*

Before he left me, he said it was 'visionary'.

I can't believe that things have turned out like this. I have this notion of Scotsfield now as a sort of Athens, a post-conflict type of

*golden place that will show everybody else the way. A sort of . . .
what's the word . . . I saw the type of thing I mean in a video the
other night* (Gladiator, *actually, by Ridley Scott!*) – Elysian Fields,
yeah!

A long way from the drab old seventies and that's for fucking sure,
compadre!

Martin Luther King

Whether it was because of Harvey Weinstein getting my goat up (they
eventually told me to stop calling his office – not just 'told', in fact, but
'warned') or the all-pervasive influence of the reverend MLK's unshak-
able self-belief, or whether it was just a hangover from the acid days,
even today I'm still not sure. But I had started actually taking photos
out at the reservoir, which I was now convinced provided the perfect
site. Sending them to the council, along with a recommendation that
'The Memorial', as I had taken to calling it, be erected right there or
very close by, perhaps in memory of Campbell Morris and others who
had died along that stretch of water.

Now that I had become quite buoyed up by the council's initial
enthusiasm, on this particular occasion when I didn't receive a reply by
return, I became quite irritated, which was ridiculous, of course, and
began to telephone them regularly, requesting that I be put through to
the various departments. 'I mean, it's not that difficult!' I remember
saying. 'It's not like you're the Harvey Weinstein Corporation or
something! So come on, please. Thank you!'

Maybe if I had showed more understanding I might have succeeded
better than I did. I ought to have learnt from my experiences with Principle Management and, indeed, the Harvey Weinstein office. But no,
the truth is, I got carried away. I couldn't stop myself thinking of the
temple's almost shocking polished whiteness, the imperious colonnade
as it rose up like magic out of the green-topped trees.

With its triumphant banners and chiselled names – among them my
own, of course, I who had committed the most grievous sin of all.

Because, as I explained in some depth to the guy on local radio – the
news had begun to get around and they had asked me in for an infor-
mal chat – everyone involved would have their contribution acknowl-
edged in this way. At first I had refused to take part in the programme,

mainly because I didn't have anything concrete as yet. But in the end he got around me, persuading me of its importance and so on and so forth.

It was a wide-ranging interview, covering the various aspects of my life. Before the green light went on, he specifically asked me not to confine myself to the topic of 'the troubles' and the proposal to build the temple but to cover as much ground as I possibly could, with particular reference to my movie-making aspirations and the creative work I'd been involved with at the college. I must have been talking for almost fifteen minutes, without a single break, before he said: 'Right then, that's it then, Joey!' and threw the phone lines open.

There was quite a heated debate then, with the listening public breaking down pretty much fifty–fifty into those who had 'really enjoyed it' and those who most definitely had not. Including a number of parents and kids from the college who announced, quite aggressively indeed, that in their considered opinion I should never have been permitted to go on the airwaves at all. But the outcome of it was – and, boy, does this seem crazy now, considering what it started – someone, quite flippantly, I think, to begin with, suggesting that instead of running to the council with suggestions – 'and I think it's a wonderful suggestion, this memorial', he'd added – had Joey Tallon not given any thought to actually running for the council himself, to putting his name forward as a candidate in the forthcoming local elections . . .?

'Well, no, I haven't . . .' I began.

But the moment the words were uttered it was like some glorious Roman candle going *'puf!'* inside my head.

And all that evening, after I got home to the caravan, I couldn't bring myself to sit still, picking up a book – *Steppenwolf*, as it happened – and the minute I saw the cover, succumbing to complete hilarity. Before flinging it *smack!* against the wall. What a lot of nonsense and blather those books now seemed to contain! A lot of piffle and fuck! *Zen! The Yogi dyes his garments! The fish in the water is thirsty!* Who gives a fuck about fish! For life, if it's about anything, is about living and doing, not sitting there cross-legged staring down at your big fat gut! In fact, it's about running for office!

With, of course, poor old Mangan getting the brunt of it again! 'Tell me,' I said, 'tell me honestly right here and now: do you think if I ran I'd have a chance of getting in?'

He stared at me and stammered for a minute, like it was some major oral examination that would end in total disgrace if he flunked it. Then he started picking at his nail and going: 'How would I know, Joey? Sure I know nothing about councils or politics or the like of that!'

'Oh, for Christ's sake, you must have an opinion!' I snapped. I could be really ratty with old Mangan at times.

But by the time the light failed, standing there in that rickety old caravan or mobile home or whatever you want to call it, I had made up my mind. *What?* I thought as I looked at the paper – Bono was on the front of it wearing this stupid-looking Fidel Castro jacket and army hat. *So it's OK for Mr 'Streets Have No Name' not only to go over to America blathering shite about Martin Luther King when he's not even from that country but now start acting like he's black and knows all about hip-hop music?*

I suppose how I saw it was as another tiny little 'eureka'.

'Yes!' I went as I fiddled with my mobile phone. 'It's OK for him to go off doing things like that, but when the ordinary Joe from Scotsfield comes up with a little project of his own, all of a sudden it's a problem? Well, somehow I don't think so!'

I don't fucking think so, Joey Tallon!

The House of the Living Dead

Having made the decision, I started work on my campaign in earnest. Now that the word was out!

Except that saying 'the word was out' is like saying: 'That Martin Luther King, he demonstrated some potential as a politician.'

For it had got to the stage now that I couldn't go up the street without someone calling: 'I say there, Joey! Good luck now in October!' and me starting to get like the rest of them in response.

Like the rest of the politicians, I mean, of course! For a start, going straight into the barber's and getting myself a haircut!

'No Mohawks this time then, Joey?' he said, and I wished he hadn't. Because it reminded me of the bad old days. It brought me back to . . .

I just wished he hadn't said it, that's all.

'Just cut it short and decent,' I said as I leafed through a magazine.

Guess who was in it? 'Oh, for fuck's sake – *Bono*!' I said. This time appealing for peace in Northern Ireland.

Although I had to admit it was a very good cause. Who knew? Perhaps I'd meet him if I got elected. Chat about old times and the Breakaway festival.

'The trouble I had chasing after you, Bono, my man!' I'd say, and we'd have a laugh and head down to Lillies Bordello for a chat and a coupla shots of Jack Daniels.

But then it would be on to more serious matters. Maybe he could write a song, to be played on the inaugural night. 'The Temple Song' maybe, or 'The Achilles Lament', after the poem by Michael Longley that I had included in my manifesto. Who knew – it was just an idea.

After that, I went from strength to strength, everyone telling me how good they thought I looked with my neatly trimmed hair and, of course, all the weight that I'd lately lost. I had bought a suit – actually, the truth is, the St Vincent de Paul Society had assisted me with its purchase but I didn't want anyone to hear about that – and once I'd donned it, in its charcoal grey I looked every inch the up and coming politician, even if I say so myself.

The man with his finger on the pulse!

The caravan was full of newspapers now, and you couldn't look out your window but there I'd be, chatting away to people as they told me all their problems. I really was beginning to become excited – no, not just excited, *empowered* – by this new-found direction. It seemed so *real*! So practical and of . . . *value* that I don't know on how many occasions – after talking to a farmer about, maybe, a sick calf or to a housewife about, say, a housing extension grant – I was on the verge of going – no, not going! – *running!* – back to the caravan and gathering up all my so-called 'paraphernalia of enlightenment' – *St John of the Cross*, Rabindranath Tagore, Hermann Hesse and *Siddartha, Abraxas* – . . .

And making a great big pyre of the whole fucking lot!

Before returning once more to the square, barking through my loudhailer (which I regularly used to assist me with my speeches, whether in the square or anywhere else): '*No! Living is not about thinking! It's about engaging for the good of others! About grabbing life by the hasp of the arse and going: Yes! Yes, I say! Let's . . . do! Not think, my friends, but do!*'

I spoke every Saturday and, bit by bit, the crowds began to get bigger. What was gradually becoming plainer to me was that I had stumbled by accident upon my destiny. It was the most beautiful, rewarding feeling, particularly because of the way it had happened – with a simple, unassuming letter to Scotsfield Urban Council.

'Yes!' I said one day in Doc Oc's. 'All your life you think you're one thing! And then you discover . . .!'

What did I mean by that? I reflected. Then I slapped the counter, saying (privately, however, not to the patrons!): 'I mean that, all along, I have seen myself as being *outside* the establishment! Which is really a load of delusional nonsense! For I belong *inside*! And that realization is my "coming home"! The rebirth that I've been awaiting all along!'

I literally beamed at my reflection in the mirror as I adjusted the thin knot of my spotted grey tie.

I walked home that night. I had cut down dramatically on my drinking; all of that belonged in the past, and as for spliffs? Marijuana – nothing more than the crutch of a sad, Charles Manson-type jailbird who'd been looking in all the wrong places for 'the answer'. 'If only Eamon Byrne could see me now,' I mused as I stepped along the road. 'He really would have himself a laugh!'

The great thing was that now I slept like a top. The old days when I'd been unnerved through thinking about Boyle – they might as well have belonged to another age.

I looked out the window to see a great big sun like a slice of blood orange coming peeping over the hill, and it really did feel like the new beginning to end them all.

Pride in the Name of Love

I just could not wait to get into those chambers, take my seat on the council and get down to the nitty-gritty of helping ordinary Scotsfield citizens with the management of their day-to-day lives. Which I made sure to make clear in the *Scotsfield Standard*. I couldn't believe it when they called me up and asked me. They had got my number from LLR. 'Would you be prepared to do an interview for us,' they said, 'dealing with your policies and your attitudes to living in Scotsfield town generally?'

Nervous as I was, I was happy with the way that it went. I reckoned I looked pretty snazzy, smiling out from the very front page in my executive suit with, very much to the fore, the words 'New Spring Manifesto' clearly visible on the the poster.

I don't know how many times I read the interview while sipping coffee at the bar in Doc Oc's, having decided now to turn my back on alcohol, this time for good. Definitely. With not even so much as an alcopop passing my lips. Absolutely nothing. Come hell or high water, I was going to stick to that.

The number of people who clapped me on the back as they came and went was absolutely unreal! All I kept thinking as I sat there reading was: *Boy! Wouldn't they all be proud of me now!* (I could see me telling Bono how like his song *'Pride [In the Name of Love]'* it all seemed. Because that's what they all said to me: 'We're proud of you, Joey, because of what you're doing – *in love's name*!')

Meaning my love for Mona, of course, and my mother and father, as well as those old pals The Seeker and Bennett, all of whom I saw in my dreams that night. Again I had slept like a lamb, and I can't tell you how good it felt to be experiencing that at last! 'A noise outside? Oh, don't be ridiculous,' I'd say. 'Those "noise-imagining" days are gone forever!'

As my eyes closed over and I stood with those old pals in the hush of a sylvan glade. With the temple already built – even more imposing than I ever had imagined – my father Jamesy beside my mother, bawling through the loudhailer: *'Come on up here, Joey! Come on up here to the temple and talk to your old friends and us – the lovebirds!'* Beaming as he squeezed his beloved wife's hand.

The massive oaken door creaking open as one by one they started appearing in the Great Hall – not only my friends, but also many others who had lived in the town at one time or another. But every one, without exception – it was *wonderful*! – all looking fresh as daisies!

'Yes! It's him we have to thank for building our house!' barked Jamesy. 'This Temple of the Living that commemorates the dead!' as this great big smile cracked from ear to ear.

It was going absolutely fantastic. I could have sworn I caught a glimpse of the salesman flitting about inside and was about to call his name: '*Campbell Morris!*'

But then something happened and I . . .

I was so disappointed when I woke up and found myself covered from head to toe in that familiar old sweat. Then I heard something moving outside and ran over to the window.

I could make out Mangan shuffling back from the pump, pulling his old coat around him as he climbed the step into his caravan, closing the door behind him.

I sat slumped by the window and tried to make out how it had happened . . . that I should wake up all veined and sweaty like that.

Then the dream started returning again, and I remembered how everything had been going so well, until I'd seen the salesman in the shadows.

I wished now I had forgotten the details, which began to reconverge as vividly as if I'd been filming them myself in Technicolor Deluxe – the palmprint of blood plainly visible on the Doric column and the streak on the white wall behind the salesman as he stumbled, his voice not a voice at all but a strangled gargling so similar to the one I remembered from that day long ago when myself and Bennett stood outside Willie Markham's window. The dying man blurred but visible through the glass, his body convulsing as his wife fell across him, hopelessly trying to console him. But none of it doing any good, his choking worsening as his relatives went on sobbing helplessly.

Bennett turning to me and using the same words as the salesman did now, staggering like a drunk man down the spotless white temple steps: 'The house of the living dead,' he groaned fearfully, 'the house of the living dead.'

Then, in the dream, Mona bursting out crying and Jamesy through the loudhailer barking 'No, no, no.' But 'Yes' said Campbell Morris as Bennett emerged, his face not a face but a writhing embroidery of black-headed earthworms engorging and mutating repulsively out of the circular black pit of his shirt collar. His voice, however, the very same as it had always been – no rattle, no nothing, but affirming, almost matter-of-factly, what the salesman had said: 'Yes. That's what it is. It's that all right. The House of the Living Dead. And it's us that's done it, everything bad that happened around here – it's us that has done it. Nobody else – us!'

He stood right in front of me and smiled. Then began to change into someone very familiar as the worms slowly faded, and The Big Fellow pushed back his fedora to sigh, with just so much weary exasperation: 'We did it all right. We're guilty. But you know that, Joey, don't you? Oh, Joey Tallon knows it all right, for there's no one more guilty than him.'

It was after that – and I cannot emphasize enough just how much of a state I still was in, even after calming down, having rationalized it all as best I could – that I decided to make it clear that I had been focusing excessively on the misdeeds of others as a means of exonerating myself. Avoiding the consequences of my own, every bit as grave, past actions.

I went over to Mangan at once and explained myself – not wearing my suit, but attired in nothing apart from my underwear – laying my heart as bare as it is humanly possible to do. And trying my best to sit still but unfortunately not being able to achieve the desired level of calmness, smacking my palm with my fist as I proceeded vehemently: 'No! I *know* what I did to Jacy, Mangan! Nobody is more aware of that than me! I understand the trauma she went through and the suffering it must have caused her! And I hate myself for what happened! I really and truly do! For yes, I *am* as guilty as anyone! No, Mangan! I'm not as *guilty* as anyone! I am *twice* as guilty! You see those who murdered Tuite? Detective Sergeant Tuite of the Heavy Gang long ago? Do you remember him? So you remember who dumped him in the tannery pit? Who carved and branded his flesh with initials? *I'm* as guilty as them! As guilty as everyone who laid a hand on the salesman, on poor old Campbell Morris! As guilty as them all and make no mistake!'

I whirled, puncturing the air with my finger. Mangan stumbled backwards – I think he must have thought I was going to hit him.

'Except . . . far more guilty!' I pronounced, almost with a hint of triumph.

The last thing I had intended to do when I'd finished all that was weep. But I did.

Mangan was very understanding. He told me to take the day off school (I was glad he encouraged me in that as I'd been absent a lot of late on account of the campaign. And, to tell the truth, was reluctant to get involved in any more rows with Carmody about it or anything else. The campaign, I mean. Even Eddie the supervisor seemed to have given up on me, giving me the cold shoulder whenever we'd meet on the street.)

Mangan suggested that maybe I ought to stop thinking about things for a little while. While leading me to the door he placed a reassuring hand on my shoulder and said: 'Maybe you shouldn't write any more letters, Joey. And maybe stop all these phone calls for a few days,' he advised, adding, almost apologetically: 'Them auld politicians! Sure they're only out for all they can get! Forget about them, at least for a little while! Put them out of your mind – for today, anyways! It might be better for yourself! It's all only making you upset. You'd be far better taking some time off to rest.'

I was glad he had said all that, for I needed some advice. Some solid practical advice that had nothing to do with 'thinking' or 'considering one's options' or endlessly trying to work things out. I lay on the bunk bed and decided – the relief was absolutely immense – that I didn't care any more. For everything that Mangan had said I knew to be absolutely right. Spot-on guidance. That that was *exactly* what I needed to do. Forget for a while about politics and 'thinking', plans and politicians. Everything.

'Forget about everything, Joey,' I said. Then I just drew the curtains and fell back down on the bunk, only this time not on my own but lying in the arms of Mona. She was wearing her floaty skirt and gazing at me with the saddest eyes. As I parted the black curtain of her hair and lay there sucking my thumb, my head resting on her stomach, a cold hard fact got a grip of me and would not let go till I faced it squarely. And that was to accept that soon – for definite, this time! – this would have to come to an end. That I'd have to burn her wig and skirt and the old-fashioned floral-patterned apron. Even her ear-rings would have to go in the bin.

'But not yet, Mona,' I whispered. 'Not yet, Mona of Dreams,' sucking away there (*tttht! tttht!*) on the moon of her belly as my heavy eyes closed (I had taken a sleeping tablet) and I tried not to see them, the fluid symbols swirling at the edge of my vision: POLITICAL CANDIDATE'S SECRET FANTASIES!

At first an indeterminate newsprint grey that gradually began to bleed into the most fantastic colours, the rubrics assuming a life of their own as in the manner of laboratory plasma they melted in and out of each other, like living liquorice flicking out across the cosmos before reassembling almost decorously, annotating in the most fastidious and elegant of calligraphies the observation: *'It was established today that Joseph Tallon, the Temple of Colossal Dreams Candidate in the forthcoming council elections, has been for a considerable period of time – on and off over the past twenty-five years, in fact – engaged in an intimate relationship with an inanimate object, i.e. a life-size doll of synthetic rubber, of the type normally associated with perverted and bereft old men for whom any normal type of intercourse, be it social or sexual, with the female gender is, generally speaking, impossible.'*

I was so disappointed when my sleep was broken again. I could have sworn I heard something . . .

But it was nothing, I knew that in my heart. Just Mangan and his bucket again. I sat on the edge of the bunk and buried my face in my hands. I looked at Mona and my stomach turned over. Her head was tilted sideways with her wig about to fall off. Her lipsticked mouth was hanging open and her glassy eyes were empty. Sometimes they said: 'I love you' but other times they said: 'You're *afraid*, aren't you, Joseph?'

The only person who knew about them, these deep-rooted fears, psychosexual anxieties or however you might wish to describe them (chief among them bundling Mona into a box every time you heard the slightest sound!) – apart from Mangan, of course – was Bonehead. In the end – when we moved in here, especially – we told one another everything. And I really do have to say it: the old fucker could be so understanding!

He's always had this gift of making a joke out of the most horrendous events. He'd be chuckling as he pulled yet another meal out of the oven (what a fantastic cook he turned out to be – 'Kedgeree!' 'Tagliatelle!' 'Fajitas, Joesup!' – the place full of recipe books!), grabbing the dish with the oven glove and running over to the table as he said: 'Well, all I can say is, that's what you get for wanting to be famous, Joesup!', always then adding something light-hearted like: 'Boy but this pasta looks the business!' or 'Taramy-salata! Just the fucking job!'

He's right, of course – it *is* what I get. Although a poorly lit, hamfistedly shot ten-minute sex video called *The Lovebirds* was hardly what I'd had in mind when it came to becoming famous!

'The Showdown' or 'The Incident'

The funny thing is – and I've often heard it said – that when you're reviewing your life, trying to take stock, evaluate or whatever – especially when in your heart you know only too well what you think of that idiotic itinerary – it's as though it's not yours at all but belongs to somebody else. Not quite a stranger; more, perhaps, a distant relation. And that everything that occurs does so at one remove, as though being observed through the frame of a viewfinder. That's the way I've begun to see it now, especially those last few months leading up to the election. But not, however, in the style of Cassavetes. No, no cool black and white this time, I'm afraid. That would be much too clinical! Too clinical by far and hopelessly untrue to the spirit of the time. Which was wild, really, pulsing at all times with possibilities that seemed limitless.

Days that existed almost in a different universe from the singularly drab and uninspiring notion of monochrome. How best, in cinematic terms, to describe them? Lush and sumptuous? Extravagant, majestic. Breathtaking, stunning.

Beautifully shot with deep focus cinematography – a great big matinee – a cinemascopic epic!

There is one thing I am ashamed of, though, and perhaps this episode could be viewed through Mr Cassavetes' monitor. Put together, maybe, as a short, sharp sequence snappily titled: THE SHOWDOWN, maybe, or A SERIOUS ALTERCATION!

But which might, possibly, on reflection, be inappropriate also, lending, it could be argued, an air of confrontational majesty to an incident which, although not of major importance in my life – certainly nothing when compared to 'The Night They Bombed Scotsfield' or *The Cyclops Enigma*: Chapter 3 ('Abduction!') – does not rank among my most edifying performances.

Because, no matter what way you look at it, I did ultimately let the kids down.

Sure I can blame Fr Connolly and Carmody, but, essentially, if you examine it, what happened was that I began to lose interest in my seminars and classes, preferring instead to work on my *Life and Times*, which I viewed as a sort of extension of my manifesto. And which, *mirabile dictu*, as the great authors say, by some process of osmosis eventually became my first – and *last*, it would seem – published novel; eventually, by consensus, entitled DOUGHBOY.

It grieves me, though, to think of it now, and perhaps that's one of the reasons we prefer to peer through a viewfinder. Maybe that's why we *become* 'the camera'. So that we can pretend it's happened to someone else and isn't directly related to our experience at all!

Such being the case with this scene starring 'The Candidate – Joey Tallon!', or whatever you might like to call him, as he stands in a seminar room of the community college (on a flying visit, as he explains) dressed in his charcoal grey executive suit, his hair neatly combed and a – *can you believe it?* – *starched* handkerchief in his breast pocket, delivering a speech on political film, quoting Cocteau, Godard and Pasolini, with specific reference to the Irish 'troubles' and referring intermittently to an impressive chalk drawing of 'The Memorial' on the blackboard.

'What I have in mind, guys,' he continued, 'is a great big temple rising out of the sea like something, say, from *Jason and the Argonauts*, but with the doors flying open – those massive portals of gold, set with shimmering emeralds – to reveal within the piled bodies of the dead! The faithful departed, keening and screaming, yeah? Say, Campbell Morris! Bennett! Eamon Byrne, The Seeker! And Detective Tuite! But not only them! Yes! We open lots of different doors and in there we see . . .'

In actual fact we don't see anything, for at that very moment another, more immediate door, is flung open, i.e. the one leading directly into the seminar room where 'The Candidate' happens to be speaking, and standing there and looking very irate indeed is none other than Fr Connolly, accompanied by supervisor Eddie and, of course, a trembling Dr Maureen Carmody, who demands that The Candidate vacate the classroom and direct himself towards her office at once, these latest 'impromptu think-tanks' being 'the very last straw'!

I still hadn't mastered political skills. Latterly, if faced with a similar situation my strategy would have been to remain seated, placidly, compliantly indeed, carefully considering each point as it was advanced, patiently examining my fingernails and weighing up a number of possible responses, empathizing with every aspect of the argument, regardless of how repugnant I might privately have been finding it.

Instead of flinging back the chair and bellowing: '*Well, fuck youse then! You don't want me to teach? You don't want me to tell the truth? Then shove your job, you hear me, Carmody? And fuck you too,*

*Eddie! Yeah! Youse do that! But listen up! You think this will stop me?
Well, then, think again! I won't be muzzled, you hear me, Father? I
won't be deflected from my course, from telling the truth, yeah?
Because that's what it's all about, my friends! And, just before you
interrupted me – do you ever bother to knock, by the way, Mrs Dr Carmody? Don't you think maybe that is something that you should do?
You hearing me, Father? Don't you agree there, Eddie? Because, yeah,
what I was saying before you came in was that cinema is truth. Yeah,
that's what we think! But it isn't you see! We are told that it's truth!
But that's just . . . another lie! Cinema is just one man – or woman,
excuse me! – who's looking through an eyepiece! Or staring into a
viewfinder and saying: "Yeah, this is what I see so therefore it must be
the truth!" Bollocks! Bollocks, Dr Carmody! It's his truth, maybe – or
hers! – but that's all it is! Nothing more, nothing less!'*

I paused for a minute and then said: '*Huh?*' to see what kind of reaction I was getting. Then said: '*Huh?*' again. When they showed no sign
of making any response, I started rummaging around in my shoulder
bag. I could see Mrs Carmody leaning over. 'Don't worry, Dr Carmody, I got it right here!' I said, which was a lie. I wasn't even sure if
I'd put it in that morning.

But I was in luck.

I slapped it down on the table, as battered a manuscript as ever was
assembled by an aspirant author – *The Life and Times of Joey Tallon*
– complete with the clichéd teacup rings and cigarette burns!

'Yes! There it is, my friends! You wanna find truth, you got it right
there! And once you got it, you can't stop its march! Not you, my
friend, Fr Connolly! Nor you, Mrs Carmody the doctor! And you
know why I say that? Because I know where it comes from now! And
we don't need Mr Charlie Manson! We don't need Mr "Surrender"
Hermann Hesse! Me and the padre we got a good old friend, right,
Father? And his name is – guess what, Mrs C.? His name is T. S. Eliot,
and what that guy has got to say is – Fr Connolly will remember – "*We
shall not cease from exploration, and the end of all our exploring will
be to arrive where we started and know the place for the first time!*"
You can dig it, Father, can't you? You remember that from way back
when! Sure you do! Yeah! Course you do!'

Fr Connolly didn't say anything as I gathered up my manuscript and
put it back in the bag. I eyeballed the three of them. 'See, that's the way
it is, my friends,' I continued. 'Truth is what it's about and always will

be! And that's to be found right here in Scotsfield. You don't have to go to India, man! Because what you're looking for is right here beside you! All you've got to do is be able to see it! You getting my drift? Fr Connolly? Eddie?'

As far as the 'Youth Awareness' scheme and its associated responsibilities were concerned, not to mention his enthusiastic efforts in the field of pedagogy, with particular regard to cinema studies, it might be said that at that precise moment the credits began to roll on The Candidate's career.

Either way, he was never to be seen in the vicinity of Scotsfield Community College again. Notice regarding his 'dismissal' arrived some two weeks later, of such little consequence to him now that the envelope remained unopened. For her part, Dr Carmody was reputed to be on tranquillizers for some considerable time after what she privately referred to, in muted, almost hunted tones, as the 'Incident'.

The Man in the Top Hat

'Hunted' not being an epithet which could have been comfortably applied to the behaviour of The Candidate, who, after the 'incident' or the 'showdown' or whichever noun you think most apposite, had begun to declare himself, in an assortment of public places including the square, the churchyard and the 'fairgreen', as 'empowered' by developments in his life. These declarations were, without exception, passionately imparted, some through a megaphone and others not. But all of them quite audible and impressive as oratory, a fact to which the ever-swelling groups of people that had begun to gather about him testified. Also of assistance, in this regard – it had already been advanced in the pubs and so forth – was his presenting such a colourful and unusual spectacle on what would otherwise be drab wet Wednesday afternoons. Now sporting, as he did, a specially tailored headband (an old friend of his mother's had run it up for nothing) which displayed the logo, beautifully dyed and stitched: *Vote for Joey! The Man You Know-ey!*'

In cinematic terms, it might well be suggested that he had become, almost overnight – the details of the 'incident' were already the stuff of legend – something of a knockabout silent movie star. A Harold Lloyd perhaps, if not Buster Keaton himself! Visible, as time went on and the election month of October drew near, at practically every moment of the day, swinging his loudhailer and exhorting the by now – or so it would appear – hopelessly besotted citizens of his hometown to bestow on him their 'number one', so 'I can give you back the gift of truth!' His campaign now becoming so successful that the *Scotsfield Standard*, in a comparative study of all the candidates, without a hint of irony proclaimed in broad black type on their very front page that they had recently, after some initial scepticism, come around to rating his chances 'very, very highly' indeed. Their brief analysis accompanied by a photograph which depicted The Candidate in his by now familiar spot, raising his fist and barking through his 'trumpet', stirringly reminding passers-by of the 'collective guilt' of Scotsfield and each individual's duty before the 'restless dead'.

'*Let us remember the ghosts of '76!*' he feverishly insisted from his perch outside the post office once again; this had, in recent times, become a notable feature of his speeches – his emphasis on his refusal to be 'muzzled'.

The most recent innovations, regulars to his 'public clinics' and 'reconciliation half hours' noted, were pictures and photos of long-forgotten victims, and beside them neatly pinned newspaper cuttings reporting their deaths, including: '*Blood in the snow marked the spot where the first New Year victim of the North's violence was killed last night. The little baby boy died in his mother's arms, caught in the blast of a massive car bomb in North Belfast*' and '*British Ambassador murdered in Sandyford. This is the first time in the history of the state that such an act has occurred. Mr Ewart Biggs, who, along with his secretary Judith Cooke, met his death in the explosion yesterday, was the most closely guarded diplomatic representative in the country.*'

'Let us never forget,' he continued, 'just how bad things were! Let us refuse to be gagged and each of us live up to our own responsibilities! As I will to mine, ladies and gentlemen! Make no mistake! Joey Tallon will show you the way! He will not shirk from facing his demons as he pleads with you now to confront your own! In that way shall the ocean be seen to part and out of its depths the Temple emerge! The Temple of Colossal Dimensions, my citizens!'

Worshippers in the churchyard were quite amused but not a little impressed by his erudition when they emerged from Mass one Sunday to find him there, snug in the fork of a tree outside the gates, reciting Gogol (down the megaphone) and now sporting a top hat ('Vote for

Joey!') covered in tricoloured crêpe paper, of the sort often purchased at football matches. *'Yes, I tell you! The spring which has been held back for a long time by frosts has suddenly arrived in all its beauty and everything has come to life everywhere! Patches of blue can already be seen in the forest glades – if you don't believe me take a walk out to the reservoir – and on the fresh emerald of the young dandelions show yellow and lilac-pink anemones bowing their little heads! What freshness in the air! What excited twitterings of birds in the orchards! Paradise, joy and exaltation in everything! The countryside resounding with song as though at a wedding feast!'*

There could be no doubt that he was talking some sense, a lot of people found themselves agreeing. 'You have to give him that,' they said and went home thinking deeply about the horrors of the past. *'I will not be muzzled!'* becoming a bit of a catchphrase locally.

But the novelty aspect aside – and even that was bound to work to his advantage, bringing in a lot of the young voters, to whom he had now become a kind of anti-hero – there could be no doubt but that Joey – 'Vote for Joey! The Man You Know-ey!' – Tallon was making his mark politically.

'I wouldn't be a bit surprised,' an irate – and visibly threatened – council official was overheard remarking in Doc Oc's, 'if the fucker managed to scrape in by the skin of his teeth! It will be God help the fucking town then! God only knows what he's capable of coming out with!'

An eventuality which would most definitely send shock waves through every incumbent member of the urban district council. Something which, in the opinion of many casual commentators in the shops and public houses, they richly deserved, so indolent and complacent had this current crop of public representatives become!

The Art of the Possible

All of which was essentially, of course, in the global scheme of things, just so much small beer, and didn't exactly entitle Joseph Tallon 'The Candidate' to qualify for Malcolm X or Martin Luther King status. Or even for that enjoyed by Tony Blair, Bertie Ahern, Gerry Adams or any other politician currently in the news.

But there wouldn't have been any point in telling him that. Oh no, I'm afraid there would have been absolutely no point in the wide world, and if you'd had the temerity to do such a thing, especially at one particular point in his campaign when it was really beginning to catch fire, you might have received a sound thrashing for your trouble. At the very least, a severe tongue-lashing.

For now, with the reception he was receiving town-wide (all the primary schoolkids had taken to sporting the badges which he'd got made up cheaply by a local firm – a branch of the *Scotsfield Standard*, in fact, who'd gladly accommodated him, wanting to hear more about his cause), whatever reticence might have been evident in the early stages began to slowly but surely dissipate, until it gathered momentum and practically vanished altogether, in its place now unmistakably evident a steely and vigorous new confidence.

The like of which he'd never experienced before but found, he had willingly taken to reminding himself, very much to his liking! And which literally shone out of his pores ('Oh glowing man, thy name is Tallon!'), he thought as he presented himself one electric-sparking day – the campaign was literally galloping along now! – at the front desk of Scotsfield Library and handed to his old friend Una Halpin a reading list so comprehensive that her eyes almost popped out of her head!

'Joseph, Jesus and his mother Mary!' she gasped as she placed a comforting palm on her breast. 'Who on earth can this be before me in a lovely charcoal grey suit and a gorgeous spotted tie? Surely it can't be Joseph Tallon? Is it really you, Joey?' she croaked. 'And you really and truly are standing for election?'

The Candidate beamed from ear to ear as he clutched his thin lapels.

'Yes, it's me, all right,' he replied, 'and I trust you'll be giving me your number one, Una, whenever the big day comes around!'

Which wasn't so very far away now! A mere matter of weeks was all it was!

Una still couldn't believe it. He had lost so much weight! And he looked so handsome now! All that jowly beer fat was gone, every inch of blubber put there by the pies which she had seen him wolf down in Austie's so many times when on her lunchbreak! Where had he gone, that sixteen-stone hulk who used to come barrelling down the street, glowering at everyone and quoting one minute Hermann Hesse and the next Charles Manson? Something she felt responsible for, having ordered that copy of *Helter Skelter* (companion volume to *The Family*) for him so long ago. But she needn't feel that way, not from this day on, she knew. But where had he gone, the old, sad Joey Tallon, forever pursuing his interminable quest? *Where, please tell me?* she found herself thinking.

Her visitor could have smiled and said: 'He's gone all right! Yes, vanished! Gone for ever to become . . . "The Candidate"!'

If he had been aware of her thoughts, that is. Except that he wasn't, being much too preoccupied with drawing her attention once more to his extensive list, which she peered at now through her specs.

'Obviously I won't have time to read them all,' said The Candidate. 'Not before the election, at any rate. But I really have been bitten by the bug, of that there can be no doubt, Una! I have become completely obsessed by my pursuits in the world of politics. The art of what's possible, Una. Yes, it's wonderful!'

Una smiled as he stroked his chin, thinking. What he had meant by that statement was how wonderful it is that it can confer on you such power. He had given this subject much thought of late.

Long into the night he would find himself writing, before pausing then in the first light of dawn and reflecting on the years already past. 'Ah, youth!' he would muse. 'Listening to Santana and reading Carlos Castaneda, before moving on to Mr Hesse and our old friend Rabindranath Tagore. Not to mention Mr Ginsberg and the best minds of our generation!'

Then, having completed his reflections, realizing how childish – so *immature!* – it all seemed now and how what he wanted was nothing so much as to distance himself from it. To observe it all through a viewfinder. Almost without realizing it, he had removed the tattered paperback from the inside pocket of his jacket and was smiling approvingly down at its cover, when he once more became aware of his surroundings as he heard Una say: 'Is that what you're reading at the moment, Joseph?'

He nodded and ran his palm across it. 'Yes,' he replied, '*The Prince* by Machiavelli. Here, between these pages, Una . . .!'

He hesitated, aware now that his sudden intensity had taken the librarian aback somewhat.

Una smiled and coughed politely. She really liked Joey but she had known him since he was a child and realized that the last thing you wanted to do was get him excited . . . encourage him to warm to his subject, in other words . . .

'Now, Joey. Let's have a look at these, shall we,' she began as she smoothed out his reading list, 'and see what we have and what we haven't!'

As it turned out, the shelves of the library were more than adequately stocked with many of the titles included. Of which there were, *in toto*, forty-six.

And when The Candidate swung through the glass doors of that quiet and scholarly oasis in the town of Scotsfield and swept out once more into the bustle of the afternoon street, there was a grin on his face that felt like it might have been three feet wide. For, right at that moment, there was one thing he knew and that was, come the dawn's early light – for he fully intended to read and read and read . . . What was the word that Johnston Farrell had used once upon a time? he magisterially inquired of himself . . . *voraciously*, that was it! – he would find his hunger sated once more.

But this time filled to the gills not with pies or the 'muck food' of ethereal mystics but with facts and figures and analyses and strategies. Knowing that in the career that lay before him – it was almost predestined now! – there would be no one in that council chamber who would be able to match his oratory. To use a phrase he'd already noted – in Winston Churchill's diaries, in fact, which he'd just casually plucked from the library shelves – no one who would be able to 'steal a march' on him.

He was in another world, his eyes practically closed as he came striding past Austie's pub, a hush having descended within those imaginary council chambers, his stentorian voice resounding as by the words of Gogol, the 'Little Russian', they found themselves helplessly humbled, now hopelessly cowed by The Candidate's mesmerizing brilliance.

'Colleagues!' he boomed – the floor was his! – '*The spring which has been held back for a long time by frosts has suddenly arrived in all its glory . . .*'

Joey smiled as he came past Jackson's Garage, where psychobilly punks The Mohawks had practised once upon a time. He sighed wearily, but contentedly. There was a tear, he had noticed, in one of the older members' eyes.

Earnest Reading, Gooseberry Shaving

Except that, in the words of Joseph Mary Tallon 'The Later' as he sits at his desk in the hallowed halls of Dunroamin', for all the difference any of these breathless endeavours were going to make to the world – be they the delivery of phantom speeches or his earnest late-night readings of tomes ('Hmm! This looks interesting! *The History of Western Civilization* by Bertrand Russell! Now what do you suppose we might find in here?) – he would have been as gainfully employed shaving the hairs off gooseberries or firing pellets at the moon through the high holy cheeks of his arse.

Although, you couldn't, of course, have whispered such a thing!

Why, The Candidate would have taken your head right off if you'd dared to voice that opinion, *sotto voce* or otherwise. Having fallen into his caravan, laden down with books (some of them up to 1,000 pages long!) convinced now – and this time without the slightest doubt! – that he'd at last succeeded in finding his way home.

You can imagine the face of poor Mangan, finding himself practically strapped to the chair, Sir Joseph pacing the floor of the house, thumbs hooked into his waistcoat pockets, proceeding: 'You may think, Mr Mangan . . .' as he circled his quarry portentously – and somewhat *forebodingly*! – until at last his exhaustive catalogue of assertions was concluded and he retired for the evening, Mangan's sleeping head having long since slumped forward on to his chest as the first light touched the window and the choral approvals of the early morning birdies went chirping out over the foggy, waking fields.

The Petition

He was off again, head down, folder clutched. Had anybody taken it into their heads to time him, it would have been estimated that he spent at least two entire working days in the composition of his REC-ONCILIATION PETITION, which he had decided to title his document. All of his remembrances were written out by hand.

'I hope I haven't left anyone out!' he murmured to himself as his eyes scrolled down the sheet of foolscap webbed with the names and dates of the seventies. 'And the eighties indeed!' he sighed, contentedly however. For he felt it was a job that was going well.

The names included were Majella O'Hare, Lord Louis Mountbatten, the Hanna family, Billy Reid and many, many others.

So many, in fact, he had to go and ask Una Halpin for another sheet of foolscap – and he'd already filled at least nine or ten!

'But it's worth it to do the job well,' he told himself.

When it was at last complete, he stamped right across the top (having purchased an ink stamp for that very purpose):

THE RECONCILIATION PETITION

and went off to get his tea.

Blushing as he came past the Fuck Me hotel, full certain that the lady in the red coat he saw climbing into the car was . . .

But it was a false alarm. It was someone else in a red leather coat.

A Very Serious Story

Even allowing for the growing eccentricity of The Candidate, it must be considered a mite audacious for a fledgling politician to set about the task of penning his memoirs before ever having assumed office at all! But *The Life and Times of Joey Tallon* already, of course, existed as a manuscript and was simply now being 'reimagined' – it is possible that some might contend 'plundered' – and extensively rewritten in a style more suited to its subject, now displaying, most dramatically, the new-found confidence and sense of *real* and *tangible* destiny that resided within its author!

The extravagantly adorned prose at this point included a most vivid description (disturbingly familiar) of a fin-tailed American automobile winding its way through rapturous streets as flag-waving subjects tossed kisses by the score, while in upstairs windows helpless matrons wept, grown men's eyes glittering with respect as exultant cries of 'Joey!' went raising up to the heavens!

> Radio and TV reports of 'this magnificent cortege' are going out across the world to millions and millions of people, whose affection for 'this young leader' is like nothing the world has ever before known. 'Who can know,' the announcer inquires on this amber-coloured day that will live in the memory, 'what can be possibly in store for this unique politician whose charm and good

looks are already legendary? Who can even begin to say what achievements – so many of which already have been logged by the historians – we, his lucky public, may have yet to look forward to. This wonderful man whose kindness and wit and wisdom and – *oh my God!*

The single shot rang out from nowhere, its shocking report reverberating in the heavy heat of the summer afternoon, as the author yawned and closed his memoir for the night. Stripping off his clothes then and retiring to his bunk, suddenly pausing –

He could have sworn he'd heard something. He looked out, but there was nothing, only Mangan, returning from the pump. Closing his door before retiring for the night. That was all.

Nothing save the most imaginable world of peace.

That was something he felt sure of as he slipped in between the covers, gratified, once again, to find himself effortlessly drifting off to sleep. Once more to dwell in that land where candidates slumber, as happy and untroubled as the most valued and cared-for children. It was as though, in recognition of his hard work and belief, he found this new life bestowed upon him.

They were delirious times. And there was nothing he liked more than getting home those evenings, his canvassing successfully completed once more – the numbers who pledged their votes seemed to be literally growing by the hundred. And, after consuming nothing stronger than a nice cup of cappuccino – you could buy it now in packets! – to sit down at the table and continue with his life story, compiled in a thick ledger marked: THE LIFE AND TIMES OF THE CANDIDATE. The great thing was that now you never got stuck. Unlike the way it had used to be, right back in the dark old days of 'the beginning'.

When you had screwed up so many balls of paper you could barely see out your window. The confidence he'd been experiencing out there in the political arena was now, without a doubt – if there ever had been the whisper of one! – transferring itself to the world of creativity as well.

By Christ! he kept thinking as he continued. *There's going to be a lot of producers that are left with egg on their faces when this little baby hits the decks! So screw you, Harvey Weinstein! What's that, Bono? You'd like first option on the movie soundtrack? Well, I'm afraid that's too bad because it really isn't possible! See you around, though, maybe the Clarence Hotel, yeah? Ha ha! Dream on then, Macphisto – you had your chance, compadre!*

Jacy's name was inscribed on the very front page. He'd spent ages on the calligraphy alone. He didn't want just any old dedication. He wanted it to be special. In case – miraculously, but miracles did happen, he knew that now! – she might one day see it and think: *He's trying to explain so we can both attain closure.*

He held it up to the light and gave it the once over. 'To Jacy,' it read, in elaborate but very delicate lettering, like you often came across in the classics at the beginning of a chapter. Ornate and special, just like her. He softly repeated the words as he read: 'To Jacy.'

That was what it was, all right – a means of establishing closure. Of saying farewell to the past for good.

Of course, *some* of it was mischievous – the 'Assassination of President Joey' section, for example – but almost all of the remainder told a somewhat harrowing story of a young boy growing up in Ireland. Digressive, perhaps, maybe a little overblown. But never, in its intent, anything other than serious.

At least, that was what the credulous author had been thinking when he wrote the fucking thing: Yes, in *The Amazing Adventures of Blobby McStink*, I've written what I can only describe as an extremely serious story!

But it didn't seem to interest the publishers much. As soon as they got their paws on it, they were by all accounts falling around the Kingfisher office reading it, thinking it absolutely hilarious! It was one of them, in fact, who had suggested the revised title, chortling: 'Why don't we title it *Doughboy*? For its deep-fried dumpling of a slow-witted protagonist must certainly be in the front line of idiots!'

The Coiled Spring

'What?', I imagine, is the most likely reaction to the disclosure of this piece of heretofore somewhat obliquely adverted to information. 'You mean the novel really *did* get published? And isn't yet another "imagining"?' I can already hear startled readers exclaiming: 'Really and truly? Genuinely published? And not by some backstreet outfit on brown paper bags?'

Of course it did! Really and truly! No shit, *amigos*! By *Kingfisher* of London, a subsidiary of a major London outfit specializing in literary fiction! How else do you think myself and Bonehead ended up here, in this tranquil rural haven of unbridled peace and contentment?

Albeit full of empty bottles. Bonehead's forever dragging crates of them out the front – he says I drink enough for ten men now – the refuse collector giving out one day: 'Jesus Christ,' he says, 'what the fuck do youse be at in there, drinking wine and whiskey like it's going out of fashion! Still, fair fucks to youse, lads, I'd do the very same myself if only I had the dollars!'

But it never does do you much good, no matter how much you drink, does it? For in the end it only makes you worse, and most of the time I'm like a coiled spring emotionally. 'Thanks to what?' I hear you say. 'Attributable to what, this emotional crisis? The failure of your political campaign? The demise of "The Candidate" and the collapse of his nascent empire?'

No, it's more to do with the collapse of 'The Emerging Novelist' and the consequent sad and somewhat reluctant birth – whether Bonehead can bring himself to accept it or not – of 'Mr Failed Writer', the man no one wants to bring to the party.

But there it is – the arrival of one unfulfilled artificer into the well-appointed spaciousness of our beautiful new home, Dunroamin'. A Tudor-style residence twenty miles from Scotsfield set back from the road with many attractive features, all secured (to rent, of course!) with the aid of my staggeringly large advance! And on the strength of one's future royalties (substantial, in fact!).

Bonehead, on my instructions, managed to secure it from the auctioneers without a deposit. 'I wore them down, Joesup!' he says. 'I wasn't going to take no for an answer! "Do you know who wants to rent it?" I told them. "It's a very famous novelist! His name'll be in all the papers! His first book will be coming out soon and it's going to be a best-seller! So come on now, hand it over!" They couldn't wait to give it to me, Joesup! They could tell straight away I'd lived in plenty of houses! *No tinker here!* you could see them thinking. *This writer has got to be class.* Jailbirds? Not us, Joey! Not any more! Them days is gone!'

You'll have to forgive me, Bone, for describing you in the third person. I find it's conducive to clarity of thinking. And, believe you me, now that I've made my decision – to once and for all to embark on shooting my aforementioned 'mini-disaster movie' – I think I could be doing with a little of that.

Which is a pity, really, that it has come to that. Me taking such a decision, I mean. And, believe you me, I fucking well have. Make no mistake about that!

For back then, when I'd heard that the book had been accepted, it really did look like I was going to make it as a novelist! That 'literary art' was going to be . . . *the one!*

Why, in the seconds before the editor Gail Marchant dropped her clanger and made me realize they hadn't understood the book at all, I'd been on the verge of saying: 'Oh, fuck all these politics! It's *writing!* That's the only true answer! I'll live my life by *writing* now! That's what I'll do! Yes, by Christ! I've found the answer at last!'

And now here I am, back to square one. I still can't believe the words she used that night of the launch – and her such an intelligent lady. 'Oh, Joseph!' she says – definitely not drunk! – Not even *drinking* as far as I can remember. 'I can't thank you enough for sending us your novel! A talent like that to come completely out of nowhere! It doesn't happen very often, I can assure you! But what gets me is just how funny it is! I've not read anything quite like it! Absolutely hilarious, Joseph! Magnificently overblown Celtic whimsy!'

For one giddy moment or two, I really did think she was joking. Then I looked in her eye and realized she wasn't. 'No, he really had us in stitches, that sad old Doughboy McBlob! You've really done it with him, haven't you? Poor old sad old Doughboy! He's never going to get it right, is he? And yet somehow you love him, poor thing!'

I didn't know what to say, especially when I heard the last part. All I remember after that is sitting there in the dark of the men's room, expecting at any minute to throw up. Then I could hear Bonehead banging the doors of the cubicles shouting: *'Are you in there, Joesup? Are you in there? I was looking for you!'*

Which was the last thing I wanted to hear, because it started me thinking about Jacy all over again, her face as she spoke those words in the way that I'd been longing for so long to hear: *'I was looking for you, Joey. I was looking for you.'*

Then I'd reach out as she tossed her blonde hair back, before giving me that smile as she said it once more: *'Joey, my Joey, my Joey the Breeze!'* just before the hammering started again on the cubicle door and Bonehead came falling through it with his whiskey.

'The Wind of Change Is Blowing' . . .

. . . became, more or less, my slogan throughout that airy and buoyant 'Candidate' era, those frenetic, exhausting days – and, make no mistake, they were that all right, but what truly magnificent, incomparable times!

Up at six every morning, throwing open the window in order to be anointed by the wholesome, untainted air, throwing on the shoes followed by the charcoal grey suit with its matching spotted tie, then away off into town to wolf down some brekkie before going on my rounds to meet the punters. I don't think I've ever felt so contented as I was for the duration of that entire campaign, cycling through the town and countryside with megaphone in hand, outlining all my policies on the move.

I became quite a novelty, actually, pedalling the backroads of the hinterland, with sticky-faced children appearing at windows and calling out to their mothers: 'It's "that man" again, Mummy!'

Not to mention the observations of farmers leaning across their gates as they started arguments over this, that and the other. 'But what are you going to do for us?' you'd hear. 'The farmer is the backbone of this country, Joey!'

'I'll do what I can for you, lads!' being as a rule my parting shot, along with, of course: 'Don't forget now! Vote for Joey! The man you know-ey!'

'We sure will!' you'd hear them calling. 'You can bet your bottom dollar on that, Mr Joey Tallon!'

A really terrific development also was Boo Boo offering me the loan of his garage – he didn't use it at all now that he'd moved to Dublin full-time with his recording studio. We had a really great rap one weekend he was home, and he was full of enthusiasm for my candidacy. 'You'll be like Screaming Lord Sutch, man, the guy who used to run for election in England! It'll blow the fuckers' minds! It's "The Scotsfield Shakedown", and it's Joey Tallon making the running!' he said. 'They're far too complacent down here in the bog! You keep her going, Joey! Rockabilly, yeah?'

'You got it, Boo!' I cried. '*Rockabilly!*' as I gave him the soul-brother handclasp and bought him another coke. He wasn't drinking now. 'Cleaning up my backyard, Joey! It's all salads and still water now in the music biz,' I was told.

What changes were coming about in the country generally and in the quiet little town of Scotsfield! Boo Boo McGann the psychobilly man driving this great big motor (a Ford fucking Mustang, no less!) like he was the head of Island Records. His studio was used by all the major international acts.

'You might as well have the garage for the rest of your campaign. I mean, it's no good to me, and you really need a base!'

So that's how the Joey HQ came into existence. I really went to town on it that night, after Boo Boo gave me the go-ahead. Cleaning it from top to bottom – you want to see the state it was in; I mean, it hadn't been used for years – and painting JOEY'S HQ in red letters three feet high! It really did look fantastic!

Then I covered nearly every inch of the walls with photographs from the seventies and more coloured posters I'd got from the printers depicting me on my bike with the loudhailer and novelty hat, splashed across the top two simple words: THE BREEZE.

So everything was in place. I had nothing to do only wait. But boy, let me tell you, was I one happy man when the punters started flocking in, either to sign the Reconciliation Petition or just chew the fat in general. Every so often I'd bellow into the loudhailer: *'Don't pass by Joey's HQ! Come in and remember those who are gone! Show your solidarity with all the dead souls! Bobby Sands! Sir Norman Strong! Come on now, ladies and gentlemen! Remember the words of the poet! Get in here now and kiss Achilles' hand!'*

I swung the megaphone and grinned at a passer-by.

'You! Come on now, sir!' I exhorted him. 'Get your butt in here and sign! Joey, Joey, please don't go-ey! *Passer-by, you will rue, walking by Joey's HQ!* Do not pass, I entreat you, friend!'

Another idea I hit on was the masks. I got the inspiration from the *National Enquirer*. You can't beat the Americans when it comes to gimmicks! Some dude running for governor had come up with it during the last election. Got replicas made of his own fucking face!

'This is terrific!' I enthused when they handed me over the very first one. 'It will give the campaign a whole new impetus!'

I pulled the elastic band over my head and looked in the mirror.

'For the love of fuck!' I chortled. 'This is the best yet!'

'There's a great demand for them, Joey,' the guy in the workshop told me. 'A lot of the kids go mad for them. Whether it's Robbie Williams or David Beckham or whoever. You know yourself!'

'I sure do!' I replied as I struck a few poses and wagged my plastic ears.

Well, honestly! The more I looked at that mask in the mirror! Such a great big potato head as I happened to be saddled with on the day of my birth! If you could imagine, say, your man on the cover of *Mad* magazine – but without the scattering of freckles – then you've managed to get a pretty good picture of what that reflection looked like!

But did they turn out to be a hit or what! All you can say is, it was starting to look like 'Joeytown' now! Everywhere you went, potato heads! It was fantastic, really and truly it was!

'Vote for Joey! The man you know-ey!' I heard one day as I was coming back after lunch. 'What the fuck's this?' I said as I turned around to see . . . *myself*! Until one of the kids pushed back his mask and gave me the thumbs up, grinning!

They'd call in regularly on their way to school, and I have to say it – there really were some terrific discussions in that old HQ! Both with the schoolkids and the old-timers, who'd often take it into their heads to pop in on their way back from the pub to rap away and marvel at all the progress. 'I can't get over it,' I remember an old fellow saying. 'The place is getting like fucking New York, Joey!'

They were particularly proud of what I was doing, they told me. 'It's people like you this country needs,' they said. 'Go-ahead people that are not afraid to speak their mind! Sure in the old days we were afraid to open our mouths for fear somebody'd be talking about us!'

Encouraged by such comments, I'd grab the megaphone and stand in the doorway, shouting: '*Remember blood in the snow! Remember poor Campbell Morris! Look, I implore you, into the depths of the animal pit! The dead! The dead! Remember the dead! Don't let them be forgotten, those souls without names! Vote for Joey! Joey's the man who will see that they are remembered! Hello there, missus!*'

Sometimes, when things were lax, I'd just take out a book and spend a little time reading. The more I read of *Dead Souls*, the more I began to realize that that was the way I wanted to go about the business of telling my own story – to describe my past in the way that the 'Little Russian' had. I just couldn't get enough of him and had Una Halpin tormented for every scrap he'd ever penned. 'Get me more!' I demanded. 'He's teaching me so much!'

After having eaten up *The Nose* again – one of the first books she had ever ordered for me, actually, all about this fellow's conk hopping down off his face and running around the town, before ending up living with other noses on the moon – I got so fired up by all these ideas that were gathering inside that I literally began 'feeling' the words, if you can understand my meaning, in the end having to close the garage. Because such a 'movement' within me, if I might call it that, was something that I'd never before experienced. Not quite so intensely at any rate. It was a sensation you imagined took hold of authors when you heard them announcing that the 'Muse' had struck.

And, boy, had she struck or what! I nearly knocked over five or six people as I cycled off out to the caravan!

I don't know how long I'd been writing, but when I looked again, the sun was coming up, and if I'd been delirious before, I don't know how you might describe what I was feeling now.

All I can say is that the words were just continuing to pour out of me, crashing away there like some majestic waterfall.

When – what do you know? – this *rat-a-tat-tat* comes hammering on the door.

'All right, Mangan!' I called. 'I'll be with you in a minute! Just go and get your water, can't you? Can't you see I'm busy in here?'

I proceeded, preoccupied with my creations. But then – I couldn't believe it! – he starts up again!

'For Christ's sake, damn you! Can't you wait?' I shouted. Adding: 'Ah, hold on, will you, for the love of Jasus!'

But no. He couldn't. *Rat-a-tat-tat, rat-a-tat-tat,* except this time he really annoyed me!

'Right! That's it! I warned you, didn't I?'

But I might as well have been talking to the wall, and of course I should have known that. For the next thing I look up and he's outside the window, pressing his face to the glass.

Except for one thing. It wasn't Mangan's face. It was mine! Mr Potato Head! Complete with plastic ears!

'Ah, for Christ's sake!' I groaned.

I mean, what could you say? What could you fucking say, you know?

'Joey, Joey, will you let me in?' he says then, plaintively tapping away and wagging the ears.

I have to be honest, though, they really did look hilarious!

'You drunken auld bollocks you, Mangan!' I laughed – it was impossible not to do so – and went over to the door to open it, growling irascibly as I strode back to my desk, still grinning away, but privately, of course.

Launch Party Contretemps

Which, I suppose, if you were so disposed, you could feasibly interpret as further evidence supporting the 'Johnston Farrell theory' regarding the peculiar character of one Joseph Mary Tallon. Yet another indication of just how intemperate and unsociable that erratic loner and would-be scribe could be, of whom the fêted artificer Mr Farrell had already written so eloquently and perspicaciously to that effect in his much-acclaimed masterpiece, *The Cyclops Enigma*.

He could focus his genius now on this little development, could he not? In searing, indicting prose analyze the continuing heartlessness of Jake Carradine! I beg your pardon – Joseph Tallon. Tell all his readers of how he kept his poor neighbour waiting. Of his harsh, cruel treatment of a helpless old tinker who'd never harmed a soul in his life. He could write about that then, couldn't he? Of course he could!

This time, who knows, maybe scoop the jackpot altogether and wind up on the *New York Times* bestseller list. Doing coast-to-coast TV!

'Yes, it's Johnston Farrell with episode two of The Joey Tallon Story! The Potato Head Visitation!'

Why, a man of his skills could stand to make millions by reworking an action-packed tale such as this! In its way much more surprising and full of more exciting twists and turns than that other silly kidnapping caper of his!

Meaty, intense stuff providing him with an opportunity to deal with the material in his own much-lauded 'individual and hard-hitting' approach. But most of all – in keeping with this so-called 'style' – to ensure that nothing ending up between two covers bears the tiniest resemblance to what might generally be regarded as 'the truth'!

And by that I don't mean exactly the 'events'! Or the chronology of things – *as they happened*!

I'm not that fucking well pedantic!

I mean, like I've said, the real and, more importantly, *emotional* truth!

For who gives a fuck what *really* happened? They're just the *facts*, for Jesus's sake! That's what I was trying to tell him on the night of the book launch, but of course he pulled the usual stunt. Pretended to be 'bewildered'.

'You fucking cunt!' I said. 'You were pumping me all along! And now you're trying to do it again! I'll have you! I'll fucking have you, Farrell! Call yourself a writer? You know what you are? You're a fucking bloodsucker!'

The funniest thing about Johnston, though, are these new mannerisms. That English sort of refinement, I guess, that he reckons should accompany the fame.

'No, no,' he says, 'you don't understand! I would always treat a person's story with respect! I did actually try to be fair to everyone in the drama! Which is why I'm devastated by your attitude, Joey! I really am! I always thought we –'

That was more than enough. I sneered and turned my back on him. But not before saying: 'And you'd do it again, wouldn't you? Write it all over again so you would! You and your lies! You think you understood her? You don't know the first thing about her, man! You got it wrong! Way wrong! Like everything else in your fucking book!'

I could see them all looking away, wishing to God there was somewhere they could hide. And I'm sorry it had to work out like that. For they were really fine people. Even Johnston, before his head went *whoomph!* and he got to thinking that *The Cyclops Enigma* ('The first in a series of "Jake Carradine" thrillers set in border bandit country in the feral, explosive mid-1970s, this book will blow your mind!') was the successor to fucking *Ulysses*!

A perception which I did little to propagate, I have to say! All I can remember is coming back across the floor and stabbing my finger at him. 'No,' I went on, 'you'll get no more stories. Because this time I'll tell it *myself*! I'll write my own life story, no matter how illiterate you might think I am, and *this* time see to it that the truth *will* be told!'

'I don't think you're illiterate, Joey!' was all I could hear as I walked away.

'Leave it,' I called back, 'Mr university graduate! The *truth*, that's what you're gonna get this time around! The fucking *truth*, man, got it? Something that you'll never know about, you or your travesty of a book, you and your dime novel ephemera!'

I think I must have knocked something over, glasses or some shit, for all you could hear was '*Oh!*' and them all looking over as I stumbled down the stairwell, the very last thing I heard being: 'It just wasn't quite good enough now, really!' All these black cocktail dresses with shocked pale faces going *'Tsk! tsk! tsk!'*, shaking their heads as Bonehead shouted after me: *'Hey! Joesup! Wait for me!'*

Beaming with pride and pulling on his coat as the two of us fell out into the night. He threw his arm around me, with the traffic swooshing past, bawling: *'Ha ha, Farrell! You dirty auld fucker! You couldn't write your fucking name! Haw, Joesup! Come on now, Rooster Cogburn! Get up there, Moshe Dyan! The one and only Big Joey Tallon from fucking Mountjoy jail!'*

Of course, now that I can look back with some degree of objectivity, it's plainly obvious that that isn't strictly accurate – Bonehead's somewhat ungenerous appraisal of Johnston's literary abilities, I mean.

For, regardless of what I have said myself and what we might like to think, there is incontestably a certain amount of rigour and skill that's necessary when you approach the writing of thrillers or crime novels – and, believe you me, neither happen to be in my possession. So, hats off to you then – however belatedly – Johnston Farrell, and all your midnight oil-burning fellow wordsmith travellers!

All I can say is, I hope you're out there doing your job better than I've been managing here tonight! And that your publishers will endow you with wagonloads of cash, which I certainly won't be getting for the discursive ramblings I've been tapping away at here for hours, regardless of my extensive researches in the depths of the famous 'Archibe' (!).

Perhaps what I ought to do the minute I'm finished is mail it off to Johnston, with a letter enclosed eating lots of humble pie. Thereby wheedling my way into having my story reinvented by a gifted, proven master! In particular, perhaps – if the maestro should deem it worthy! – the following little set piece. Anticipating his assent, already, somewhat grandiosely perhaps, entitled:

VISITORS AT DAWN!, from **The Potato Head Visitation**

The Candidate continued standing in the middle of the floor of his caravan thinking to himself about the next part of his novel, every so often raising his hand to caution his elderly neighbour, who was continuing to potter about noisily behind him as he made his way back to his desk, at which he then sat down to resume his labours. Not just a little irritated by the persistent interruptions, which took the form of irritating coughs, unnecessarily loud sighs and the idle and deliberate squeaking of shoes. Eventually it reached the point where he could endure it no longer, snapping: 'Will you for fuck's sake sit down, Mangan! I told you I'll be with you just as soon as I complete this sentence!'

For the briefest of seconds, he could have sworn he heard laughing in reponse to his injunctions. Not so much laughing as muffled chuckling, in fact. But almost instantaneously he dismissed such fanciful notions, his calm appraisal of the situation being that when you were up half the night typing, it was only to be expected that you might find yourself prone to the occasional lapse of judgement. Even to the extent of imagining . . . well, silly things, to put it mildly.

Such as *a chicken*, for example, aimlessly fluttering about your abode. Was it any wonder, he considered, that you might find yourself saying: 'It's absurd, these things you find yourself thinking when you fall victim to the unspoken pressures that tend to go along with creative work!'

Then, to your astonishment, discovering that you hadn't been imagining them at all! Perceiving that there were already some feathers – plain to see! – decorating the cornflakes bowl and others coming floating down from the top of the wardrobe where the so-called 'imaginary' chicken was brashly flapping its wings. The Candidate, taken aback by this new 'reality', made sure to take a long hard look at the bird. It was scarlet in colour with a small rose comb and beneath its chin a livid quivering wattle. Where had it come from? Why, Mangan, the mischievous rascal, he suddenly realized, had obviously brought it along as a present!

Such noise in his life Joey had never heard coming out of any animal! He stood looking at it for another moment or so, considering what his approach might be to the situation. In the end he decided to confront Mangan – to clear his throat, then reprimand him forcibly. Which he was on the verge of doing when he heard a familiar voice.

'It's a Rhode Island Red, Joey,' said Boyle Henry, pushing back the plastic mask.

The blood drained from Joey's face as he saw the senator smile. His visitor contemplated an unlit Hamlet.

'Did you hear a knock?' he said impassively. He went over to the door.

'Ah, hello there!' he exclaimed breezily as he opened it.

Hoss Watson and Sandy were standing outside. Joey saw that Jacy was with them, pale in her imitation leather coat.

'Look, Joey, it's the Three Stooges,' said Boyle. 'Come on in out of the cold.'

She was as beautiful as ever, all right, even though she had put on a lot of weight and was dressed in a hooded jersey shirt and sweatpants. Her lovely blonde hair was black at the roots now and looked like it hadn't been washed.

'An old friend of yours, Joey. Remember her?'

'Boyle, no!' she pleaded anxiously. 'Don't go through with this! It's unnecessary! Can't we just go now, please?'

'Go? What are you talking about, go? You have to say hello to your old friend, don't you? You seemed very keen a couple of nights ago.'

'I didn't mean that. You talked me into it.'

'Fucking women. Can't stick with anything. Make a decision, then go and fucking change it. Hormones, maybe. But what the fuck. Come on now, Jacy. There's a good girl.'

He shot Joey a glance. 'You want her to stay here, don't you, Joey?'

Before Joey could answer, Boyle gave Jacy a hug and said: 'You see? Of course he does, baby! You two have a lot to talk about!'

He smiled over at Joey. 'After all, it's been a long time, Josie!'

Jacy averted her eyes and dragged on her cigarette.

'Come on now, girl!' barked Boyle Henry as he slapped her backside smartly. 'Shape up out of that!'

He reached into the pocket of his cream-white suit and produced a cellophane package, winking over at Joey as he pulled up a chair.

The Film-makers

The dawn had long since passed and everyone was a little bit drunk. Boyle hummed to himself as he poured himself some more vodka, before returning to combing the white powder. He asked Joey whether he would like a sniff.

'No, Mr Henry, I've given drugs up,' he replied.

Boyle sighed, looking pained. 'Do you not approve? Is that what you're saying?' he asked.

Joey shook his head. 'No. It's got nothing to do with that. I've just given up, that's all. For a long time now.'

'Well, is that a fact?' Boyle said.

'Yes!', blurted Joey, louder than he'd intended.

Boyle paused, then frowned. 'Don't get snotty now, Joey! That mightn't be such a good idea!'

'I'm not getting snotty,' Joey protested.

'It's nice to be nice,' said Boyle, snorting some coke. 'Isn't that right, Hoss?'

'Yes, Mr Henry. It's a very good thing to do.'

'It just that your attitude puts me in a very embarrassing position, Joseph, that's all I'm saying,' went on Boyle. 'You see, now you know that I take drugs, you might go off and tell people.'

'No! I wouldn't! I wouldn't do that!' said Joey.

'Would you not?' asked Boyle, sniffing again as he raised his eyebrow.

'No. That's one thing I definitely wouldn't do. Because I know it would . . .'

'Would . . .?' quizzed Boyle.

'Affect your position . . .'

You could barely hear Boyle as he said: 'Affect my position?'

Joey nodded. He hadn't meant to say that either.

'Thanks, Joey. Thanks for saying that. It's just that I'd be worried, you see. I'd be worried you might put it in one of your films. One of these films you've been making.'

Before Joey got a chance to reply, Sandy McGloin announced: 'Do you know what, lads? I'm hungry!'

Boyle contemplated his cigar and said: 'Are you, Sandy?' Then he glanced towards Joey and said: 'Did you hear that, Joey?'

Joey nodded. Boyle came over.

'So what do you propose to do about it?' he asked, sucking his teeth.

'I don't know,' said Joey.

'You don't know?' said Boyle. 'Well, maybe this will help you clear your thoughts!'

The crack of his hand rang out sharply then lingered for a bit in the air. Joey's face stung. The smoke of the Hamlet was obscuring Boyle's face but you could still see the movement of his lips. They weren't unlike, Joey thought – absurdly, perhaps – two small independent creatures communicating in the undergrowth.

'Just tell us, Joey, where we can get some grub then, Joe Boy,' Boyle said, 'for Sandy.'

'I think there's some bread in here, Mr Henry,' said Joey, his face still flushed as he stumbled awkwardly to the cupboards, trying hard not to look in Jacy's direction. She was shivering.

'Boyle,' she said, 'I'm not feeling well. Can we go now?'

'Well, maybe if you didn't drink so fucking much you mightn't feel so bad!' snapped Boyle.

She cast down her eyes.

'I can see your bum, Joey,' said Hoss.

'Look at Joey's bum,' said Sandy. 'Jacy, look at Barbapapa's bum.'

Joey stood up and handed Boyle the loaf of bread. Boyle broke off a chunk and started feeding it to the chicken. He said: 'He likes it. He likes his bread.'

He was staring right at Joey now, steadily tapping his foot. He lifted the Rhode Island Red.

'Have you had enough to eat now, chicky?' he asked as he gently stroked the dome of its head. The bird shook its head like a peevish dowager.

'Here, Joseph,' he said.

'What?' Joey replied.

'Do it, will you?'

'Do what?'

'Wring its neck! What the fuck else would you do? Isn't it a chicken, for fuck's sake?'

Joey hesitated.

'I can't,' he said. 'I can't do that, Mr Henry.'

Boyle stared fixedly at him.

'What did you say?'

'Please, Boyle!' interjected Jacy. 'That's enough! Let's go! You've made your point!'

'You want to leave him, do you? You want to leave your old friend like that? You *are* her old friend, aren't you, Joey?'

'Yes, Mr Henry,' he said.

'Well then, don't disappoint us. Do it.'

'I can't,' he reiterated.

'I see,' Boyle replied. 'So I have to do it myself then. Is that what you're telling me, Joey? Why is it I always have to do everything?'

Joey didn't answer. Boyle said nothing and reached into his pocket, sighing melancholically.

'It's just as well that I came prepared then, isn't it?' he said as he flipped the cutthroat razor open. He ran his thumb along the edge and turned to Hoss and Sandy.

'Say goodbye to the chicken,' he said, 'Say goodbye to the chicken of forgiveness.'

'Goodbye,' said Hoss as he wiggled his fingers.

'Goodbye,' said Sandy.

It didn't take him long to completely decapitate it. He put the bird down and it ran around for a few seconds before collapsing.

'Get me a tissue,' said Boyle, and swiped the blade clean. Then he smiled and said: 'It's time to go to work. You ready, Joey? Get those duds off! Hoss, we ready to roll?'

'Ready when you are, Captain Birdseye!' replied Hoss as he grinned behind the camera.

Hooray for Hollywood

It was Hoss who did the bulk of the filming, his celebrated sense of humour, despite his good fortune and Armani suit, clearly having lost none of its spark. He winked at Sandy, who twinkled and shook his head. Hoss camply placed his hand on his hip and said: 'I know what you are probably thinking, Joey – this is a violent movie, right? Would I be right now in saying something like that? A video nasty, maybe?'

Sickened, Joey nodded, for there could be no denying the idea had fleetingly crossed his mind.

'Not at all!' snorted Hoss good-humouredly. 'Sure what would we want to make another one of them for? We've already done that! It's . . . *in the can*! Right, boys?'

'Right!' chirped Boyle, sniffing a little and rubbing his eye.

'100 per cent!' piped Sandy, as he flicked some coke up his nostril.

'If you don't believe us, Joey, all you've got to do is go over to Mangan's caravan just as soon as we're wrapped up here. Jasus but he's a great actor! I can see now why you picked him! I say there, Boyle, you pay attention! We're getting ready to shoot here!'

'Please, Boyle, what more do you want?' pleaded Jacy, hoarsely.

'Now, baby, baby! Don't go spoiling things!'

'That's right, Jacy!' laughed Hoss. 'Who knows, we might win ourselves an Oscar? Whaddya think, Joey? Think we might make it to Tinseltown? I reckon we're in with a fighting chance. They love comedies over there, you know!'

'So that's old Mangan fucked then!' said Boyle.

'That's one thing you can be sure of!' laughed Sandy. 'Pissing down his leg like that! I mean, for God's sake!'

'Who's going to give you Oscars when you go and spoil it like that?' scoffed Boyle. 'Not a hope in hell!'

'All the same,' said Hoss, 'make sure you watch it now, Joey! You owe it to him! After all, it was you who introduced him to the big time!'

'And encouraged him to open his big fucking mouth!'

'I dare say he's regretting it now!'

'*We* won't, though! We'll make our money out of this little baby!'

'Short and all as she might be!'

'OK, folks! That's enough talk! Come on, get ready!' called Hoss, as Sandy took Jacy's hand and led her over to the bed.

'OK, Joey! Take off your clothes!'

'Hooray for Hollywood!' sneered Boyle, sniffing again.

The blood rushed to Joey's cheeks as he tried to steady his fingers, unbuckling his belt.

Unusual Cinema

Transgressive films, of the type specified by Hoss, are generally expected to be affairs of an extremely shoddy nature, blurred and grainy with shaky hand-held camerawork and hopelessly indiscriminate editing.

The Mangan video, which I'd watched after they'd gone, proved to be very much that, its hideous texture and content heightened, if anything, by the fact that I was close to exhaustion while viewing it.

The tracking for some moments was slightly askew. The exposure, predictably, was bad. The frame blurred into a washed-out umber then ran into leader tape. There was no sound. A hair on the lens remained in shot throughout. There was a hand visible on screen – it appeared no less than three times; I wasn't sure to whom it belonged. There was a lot of wind noise and a couple of shots photographed from a half-cocked angle on the floor where everything was happening on its side.

Then, out of nowhere, the old tinker's chalk-white face loomed into the frame.

There was a leather belt fastened around his neck and they had affixed wooden clothes pegs to his nipples. There were congealed blots of candlewax spotted all over his chest and his face throughout was contorted in extreme pain. A pair of anonymous hands gripped his wrists and the camera homed in on a pair of pliers. Two fingernails were expertly, almost lovingly, removed as he writhed in agony – in complete silence. The entire thing didn't last more than three minutes. It was only when you thought it was over and were expecting the tape to fade to black that you heard the sound of a cord being chucked, realizing that it was an electric drill, buzzing eagerly away out of shot.

They didn't use it on him, however. They didn't have to. You could hear the faint sound of laughter – I suspected it was Hoss – as the camera closed in and tracked along the golden yellow trail where you could see he had lost it. I covered my eyes, then sat by the bunk to hold on to Mangan's hand, consoling him as best I could. Every so often he kept repeating, as some fearsome, abstracted mantra: 'They said if I opened my mouth about what they were going to do to you, if I said anything at all, that they would come back! Joey, I thought they were really going to do it! They were laughing, Joey! All the time they kept laughing!'

I whispered: 'It'll be OK, Mangan,' coughing up all sorts of phlegmy black shit and trying my best to sound convincing. The only things I'd been able to find to cover myself were a torn old jacket and a pair of enormous corduroys. I went over to the window and looked out at what remained of the caravan. Coils of black smoke were roiling up into the reddened sky. The air was thick with the smell of gas – the cylinder had exploded not long after they'd set the blaze. I started back instinctively as the entire structure groaned then slumped a little more before eventually caving in on itself, a ravaged cripple of broken glass and scorched galvanized steel. All of a sudden a great twisting funnel of black toxic smoke swept up out of nowhere, bloating into the acrid air as yet another window blew out. The PVC sheeting peeled like layers of crackling skin, the poisonous stench of melted polystyrene close to inducing a faint as my stomach succumbed to vicious cramps, a roof-support beam crashing to earth as the video ended abruptly and immediately began to rewind.

Out of nowhere then, large as life, none other than Oprah Winfrey appearing on the screen!

'I've just got one question to ask today,' she said. 'Do you think the world is in trouble?'

A Political Career Reconsidered

The answer in my case being a definite *'Yes!'* when, a very short time afterwards, I picked up the the *Scotsfield Standard* and there – to my relief! – given pride of place in the 'Local News' section, discovered my letter of resignation, advising all the good people of the borough and its hinterland that I would not, regrettably, be standing after all as a candidate in the forthcoming elections. And that the 'New Spring Manifesto' and 'New Spring Party' could henceforth be considered 'effectively disbanded'.

I was just about to put the fucking thing down when a photograph tucked away on the inside front page happened to catch my attention. I gaped in astonishment for I truly could not believe my eyes. Yes, there he was, smart and dapper as ever, Boyle Henry, council chairman, senator, financial speculator, hotelier, presenting a bursary cheque to 'local boy' Johnston Farrell in recognition of 'continued good work' in the 'field of the arts'.

'Perhaps you should do the script of his next movie, Johnston,' I found myself muttering bitterly.

The Lovebirds

Again, it had been Hoss's idea. He stood in the middle of the caravan floor, stroking his chin, with the camera swinging by his side.

'That's the way I want it,' he told us, 'like the ones they'd show in The Ritzy. What's this you call him, your man? They often showed them for a laugh.'

He clicked his fingers, staring over at Sandy, who gazed insouciantly back.

'Search me,' he replied. 'I never bothered going out there much.'

'Oh, bollocks! You know him, Boyle! Riding the women and climbing out windows!'

Boyle paused for a moment or two.

'You know, I think I know who you mean,' he said.

'Course you do! What's this you call the fucker? Robin Askwith! That's him!'

'Now you have it!' beamed Boyle, and returned to his stash, rewarding himself with a sizeable pinch.

'Do you mind him, Joey? There wasn't a woman in the town but he'd given a poke! Do you think you might be up to it?'

I said nothing. I could see Jacy through the corner of my eye. I turned away. I felt sickened.

'Well, you'd better be, that's all I have to say! After all, this movie will be getting major distribution! Isn't that right, Mr Henry?'

'Oh yes!' Boyle said. 'There'll be very few in the town who won't be getting to see this little baby at some point or other!'

'I'm sure they're all looking forward to it.'

'Especially Mrs Carmody,' said Boyle, sneezing. 'Oops!' he laughed.

'I'd just like to see her face when she sees Tallon's todger going inside this!' chuckled Hoss as he dragged the doll over and threw it on the bed. 'There she is, the star of the show!' he trumpeted.

Her long black wig had almost fallen off, her mouth wide open in a pink oval 'O'.

'We're ready now, Joey, so chuck your plonker and let's *go, go, go!* Jacy, get over there and tidy the bitch! Look at her, for the love of fuck!'

Jacy came over to the bed and was kneeling so close to me that I almost fainted. I closed my eyes tightly and prayed for it to be over. It was then that I heard her whisper: 'I'm sorry about this, Joseph. I'm sorry that it had to happen. I didn't want to come here. I'm sorry.'

When I looked again she was standing over beside them, but when I tried to catch her eye, she looked away.

'Get over here, Jacy!' Boyle Henry called, before growling disgruntledly when she refused the coke: 'I seen the time you were glad of it!'

She raised her voice then – a thing I never thought I'd hear her do – to him.

'Well, that was then, Boyle! This is now!'

I don't know what she said to him then. I couldn't quite make it out. He kicked the chair away and stood up, paling.

'Don't you fucking talk like that to me! You hear me? After all I've done for you!'

Her voice trembled.

'What have you ever done for me? You've never done anything for me in your life!'

'Shut your fucking mouth! I've done plenty for you, you ungrateful bitch!'

He glared viciously at her. Then over at me.

'What the fuck are you looking at, Tallon? Have you got something to say? Huh? Have you got something to fuckingwell say?'

Hoss laughed heartily and put his arm around my shoulder.

'Don't mind those two, Joey! Sure you know what they're like! Bickering away and the next thing you know they'll be like lovebirds again! Hey, *lovebirds*! That's a good name for our little movie! Isn't that right, Boyle? It sure is, buddies! OK then, Joey! Whenever you're ready! Ladies and gentlemen – it's – *The Lovebirds*!'

'Slap her in there, Tallon!'

'Ride her, Joey! Ride Mona crossways!'

'You have her now, young Joey! You're home and dry with Mona!'

'He's home now all fucking right! Would you look at the big fucking pimply arse!'

Overheard

I never went into Doc Oc's again, so whether they ever did get a copy of the video in there, to this day I still can't be sure. But plenty of people saw it all right – you could tell by the looks I was getting. The nudges and the winks and the guffaws: *'Look! There's Tallon, the fucker!'* even more pointed than before. I didn't stay around too long after that. It's just a pity I hadn't left before I did. Then I mightn't have been sitting in the bar of the Scotsfield Hotel, my ears pricking up as soon as I heard her name.

'Jacy? You mean Boyle Henry's bit of fluff? Oh, she's gone back to the home place in Wicklow, I hear. Got fed up being rid, shouldn't wonder.'

The 'Doughboy' Manuscript

After that, things weren't so good, I have to say. It was as if the earlier days in the prison had returned now with a vengeance. Only for Boo

Boo I don't know what I'd have done, for I'd nowhere else to go. He gave me the run of his flat in Dublin, and for weeks on end I never went out, drinking and toking worse than ever before but writing away like a lunatic. It was the only thing I felt I had left, with pages by the score shooting out of the printer. Hoping against hope that what I'd come up with would make some kind of sense. Never expecting for a moment that the manuscript would be published. Much less become a runaway success, for whatever reason!

Although, looking at it now – I have the reworked manuscript here, or at least a good portion of it – I suppose some of it is, in a way, quite funny. A chapter or two, at any rate. 'Rollicking', as they'd described it. 'Full of irreverent Irish whimsy!'

But, as for the rest, I find it impossible to read. Too fucking painful, if you want to know the truth. In the end this became the final title:

THE LIFE AND TIMES OF DOUGHBOY McBLOB
A NOVEL
by
Joseph M. Tallon

'You know, I've been thinking!' said Mrs McBlob to herself. 'I've been worrying myself about nothing, maybe! Perhaps when I get home the neighbours *won't* be saying: "That old Mrs McBlob! She'll be coming home soon with a heap of junk wrapped up in her arms! A pile of old rubbish put in her by her husband, that no good, round-shaped human that goes by the name of Jamesy Tallon. A shawlful of blobby old rubbish that will end up just like its father, no good for anything only playing cards and drinking and riding anything that comes about the town. The same as he did to Mona that tossed herself in the reservoir."'

She paused and placed her index finger on her chin, striking an attitude of quizzical contemplation.

'How am I to know for certain that those are the words they'll use?' she asked herself. 'They might not say those things at all. They might say absolutely nothing at all along the lines of "that big fat lump" or "stupid big hunk of lard letting on to be a baby"! For all I know they might say the nicest things before looking into the cradle to smile. And say: "He's a lovely wee baby, this ba you've brought home. After all you've been through, you've done Scotsfield proud in the end! Why we can't wait now just to see him grow up and roam about in his lovely wee shirt and tie."'

'Yes,' she heard other neighbours say, 'in a gorgeous starched white shirt and a lovely little neatly knotted red tie. Who's to say that he won't be like that? And why wouldn't he be when there's nobody to make him go bad! In other words, now that that other useless fucker's long gone, on a slow boat to China with his fat arse slung behind him!'

'Yes!' she heard a familiar voice agree – it belonged to one of the neighbours but she couldn't quite place it – 'Daddy Doughboy gone to sea, never again to come back and see me – not that we care, the ne'er-do-well auld cunt!'

When all those thoughts that had begun to gather gradually in her mind had consolidated themselves as she sat there in her pink lambs-wool bedjacket, Mrs Dough was as a woman transformed.

Even all the nurses would soon be remarking on it. 'Do you know,' they would say over tea during lunchbreak, 'I can't get over this fantastic new attitude that Mrs Dough has begun to manifest. When she came in here first she'd a face on her that would sharpen a hatchet! Looking at you this way, looking at you that way, thinking: *Youse all hate me and call me Mrs Stink! Don't think I don't know that that's what youse've been saying! All because I have a little bit of pudge around my hips and my thighs and because I've lately succumbed to the nerves and have been scoffing far too much porridge!*'

'And us not saying a word!' the nurses would protest, with expressions of the purest distilled innocence. Before adding: 'Sure it doesn't matter now, for all of that is past. Now you wouldn't know her if you happened to skip past her bedside. Why, she's a woman aglow, that Mrs McDough! And the way she looks at her baby! Do you think you'll catch her grimacing now, grinding her teeth and muttering darkly: "He hasn't a chance! All he'll ever do from the day we leave the hospital is get fatter and fatter and stink the place out! Baba McStink the stinky baba-pie! That's all *he'll* ever be known as!"'

You most certainly would not, and all of the nursing staff knew it. As indeed how could they not when they stand there at the foot of her bed, sighing almost dreamily as they attend to her exclamations. Mrs Dough-Dough *in excelsis*!

'I love him!' she cries as the baby googles there like mad. 'I have nobody to blame for my silly old nerves, only myself this past while, going and imagining all those silly stupid things! Why, my neighbours all along were the best in the world! It was Daddy Blob Jamesy who was to blame for it all! He's the one that did it! It was him going away made me think all them things and then start shaking with the cold in my own wee private kitchen, even on the hottest of summer days!

'Just like he did with Mona! He did the very same to her! Sure isn't that why they called her "The Jelly"? After she took to shaking so bad that they started to forget what she'd ever been called and now said when she'd appear: "Here comes The Jelly! Yes! It's the human Chivers Jelly! Get into Austie's, Miss Galligan, and purchase yourself a gin! No – *ten*! Ten gin and tonics for Jellygirl here! And then let us see how a lady can shake!"

'Now I can see that I was wrong,' she continues, 'I will take pains to rectify matters. The first thing I do when I arrive home to Scotsfield will be to go and visit Mona. I'll bring baba down as well, wrapped up in a nice warm shawl, and also I'll bring a pressie! "Here, Mona," I'll say, "we should never have fought, but hence we never shall again." And it's all because of little ba here, whose magic makes a dark place bright. Isn't that right, young ba? Isn't that true, goo? And then we'll get out the wicker basket and trot off to the reservoir. But not to kill ourselves though! There to enjoy the beautiful Picnic of Dreams. The most beautiful little munch munch that ever was held, with toasties and bun-buns and lots of soft-boiled eggs! Isn't it true, wee goo? That's what we're going to do! You and me and Mona and all our friends! Come on now, goo! You know that it's true!'

And, some days later, very true indeed it was as her little babalicious slept in her arms, before waking up to see his neighbours, all trooping in one by one to pay homage to this new arrival. Mammy Dough had just been out at the clothes line when Mrs O'Hanlon from number six spotted her. 'Ah, hello there', said Mrs O'Hanlon. 'And what's this I hear is inside? A little bird has been telling me that there's a new addition in yonder kitchen!'

If there had been quite a few sunny days in the autumn of 1960, there were none that matched this one, the sun that provided the light in which it swum shining right there out of Mrs Dough's eyes.

'Yes,' she beamed, 'he's right inside and awaiting your generous appraisal!'

'Excellent!' chirped Mrs O'Hanlon, as they were joined by friends and colleagues.

'Do you know what it is?' said one of them, twinkling. 'It must be like winning the Irish Hospital Sweepstakes!'

'Oh now indeed!' said Mammy McDough as she wiped her hands and, proud as a kiddie on a glorious Christmas morning, proceeded to lead them all inside.

The first thing they noticed was the beautiful cradle. It had been purchased by Sally Stink, her considerably younger sister (but, ironically, if such a prospect be humanly conceivable, almost twice as fat and at least a half time again as stinky as her sibling), and had been very expensive. But well worth it now, thought Doughboy's mammy privately, now that the nerves were over and everything around her transformed. In fact, she allowed, nothing less would have actually done her now. It was the very least she expected at this point, an expertly carved and handsomely decorated little cradle!

After all, she thought, *it won't be very long before he's running around in his white shirt and red tie, making me proud every minute of the day! So I have to make sure that he gets a good start! I have to ensure my boy's encouraged and thinks well of himself from the very first day! So he can be such a proud example!*

A hum of happiness seemed to fill the kitchen. One of the men said: 'Will you get out of the road there, ma'am, and let us in to see wee baba babbikins! Do you think us men are not interested in young fellows the like of this? Well, let me inform you, missus, that we are! And it won't be long before Junior's above there on that football field scoring goals and points! Along with me and the chaps! Am I right there, boys, do you think, when I say that?'

A man called Owen Dunne seemed happiest of all. He lived in number two. His expectant smile gave the impression of stretching right across the kitchen as his lips retracted to their former state of repose before gradually, almost sensuously, pursing to form a smallish circle out of which bright polished notes the size of little diamonds now trilled as if in an effort to form an extemporized tune, along the lines, perhaps, of 'Here Comes the Baba!', although, of course, it was actually them – the neighbours, that is – they were making the shape of a conga now! – who were coming in to see *him*!

The Sun Goes Out

Mrs O'Hanlon was first to vomit.[*]

It shot out of her like a lasso and hit the wall directly beneath the wedding photograph which depicted Mr and Mrs McDough standing outside the church just minutes after they had been married. It made a loud smack. After that it was Mrs Greene's turn. She came tumbling across the floor with her bony hand clamped tightly over her mouth.

'I suppose the funny part,' Owen Dunne was often to say later, 'was us thinking that what we'd see would be grand!'

And when she heard that, Mrs O'Hanlon would ruefully shake her head and say that, yes, they had been fools.

'Because then,' she'd continue, 'when you see what he really looks like, it makes it harder then to accept. But Jesus, Mary and Joseph, did you ever in all your life? I mean, deep down, I was a little bit prepared . . . I mean, I had my suspicions . . .!'

'But a roly-poly pile of . . . not to mention the great big stink!'

'Oh man, dear but the father would be proud! He'd be proud of what we seen there dumped in that cradle! A steaming pile of soggy old pastry going around masquerading as a baby!'

'When you think of it, then, wasn't Galligan quare and lucky to do what she did?'

'Which? Drowning herself in the reservoir, you mean? Or aborting the little child?'

'Well, both I suppose you'd say, really. But I meant, really, killing the infant.'

Owen Dunne nodded.

'Aye. I dare say you're right there, missus,' he said. 'If that's all Mrs Blob could manage, can you imagine what they'd have pulled out of Chivers? Can you imagine what *she'd* have produced?'

'A great big enormous heap composed entirely of wobbling jelly!' retorted Mrs O'Hanlon. 'That'd leave old Dough in the halfpenny place!'

'A giant big ba sitting there on a plate which you could only call The Jellybaby King!'

[*] Some editors found this *amusing*! 'A metaphor for the character's intrinsic self-loathing and congenital malignant shame?' they said. 'Really, that never would have occurred to me!'

328

Mrs O'Hanlon sighed with resignation.

'I suppose what this means now is that the nerves will be back,' she said, 'which in a way is probably all for the better. You wouldn't want her to start raising her hopes and then ending up all disappointed!'

'That's right!' Owen Dunne agreed. 'That way she'd deal with it better, knowing there's no use worrying about young Blob or Stink or whatever she calls him!'

'Knowing that no matter how hard she tries or whatever it is she might do to try and improve him, that in the end he will always be that – a great big humming mass of mush on a plate!'

'Or jelly or whatever!'

'Exactly!'

They were right, of course, and no one knew it better than Mrs Blob herself, who, although only a few days had elapsed, could not believe she had ever permitted those original 'hospital' thoughts to occur. Falling over a few saucepans and plates (she had taken too many tablets) she could not stop herself from giggling as she exclaimed, shakily: 'Imagine me thinking like that! Well, honest to God I'm a fool! Imagining the world had become all bright and gleaming and that Stinky in there was somehow special! I'll soon give him special – with this wooden spoon!'

Which was exactly what she did – and the yowls of Doughboy, with his pitiful little shrieks!

'Stop that!' demanded his mammy. 'Stop your yowling or you'll get another one and more! For you'll not turn out like him! You needn't think you'll make us ashamed! Do you hear me? You hear what I'm saying, Stinkbag?'

Then, when she was exhausted pounding the bedclothes of the cradle, Mrs McDough just fell down and wept. A large tear cracked on the lino and some of its saltwater dribbled on to her lips. Which she didn't mind all that much because all she had to do to get rid of it was flick it with her fingers. Not once or twice but three times, in fact, and finding that she liked it so much deciding to continue, locating a steady rhythm and then continuing to play a little tune.

One that moved along nicely as some words formed themselves in her mind. Words that included: *'Has the sun gone out? Will it stay that way? Has the sun gone out? Will it stay that way?'*, a riddle to which she herself provided the answer by doubling over and crawling across the lino in the general direction of the scullery as Blob of Stink (now urine-saturated from head to toe!) kept on howling and wailing as his mother repeated: *'Yes it has! Oh, blub blub, yes, oh yes, it has!'*

The sun has fucking gone out all right.

Through the Park, Bonesy!

Hilarious indeed. Your mother on the floor with her mouth covered in spit, crawling around in a nightmare. Rib-tickling 'puckishness' that will 'have you in stitches' as the *Sunday Telegraph* attested.

One of the reasons, no doubt, why Bonehead has accorded these chapters pride of place in his collection, marking them thus: '!!', and allotting them their own special plastic pocket, with each section numbered as well as labelled!

'Don't take it all so serious, Bone!' I told him one day, trying to communicate how I'd been feeling of late. 'After all, you were the one who said art didn't matter, that day you came to visit me in the caravan! You were the one who insisted it was all worthless!'

'Ah, but that was different, Joesup!' he says. 'Look at the way things has changed-ed since then! That was before your book was a success! You've showed them now just what can be done! You keep on like this and you'll change the frigging world! Because you speak for us! You speak for the Joey Tallons and Boneheadses! It's not like it was way back in them days! We've a stake in the world now, and we're going to see it changed-ed! No, *you* are, Joesup! And I'm going to help you! Pat Joe Stokes will help you, by Christ!'

I first became aware of this dynamic new attitude a day or two after the *Doughboy* launch. 'I know we disgraced-ed ourselves, Joesup,' he said, 'but now's the time to make a fresh start! Now that you're an author and famous book-writer, you will have to start acting responsible! Remember, they'll be expecting another novel from you, and you will have to take yourself in hand if you're going to get down to writing it! What you're going to need is, Joesup, some organization!'

I had to laugh when I heard that. 'Aye, Bonehead,' I says, acerbically – I was still fizzing with a hangover – 'but not just organization! Total organization!'

'You're abso-ma-lutely right!' he says, not having a clue what I was on about and haring around the place like a butler demented.

It wasn't long after that that the 'accent' appeared, with him answering the phone and taking down messages: 'Yes, sir! I shall see that Mr Tallon receives it,' fulsomely assuring them he'd attend to things 'promptly'!

All I can say about that is, I wish I were him. To possess even a fraction of this steadfast orientation he's somehow channelled into.

'I can't believe it, Joesup!' he announced to me one night. 'If only the fuckerses in Mountjoy could see us now! Do you think they'd be able to believe it, Joesup? Well, that's tough! They should have writ their own fucking books! Oh but, Joey, wasn't I the awful eejit, saying writing was a cod? And I definitely admit that I said it! I acknowledged-ed it. Is that the right word, Joesup?'

That's another habit 'recently acquired' – slipping in words he'd never have used before in a fit!

'Who'd have believed it, a pair of cowboys like us!' he laughs as he wrings his hands, then goes off again, chuckling, his echo following him all down the hall. *Fantastic! Fucking absomalutely fantastic!*

He's going to be crazy about me taking the car without telling him, I know that. But don't fret, Bone, I've been into the bank and sorted everything out, so you've no need to worry, there'll be no problems there. Why, with all these royalties coming in (*Doughboy*'s exhausted its third printing and there's talk of them doing a fourth) you should have more than enough left over to buy yourself a new motor *and* employ a chauffeur!

I'll never forget the first time we clapped eyes on it: an ice-cream pink 1976 Pontiac Ventura, with radial-tuned suspension and a Landau top.

'Well, fuck me, Joey!' he says. 'Look at that! One hundred and thirty fucking horsepower! Oh, Joesup, we've got to have it!'

'That's right!' I remember laughing. 'Who knows where that beauty'd take you!'

'Aye,' he replies, 'California or some of these places, maybe!' completely oblivious, of course, to my reaction when he said it as he climbed in behind the wheel of the Ventura. I flopped down in the passenger seat beside him and grudgingly harrumphed: *Through the park then, Bonesy!* and I swear to fuck he near pissed himself laughing as he turned the key in the ignition!

The Decision

What you never ever think about when you're considering the inevitable – too consumed by dread to allow it, I suppose – are the advantages which may derive from the simple *taking* of the decision, but which don't really assert themselves properly until it is an actual *fait accompli*. Most notable amongst them, perhaps, the almost instantaneous sedation of the hyperactive vocative, those obstinately persistent self-interrogations now – with the fiercest of efficiency – contained. The *'why'* of this, the *'where'* of that. The nebulous seventies' blatherings of Mr Hesse and his would-be insightful 'ancient' friends.

Another great thing is the sheer *clarity* of thinking that somehow seems to blossom once an unfaltering resolution has been firmly established, precipitating a concomitant equanimity that in turn generates a precision and exactness of purpose that empowers you to impose on disjointed ideas a shape and logic which before would have been pretty much unthinkable. The fact that drugs and alcohol have been absent for some considerable time (i.e. two entire days!) is not, it is to be assumed, without significance.

A development which I don't expect you'll be displeased about, Bone, considering some of the outpourings that you've been subjected to of late, although I don't for a second mean to blame all of it on booze and narcotics.

You ought to have hit me when I came in the other night. 'You want a drink?' you should have said. 'Then have yourself a fucking drink! Here then, you fucker, have this one, why don't you?' and struck me with the bottle right there and then. But you didn't, did you, you decorous old bollocks, for that's what you are at the back of it all, too fucking decent by half! What did I say to you? I suppose you won't even tell me that!

All I can remember is turning the CD player up – what time was it? Long past three, I know that much – slobbering like a half animal as you did your best to placate me. That was when I turned on you, wasn't it? Like I'd been doing all day in the pubs to anyone who was dumb enough to come near me. Or *encourage* me in my work – even dumber still. Like you did, Bone, and you see the thanks you got. A Joey Tallon special 'speech from the dock', which I've no problem regurgitating now I've delivered the fucking thing so often.

'What would you know, Stokes? What would you know about anything, you half-tinker simpleton? You think you know about writing, do you? You think that's how it happens then, huh? A few well-chosen words and – bingo! Out springs the follow-up novel! Well, I'm sorry, Bone, but you got it wrong! You got the wrong guy this time, I'm afraid! Maybe that's the way it happens for someone else, but not Joey Tallon, the small-town innocent who happened to get lucky, waking up one morning to find himself famous! Me, a writer? Now *there's* a fucking joke! *Another* illusion, just like Jacy! Surprised to hear that, are you, Bone? You thought I didn't know she'd never lived in California? Sure I did. All along. I just happened to think that if you believed – *enough!* – that somehow that would make it happen! How about that for a fucking illusion? That good enough for you? Huh? Well, Bone? You lost your fucking tongue or something?'

You tried to say something but didn't get a chance, and all I can remember then is you capitulating resignedly and the dawn coming up as I read through the letter I must have spent two hours composing – there were pages and pages and pages of it – out of pure unconscionable spite not addressing it to you but McQuaid, the old geezer who lives up on Tynagh Mountain.

He never got it anyway. I changed my mind and tore it up.

Which is just as well for it was the most objectionable litany of incoherent nonsense, with the predictable sprinkling of sententious pronouncements and any number of half-finished simpering parables regarding this 'illogical, irrational world, devoid of apparent meaning' and the 'yearning for communion' that, I seemed assured, exists within us all. With particular attention – and three whole pages – being paid to Jacy and what I'd christened 'Our American Journey', regarding how we might now make it 'real', forever in our 'minds', with our two precious souls vanishing out amongst the stars, there to be eternally entwined *'in the wondrous place that beckons, far beyond the Cave of Dreams'*. Which all along had been the womb, apparently, a prognostication bombastically inscribed in elaborate, emphasized calligraphy.

Whatever anyone was supposed to make of that, especially a poor old inoffensive old bollocks like McQuaid, who you can be pretty sure is going to be the one to find me, all right, and that it's not going to be very fucking pleasant. I just wish it could be some other way, for distress around here has more than exceeded its quota. And 'then some', as the Yankees say.

But at least, if nothing else, he'll have been spared my stupid original 'letter of explanation'. That over-emotional assault upon the intellect with its grossly inflated metaphors and unremitting, self-pitying prose now happily replaced by this much leaner, infinitely more direct elucidation: *I'm going, Bone, I'm finishing it, and I'm sorry I didn't tell you! I hope you forgive me and that this makes sense. My final penned masterpiece which I hope you'll file, prophetically entitled:*

'THE CRASH!'

. . . the entire mountain shuddering as the Pontiac came screaming past the old man's window, making straight for the dilapidated wooden cabin. It glanced off a telegraph pole and almost hit the ditch, the tyres screeching as its speed increased. The old man at the window knew there was nothing he could do. He looked on in horror, the colour draining from his face as it went ploughing right into the deserted shack, the noise of the impact horrendous. He fled from the cottage, but knew it was pointless. No one could possibly have survived such a collision.

By the time he reached the appalling scene the American-style car was a complete write-off, with the windscreen shattered and the pink hood smeared with blood. 'Joey Tallon,' he gasped as the dying man smiled from where he lay prone on the earthen floor with his skull split open.

It was a strange smile, the old man reflected, and he couldn't quite determine where it was coming from. But then, of course, he couldn't see the Big Fellow . . .

. . . Who stepped from the shadows and said, quite softly: 'Well, Joey Tallon. You took your time.'

Then he stood in the doorway, not making a sound. Staring out across the verdant valley, with its light, drifting mists and eerie evanescent stillness, powerfully evocative of both 'The End' and . . .

The Beginning . . .

. . . where Joey opened his eyes to see that yet another fine day had dawned in the Place of Wonders, the wondrous place. What freshness in the air! What excited twitterings of birds in the orchards! Joy and exaltation in everything! The entire countryside resounding with song, as though at a wedding feast!

Everyone had got up early and they had all been for a walk in the spring rain so as to give Mona and Mrs Tallon time to get everything ready for the 'Picnic of Dreams', a daily occurrence which took place at 12.00 p.m. sharp. They had prepared the most beautiful array of treats that you could ever imagine: wooden bowls of peeled boiled eggs, fresh salads, fruit, nuts, pastries and mouth-watering confections of all sorts, plus a bewildering assortment of coloured fruit drinks neatly laid out on the gingham cloth which they had spread beneath the 'Tree of Everlasting Apples'. The sky was streaked with stripes of pink and the sun was the most gorgeous-looking crimson ball. Mona was nibbling on a watercress sandwich and waiting for Jamesy. You could hear him singing 'Harbour Lights' the way he used to long ago. It was beautiful and Mona felt sure that this was the day when everything would come right. 'I just feel it in my bones,' she said to Mrs Tallon, who wrapped a clean fresh cotton towel around a plate of cooked ham and said that she did too. 'I think you just feel it, don't you, Mona? Some days you just know and that's all you really need.'

They half expected Joey to appear out of the trees at that very moment, specially attired for the occasion in his lovely white starched shirt and red tie. *'Jamesy!'* called Mona. 'Come along now, Jamesy, we're expecting you-know-who any minute!'

Everyone apart from Joseph was present. The Seeker had been sitting there on the stile all morning, serenely turning the pages of T. S. Eliot's *Collected Poems* and dressed after the manner of St Francis of Assisi in his hooded brown *djellaba*. Bennett was close by, not bothering to speak, listening attentively as The Seeker cleared his throat and, somewhat ponderously, read aloud: *'We shall not seek from exploration and the end of all our exploring will be to arrive where we started and know the place for the first time.'*

As they looked up, Mona and Mrs Tallon could see the English salesman Campbell Morris approaching with a copy of *Dead Souls* under his arm. 'Yoo hoo, Campbell!' called Mona, waving. He waved back. They really had become quite friendly with Campbell. 'He's such a lovely man,' you would often hear Mona saying.

They waited for almost three hours but there was still no sign of Joey. In the end they just gave up and went home, Mrs Tallon folding the picnic rug and sighing, a little tearfully: 'We'll try again tomorrow!'

Who knows, he might come then!'

'Yes,' agreed her husband as he put his arm around her, 'I'm really sure that he will.'

But in their hearts they knew he never would. For ever since their earliest days in the wondrous place Joseph had increasingly grown into a stranger, and somewhere deep down they had come to accept it. Back then Mrs Tallon had tried so hard to get through to him, gone down regularly to the harbour each night where she'd find him staring out to sea.

Once, trying to reach him, she had touched him on the shoulder, whispering his name only to find him facing her, glowering like an Antichrist. 'Who are you?' he bellowed. 'Don't you dare touch me! Don't lay a finger on me! You hear? You fucking hear me?'

And since then she never had, to all intents and purposes leaving him to himself and his musings, his self-styled 'meditations' which were little more than vainglorious gibberings, endless repetitions, including: 'I'm in the wrong place!', 'I can't stay here, don't you understand?' and 'I have to go to America, you see!'

Sometimes you'd hear him going on about Iowa, waylaying people and insisting that they listen as he rambled incoherently about 'magic'. 'The most beautiful magical journey,' he called it, 'and I'm supposed to be on it! I'm in the wrong place, can't you see that? Why? Why can't you see it?'

Occasionally he would become hysterical and inevitably people began to lose patience, tossing him aside as they went off about their business. 'It was sad,' they would often reflect later, having come upon him by the side of the road, perhaps, with his hair all matted and clearly the worse for drink, muttering to himself along the same old lines. Then rumours began to circulate about his having become 'deranged', a perception chiefly prompted by the peculiar smile they had noticed on his lips of late. Which was indeed sad, because the truth was that Joey Tallon wasn't deranged. He was, in fact, as he insisted, simply in the wrong place. And which was why it was logical for him to continue going on his nocturnal visits to watch the harbour lights twinkling, repeating: 'She'll be definitely coming tonight.'

And to plan for the moment they'd be setting off on their 'journey'. To the United States of America, where the surf of Big Sur would crash on Californian sand, the blue sky of Iowa rise over patchwork fields and white wooden chapels. And the woman he loved more than anything in the world put on her shades and shake her blonde hair free, standing by the side of the Pontiac, smiling, as she said: 'It's the end, you know that, Joey, don't you? The end of the beginning and the beginning of the end. It's beautiful, Breeze.'

'I know that, Jacy,' he'd reply, consumed almost totally by a sweeping wave of happiness, her hand in his as she rested her head on his shoulder, contemplating the tranquillity of the flat Midwestern plains. He could see it all clearly, like some secret mini-movie in lush and sumptuous Technicolor.

'It's like . . . total *belonging*, Breeze. You know what I mean?' she whispered. 'It's like *home* or something.'

'I know,' he replied. 'I know what you mean. I've been searching for it all my life,' her hair in that huge but inconceivably easeful silence blowing as though before some ancient wind, the golden corn all about them swaying, as it might in a child's golden Paradise vision.

The author would like to express his thanks to Jon Riley and Jeff Kellogg, editors, for their invaluable assistance while working on the manuscript.

Bibliography

Carey, Tim, *Mountjoy: The Story of a Prison*. The Collins Press, Ireland.

Kerekes, David and Slater, David, *Killing for Culture: An Illustrated History of Death Film from Mondo to Snuff*. Creation Books, London.

Thanks to Paddy Goodwin, Solicitor, Drogheda, Ireland, for legal advice.